KANE
a slater brothers novel

Stacey,

Enjoy #FBBF16

:)   — L.A.

AMAZON BESTSELLING AUTHOR
L. A. CASEY

Kane
a slater brothers novel
Copyright © 2015 by L.A. Casey
Published by L.A. Casey
www.lacaseyauthor.com

Cover Design by Mayhem Cover Creations | Editing by Jennifer Tovar
Formatting by Mayhem Cover Creations

This book is licensed for your personal enjoyment only. This book may not be re-sold or given away to other people. If you would like to share this book with another person, please purchase an additional copy for each recipient. If you're reading this book and did not purchase it, or it wasn't purchased for your use only, then please return to your favorite book retailer and purchase your own copy. Thank you for respecting the hard work of this author.

All rights reserved.

Except as permitted under S.I. No. 337/2011 – European Communities (Electronic Communications Networks and Services) (Universal Service and Users' Rights) Regulations 2011, no part of this publication may be reproduced, distributed, or transmitted in any form or by any means, or stored in a database or retrieval system, without prior written permission of the author. The scanning, uploading, and distribution of this book via the Internet or via other means without the permission of the publisher is illegal and punishable by law. Please purchase only authorized electronic editions and do not participate in or encourage electronic piracy of copyrighted materials. This is a work of fiction. Names, characters, places, brands, media, and incidents are either the product of the author's imagination or are used fictiously. The author acknowledges the trademarked status and trademark owners of various products referenced in this work of fiction, which have been used without permission. The publication/use of these trademarks is not authorized, associated with, or sponsored by the trademark owners.

Kane / L.A. Casey – 1st ed.
ISBN-13: 978-1511505192 | ISBN-10: 1511505192

DEDICATION

For my mini me, thanks for being such a cool kid.

TABLE OF CONTENTS

Chapter One	1
Chapter Two	7
Chapter Three	19
Chapter Four	32
Chapter Five	41
Chapter Six	50
Chapter Seven	58
Chapter Eight	64
Chapter Nine	106
Chapter Ten	120
Chapter Eleven	137
Chapter Twelve	155
Chapter Thirteen	169
Chapter Fourteen	198
Chapter Fifteen	209
Chapter Sixteen	216

Chapter Seventeen	227
Chapter Eighteen	250
Chapter Nineteen	262
Chapter Twenty	269
Chapter Twenty-One	283
Chapter Twenty-Two	298
Chapter Twenty-Three	304
Chapter Twenty-Four	315
Chapter Twenty-Five	320
Chapter Twenty-Six	333
Chapter Twenty-Seven	353
Other Titles	368
Acknowledgments	369
About the Author	371

CHAPTER ONE

I had a headache.

A pounding headache.

My stomach was queasy and I felt a little dizzy.

I felt like shite.

I felt like this because I was scared.

I was so damn scared... and all because of a damn plastic stick!

I tried not to look at the stick that would decide my fate as I sat in the main bathroom of the Slater brothers' house. I focused on the tiled floor and the grout that cemented them in place just to avoid looking up. I counted the tiles and each time I only got to ten or eleven before my head automatically turned to look at the counter.

No.

I hissed at myself and stilled my movements before I could take a peek. I didn't want to know what the stupid stick said, but I had to know. It was eating away at me and had been for the last hour and a half. I looked up at the ceiling and blinked.

I wish you were here, Ma.

I needed my mother. I needed to vent to somebody about the fucked-up day I'd had. I swallowed and pictured my mother in front of me, and I mentally unloaded everything to her. I told her everything.

Today was a pretty eventful day to say the least.

It was moving day for Keela and Alec. They moved out of their box-sized apartment into a beautiful house, directly across from the brothers' place in Upton. As a leading member of the fucked-up friendship group we upheld, we were all drafted to help pack up boxes in the old apartment and then unpack them in the new house.

Everyone had some fun packing up, but we also had arguments... and a lot of other bullshit to deal with. Keela had more bullshit than anyone to deal with.

My girl was stressed, and I put it down to moving because that *was* stressful, but she revealed to me that she wasn't doing good and it wasn't just because she was moving to a new house. She was having nightmares about an incident that happened with her uncle and the brothers thirteen months ago. Keela never liked to talk about what happened. I knew the gist of what went down, but not everything. I didn't know what caused Keela to be so scared... scared enough to still be having night terrors so many months later.

Her nightmares weren't her only problem though. She wasn't comfortable with how fast Alec was moving with their relationship. She wanted to enjoy him in the dating game, but he wanted to get married and have babies right away.

The kicker?

Alec knew none of this. Nothing about her nightmares and diddly-squat about her hesitation with what she wanted out of their relationship. This all came out of course... during a surprise housewarming party that Alec arranged. Keela wasn't impressed at all. She had a bit of meltdown, and if things weren't bad enough already, her uncle, cousin Micah and Micah's wankstain of a husband, Jason, showed up.

You know, the Uncle who was really a gangster, the cousin who put the B in Bitch, and her husband who was the biggest dickhead ever? Yeah, those bastards. They showed up, and they caused arguments and physical fights. They had found out about the party thanks to my bastard little brother, Gavin. He was somehow close to Brandon and Jason now, however *that* situation was too fresh for me to think about right now. I needed time before I even thought about the little fucker that I helped raise.

The whole situation was bad, but what really put the cherry on top of our fucked-up-day-cake was the stupid thing myself, Branna, Bronagh, and Alannah did in Keela's bathroom for fun.

Before the shit hit the fan, we had some drinks to unwind from a long day of packing and unpacking and we thought it would be funny to take pregnancy tests. And it was funny... until Keela showed up and knocked the pregnancy tests into the sink and mixed them up. That wouldn't normally be a problem, but guess what one of the test results turned out to be?

You guessed it.

One of us was fucking pregnant, and we had no clue who it was.

We had Keela to thank for that.

It got scarier when Alannah ruled herself out of the line-up because she swore there was no tick in her clock for at least six months. So that left Bronagh, Branna, or myself to have the pleasure of being with child.

Ha! Pleasure my arse.

I prayed it was either Bronagh or Branna who was pregnant, simply because those two were in committed relationships, while I wasn't. The closest I ever got to being in a relationship was the hate/hate thing I had going on with Storm—and he was a dog. And he hated me.

We were going to see who the unlucky lady was, but Keela ran out of pregnancy tests, which, of course, was just fucking typical. She was on her way to go get some more tests when the bastards I mentioned before showed up and things got put on the back burner for an hour or two.

Things were calm now though, and Keela went on her way to our local supermarket with Kane Slater—he was a prick in plain sight—to get more tests. I was impatiently waiting for them to return and so were the lads.

All three of them—Nico, Ryder, and Alec—were sat in the sitting room of Alec and Keela's house trying to piece a fucking shattered vase back together. I knew it was a lost cause, but I still came over to Ryder's house for glue when he asked for it.

I had to go to the bathroom though, and that's how I ended up sitting on a toilet staring at a pregnancy test. I spotted the box on the counter and it had one test left in it. I knew Branna would've wanted to use it, but I had to know if it was me who was pregnant.

I just *had* to know.

Plucking up the courage to actually check what the result was turned out to be more difficult than I anticipated. I was about to peek at the test results when my phone buzzed for what had to be the tenth time in the last five minutes. I didn't look at it when it first rang because I thought it was Gavin. Giving up I took it out of my trouser pocket, glanced at the caller ID and saw it was Keela.

I clicked answer.

"Aideen! Finally!" Keela's voice cried.

I froze. "Keela? What's wrong? Are you okay?"

"No," she whimpered. "It's Kane, he collapsed."

My heart stopped beating, my stomach churned, my throat closed up, and my head spun. I was acutely aware of how I felt at that moment—I was absolutely terrified.

"What the hell do you mean Kane collapsed?!" I shouted into the speaker of my phone.

"I mean exactly that. We were in Tesco and he just dropped. No warnin' at all—he just fell. The ambulance is here and the paramedics have him on a stretcher. I'm goin' to head to the hospital with him. Can you let the brothers know and tell them to get their fuckin' arses to the hospital right away? None of them are answerin' their bloody phones."

My voice was raspy as I asked, "What about the girls? Did you try them?"

Keela hissed, "Their phones are ringin' out too. I'm goin' to fuckin' kill them all. I'm scared shitless and none of them are answerin' their poxy phones."

I blinked my eyes and was surprised when tears fell onto my cheeks.

What the hell?

I quickly wiped under my eyes then took a few deep breaths to calm myself. I would be no good to anyone if I freaked out. I was pretty focused until my best friend showed signs that she was cracking. I squeezed my eyes shut when I heard Keela sniffle on the other end of the phone.

"It'll be all right, Kay," I said, hoping the comfort I offered helped her, because it did shit for me.

"Just get the brothers and meet me at the hospital, *please*."

She hung up and for a long moment I sat unmoving and tried to process what she'd just told me, but I couldn't. I just couldn't. It was probably best because I quickly sprung into action by jumping up and running out of the bathroom and out of the Slater household without a backward glance. I sprinted across the road and crashed into Alec and Keela's front door slamming it open in the process.

"Lads! Omigod, lads!" I screamed as I ran into the sitting room.

"Aideen!" Ryder shouted and grabbed hold of my shoulders when I stumbled into the room. "Calm down and tell us what's wrong."

I inhaled and exhaled a couple of times trying to get my breath back. When I did, I looked from Ryder to his brothers and back again.

"Keela called me from the supermarket."

Alec moved closer. "Is she okay?"

I nodded my head. "*She* is."

Nico moved closer, too. "And Kane?"

Tears gathered in my eyes. Again.

I shook my head. "She said it happened so fast. He was standin' beside her one second and on the floor the next."

All the brothers widened their eyes and from behind them Branna and Alannah gasped.

"She tried to ring, but no one answered their phones," I continued. "She is on her way to the hospital with him. We have to go there right now."

The next few minutes were a blur of activity with the lads shouting and the girls crying. We all ran out of Alec and Keela's new house and piled into cars. I went with Ryder and Alec, and Nico went with the girls to get Bronagh.

"He's goin' to be okay, isn't he?" I asked the lads as Ryder flew down the bypass with Nico following close behind before he turned down the road to go get his girl.

I felt a comforting hand grip tightly onto my shoulder. "He *is* going to be okay."

I hadn't talked to God in a long time—not since my mother died when I was little—but on the drive to the hospital I prayed we'd find out what was wrong with Kane and if he was okay. I prayed harder than I ever had before, and I begged Him to let Kane be okay.

I jumped when my phone rang, but I quickly answered.

"Hello?"

"Where are you all?" Keela cried.

She was sobbing; I could hear it in her voice.

I broke down with worry. "We're nearly there... is he okay?"

The brothers held their breath when I asked the question we were all thinking.

Keela bawled, "I'm tryin' to find that out, but I'm not related to him so the brothers need to be here."

"Why?" I asked, terrified to hear her reply.

"Because they won't tell me if he is dead or alive!"

CHAPTER TWO

When we pulled up to the entrance of the A&E department of the hospital, both of the brothers jumped out and sprinted through the automatic doors that led to where Keela was... and to where Kane was.

I froze to my seat. I couldn't move at all. Keela said on the phone that she didn't know if Kane was dead or alive. I knew that didn't mean he *was* dead, but it meant he *could* be and the possibility of his death was enough to frighten the life out of me. I couldn't be there to hear if he was dead. I think I'd cease to function if he was gone, and I couldn't even fully explain why I felt like that because Kane... well, he pissed me off all the time.

It was a good thing I lingered behind after the brothers bailed because Ryder didn't even pull the handbrake up on his Jeep or take the keys out of the ignition. He never even bothered to shut the driver's side door. He and Alec just ran. Rightfully so, it was their brother who was lying in a bed somewhere in the hospital after all.

I looked at the hospital and quickly snapped my head back forward. I hated that hospital. I hated all hospitals though. My mother died in a hospital, and even though I was young when it happened, I'd always thought of hospitals as being horrible places that take people away from their families. I knew now it wasn't the case, but the initial fear of hospitals had stuck with me. I just hoped when I entered the building that I wouldn't be leaving with the people around me making funeral arrangements.

That would kill me.

When I gathered my bearings, I slid into the driver's seat of Ryder's Jeep and reached for the handle of the door. I gripped it tightly, pulled it shut, and then I put the car in gear. I heard a couple of beeps behind me, but I didn't look in the rearview mirror. I didn't pay them much attention at all, to be honest. I felt numb and oblivious to everything... except for the hand that banged on the window next to me.

I screeched and gripped tightly onto the steering wheel.

"You have to move!" A male hospital traffic warden frowned at me through the glass. "This is a drop-off zone *only*. Move it, lady."

Fuck you.

I nodded my head to the man, pulled out of the no-parking zone, and slowly followed the signs to the multi-story public car park to find the first three floors of the car park were full.

Apparently, everyone and their auntie in the Tallaght area were fucking sick today.

I was pissed off when I got to the fourth floor of the car park, but I found a spot next to the elevator and stairs so that relaxed me a little bit. When we first got here, I was more than happy to let the brothers take the lead and run into the hospital, but it had been ten or so minutes since I had any sort of information and now... now I was antsy. I wanted to know if Kane was okay.

He *needed* to be okay... he just needed to be.

After I had parked the car, I locked it up, got a parking card from the machine and left the multi-story car park to head straight for the A&E. I glanced up at the *Accident & Emergency* sign as I walked into the hospital and swallowed down my nerves.

I looked around for the brothers and Keela but didn't see them. "Crap," I murmured out loud.

What in the hell was I going to do now?

"Can I help you, miss?" a security guard asked me from my left.

I nodded my head and walked over to the man. "Yes, please. Me friend was taken through A&E not so long ago; he arrived in an ambulance. His name is Kane Slater, me friend, Keela Daley—she's a little redhead—came in with him. He collapsed. Two of his brothers came in here about ten minutes ago lookin' for him, you couldn't miss them. They're both tall, over six foot, one has a buzz cut on both sides of his head with longer brown hair on top, has a dragon tattoo down his right arm, really good lookin' like his brother—"

"Ah, yeah. American blokes, right?" the security guard cut off my rambling. "Pretty sure the lad you just described threatened to break me nose if I didn't let him and his brother through the doors to see their little brother."

I winced. "Alec is usually really nice, I swear."

The security guard snorted. "I'm sure, but unfortunately I can't help you. You have to be family or a patient to get through the doors behind me."

Crap.

"Well, it's funny that you mention family because—"

"Aideen!"

I jumped when a voice shouted my name. I spun around and almost burst with excitement when I spotted Nico running through the automatic doors of the A&E closely followed by a worried looking Bronagh, Branna, and Alannah.

"*He* is family!" I said to the security guard. "He is Kane's- I mean the *patient's* younger brother."

The security guard looked at Nico when he came to my side and put his hand on my shoulder.

"Any news?" he asked me.

I shook my head. "I was parkin' the car, and now I'm tryin' to get back to see what's happenin', but I need to be family."

Nico glared at the security guard. "She is family. They *all* are," he said and gestured to the girls beside him.

The security guard groaned. "You expect me to believe all four of them are—"

"My wives," Nico cut the security guard off.

I looked at Nico with wide eyes and so did the other girls.

"What?" the security guard said after a pregnant pause.

With a straight face Nico gestured to me and the other girls. "They're my wives. My *legal* wives... we aren't Catholic."

Oh. My. God.

The security guard blinked at Nico, then looked at me and the other girls before looking back at Nico. I was convinced he was about to call bullshit on Nico's lie until he opened his mouth and said, "You lucky bastard."

Wait, what?

Nico nodded his ever-expanding head and sighed. "I know, it's damn hard to choose which one of them to sleep with at night, but we devised a schedule to keep things fair. I don't want them fighting with each other just to get my attention, you know? I mean, I can barely keep up with them. Sex with each of them daily is *a lot* of work, but someone has got to do it, you know?"

I felt my eye twitch as I watched Nico effortlessly lie to the security guard who was gazing at him and lapping up his every word like he was talking to Jesus Christ in the flesh.

"Fuckin' hell," the security guard breathed.

I looked at the girls and found all three of them shaking their heads at Nico then rolling their eyes at the more than gullible security guard.

"Yeah," Nico breathed. "Can you let us by to go see my brother? I can't leave them out here alone. Getting backlash from one woman is torture, but four of them? You'll be sentencing me to death, bro. *Death.*"

Oh, a Slater *was* going to die today and my money was on it *not* being Kane.

"Man, of course," the security guard said and reached out and patted Nico on the shoulder like he was 'the man.' "Go right on in. Your two other brothers are down the hall and in the last waitin' room on the right."

Nico patted the security guard on the shoulder. "Thank you, bro.

Thank you."

Oh, for God's sake.

I grunted as I took Nico's extended hand, and I wanted to smile when he hissed as Bronagh took hold of his other hand.

"It'll be okay, *husband*," she growled. "We'll take it easy on you today."

"Yeah," I chimed in as the security guard swiped his keycard and opened the doors for us. "We'll take really good care of you, *baby*."

"Lucky son of a bitch," the security guard said from behind us.

We walked in sync then when the doors behind us closed, each of us girls landed a punch or a slap to different parts of Nico's body.

"Ow, ow, fucking *ow*!" he hissed and jumped away from us.

He turned to face us and walked backwards with his hands raised in front of his chest. "I couldn't think of anything else to say to get us back here."

Alannah narrowed her eyes at Nico. "You couldn't think of somethin' better than sayin' the four of us were your *wives*?"

Nico gnawed on his lower lip. "No."

Liar.

Bronagh all but hissed at Nico. He refused to look at her, which was the smartest thing he had done in the past five minutes.

"It got us back here, didn't it? Let's just find my brothers and find out what's happening with Kane," Nico sighed and turned around. "Which room did that security guard say Ryder and Alec were in?"

"Last one on the right," I murmured.

We all picked up our speed until we reached the waiting room door. Nico walked straight into the room and so did the other girls who were hot on his heels. I hung back for a few seconds, and I had no idea why. The only thing I could think of was that I was afraid.

I was so damn afraid, and that fear worried me.

I wasn't sure what it meant. I mean, did I care for Kane if I was this concerned about him? Did I *like* him? Or did I just not want him to be dead for the sake of everyone else? I went with the latter because it was the only choice that didn't cause my mind to explode with even more stupid questions.

I jumped when Bronagh's head popped out of the doorway. "Hey, are you okay?"

I blinked. "I'm fine."

She reached out and took me by the hand. "Come in, then."

I let Bronagh lead me into the waiting room, and when all eyes fell on me. I looked down at my feet as I waited to hear an update on Kane. Bronagh placed her hand on my back and said, "No news on him yet."

That pissed me off. I—I mean *we*—needed an update on Kane.

I balled my hands into fists. "Give me one minute," I growled.

I turned and pulled the door open, stepping back out into the hallway, and looked up and down. I spotted a nurse reading a clipboard as she walked in the direction of the doors that led back out to the A&E reception.

"Excuse me!" I shouted and briskly walked down the hallway towards the nurse when she stopped and looked over her shoulder.

"Can I help you?" she asked when I stopped in front of her.

"Yes, please," I replied. "I'm with the family of Kane Slater, and we have received *no* information on his current status. He arrived here around twenty-five minutes ago, and his brothers in the waitin' room down the hall behind me are getting *very* impatient. Each of them are over six-foot-tall and combined, they probably weigh the same as a full-grown bull. Please come and give them an update before they... get *upset*."

The nurse swallowed, but nodded her head at me.

"Thank you," I breathed, relieved she believed the brothers would be dangerous.

I mean, they could easily go crazy, but I knew they wouldn't. My white lie would get us the update we needed though so I didn't care what was running through the nurse's mind.

I re-entered the waiting room and again all eyes fell on me, but when their eyes switched to the nurse behind me everyone stood up. Everyone.

"*You*," Keela growled to the nurse.

I raised my eyebrow.

Did something happen that I didn't know about?

"Oh, damn," the nurse whispered.

"I *told* you we wanted a different nurse!" Keela snarled.

The nurse shrugged her shoulders. "We're short on staff today, it's me or nobody."

"You might as well be nobody, you evil cow!" Keela bellowed.

Oh, hell.

Keela. Was. Pissed.

I moved over to my friend. "What's wrong?" I asked, my voice low.

"That *bitch* refused to give me any information on Kane. She made the security man outside keep me in reception from the moment they wheeled him through the double doors. If Alec and Ryder hadn't showed up, I would have still been kept out there."

"It's protocol!" the nurse snapped. "I told you that. It's the hospital's rules, *not* mine."

"I'll show you fuckin' protocol," Keela snarled.

I remained in front of Keela. "Calm it," I grunted then lowered my voice to a whisper, "just until we get the update on Kane from her."

Keela instantly calmed herself, but I could see she wasn't happy about it.

I nodded and turned back to the nurse. "So," I began, "how is he?"

I held my breath after the question left my lips.

The nurse flipped up a few pages on her clipboard and read a few lines then looked around the room. "Mr. Slater is stable. We have him on oxygen, an IV drip for fluids, and we're running his blood now to see what could have been the cause of him collapsing."

I blinked and exhaled a slow breath as I let what the nurse said sink in.

Kane was stable. He was alive!

Thank God.

"Why couldn't you just tell me that?" Keela suddenly screamed at the nurse. Alec had to jump forward and wrap his arms around her body to keep her from attacking the nurse. "Why couldn't you just say he was alive? How fuckin' dare you keep that information from me! You made me think he was *dead*! You made me tell his *brothers* that he might be dead. How fuckin' *dare* you!"

The nurse was on the verge of tears and I didn't know if it was because Keela was screaming at her, or because she felt bad for keeping precious information away from the family of a patient. I didn't care though—I wanted the bitch to cry. She worried us sick until we got here and the brothers could prove they were a blood relation.

"I-I'm sorry," the nurse stammered.

Keela tried to get at her with her extended arms. "You're sorry?" she bellowed. "You fuckin' will be!"

The nurse took a wise step backward. "Ma'am, you'll have to calm down or I'll call—"

"Don't," I cut the nurse off with a growl. "Don't threaten to call security and put her out of this hospital when our family is lyin' on a bed in this hospital. I'll put *you* in a bed next to him if you do."

"Shit," Nico said and quickly moved across the room and stood in front of me, pressing his hands on my shoulders, he nudged me backwards a few steps. He glanced over his shoulder at the nurse. "You better leave; your presence is just further upsetting my girls."

The nurse mumbled something then scurried out of the room, closing the door tightly behind her.

"You should have let me hit her!" Keela snapped at Alec when she turned in his arms. Alec said nothing, just wrapped his arms tightly around her body and held onto her until she calmed down enough to hug him back.

We were all quiet for a moment until I said, "He is okay."

Nico put his arms around me as I burst into tears. Bronagh joined us, and Nico took an arm away from me and wrapped it around her, pulling us together. I put an arm around Nico's waist and then Bronagh's as my tears flowed.

I could hear the other girls cry with relief, and I could hear a lot of patting going on. I opened my eyes and looked up as Ryder leaned in and pressed his head against the side of Nico's head and patted him roughly on the shoulder. I cried harder when I saw tears on Nico's cheeks.

I had never seen him cry before.

Ever.

I stepped back so he and Bronagh could comfort one another. I knew he needed her at that moment and I was glad they had each other to make this easier. The hard part was only beginning and we would all need one another to get through it. We knew Kane was okay, but we didn't know what happened to him, or why.

I sat down on one of the many plastic chairs in the waiting room and bent forward. I placed my elbows on my knees and my face in my hands. I closed my eyes and focused on breathing. I suddenly felt like I was going to be sick. I wasn't sure if it was from the immense relief of finding out Kane was okay or if it was because of something else.

"Aideen?"

I looked up when Keela called my name.

"Yeah?" I asked.

Keela sat down next to me and put her hand on my back. "You don't look so good."

I snorted and sat upright. "I feel like I'm about to puke. I think it's me nerves. I was just... so afraid."

Keela leaned into me and rested her head on my shoulder. "I know. Me too. When he fell... and the noise of him hittin' the ground. I didn't know what to do."

I hushed her. "You got him here, that's all that matters."

Keela nodded her head and sniffled.

I frowned and turned so I could put my arms around her.

Out of all of us, she really didn't need the stress of Kane being ill hanging over her. She had enough going on inside her mind without adding this to the list. I hugged Keela and whispered soothing things to her.

Alec took over for me after a while, so I got up, hugged everyone else in the room, and then sat down in a chair closest to the door of the waiting room. A few hours passed by and I found myself looking out the window of the waiting room, watching the moon as it inched its way across the night sky.

I blinked my eyes and looked at the door when it opened and in stepped the nurse who nearly became Keela's punching bag only hours before. I was the only girl awake right now. Bronagh was sleeping on Nico, Keela on Alec, and Alannah and Branna both had their heads on Ryder's thighs as they snoozed. The lads were watching some American football match with the television on mute in the room, but when the door opened, they all turned their heads towards the door.

The nurse nervously swallowed. "My shift just ended, and I'm supposed to tell you that visiting times are over, but I know you haven't seen your loved one yet. So I pulled a few favours with the night staff, and they're letting some of you stay with Mr. Slater in his room, and the rest of you can stay in here then switch in a few hours. It's my way of saying sorry. I-I'm sorry I upset your friend so much, I was only doing my job."

I reached out and gripped the nurse's hand. "Thank you *so* much and I'm sorry. I speak for Keela, too. We acted wrongly. We were just..."

"Scared?" the nurse finished my sentence and gave me a small smile.

I nodded my head in answer to her question.

"I understand," she said then handed me a sheet of paper. "This has the name of the ward Mr. Slater is on and the number of the room he is in. You will all have to leave this room by morning, as other loved ones of patients in the A&E will need it. The waiting room in the ward he is on is like this so it will accommodate you all if needed."

"Thank you," I said and cleared my throat. "We really appreciate this."

The nurse inclined her head, gave a tight-lipped smile to everyone then left the room. Things were quiet until Alec said, "We should let Keela threaten people more often if it gets us results like this."

I snorted and shook my head at him then read the sheet of paper the nurse gave me.

"He is on St. Peter's Ward in room nine," I said and looked at the brothers, then to the girls. "You all go up to see him. The four of them will stay asleep until we switch."

Ryder blinked at me. "Are you sure?"

Was I sure?

"Of course," I said, biting my lip. "You're his *brothers*."

The brothers said nothing for a moment, but nodded their heads in agreement with me and carefully moved the girls off their bodies so they could stand up. Nico had a bit of trouble untangling Bronagh from his body so Alec had to help. Watching them made me laugh. I placed my hand over my mouth and shook with silent laughter until he was free from his sleeping beauty's grip.

He kissed her head, took off his jumper, and laid it over her to keep her warm. He walked over to me then and playfully kicked my leg when he saw I was smiling. "She has the grip of an anaconda; don't judge her by her size. She may be small, but trust me when I say she is strong. Very strong."

"I've no doubt, *husband*." I winked.

Nico snickered then laughed a little when Ryder and Alec asked what I meant by calling him husband. I grinned, too.

Good luck to you on explaining that one, buddy.

"I'll explain along the way, come on," Nico said grinning as he took the sheet of paper the nurse gave me.

Ryder winked as he passed me by and Alec fist bumped me. They gently clicked the door shut behind them as they left and when they did, a veil of silence coated the room. I could hear the girls breathing, and every few seconds Bronagh would snore a little, but other than that, it was silent.

I leaned my head back against the wall of the waiting room and sighed. I folded my arms across my chest, and tucked my legs under my behind then closed my eyes and relaxed as much as I could. I was uncomfortable, but that wasn't what had me uneasy. Kane did that just by being here in the hospital; it wasn't so bad because he was alive and stable. He wasn't okay because he was in the hospital, but he *was* alive and that was the main thing.

I would take alive and ill over dead and buried any day.

CHAPTER THREE

"Aideen?"

I groaned low in my throat and wrapped my arms tightly around myself, trying to hold onto sleep for a little while longer.

"Aideen? Hey, wake up."

I felt a nudge on my legs and it caused me to wake with a jolt. I scrunched up my face then slowly blinked my eyes open. I pulled my head back a little when I found a huge clump of tin foil shoved in my face.

"It's a breakfast roll, eat it. You need food."

I blinked at the tin foil then looked up at the person holding it. I stared at Keela for a moment then took the tin foil covered roll from her extended hand. I sat upright and groaned when my back clicked. I carefully stood up and stretched out my body, making noises close to that of a baby dinosaur.

"Fuckin' shite chairs," I grumbled and placed my free hand on my now aching back.

My legs, back, arms, and my neck were stiff and sore. My damn neck felt like a five-hundred pound wrestler had leaned on it all night long.

"You know what?" I mumbled to Keela who sat down next to a still sleeping Bronagh, Branna, and Alannah.

"What?" Keela asked as she opened her own roll.

I sat back down on the God forsaken chair I slept in all night and rolled my head on my shoulders. "I wonder if people ever end up in A&E from these chairs. Imagine that, comin' to see someone in hospital but throwin' your back out in the waitin' room."

Keela shook with silent laughter.

I opened the breakfast roll and when the smell travelled up my nostrils I groaned out loud. It smelled delicious. My stomach agreed because it grumbled as if to say, 'feed me.'

The roll was a full Irish breakfast roll that consisted of eggs, black and white pudding, sausages, rashers, hash browns and some ketchup. My mouth watered as I brought it to my lips and sunk my teeth into the yumminess.

I again groaned out loud and closed my eyes as I chewed and swallowed down my first bite. I repeated this action until my roll was completely gone and my belly was full and satisfied.

"Damn, Aideen," Branna's voice murmured.

I blinked my eyes open and looked across the room. All the girls were awake now, and each of them was staring at me. I flushed with embarrassment.

"What?" I muttered.

Alannah grinned. "It sounded like you were havin' an orgasm."

Oh, my God.

"Lana!" I cried.

All the girls burst into laughter.

"It did," Keela agreed still laughing, "but it looked like somethin' out of Bear Grylls. You destroyed that roll in less than three minutes flat, babe."

I frowned. "I was hungry."

The girls laughed again and each took their own breakfast roll from Keela who took them out of a plastic bag on an empty chair beside her.

"Where are the lads?" Bronagh asked as she opened her roll.

Keela shrugged her shoulders. "They weren't here when I woke up half an hour ago. I thought they'd be outside so I checked when I went to the deli to buy the rolls, but they weren't out there either."

I yawned. "They're with Kane. When you were all sleepin' last night, the nurse Keela tried to kill came in. She felt bad for upsettin' Keela, and pulled some strings with the night staff. They let the brothers go be with Kane and let us stay in here. We have to leave soon though because they'll need this waitin' room for other families of A&E patients. Kane is on St. Peter's Ward and they have a waitin' room there that we can use."

Bronagh cheered a little as she bit into her roll.

"What?" I chuckled.

She chewed and swallowed her food. "St. Peter's Ward is on the first floor. All wards on the first floor aren't trauma wards, so whatever is wrong with him isn't too serious—trauma wise, anyway."

I blew out a big breath of relief.

"Are you sure?" I asked.

Bronagh nodded her head. "It was on one of those hospital adverts on the telly last night. All the wards were listed and what floor they were on. I pointed it out to Ryder and said I hope Kane is in a ward on the first floor so we know it's nothin' too serious."

I was delighted with that news.

"Thank God," Alannah breathed.

We all nodded our heads in unison as we agreed with her. I was about to speak when the door next to me opened. I turned my head and watched as Nico, Alec, and Ryder walked into the waiting room looking tired but put together, which was better than how I felt.

"You're all up." Ryder smiled.

"Thanks to Aideen and her vocal abilities." Alannah grinned.

I glared at her and the other girls when they started laughing.

"Do we want to know?" Nico asked, amused.

"No," I growled. "You do *not*."

Nico snorted and stretched his arms over his head. "We're going home to shower and get some food then come back with some stuff for Kane. Are you all ready to come with us?"

I frowned. "You want to leave him on his own?"

Everyone looked at me.

Alec sat next to me and dropped his arm around my shoulder. "He hasn't woken up yet, he's still out cold."

I shrugged. "So? That doesn't mean he *won't* wake up today, and what if none of us is here when he does?" I asked and shook my head. "No, I'll go up and sit with him, then when you all come back I'll leave and go get showered and stuff."

I caught Nico grinning and looking down. Alannah looked away smiling, too.

"What are you grinnin' about?" I asked Nico then looked at Alannah.

Both of them said nothing; they only shook their heads with their silly smiles still in place on their faces. I narrowed my eyes at them, but shrugged it off as I stood up. "Go on, get goin'. I'll go up to his room and wait."

I hated when everyone else started to smile at me.

"I'm not doin' this because I care or anythin'. I just don't want to listen to him complain that he was on his own when he wakes up. That's all. I'm doin' this for me own benefit when you really think about it. I'm savin' meself a future headache."

The fuckers just continued to smile at me. Alec was smirking though, and I wanted to wipe the stupid look from his face. I shook my head, dug the car parking card and keys out of my back pocket, and handed them to Ryder.

"Fourth floor in the multi-story car park, closest spot to the stairs and elevator."

Ryder winked at me.

"He's in room nine, right?" I asked the brothers.

They all nodded, still smiling.

I opened the door and walked through it. "I hope your faces get stuck like that," I threw over my shoulder.

Their laughter didn't fade away until I got into the elevator next to the waiting room. I shook my head as I pressed the button for the first floor and watched the elevator doors close. They reopened a few seconds later when it brought me to the first floor. I nervously swallowed as I stepped out and looked up at the signs on the wall in front of me. I saw St. Peter's Ward was to the right so I turned and walked down the hallway and straight through the set of double doors for the correct ward.

I walked by the nurse's station and avoided eye contact with them. I didn't want any of them to stop and ask me questions. I continued to walk down the hallway and followed the room numbers. Room number nine was down at the very end of the hallway with the door closed. I swallowed as I reached for the handle, pushed it down and nudged the door open.

I looked at Kane as I entered the room and closed the door behind me. I stood motionless and stared at him for a few minutes. He was too big to be in the bed they had him in. He'd lost weight and muscle mass over the past year, but he was still a big lad, and seeing him lying down on a small bed with a hospital gown on looked weird.

I walked over to the large chair next to the head of the bed and quietly sat down. I flicked my eyes over Kane to see what else was different about him. He had an IV drip in his arm to give him fluids, I assumed, and a dressing on his forehead. It was spotted with little red dots. I figured that was from when he fell and hit his head.

Other than the drip and bandage, he looked okay. He was pale, and his face looked sullen even in sleep, but that was how he always looked. At least how he looked over the past year. I leaned forward and pressed my hand on top of his.

"Kane?" I murmured. "It's me, Aideen. I just want you to know... you aren't alone. I'm here with you."

I removed my hand from his and sat back in the chair when he gave me no reaction. He was deep in sleep, so I decided not to speak anymore. He needed his rest. When he decided to wake up that was when the real tiredness was going to start because everyone would be breathing down his neck.

I relaxed into the big chair and was so pleased to find it had cushions. It wasn't plastic like the ones in the waiting room—it was a real chair. I snuggled back and folded my arms across my chest. I was aware that my eyes felt heavy, but not surprised, because I had the worst night's sleep on the chairs in the bloody A&E waiting room.

When I was sure Kane wasn't going to wake up, I closed my eyes, and like the flip of a light switch, I was out.

I awoke later when a God-awful pain struck my stomach and caused it to churn and roil. "Oh, fuck!" I grumbled as I jumped up out of the chair and ran over to the sink in the hospital room.

I vomited into the sink until I was dry heaving and nothing else came up. I ran the water in the sink and splashed some of it on my face. I filled my mouth with water, gargled some of it, and spat it out before I shut the tap off and got some tissue papers to wipe my face and mouth dry.

I felt disgusting.

"Aideen?" a raspy voice behind me grumbled. "Are you okay?"

I spun around.

"Kane," I whispered and moved over to the side of his bed. "Hey, you're awake."

Kane blinked up at me. "You were throwing up."

I waved my hand. "Don't mind that, I'm fine."

Kane frowned, then reached up and touched his bandaged head. "What the hell happened? Where am I?"

I frowned. "You collapsed. You're in the hospital, but you're okay. This is just a precaution."

Kane furrowed his eyebrows in confusion. "I don't remember much. I was with Keela and we—" I jumped when he gasped. "Did it happen while I was driving? Oh, God, *Keela*! Is she okay? Is she—"

"Shh. Stop. She's okay," I cut him off and took hold of his hand in mine. "It happened while you were inside Tesco. The car was parked and you were both in an aisle inside the shop. She is okay."

Physically okay, anyway.

"Thank God," Kane breathed in relief. "That's good."

I nodded my head and let go of his hand when he glanced down to my hold on him. I busied myself with moving a chair closer so I could sit and talk to him.

"I'm... I'm a little surprised you're here," Kane said after a few seconds of silence.

I looked up at him and frowned. "Why?" I asked, slightly offended.

He shrugged his shoulders. "You don't like me, Aideen."

I huffed. "So? That doesn't mean I want to see you dead."

Kane smirked. "If I remember correctly, the last time we were alone together, you said you'd kill me yourself if I—"

"Do you want me to hurt you while you're in this state?" I snapped. "We agreed to *never* talk about *that night*."

Images of our bodies moving together from *that* night filled my mind, but I stopped that train of thought. I forced myself not to think about what happened. I pretended if I didn't think about it, then it didn't happen.

Kane lost his smirk and glared at me. "You agreed. Not me."

I groaned. "Please, Kane. What good will come from people knowin' what happened between us? I can tell you. Nothin'. Nothin' will come of it because it *was* nothin'."

"Kick a man while he's down, why don't you," Kane growled.

I placed my head in my hands. "I didn't mean it like *that*—"

"Then what way did you mean it?" Kane cut me off, his voice raised.

I kept my head down. "It was drunken sex, Kane. It was a mistake."

"Yeah, well that *mistake* may be growing inside your body right now. I'm not stupid, Aideen. I may not remember fainting, but I remember everything else about yesterday. You might be pregnant, and we didn't use protection *that* night. I can put two and two together. I'm not as dumb as you think I am," he hissed. "Did you take a pregnancy test yet?"

I felt my eyes well up as I nodded my head. "I did, but then Keela phoned and told me what happened with you. Everythin' was a little crazy after that. I forgot to look at the results."

Kane's voice was stern. "Go take one now. Ask a nurse for one; they will have them in their supply rooms."

I looked up at him and frowned. "I can't do it here."

"Why not?" Kane asked, his face twisted in rage. "If you are pregnant it's just a *mistake*, right? What do you care about taking a test in a hospital?"

I wasn't sure why I was so upset, or why he was so angry with me. He agreed what happened between us all those nights ago was just an impulsive act. He knew we weren't suited as a couple just as much as I knew it. We were the polar opposites of one another, and butted heads more times than not. We weren't good together. We didn't even like one another.

"Please, Kane," I whispered. "I'm... I'm scared, okay?"

Kane remained silent for a long moment. "Fine. I won't tell anyone we *fucked*, but I want you to go home and take a pregnancy test today and then come back and tell me the results. Do you understand me, Aideen? If you're pregnant, that's my kid in there too and I *will* have a say in what happens. Understood?"

I was frozen to my seat as Kane spoke. I had never heard him use that tone of voice before. It was cold and threatening and not at all the Kane I knew.

"You seem pretty confident that if I was pregnant the baby would be yours," I began, "I want to know why you'd just assume it's yours? I could have been with someone else around the same time."

I wasn't with another man before I fell into stupidity and slept with Kane. I would normally never lie like that, but his arrogance and controlling demeanour both scared and pissed me off.

"*Were* you with someone else?" Kane snarled, his hands balling into fists.

I kept my head down so he couldn't see the truth in my eyes. "It's not relevant unless I turn out to be pregnant. I'll keep you posted."

Kane sat up in the bed and I heard how laboured his breathing was.

"Aideen."

One word and I was shitting myself.

"I understand you, okay? I'll do as you asked and take a test then let you know the results. Jesus."

"Good," he quipped.

I didn't know what to do then. I was surprised with how I felt in his presence. I was uncomfortable being alone with him. There was no room for jokes or insults between us right at this moment, it was just a dark space filled with nothing. He wasn't the same person I was so used to being around, and I could tell all this from the tone of his voice.

"I'm going to go now," I said, my voice low.

I slowly eased myself up from the chair but halted when Kane said, "No... just stay awhile, okay?" He sighed and like the click of my fingers, he was changed back to the Kane I knew. "I'm sorry... you just... made me a little angry."

That tone was him when he was a little angry?

Damn.

I was so screwed if I ever really pissed him off.

"Will you look at me?" he whispered.

It took me a minute but I lifted my head and brought my gaze to his.

"There she is," he murmured.

Oh, God.

His mouth was in a frown and he was still a little pale, but fuck, he was gorgeous.

Scars and all.

I hated with everything in me that I found him attractive. Hating somebody and still finding them stunning in appearance was torture. Utter torture.

"Things are so fucked up," I breathed and sat back in the chair. "One of us girls might be pregnant, you're ill, Keela's head is turnin' against her, Nico is workin' for Brandon Daley and so is me little brother. What fuckin' else can happen to us?"

The room was silent for a few moments.

"We'll figure it out. *All* of us will figure it out," Kane said. "We always do."

I blinked. "Yeah, but still, this is a lot of shite to deal with."

Kane's lip quirked a little. "We've been through worse things, babydoll."

I widened my eyes to the point of pain. "We discussed you *never* callin' me that again."

Kane grinned. "You only get one pass. Either I keep quiet about us fucking, or I don't call you babydoll. You choose which one you want, but if I was you, I'd hurry because time's a wasting."

I hated him.

I hated every fibre in the sick bastard's body.

"The stupid sex," I growled. "Keep *that* to yourself."

Kane winked. "You got it, *babydoll*."

What. A. Prick.

"If you weren't so ill, I'd kill you meself," I angrily snapped.

I jumped with fright when laughter sounded from my right.

"He must be okay if she's threatening to kill him," Alec's voice sang with laughter.

I looked up and playfully rolled my eyes as the brothers and girls filed into Kane's room.

"Good to see you awake, you bastard," Alec said and leaned in to hug Kane. "You frightened the shit out of us."

Kane made jokes as each of his brothers hugged him, followed by the girls. After Bronagh hugged him, she walked over, closed the door of the room, and leaned against it. Nico tried to get her to move over to the seat near the window so she could sit on his lap, but she was having none of it.

"I told you no," Bronagh snapped. "Kane is awake now and I'm not blinded with fear for his safety anymore, so I can remember perfectly fuckin' well the deal you struck with Brandon fucking Daley. I was serious when I said I'm done with you, Dominic. I want *no* part of that poxy life, and if you insist on being part of it then I'm sorry to say fuckface, but I'm cuttin' you loose."

Oh, bollocks.

They were breaking up?

"Cutting me loose, huh?" Nico said, his voice cool and calm. "Like I'm some snot-faced little boy you sunk your claws into?"

Bronagh glared at him. "Somethin' like that."

Nico moved so fast that none of us had time to react. He got Bronagh backed into the corner of the room and blocked her from our view with his body.

I looked at Kane who shook his head at me. "Let them hash it out," he murmured.

I looked away from him and at Nico's back.

"You think I want to be involved with Brandy and that fucking life? I fucking *don't*, Bronagh. I grew up in it, and all my life I just wanted my brothers and me to have a normal life, but that isn't on the cards for us. As much as it sucks, this crazy fucked-up life—is my normal. I'm trying to make the best I can out of a shitty situation. And, sweetheart, the fact of the matter is that we're broke and my job at the gym and with clients isn't cutting it anymore. I don't know how, but I blew all of my money and I refuse to get loans from my brothers or to scrape the bottom of the barrel to support us. But fighting... it's what I'm good at, Bronagh. It's really good money. It won't be like it was before—you just have to trust me when I say that. Please. I'm doing this for you. For us."

Bronagh's cries were evident then, and so were Nico's soothing murmurs of his love for her and the promises he swore to keep.

"You promise me," Bronagh whimpered. "You promise it won't be like before. You won't go from country to country fightin' or be involved in shady shite. Promise if you're fightin' that it's just on that fuckin' platform in that stupid bloody nightclub. *Promise me.*"

"Look me in the eyes," Nico breathed. "I *promise* you."

Bronagh cried again, "I love you."

Their kissing could be heard then, and so could my sniffles.

"Aideen?" Kane murmured. "Why are you crying?"

I waved him off and everyone else who was looking at me. I wiped the tears as they fell from my eyes. "I don't even know why, but I can't stop."

I covered my face as I began to sob.

I was upset and mortified at the same time.

"Ah, darling, everything is okay," Alec's voice chuckled as he hunkered down in front of me and pulled me into a hug.

I put my arms around him and hugged him tightly.

When I calmed myself down and Alec stood up, I got up, walked over to Keela and put my arms around her. Keela placed her hands on my back and rubbed up and down. "What's goin' on with you?" she murmured in my ear.

"I don't know," I admitted and hugged her tighter.

We separated when a knock sounded on Kane's door. The door opened and a middle-aged man stepped in. I instantly knew he was Kane's doctor. He had a clipboard in his hand, a long white coat on his body, and a stethoscope around his neck. Classic doctor attire.

"Huh, full house in here." The doctor smiled then focused on Kane. "I'm Doctor Chance, and you're my newest patient, Mr. Slater."

"Lucky me," Kane deadpanned.

Branna hissed at Kane, "Be nice!" She then looked at the doctor. "Ignore him; he is just being crabby today."

I wiped my face and smiled at Branna's motherly tone.

The doctor grinned and shook hands with Branna, then the brothers who introduced themselves one by one. He nodded his head to all of us when we threw our names into the pool, and I wanted to chuckle. He probably wouldn't remember a single name when he left the room.

"I'm going to cut to the chase here, folks. Mr. Slater isn't very well."

"No shit, doc. Tell me something I don't know," Kane snorted.

I narrowed my eyes at his rude arse, and then mentally bitch slapped him.

"Sit back, Mr. Slater, and listen closely because the following conversation will definitely be something you don't know."

Oh, shite.

CHAPTER FOUR

"Just give it to me straight, doc," Kane sighed. "What's wrong with me?"

The doctor flipped through pages from Kane's chart then looked up at him. "I had the nurses gather information from your family members while you were sleeping last night. The nurses then filled me in on your health over the past year. Based on the symptoms you were presenting, I had the night staff draw blood so it could be sent down to the lab for testing."

I raised my eyebrow. "What type of tests were performed on his blood?"

The doctor looked at me. "Glucose and haemoglobin A1C."

I blinked my eyes when my mind recognised the tests and what they were for.

"Diabetes?" I questioned. "You were testing for diabetes?"

The doctor raised his eyebrow at me. "Are you studying in the medical field?"

I shook my head. "No, no. I'm a primary school teacher. I just read a book before about diabetes and it had different types of testing that can be run to get a positive result. The tests you mentioned were two of them."

A student of mine, Jessie, had diabetes type one and just because I was curious, I read up on it.

The doctor nodded his head to me. "Well, yes, you're correct. I wanted to see if Mr. Slater here has diabetes."

"And?" Nico pressed.

"And my theory was correct," the doctor said then looked at Kane. "You do indeed have diabetes, Mr. Slater. Type one to be exact."

None of us said anything until Kane opened his mouth and spoke.

"Are you sure?" he asked. "I mean, my blood could have been tainted in the lab, right?"

The doctor nodded. "That is a possibility, but I had the tests ran three times for confirmation and nothing changed. The result was the same all three times. You're a diabetic, Mr. Slater."

"I'm a diabetic?" Kane mumbled to himself.

The room was quiet again, but not for long because I had a few questions that I wanted to be answered.

"Type one is the one that requires insulin, right?" I asked the doctor.

He nodded his head. "Yes, that is the very one."

I frowned. "Isn't that a children's disease though?"

"Normally," the doctor said and nodded his head. "It was dubbed with the name juvenile diabetes because it's most commonly diagnosed in children, teenagers, or young adults. It can occur at any age, though."

I blinked. "Oh, I see."

"I don't understand," Kane sighed. "Wouldn't I have known if I was diabetic? I mean, I would have had some signs, right?"

"Your brothers mentioned to the nurses last night about your extreme fatigue, weight loss, vomiting and so on over the past twelve months. It is very easy to look at these symptoms as a case of influenza, a vomiting bug or even a simple head cold," the doctor explained. "There are many different symptoms for type one diabetes. Some people suffer from all of them and others have no signs at all. It varies from person to person."

We all nodded our heads in understanding and waited for the doctor to continue.

"Your body is a special case, Kane. With a lot of people, the symptoms can start like the click of my fingers and things can progress quickly. Then there are cases like yours where people can be ill for a long period of time but not need treatment straight away. Your body managed to get by with what little insulin it produced itself for the past year, but the strain has started to show and it's not enough anymore. Your collapsing last night is a prime example of that. Your body needs more insulin to survive than what it's currently producing."

I looked at Kane and saw he swallowed but nodded his head to the doctor, taking what he said at face value.

"The bad news about type one diabetes is that there is no cure for it. You will have it for the rest of your life. The good news is that it *is* manageable. You will need to take a daily injection of insulin, starting today. You will have a standard daily dose and it can be adjusted depending on your sugar level. While you were sleeping earlier, we sampled your blood sugar level so it will be a low dose today as you're not actively moving, or consuming a lot of calories. That is the trick with your injections, the more active you are or the more calories you consume, the higher your dose needs to be. Don't worry about that right now though, we will develop a schedule."

The doctor went on as a nurse opened the door and wheeled in a trolley with a yellow bucket and other medical equipment on a large tray.

"Weekly appointments and check-ups will be set up until you've got a handle on your doses. It will become routine for you and I doubt it will be difficult for you to get a grasp of. You look like a man who knows about diet and exercise. You will just have to follow a new program to balance your body's glucose level. Does that make sense?"

Kane nodded mutely then pointed his finger at the trolley next to the nurse.

"What's that?" he asked, his voice low.

"Your first insulin dose. I'll prescribe an insulin pen just because they are more convenient than dealing with a separate needle and bottle of insulin."

Kane tensed up at the mention of the word 'needle.' He sat upright and he glared daggers at the doctor. "You are *not* sticking a needle in me."

The doctor glanced at the brothers then back to Kane. "Your insulin must be injected under the skin, Mr. Slater. It cannot be taken orally because the acids in your stomach will destroy it."

Kane swallowed. "I don't care; you're not sticking a needle in me. I don't give a fuck."

"Damn," Ryder murmured. "Kane, you need this medication or you don't get better. Period. You have to take it."

Kane looked at his older brother, and at that moment he was a scared little boy. "Not a needle, Ryder. *Please*. Anything but a needle."

I was shocked.

I had no idea he was so terrified of needles. I mean, he couldn't be scared of them, he had a sleeve of tattoos so what was his problem?

Nico turned to the doctor. "He's had some... bad experiences with needles in the past."

He had? How?

The doctor frowned. "It has to be injected daily. I'm sorry, he has to receive this medication or... or he will die."

I flung my hand over my mouth and widened my eyes. That was all I needed to hear for me to take this situation very seriously.

"I'll do it," I announced and dropped my hand to my side.

The doctor and nurse looked at me. "I'm sorry, but that isn't protocol—"

I ignored the doctor and moved over to Kane's side. He was panicking and looked only seconds from jumping up out of the bed and doing God only knows what.

"Hey," I murmured, my voice low. "Look at *me*, Kane."

Kane's eyes were wild as they locked on mine. "Not a needle. Please," he begged.

I felt my eyes well up. "You trust me not to hurt you, don't you?" I asked, keeping eye contact with him even as my tears fell.

Kane was hesitant. "Aideen... I can't..."

"You trust me not to hurt you, don't you?" I repeated.

Kane began to sweat but replied, "Yes, I know you won't hurt me."

I reached out and placed my palm on his cheek. "Then let me help you. Let me do this and get it out of the way. It'll be over before you know it. I won't ever hurt you, Kane. I promise."

He held my gaze and I thought he would need more convincing, but just as I was about to open my mouth, he whispered, "Okay."

He was agreeing?

Yes!

"Okay," I breathed. "We've got this, okay? Me and you?"

"Me and you," Kane repeated.

I kept looking at him and reached my right hand back.

"Give her the damn needle. He will only let her do it so *give it to her*," I heard Nico growl in a low voice.

There was a bit of movement then I felt an object placed in my hand. "His stomach and arms are pretty toned, it will have to be in his thigh. A fatty area, like the inner thigh is best," the doctor said, his voice low as not to freak out Kane.

I nodded my head and refocused on Kane. "Close your eyes for me."

"Aideen, please... don't stab me with it."

Stab him with it?

Oh, God.

"It's going to be one little prick in your inner thigh, that's all," I said, my lower lip trembling.

Kane held my gaze. "You promise?"

"I promise, sweetheart," I replied, nodding my head.

He nodded his head back at me then closed his eyes.

He trusted me.

I looked down to his body and removed the blanket that covered him. I pushed the hospital gown up his leg, uncapped the needle the doctor handed me then reached inside to a part where I could grab a chunk of the fatty part of his inner thigh.

"Pinch the skin then insert the needle. Slowly inject the insulin, then hold for ten seconds so no insulin seeps out with any blood," the doctor whispered.

I nodded and looked down to the needle in my hand. I held it correctly then pressed it into Kane's thigh before I could think about what I was doing. I was scared if I thought about it then I would lose my nerve. I carefully pushed the insulin into his body, and then held it for ten seconds before I removed the needle.

I capped it, handed it back to the doctor then turned back to Kane. He still had his eyes closed, so I reached up and touched his face. "All done," I whispered.

Kane blinked his eyes open. "I didn't feel anything."

I smiled. "Told you."

Kane stared at me for a moment then reached out and pulled me into a hug. He said nothing, just held me tightly to his body.

"I'll come back later to discuss a check-up appointment date for next week. I'll also go through everything with him, and with you, about what to expect with his diabetes. We'll keep him overnight again and if he is responding well to the injections he can go home tomorrow."

I heard the brothers speak to the doctor then a door open and close.

"Are you okay?" I murmured.

Kane murmured, "Yes," and then let me go. I pulled back and stared down at him, frowning. He closed his eyes and remained silent.

"What the hell was *that*? I've never seen him like that before," Bronagh snapped at Nico.

Nico sighed. "It's not my place to explain *that*, Bronagh. It's up to Kane if he wants to tell you."

"I don't want to *tell* anything because we're done speaking about *that*," Kane said and opened his eyes. "And we're done discussing injections of any type. I am not doing that shit again. No fucking way."

I frowned.

He needed a daily insulin injection in order to balance his diabetes and stay well.

"It's not up for discussion, Kane," Branna started. "You will be taking the injections. I'll do them for you—"

"No!" Kane shouted and cut Branna off. "Just... *No*."

Ryder glared at Branna. "Stop pushing him."

Branna glared right back at Ryder and snarled, "*One* of us has to. Otherwise he will get sick again. Is that what you want?"

Ryder shook his head and looked away from Branna's burning gaze.

Shite.

Now, what was *that* about?

They looked at one another like they hated each other.

I shook my head clear and focused on what everyone else was saying.

"She's right, Ryder," Bronagh said. "He needs to take them. You can't baby him."

Alec butted in then. "We aren't babying him, Bronagh! We're being considerate. He doesn't like needles. End of fucking story."

"Hey!" Alannah snapped at Alec. "Don't talk to her like that!"

"Don't shout at him, Lana," Keela sighed.

Alannah glared at Keela. "Tell him to back off Bronagh then."

What the fuck was going on?

Everyone was turning on one another.

"It would help if you all stopped talking about me like I'm a fucking invalid. I *can* hear what you're all saying, and I can make my own damn decisions when it comes to my body."

Branna moved to the opposite side of the bed and stared down at Kane. "Do you want to die?" she bluntly asked. "Because that's what will happen if you don't take the insulin daily."

"Branna, fucking *stop*!" Ryder shouted.

It frightened me to hear Ryder raise his voice at her.

"No!" Branna bellowed right back at him. "I love him, damn it! I don't want him to get sick again!"

I rubbed my hand over my face.

This was bad.

I looked at Kane as everyone argued amongst themselves.

"Kane?" I mumbled.

He looked at me, his face passive. "I know what you're going to say."

"What?" I asked.

"Kane, you need to take the insulin. You'll get sick if you don't," he said, mimicking my voice perfectly.

I snorted. "Yep, that was pretty much it."

Kane frowned. "I don't do needles, Aideen. I just don't."

Why?

I wanted to ask why so badly. It seemed much more than a simple phobia of needles, but I didn't want to push him.

Ryder moved past Branna and leaned down to Kane. "What can we do to get you to take the insulin shots?"

"I. Don't. Do. Needles," Kane repeated through gritted teeth.

Oh, forget this.

"You don't," I said, "but I do."

The room went silent.

"Wh-What?" Kane stuttered, as he looked back to me.

I blew out a breath. "I'll give you your injections every day. You let me do it once; will you let me do it every other time, too?"

Kane stared at me with unblinking eyes. I felt everyone else stare at me too.

"Why would you want to help me?" he asked, his face falling.

Good question.

I shrugged my shoulders. "I enjoy arguin' with you, and I need to keep you around for that so I guess I'm doin' this for me own selfish needs. Sue me."

Kane grinned a little when his brothers chuckled and the tension in the room eased.

"Aideen, thank you, but I don't—"

"Hey," I cut him off and smiled when he looked at me. "Me and you?"

Kane licked his lips and whispered, "Me and you."

Oh, my.

Me and you.

Now that got my heart rate going.

I playfully winked. "We got this."

Kane stared at me long and hard, and I saw him crack and give in to me before he realised it himself.

"What do you say?" I pressed.

Kane looked around the room, then to me and said, "I say okay, *babydoll*."

CHAPTER FIVE

It's been eight days since Kane left the hospital, but only nine since he collapsed so that meant everyone was still taking things easy around him. Even me. I limited our arguments to one a day just so he didn't wear himself out. He hasn't been necessarily weak since he got home, but he tired easily, even with his insulin injections. His tiredness aside, we could all see the change in him thanks to his medication. It was slowly building him back up to his old self.

His health was improving everyday, but his attitude? Yeah, that worsened with each passing minute. He agreed the day he woke up in the hospital to let me give him the injections every day at home, but that was easier said than done. He was on two insulin injections a day, which the doctor said was his minimum. Kane consumed a lot of calories and was active even when he wasn't feeling good so the two injections were needed for him. It might even jump to three a day when he was eventually well enough to work out again, but for now, it was two a day and getting the insulin into him had been hell. Absolute hell.

I worked in the local primary school full time. I taught second-class students and worked from eight thirty in the morning to three in the afternoon, except for Fridays when it was a half-day and I finished up at one in the afternoon. Kane's timetable for his injections was one jab in the morning, and one jab in the afternoon, after he ate. I worked it around my work schedule, so the past week I had been arriving at Kane's house at eight in the morning to give him his first injection, then I'd come over on my lunch break to give him his second.

It was difficult and I'd resorted to doing ridiculous things just to take his mind off the impending injections. The lowest level I stooped to was flashing my boobs at him just to fight off a panic attack I was convinced he was going to have. He worked himself up over the injections, and a couple of times he repeated for me not to 'stab him' and I had no idea why. I was extremely curious as to why he repeated those same words to me, but when I asked his brothers about it, they told me to 'drop it' so I did.

For the time being anyway.

It was Friday afternoon, and I had just arrived at the Slater residence after coming straight from work. Keela let me into the house. She came over to check on Kane, but he was in his room behind his locked door so she was leaving. She stopped to talk to me since I was there and I used the time to vent to her.

"I came here this mornin' on me way to work and do you know what he did?" I asked Keela.

She shook her head.

"He wouldn't let me into his room to give him his injection. I have no idea what is up his arse, but he needs to get rid of it so I can give him his damn insulin," I stated and pushed loose strands of hair that escaped my hair clips back from my face. "I'm gettin' grey hairs stressin' out about him and worryin' about his injections. It's not even funny how childish he is being."

Keela shook her head but said nothing.

"I thought since he agreed to let me give him his injections that he would be reasonable, but he isn't. He has been nothing but difficult," I said to Keela. "He is rude, mean, and a *complete* arsehole to me. I'm this close," I held my index finger and thumb a hair away from one another, "to stabbin' him in the fuckin' eye with the insulin pen."

Keela's lip twitched. "If anyone can get him to take his medicine, it's you, Ado."

I groaned. "I don't know why, all we do is argue. Literally. It's all we do. It's all we've ever done."

Keela giggled, "Maybe he gets off on your bickerin'. Have you ever thought of that?"

No, because that was a stupid idea.

"Please, he can't stand me just as much as I can't stand him. We're happily in hate, Keela."

Keela laughed and shook her head. "You're both crazy."

"I know I'm crazy," I stated. "Only a crazy woman would put up with his hormonal arse. I'm tellin' you the woman who ends up with him will have to have the patience of a bloody saint."

"I can fucking *hear* you, big mouth!" Kane roared down the stairs as he descended them.

I growled and in a low voice, I said to Keela, "I'll kill him before his diabetes does."

Keela silently laughed and looked at Kane when he stepped off the last step of the stairs.

"What's so funny?" Kane asked her.

"Nothin'," she replied and wiped tears from her eyes.

I narrowed my eyes at Kane. "What time do you call this?"

He glanced at the clock on the wall behind me and said, "Two thirty in the afternoon."

"I call it lazy bastard o'clock," I hissed.

Keela reached out and held onto me as her silent laughter upgraded to audible wheezing.

"Sorry, *Mom*. Was I supposed to be up before noon for somethin'?" Kane asked, snickering.

I glared. "You know good and well I had to give you your injection at eight this mornin'. I stopped in on my way to work and you wouldn't open the door. Don't feed me your bullshit about not hearin' me either. I *heard* you laugh when I was threatenin' you."

Kane smirked but didn't deny the charges.

"You're unbelievable," I growled. "Do you want to fall ill? Because not takin' your insulin will result in you being unwell—no one else—just you."

Kane continued to smirk. "Maybe I enjoy self-inflicted pain."

"Keep talkin'," I warned him, "and I'll inflict all kinds of fuckin' pain on you."

"Is that a promise, babydoll?" Kane said and made kiss noises.

I screeched and slapped at Keela's shoulder. "Do you see? Do you *see* what I've to put up with? A fuckin' man-child!"

"I'm all man, baby. You see my cock enough to know that," Kane snickered, again.

Keela paused mid-way through her fit of laughter to stare at me with a what-the-fuck wide-eyed stare.

I growled, "By *that*, he means he mostly goes commando when I have to give him his injection on his thigh and *forces* me to look at his penis."

Keela walked over to Kane and high-fived the arsehole. "That's brilliant."

Brilliant?

"Whose bloody side are you on?" I demanded of Keela.

"The side of love."

Of love?

"What?" I snapped.

Keela was still laughing as she turned and walked towards the hall door, not answering me or even saying goodbye. I turned and stared at her back.

"Where the hell are you off to?" I angrily asked.

Keela lifted her hand and waved without turning around. "Me first therapist appointment is in half an hour. I need to leave here; otherwise, I'll pass out from laughin'. Laters."

I huffed, "Right. Good luck, you'll do great."

"I second that," Kane said from behind me. "See you later, darling."

"Be good. *Both* of you," Keela shouted, then laughed as she closed the front door behind her.

"No promises," Kane answered.

I turned to face him and glared so hard I hurt my face.

"Kitchen. Now," I snarled and brushed past his large body as I walked down the hallway and into the empty kitchen. I glanced around the room and frowned. I knew Branna was at work because she had horribly long shifts from Monday to Friday this month, but I had no clue where Ryder was.

"Where is Ryder?" I asked.

Kane shrugged his shoulders. "I just walked down the stairs, how should I know where he is?"

The attitude!

"You need to perk up and stop being such a cheeky prick. I'm gettin' fed up with you being so rude and snippy with me. I'm here to help you, not receive your dick tantrums," I said as I stretched up and grabbed his insulin kit from the middle shelf in the cabinet above the toaster. I also grabbed the pouch that contained his glucose meter. I needed that to check his blood sugar levels before I injected any insulin.

"Take the damn pregnancy test and I won't act like such a fucking dick to you."

I froze then turned around.

I managed to go the entire day without thinking about that *situation*.

"Is that what this is about?" I asked. "You make it hell for me to get your insulin into you, you act like the mother of all fuckers, and all because I haven't taken a pregnancy test yet. Are you bloody serious?"

Kane shot forward and got in my personal space. He glared down at me as I pressed back into the kitchen counter. I held his stare, but my nerve was slipping with each passing second because when Kane was mad, he looked terrifying.

"Yes," he growled. "That is *exactly* why I'm behaving this way. I want to know if you're pregnant. I'm done waiting."

I was done waiting too, but fear stopped me from taking a test. I put it off every chance I got. I barely plucked up the courage to check Ryder and Branna's bathroom for the test I previously took, but it was gone, and I was too scared to ask if someone found it.

I groaned, "I told you that me, Bronagh, and Branna made a deal to do it together tomorrow. It's Saturday, Branna and I have no work so it's the best time."

"Why? Why can't you do this *without* them?" Kane asked, exasperated.

I shrugged my shoulders. "We started this together, seems only right to end it together."

Kane's jaw set. "If you're pregnant the *we* started it together, not the girls."

Thanks for the reminder.

I swallowed. "We'll find out tomorrow, okay? Stop puttin' so much pressure on me. I'm scared out of me mind. If I *am* pregnant then me life as I know it is about to change forever."

"*If* you are then mine will too," Kane growled and lowered his head to mine. "Me and you, remember? We're in this together."

Damn him.

"Why do you do that? You enrage me one minute then melt me the next."

Kane smiled, and as usual, it transformed his beautiful face.

"I make you melt? Like the panty soaking kind of melting?"

He was disgusting.

I grunted. "*No.* You make me melt, as in you erase the bad and replace it with good when you're nice—which isn't often."

Kane frowned then and gave me his finger so I could test his blood sugar. "I'm sorry, okay?"

I checked the results on the meter then regarded him for a moment before I nodded my head. "Apology accepted, now pull down your trousers."

Kane waggled his eyebrows at me. "Damn. You wanna fuck? Babydoll, I am *so* game."

I raised an eyebrow. "Watch it."

Kane winked. "A blowjob then? I'd rather fuck that pretty pussy, but your mouth will do just—"

"Finish that sentence and I'll cut *it* off. I swear."

Kane laughed to himself as he gripped the band of his trousers and pushed them down. Thankfully, he left his boxers in place this time. He reached down and pulled up his boxers until his full thigh was showing. I turned and got his insulin pen from the kit, set the number of units he would be receiving then turned around and kneeled before him.

"You know something? I've never had the same woman on her knees so often in front of me and *not* have her suck my cock," Kane mused as he reached over and ran his fingers through my hair.

I shook my head. "There's a first time for everythin', germinator."

Kane tugged on my hair and it made me hiss. "Lose that stupid nickname."

I smirked. "Lose babydoll."

"Not a chance, *babydoll*," Kane teased.

I glared at him then looked down as I uncapped the lid of his insulin pen and inserted a fresh needle. "Close your eyes," I said when the device was ready.

When I glanced up and saw his eyes were closed, I reached in, pinched a fatty part of his inner thigh, and inserted the needle into his skin. I scrunched my face up when the needle broke through the layers of Kane's skin because I could *feel* the moment it entered his body. I injected the insulin, then after a few seconds, I removed the needle and held my thumb over the area I jabbed for a moment. When I pulled away, there was no blood or any insulin seeping out of the tiny pricked area.

I was getting good at it and had cut a second or two off my time since Kane came home from the hospital.

"All done," I said then got to my feet.

Kane pulled his trousers up and gazed at me the entire time. I couldn't help but laugh. "Why do you always look at me like that after I give you your injection?" I asked, curiously.

Kane shrugged. "I guess I'm a little awed that you do it at all."

"Well, someone has got to do it."

Kane frowned. "I'm never going to let anyone else do it for me, you know that right?"

I did.

I didn't know how I knew it, but I did.

"Yeah, I'll be on me knees before you for the rest of me life. I'm aware of that."

Kane burst into laughter. "Your future husband will hate me."

I giggled. "He'll just have to accept you're now part of me daily routine. In the mornin' and afternoon to be exact."

Kane grinned as he turned and opened up the fridge. "Are you here on your lunch?"

"Nope," I said to his back. "It's Friday. Half day. "

"So what are you doing now?"

I shrugged my shoulders even though he couldn't see me. "I was gonna hang with Keela, but she has her therapist appointment so I'll probably just go home. I'll come back this evenin' for your second injection though."

"You could hang out with me if you want to?" Kane mumbled as he made himself a sandwich.

I laughed but stopped when I saw his body tense.

He was serious.

I didn't want to hurt his feelings since he was actually being nice to me. I mean, this could be a once in a lifetime opportunity. He never offered to hang out with me. Ever.

"Okay, what do you want to do?" I asked him.

He shrugged. "Doctor's orders are to take things easy for a few more days until my body grows accustomed to the injected insulin. So whatever we do, it has to be indoors."

I raised an eyebrow. "If you suggest sex, I'm whackin' you over the head."

Kane chortled. "No offence, but I don't have the energy for you."

I rolled my eyes and asked, "You have Netflix, right? We could watch the *Sons of Anarchy* if you want? I need to re-watch all the seasons again in preparation for the final season because it starts soon."

Kane turned to me and bit into his large sandwich. "What is the *Sons of Anarchy*?"

I felt my jaw drop open. "Please tell me you're jokin'."

Kane shook his head.

I shook my head in disappointment and turned and walked out of the kitchen. I snapped my fingers and looked over my shoulder at Kane. "Come with me."

Kane followed and said around the food in his mouth, "It better not be some sappy love show."

Sappy? *Sons of Anarchy*?

Hell no.

"Just follow me," I said as I stepped onto the stairs, "and let me introduce you to Jax Teller."

CHAPTER SIX

I smiled as season one of *Sons of Anarchy* ended.

"So," I asked as I grinned and turned my head in Kane's direction, a little surprised when I found his body so close to mine. "What did you think?"

Kane turned his head and looked at me. "I hate that I want to watch the second season right away."

I burst into laughter. "You won't ever escape now; the *Sons* have hold of you."

Kane smirked. "*You* have a hold on me."

Me?

"What do you mean—Oh, sorry." I flushed with embarrassment when I realised I was lying on his arm and he wouldn't be able to move unless I got up—which I did.

We were both lying on Kane's bed watching his television. *Just* lying on his bed. We both started out watching the show sitting up, but I think by the third episode our bodies leaned further and further back until we were lying down. I had no idea how I came to lie on his arm though. None.

"Don't be sorry, it was nice," Kane teased.

I swallowed and tried to make a joke out of it. "Me pinnin' you to the bed is nice?"

"Pin me down and I'll let you know," he quickly replied.

I flushed crimson and hated it.

"Does *everythin'* have to be made into a sexual joke with you?" I asked, slightly irritated.

He thought on it for a moment then replied, "Yes."

I rolled my eyes. "Typical."

I gasped when hands suddenly grabbed my shoulders and pulled me back down to my laid down position. "Relax, I'm not about to jump you."

I scrunched my face up in distaste. "Like I'd let you."

"You let me before. Three times, in fact," Kane murmured.

He didn't!

"That is *not* ever discussin' *it* again, Kane," I stated.

He sighed. "Right. Sorry."

It got awkward then.

I sat up again and cleared my throat. "Come on, you're due your second injection, it's already nearin' seven."

He groaned so I pinched his side making him yelp.

"None of that," I said, "let's go and get this done."

"After you, Mother," Kane growled.

I smiled to myself as I climbed off his bed, slipped my shoes back on, and walked out of Kane's room with him lazily following behind me. We made it to the bottom of the stairs but instantly slowed our pace down as we approached the kitchen door. I could hear raised voices from inside the kitchen and it made me a little nervous.

"Is that—"

"Bran and Ry?" Kane sighed. "Yeah."

"Wow," I whispered. "I didn't think Branna and Ryder argued—not like this anyway."

Kane quietly grunted. "The last few months it's been getting worse and worse. They argue over the smallest things. It's different than when the others argue because you can *feel* the anger between them."

I frowned. "That sucks."

Kane nodded his head and frowned when the yelling from the kitchen intensified.

"I can't stand the sight of you anymore. I just have to look at you to get annoyed!" Branna's voice bellowed.

"You think the sight of *you* makes me happy?" Ryder asked then humourlessly laughed.

I widened my eyes.

"Why are they being so hurtful?" I asked. "I don't like this."

"Couples fight," Kane said and shrugged like it was nothing.

I knew it was something more than that though. Ryder and Branna fighting wasn't shocking. But screaming horrible things at one another? That was *extremely* shocking.

"I can't even stand being in here with you. You're a fucking liar!" Ryder snapped.

"How am I a liar?" Branna screamed. "What the fuck have I kept from you?"

Kane and I stood idly by the kitchen door. I felt too awkward to do anything. I didn't want to leave because it would have been obvious we were listening if they heard us walk away, but I also didn't want to hang around and listen to my friends fight with one another.

I couldn't even intervene to help calm things down because Branna and Ryder were in a relationship. They have been together for years and seeing them treat one another so badly was a little bit of a shock to my system. It just went to show that even people who were clearly meant to be together didn't have it easy.

"How about the fucking positive pregnancy test I found in the bathroom last week?" Ryder snarled. "I found it the day Kane came home, but I decided to wait until he was settled in before I brought it up. Then I figured I'd wait until you were ready to tell me you were pregnant. But. You. Never. Did."

I widened my eyes and felt my heart jump.

"Pregnant? Pregnancy test? What the hell are you talkin' about, Ryder?" Branna snapped.

"Don't bullshit me. I found the test and I want to know the truth from you. We haven't had sex in months, so it's not my fucking kid."

"You... You think I would cheat on you?" Branna asked, her voice filled with hurt.

I gripped onto Kane's hand and pulled him down the hallway. "We need to give them privacy," I breathed.

Kane was looking at me, but his eyes were distant.

"Branna is the one who is pregnant?" he murmured.

I felt like I was about to throw up but forced my feelings aside to notice Kane looked... sad. Really sad.

"Thanks for today, it was fun," he murmured. "I'm going to go back to bed. I don't feel so good."

"But your injection—"

"One will be enough for me today. See you later."

He turned and walked down the hallway then up the stairs. I was frozen to my spot as I watched him go. I couldn't open my mouth to say anything because if I did, I was going to vomit everywhere.

"Ryder," I heard Branna's voice say from the kitchen, her voice not raised anymore. "I am *not* pregnant. Me and the girls are meant to take tests tomorrow, but I couldn't wait until then. I took one a few days ago and it was negative. I didn't tell you because you were so focused on Kane."

Silence.

Oh. Christ.

Oh. Fuck.

"You *aren't* pregnant?" Ryder repeated. "The test I found was positive though. If you're not then who took it in our house? *Who is* pregnant?"

"Bronagh or Aideen. It's one of them."

Oh.

It wasn't Bronagh who took the test Ryder found, it was me... and he said it was *positive*!

I couldn't breathe.

I literally couldn't breathe.

I had to get out of the hallway because it felt like it was closing in on me.

I all but ran out of the house, closing the door behind me. I bent forward and pressed my hands on my knees and sucked in huge gulps of air.

Calm down.

I repeated the thought over and over in my mind then stood upright and looked directly across the road to the lights of the Jeep that were pulling into Keela and Alec's driveway. She was home.

Thank God!

I took off out of the garden, ran straight across the road, and up their driveway.

"Aideen!" Alec snapped when he got out of his car. "You scared the shit out of me. It's dark out. Don't do that again, I could have reacted out of reflex and hit you."

"Sorry, flower," I said, breathing heavily. "Open your door."

Keela walked around the car and frowned. "Where did you come from?" she asked.

I pointed to the house across the road.

"Have you been there since I left hours ago?" she asked, wide-eyed. "It's nearly seven."

She didn't need to know that Kane and I watched the entire first season of *Sons of Anarchy* in his bedroom all day. Nobody needed to know that.

"I gave him his second injection," I lied, avoiding answering her question directly.

Keela watched me for a moment then nodded at me. "Okay, so why are you here, breathin' like you just ran a marathon?"

Uh.

"I need... to use your bathroom," I said, then smiled.

Alec sighed as he walked forward and opened the front door of his house. He entered and turned off the beeping of the alarm by entering the alarm code onto the keypad.

"Why didn't you use the toilet in Branna's place?" Keela asked as we went inside.

Because I know you recently stocked up on pregnancy tests, and I couldn't stay over there because everyone was seconds away from finding out who was really pregnant.

I knew deep down it wasn't Bronagh who was pregnant like Branna suggested, but I refused to believe it was me who was pregnant until I saw the proof for myself.

"Go on then," Keela said, waving me up the stairs when I didn't give her a reply.

"Thank you!" I shouted as I ran for the stairs.

"Turn on the fan if you have a shite!" Keela bellowed up the stairs after me.

I couldn't help but laugh. "Okay!"

"Is *that* what you came here for? Next time take a crap in Ryder's place!" Alec's voice hollered up the stairs after me.

I heard Keela's laughter and Alec's bickering, but both of them faded away when I entered their bedroom and ran into their bathroom. I knew I could have used the bathroom on the first floor, but I knew Keela's master bathroom was the one with the pregnancy tests. She wasn't planning on getting pregnant anytime soon—she had an implant in her arm to prevent pregnancy—but she had to stock up on tests because the girls and myself used up the ones she had last week.

When I closed the door of the bathroom, everything became deathly silent. Even my breathing slowed down. It was like my body knew I was about to do something huge, and it wasn't taking a crap like Alec thought it was.

I took slow, deep breaths and walked over to the his-and-hers set up. I placed my hand on the marble counter and looked into the mirror at myself. I didn't look like the twenty-eight-year-old woman I was. I saw a scared little girl who was at a loss. I frowned at myself then shook my head.

You can do this.

I believed I could, but hell, it was still terrifying. I reached up to the medicine cabinet above the sink and opened the door. I spotted the un-opened box of the digital Clearblue pregnancy tests. I reached up and took the box in my hand, quickly undid the wrapping, and pulled out a covered pregnancy test. I removed the packaging on it and stared at the test.

This was it.

I walked over to the toilet, pushed my leggings and underwear down to my ankles, and then sat down. I knew the gist of taking a pregnancy test; I'd taken two in the past nine days, but finding out the results had never come easy so hopefully the third time would be a charm for me. I *needed* to know if I was pregnant.

It took a few minutes for me to be able to go—my nerves caused me to lock up, but luckily, I eventually peed on the stick. I capped the test end and placed it on the counter next to me. I finished my business then pulled my underwear and leggings back up. I walked to the sink where I spent a great deal of time thoroughly washing my hands. When I was finished I dried my hands and turned and stared at the test on the counter across from me.

I didn't know how long I had to wait for the test to be ready, and I didn't want to pick up the box and read it because, with every passing second, I felt more and more sick. I needed to do this, but that didn't make me feel any better about doing it. It actually made me feel worse. If I was pregnant then I was completely fucked. I was twenty-eight years of age and I was well aware that I wasn't getting any younger, but I could barely take care of myself. I had a grown-up job, and a grown-up apartment, but I didn't feel like the adult I was. I enjoyed having fun and doing stupid things regardless of my age, but *this*? This was serious because if I couldn't get a dog to like me, how in the hell would I get a baby to?

I shook my head and forced all the 'what if' thoughts away. If I was pregnant, then I was pregnant. I would deal with it—probably not in the most mature way—but I'd deal with it nonetheless. With a firm nod of my head, I walked over to the counter facing me and picked up the pregnancy test. I put down the seat of the toilet and sat on it. I stared at the back of the test and tried to pluck up the courage to turn it over.

I closed my eyes.

This was it.

"I can't do it," I whined to no one and closed my eyes.

Just fucking look!

With a firm nod of my head, I opened my eyes and looked down to the stick in my hands. I held my breath as I flipped the stick over and widened my eyes as I read the results.

Oh, Jesus.

CHAPTER SEVEN

"Oh. My. God," I whispered as I stared down at the pregnancy test before me.

The *positive* pregnancy test.

I rubbed my eyes with my balled up hands and blinked profusely, hoping the words on the digital test would change, but no matter how many times I rubbed my eyes it read the same thing: *Pregnant—3+ weeks.*

"KEELA!"

I screamed her name as loud as I could. Not long after, I heard the loud patter of clumsy footsteps come up the stairs then into the bedroom. A few seconds had passed before the bathroom door was flung open as my best friend all but dived into the room ready to face the possible danger that caused me to scream so loudly.

"What is it?" Keela asked with her arm raised in the air.

I looked up at her hand and blinked in confusion. She had the television remote in her hand, and from the looks of it, she was prepared to use it as a weapon. I wanted to laugh, but I didn't. I knew if I opened my mouth all that would escape would be a terrified sob.

"Aideen, what's wrong?" Keela asked me, her tone laced with worry.

She knelt down in front of me and placed her hands on my cheeks. I momentarily wondered where she put the remote, but I forgot about it when Keela shook my head and got my attention.

"Honey, you're scarin' me. What is it?"

I blinked and flicked my eyes towards the bathroom counter next to me where I'd flung the test in a panic. It sat a mere foot away, mocking me with its presence. Keela followed my gaze and furrowed her eyebrows in confusion when her eyes locked on the small white stick. She leaned over to the counter and tilted her head to get a better look at the test.

I knew the moment she realised what she was looking at when she gasped. I stayed put on the toilet while Keela jumped to her feet and snatched the test from the countertop. She raised the test right up to her face and narrowed her eyes at the little window that hadd already told me that my life as I knew it was over.

"It's you! *You're* the one who is pregnant!"

Even though she was in shock, I felt like Keela was accusing me of hiding a secret from her and that was the farthest thing from the truth. I was just in the same state of what-the-fuck shock as she was. To soothe her though, I blinked my eyes and opened my mouth to answer her, but a muffled and terrified cry escaped my mouth instead of words.

"Oh, baby," Keela whispered and quickly knelt back down in front of me.

I wrapped my arms around her when she pulled me into her chest and held me there. My whole body shook violently as sobs wracked through me and tears flowed from my now red-rimmed and swollen eyes.

I was pregnant... *really* pregnant.

Fuck me.

I cried harder than I ever had before and Keela held me the entire time. My thoughts were a mess, my stomach hurt, and my chest felt like it was about to cave in on itself. As much as I wanted to scream and let all my fear and shock out, I just couldn't, so I squeezed my eyes shut and focused on breathing. If I freaked out and had a panic attack, it wouldn't be good for anyone, especially Keela.

She would have a heart attack if she thought there was something wrong with me. The guards, firemen, paramedics, and the Army would be at my door in minutes if she had the slightest inkling that I was about to lose it.

What felt like an hour later instead of just a few minutes, I peeled myself from Keela's arms and wiped my tear-streaked face with the back of my hands. I knew it was a foolish attempt to wipe away the evidence of my mini break down—I could feel how swollen my eyes were from crying and I could only imagine what all the salty tears had done to my make-up and overall appearance, but I had to try to compose myself.

"I c-can't believe th-this," I stuttered.

Keela sat back on her heels and looked at me with her big eyes.

"Do you think it's a false positive?" she asked, curiously.

My heart skipped a beat for a moment, but I knew the odds were stacked against me. Not only did this test come back positive, but so did the mixed-up one I took nine days ago in this very bathroom. I heard Ryder and Branna arguing about a positive test he found in their bathroom. Another test *I* took. My throwing up and feeling like utter crap throughout the past few days pointed towards pregnancy. So did the fact that I had unprotected sex a few months ago.

Reluctantly, I shook my head at my best friend.

Keela was stunned. "You're *really* pregnant?"

That sentence churned my stomach.

I gently nodded my head and accepted this fuck-up like a woman.

A very emotionally unstable woman.

"For who?"

Oh, Jesus, the father.

I instantly began to sob again.

"For the Devil, th-that's who."

"Aideen... *who* is the father?" Keela pressed.

I had taken a few deep breaths before I whispered, "Kane Slater."

A few minutes of silence passed by, but it might as well have been an eternity.

"WHAT!?"

I winced and hunched my shoulders forward at the volume of Keela's screech. She was silent for a solid five minutes after I whispered my horrifying reality to her. I calmed down enough to speak during that time, but her delayed scream caught me off guard and freaked me out again.

"Kane Slater, as in me fiancé's *brother*? That Kane Slater?"

I blinked my sore eyes. "How many lads named Kane Slater do you know?"

Keela slapped my shoulders. "This is not the time for sarcasm, you dick!"

She was right, I knew that, but I couldn't help it; it slipped out.

"Sorry."

Keela's eyes were wide with shock. "You want to talk me through how *Kane Slater* came to be the father of your unborn child?"

My stomach churned at her choice of words. Pregnancy usually involved an unborn child, but hearing 'Kane' and *my* 'unborn child' in the same sentence made me feel physically ill. I never in my wildest nightmares thought I'd hear myself say anything even close to that sentence.

"If I have to talk you through how I got knocked up by Kane, then Alec is doin' somethin' seriously wrong in the bedroom."

Keela looked like she was about to blow a fuse and jump on me so I held my hands up and said, "Sorry, sorry."

She stared at me and patiently waited for me to speak. All that came out of my mouth was a loud groan though.

Keela dangerously pointed her finger at me. "Don't even think about it, lady. I thought you didn't like Kane. You can barely tolerate being in the same room as him without a world war eruptin', so you can understand why I'm havin' trouble wrappin' me head around the fact that you're *pregnant* by him."

I winced and murmured, "It was an impulse. All the fightin' and arguments over the past year just exploded. It was either murder one another or fuck each other's brains out—we chose the latter."

Keela face-palmed herself, which was exactly the reaction I deserved.

"You didn't use protection?"

Evidently not.

"Wait, *he* was the one-night stand you had a few weeks ago?"

I groaned, again.

"You're goin' to ask me enough questions to make me relive that night, aren't you?"

Keela folded her arms across her chest. "Yeah, I am, so you might as well start your once-upon-a-time story because I'm not goin' anywhere."

Stubborn bitch.

"Okay, okay," I muttered. "I'll tell you."

A smile stretched across Keela's sadistic face as she jumped to her feet and grabbed my hand. She pulled me upright then all but dragged me out of her bedroom, down the stairs, and into her sitting room. I sat on the large settee while she dived onto the lounge chair and crisscrossed her legs over one another and stared at me expectantly.

"Where is Alec?" I asked, curiously.

"Takin' Storm on a walk," she replied with a wave of her hand.

"We don't have much time then, he can't walk very far." I grinned.

"Aideen," Keela said in warning tone. "Don't pick on Storm."

I winced. "My bad."

Keela nodded her head giving me a rare pass then suddenly shouted, "Wait!"

I raised my eyebrows at her.

I wasn't even speaking yet.

I watched as she jumped up and ran out of the sitting room. I sat and stared at the doorway for at least a minute until suddenly Keela reappeared with two mugs.

"We need tea for story time," she chirped.

My one night-stand with my archenemy that resulted in my *pregnancy* meant story time?

This lass was all kinds of messed up.

"Pre-warnin'," I said holding my hands up, "if I consume anythin' right now I *will* puke."

Keela placed both mugs on the coffee table next to her. "Okay fine, I'll drink them while you talk. Go."

I blinked my eyes and licked my suddenly dry lips.

"Okay." I swallowed. "It was about three months ago that I fell into sin. Do you remember when I went out on that date with Skull —"

"You shagged Kane on the night you had a date with your *ex*? You slag!"

That wasn't bloody helping.

I felt my eye twitch. "Do you want to hear the story or not?"

"Every. Dirty. Detail." She grinned wickedly.

Every detail?

"Okay, you asked for it," I said and exhaled a deep breath. "So like I said, it happened about three months ago in that stupid bloody nightclub, Darkness."

CHAPTER EIGHT

About three months earlier...

"I can't believe you're givin' Skull another chance," Keela grumbled to me as she zipped up the zipper on the back of my skin-tight dress.

I grinned and turned to face her. "I'm not givin' him another chance, but I haven't had sex with him in over a month, and he gives me amazin' orgasms... Need I say more?"

Keela deadpanned. "There is more to life than orgasms, Aideen."

My girl had jokes.

I burst into laughter. "Good one."

Keela rolled her pretty green eyes at me and it made me smile.

"Don't get your knickers in a twist with me because you don't get to date anymore. *You* chose to settle down with that fine hunk of American man-meat in the sittin' room."

Keela glanced at her closed bedroom door. "I'm tellin' him you said that."

"Go for it. Maybe he'll come to his senses and leave you for me." I wickedly grinned.

Keela giggled and exited her bedroom calling out to her piece of Grade A American man-meat as she walked down the hallway.

"What?" he shouted from the sitting room.

"Aideen said you're a fine hunk of American man meat, and you have to leave me for her."

Male laughter erupted.

"I always knew you wanted me, Ado!" Alec shouted.

I continued to grin as I walked over to the bedroom door.

"Only you, big lad!" I called out, sweetly.

I squealed when I saw Keela storm down the hallway in my direction. I slammed her bedroom door shut and turned the lock. Seconds later she banged on the door with her hands.

"Pussy!" she shouted.

"You say pussy, I say smart woman who doesn't want to be hit before she goes out on a date and fucks her ex-boyfriend until she can't see straight."

Keela dry heaved. "Never mind pussy, you're a slut!"

I burst into laughter and turned to Keela's full-length mirror in her bedroom. I adjusted my royal blue dress and smiled. I loved how it looked. It was short, came to mid thigh, and stuck to me like a second skin, but my favourite part was the lace on the chest of the dress and on the sleeves. It was gorgeous.

I reached up and let my hair out of the spider grip that held it on top of my head. I swung my head back and forth a few times until my hair gained some volume and looked ruffled and sexy.

My make-up was done, but as I examined my face I found I needed a little bit more on my nose because I saw some redness. I leaned into the mirror and gasped when I realised what the redness on my nose was.

It was a pimple.

"Crap!"

I turned from the mirror, unlocked Keela's bedroom door, and walked down the hallway of my friend's apartment in search of her. I bypassed the kitchen when I peeked in and saw she wasn't in there. I headed straight into the sitting room. I opened my mouth to speak when I spotted her sitting on Alec's lap on the sofa. Kane and Nico were on either side of them watching an American football game, but when Nico caught sight of me he wolf whistled and twirled his finger around with a devilish smirk on his face.

I rolled my eyes but giggled as I turned around in a circle then placed my hands on my hips and posed like I would for a picture.

"Damn, Ado, you're looking F-I-N-E," Nico said, nodding his head in appreciation of me.

I have no idea why, but Kane reached behind Alec and smacked Nico across the back of the head. "You *have* a girlfriend."

"Fucking hell!" Nico growled and rubbed his head. "I *know* that, I was just saying she looked hot. There's no harm in looking."

"You were just smacked for lookin'," Keela mused, "clearly there *is* harm in it."

"I'll say," Nico mumbled and lowered his hand.

Keela chortled and Alec grinned as he stroked Keela's side while she sat on him.

"So, what's the verdict? Yay or nay?" I asked the group as I gestured to my look for the night.

Keela gave me two thumbs. "Hell yay!"

I laughed.

"Yay from me, too. You look beautiful." Alec smiled.

Aww.

I winked at him then looked at Nico when he mumbled 'yay' but kept an eye on Kane like he would smack him again, which I thought was funny.

"Kane, what do you think?" I asked.

Kane raised his eyebrow at me. "You care what *I* think?"

"No," I replied honestly, "but you're a lad and I'm askin' for your opinion, so shoot."

Kane blinked at me then trailed his eyes up and down my body. "Nice shape. Sexy even."

My shape was sexy?

Nope, that was wrong.

"Honey, sexy is an attitude, not a shape."

"Well, with all the attitude within your little body, you must be the sexiest woman alive," Kane said, a grin plastered on his face.

I narrowed my eyes at him. "Are you sayin' I have an attitude problem?"

Kane dropped his smirk. "Uh, no... I'm saying you're se—"

"Because if you are then you should know I only develop an attitude around *you*."

Kane looked at his brothers who were shaking their heads and giving him a look that he seemed to understand. He then turned his gaze back to me and said, "You know what? I take it back, forget I even said anything."

That was the smartest thing that had ever come out of his delectable mouth.

Keela snickered, but then narrowed her eyes at my face.

Oh, crap.

"Dude, your nose!" she gasped.

I covered it with both hands. "I know. I just saw it."

"Saw what?" the lads asked in unison.

I removed my hands from my face and pointed at my nose with both of my index fingers. "*This.*"

The lads squinted their eyes.

"What are we supposed to be staring at here?" Alec mumbled to Keela.

"The mother of all pimples," I whimpered.

Nico leaned his head forward and squinted his eyes so much he almost closed them. "I can't see it."

How could he miss it?

"Me either. You're overreacting," Kane said, and waved me off.

I was about to say something smart to him, but I caught Keela staring at my nose and it made me feel incredibly uncomfortable.

"Keela! Stop!"

Keela averted her gaze. "I'm sorry, but it's bloody huge."

I knew it!

"This isn't supposed to happen! How can I go out on me date

with Skull if I have to lug around this volcano on the end of me nose all night?"

Keela chewed on her lower lip as Alec suggested, "What about cover-up?"

I hesitated in snapping at him because that was a pretty good idea.

Kane groaned in annoyance. "You could try more make-up, or you could just sit down, have a beer, and relax. Skull won't even notice, and if he does, he will be cool with it. A situation like this is what doggie style was invented for. He won't give a fuck about any pimple if you're face down and ass up in front of him."

Did he really just say that?

"You're disgustin'!" I snarled.

Kane lifted up his arm and tipped his beer bottle in my direction. "So I've been told."

I curled my lip in disgust and looked at Keela. "I can't stand him."

"I heard that," Kane said and took a gulp from his beer bottle.

"You were supposed to, germinator," I growled.

I smirked when he stiffened.

He *really* hated that nickname, which is exactly why I still called him by it.

"Ignore Kane," Keela sighed and stood up from Alec's lap. "You look gorgeous, pimple or no pimple."

I grunted then jumped when my phone buzzed. I squealed and ran to my clutch purse that was on Keela's kitchen table. I picked it up, dug inside it for my phone, and answered it the second I got it into my hands.

"Hello?" I said a little breathlessly as I pressed the phone to my ear.

"Hello, sexy," Skull's voice purred through the phone as I walked back into the sitting room.

"You can't see me, how do you know if I look sexy?" I flirted.

Keela rolled her eyes at me, Nico and Alec snorted, and Kane just stared straight ahead at the television as he watched the football game on ESPN.

"You always look sexy, dressed up or down, so I don't need to see you to know you look good," Skull said, a smile in his voice. "I'm outside Keela's apartment complex, are you ready?"

"Good answer, and yes, I'll be down now."

I pressed the hang-up option on the screen before he could reply and hugged Keela tightly when she walked over to me and put her arms around me.

"Where are you goin'?" she asked.

I deadpanned, "Where does Skull always take me when we go out?"

Keela paled a little and whispered, "Darkness."

I frowned at her reaction. She looked... scared of something.

I knew she had a bad experience at Darkness, but no one would fill me in on what actually happened that night after Marco's stupid henchmen knocked me out. I've asked all the girls and lads but they're all mute on the subject. Alannah was the only one in the same boat as me because she said she wasn't at Darkness the night some sort of trouble went down. She said she had a bad headache that night and passed out on her bed. She had no clue what problems happened for the girls there that night; she just knew that bad things happened there.

"Yep," I sighed. "Good ol' Darkness. He is workin' from ten to closin', but whatever—I get free drinks."

Keela shook her head at me and smiled. "Just... be careful, okay?"

I winked. "I always am."

I spun on my heel and walked over to the front door. I heard a growl come from inside the kitchen mid-walk then I caught sight of *it* as it emerged.

I glared at the hundred-pound beast. "Did you eat up the contents of the fridge, you fat shite?" I asked, grinning.

He continued to growl at me, but he didn't move. He was still as he watched me. He was waiting for me to leave the apartment before he walked by.

"Leave him alone!" Keela snapped from behind me.

I laughed as I opened the door and stepped out into the hallway. I reached back to grab the handle of the door so I could close it, but it suddenly slammed in my face. I gasped then glared at the door when everyone inside the apartment burst into laughter.

I knew exactly what happened. Storm shut the door with his head to make sure I couldn't get back into the apartment. The fat fucker always did it.

"I'll be back tomorrow, you hairy bastard! You'll *never* be rid of me! Do you hear me? *Never!*" I shouted through the door then turned and walked down the hallway of Keela's building.

I walked down the stairs carefully—I was in six-inch heels, I had to be careful—and exited the building and walked straight to Skull's black Ford Mondeo that was sitting out front waiting.

"Damn, babe, you look smokin' hot!" he shouted out the window of the car.

What a romantic.

I snorted and opened the passenger side door of his car and hopped into it. I closed the door, leaned in, and let him kiss my cheek even though he tried for my lips.

"Aideen," he groaned. "You can't come out lookin' like that and not give me a little taste."

Watch me.

"If you're good, then you'll get *more* than a little taste later." I grinned as I buckled my seat belt. "Now, shut up and drive the car. I wanna dance already."

Skull bit down on his lower lip and smirked. "Yes, ma'am."

I glanced at Skull as he drove and my insides clenched when I took in his attire. He always wore a suit when he went to work—all the bouncers had to wear one since Brandon, Keela's uncle, took over ownership of Darkness—but he had his jacket hanging in the back of the car and had his white shirtsleeves rolled up to his elbows with a couple of buttons open exposing a bit of his chest. It was simple, yet so delicious to look at.

"You want dinner first, or straight to the club?"

"I already ate so straight to Darkness," I answered without looking in Skull's direction.

He groaned again, "You kill me when you behave like this."

I snorted and continued to look out the window as he drove. "Behave like what?"

"Like you couldn't care less that you're next to me; it always gets me hard."

I laughed and glanced at him. "You get turned on when I ignore you?"

"Only when you're in me presence. It makes me want your undivided attention."

I smirked and looked forward again. "We'll see how tonight pans out. You might just get what you're lookin' for."

"I better," he growled making me smile to myself.

A few moments passed by in comfortable silence, but Skull broke it when he said, "How is Keela doin'?"

I crossed my left leg over my right and rested my hands on my lap. "She's good, still workin' hard on her book. She is a perfectionist, and it's a strength of hers as well as a weakness. She goes over the manuscript with a fine-tooth comb daily but is worried about it not being 'right.' Nothin' anyone tells her will relax her about it, it's just somethin' we have to let pan out by itself."

Skull clicked his tongue. "I hope it all works out for her. She's a good girl."

I nodded in agreement. "That she is."

"Is she still with that Slater lad?" he asked.

I snorted. "You know his name is Alec, and yes, they're still together. They're engaged."

"I refer to them all as a Slater lad." Skull chuckled then said, "And people who are engaged can still break up, you know."

I smiled. "Not Keela and Alec, they're solid. Nothin' can break them."

I was certain nothing could anyway.

"Well, that's great; a solid relationship must be nice."

I raised an eyebrow. "Is that a jab at me?"

"At *us*, not just you," Skull clarified. "We're both great together in the bedroom, it's every other aspect of being in a relationship that we struggle with."

Ain't that the truth.

I sighed. "We aren't goin' to get back together, and we both know it. This 'date' tonight is for a good time and wild sex. You know it, and I know it."

"I know," Skull grumbled.

I looked at him and frowned. "Why do you seem sad about it?"

Please don't say you want us to get back together again.

"I'm not sad about us. I've made peace with how we are... I'm just gettin' too fuckin' old for one-night stands. I'm thirty-three. Wakin' up next to nameless women, and sometimes faceless women dependin' on how hungover I am, is gettin' old."

I blinked in surprise. "Really? You don't like the club bunnies?"

That was a bit of a shock.

Skull glanced at me and smirked. "I *love* the club bunnies; I'm just gettin' bored of them. I don't know, maybe I need to find a good woman and settle down. Me ma is naggin' me about givin' her some grandbabies."

I smiled. "Then that is exactly what you should do, honey. Do what makes you happy."

Skull sighed, nodded his head, but said nothing.

I grunted to myself and said, "I'm not havin' sex with you ever again now, not now that I know where your head is at."

Skull burst into laughter. "Should I repeat that to you when you're feelin' me up later in your drunken haze?"

I giggled. "Yeah, say it loud and clear. Pinch me if you have to."

Skull continued to laugh. "I love you, babe."

"I love you, too," I replied, happily.

I loved Skull, and he loved me, we just weren't *in* love with each other. That ship had sailed long ago.

"Any lads you have your eye on?" Skull asked as we neared Darkness.

I was shocked when the image of Kane Slater filled my mind. I quickly blinked the unwelcome image from my head and focused on Skull.

"Nope, no one. I'll probably do what you're doin' and look for *my* other half, or I'll just keep me own company and end up an old spinster."

A belly laugh erupted out of Skull. "You're twenty-eight, that's *not* old."

"Tell that to me students," I muttered and thought of all the kids in my class who thought I was *super* old.

The little brats.

Skull continued to laugh to himself as he flipped his indicator on and headed into the private car park for the staff of Darkness. Brandon Daley had splashed out on upgrading Darkness over the last few months. He completely redecorated the club—inside and outside.

He added a private staff car park and a brand new level to the club. Hard-core partying happened on the new bottom floor, and the fighting and *more* hard-core partying happened on the first floor. The first floor still looked the same except it didn't. The platform was in the same spot and had been completely upgraded. It was matte black now, but when blood or any fluids from the fighters touched the surface, it appeared as neon red blood splatters on the platform surface. It was brutal, but awesome looking. There was also an automatic black cage that folded down from the ceilings on Friday nights, which drew in crowds because there were no rules inside the cage. Anything went.

The booths were bigger and fancier. They were also matte black, but each table in a booth glowed different colours. A section of the club that had paint drums where people banged on them and paint splashed onto everyone within close range, and thanks to special lighting in the club, it glowed neon like the tables and platform. It looked awesome when everyone was drunk, but when you left the club, you were covered in different coloured paint splashes. It was clothing friendly though, so no one cared.

"How many people do you plan on refusin' entry to the club tonight?" I asked as we parked and exited the car.

Skull got his suit jacket from the back of the car and folded it neatly over his arm as he locked the Mondeo up.

"A lot." He grinned. "It's Friday, which means fight night. Only regular faces get in to see that, or new faces that the regulars vouch for. You know the drill."

I actually didn't. I never had to worry about gaining entry to Darkness. Back when Skull and I first started going out I'd never heard of the club, which wasn't a surprise. It was exclusive and for good reason. I only got in because I was Skull's girlfriend.

I knew Brandon had some sort of licence for the fighting that went on, according to Skull, so a lot more people knew about its existence now. But it was still hard for people to get in unless you had a hook-up like I did.

"You win some, you lose some," I smirked. "Let's get our drink on."

Skull slid his hand into mine and gave it a tug. "Come on, pussy cat, let's get you hydrated. I want you nice and wet."

I laughed as I followed Skull through the doors of the nightclub and down the stairs where darkness consumed us.

"Aideen? I can barely hear you, are you okay?" Keela's voice blared through the receiver of my phone.

"I'm fine," I shouted and leaned my head against the wall of the toilet stall I was in.

"The reception is bad; can you hear me?" Keela asked and continued to shout.

I nodded my head even though she couldn't see me. "I'm in the toilets on the first floor in Darkness, that's why the reception is shitty. If the phone cuts off, you know why."

I heard Keela mumble something to someone before she returned her attention to me. "If you're fine, then why're you callin' me? It's half two in the mornin'!"

Was it that late?

Oops.

"Sorry, I thought it was earlier," I said and smiled. "I love you."

Keela laughed. "Are you drunk?"

I shook my head. "Nope. I mean, I was, but I'm soberin' up now. I'm tired of dancin' so I think I'm gonna go home. Me feet hurt."

Keela laughed again. "Make sure Skull puts you in a taxi."

I blinked. "I will, but first. Guess what?"

"What?"

"I said *guess*."

Keela groaned. "Aliens have taken over Earth?"

"Close. Skull and I didn't have sex."

Keela choked on air.

"What?" she rasped. "*Why not?*"

I shrugged my shoulders. "We had a talk on the way to the club and it turns out he wants to settle down. He thinks he is gettin' too old for one-night stands. He wants to find his main chick."

"Wow."

Yep. Wow.

"I know—it sucks for me though. I wanted sex tonight. I'm so disappointed."

Keela snorted. "I'm sorry for your vagina's loss."

I dramatically sighed, "So am I. No one can turn her out like Skull can."

Keela burst into laughter making me smile.

"I'm goin' to go home. I'll text you when I get there, okay?"

"Okay, I'm going back to bed. I'll set me phone to vibrate and when I hear it vibrate from your text I'll know you're okay."

I used my left hand to grab some toilet roll and wipe myself. I stood up, pulled up my underwear, and adjusted my dress. I turned and flushed the toilet and laughed when Keela cursed.

"I fuckin' hate when you call me in the jacks!"

I snorted. "I know, sorry. Love you. Bye."

I hung up giggling while Keela went on about how disgusting I was. I bent down and picked my clutch up off the floor, stood up straight, and adjusted my dress once more then dropped my phone into my bag. I exited the stall and went straight to the sinks where I washed my hands.

The bathroom was crowded, and I could hear multiple females talking and laughing. I was so tired that everything felt like it was far off in the distance instead of happening around me. I glanced left and right and looked at all the baby faces of the women in the bathroom and groaned.

Maybe I *was* getting too old for this shite.

I sighed to myself, gripped my clutch and walked out of the bathroom. Instead of looking up at where I was going, I looked down at the ground. As a result, I walked head first into another person and the force of the impact knocked me back onto my behind.

"What the fuck?" a female voice hollered. "Watch where you're fuckin' goin'!"

I groaned and rubbed my head. "Sorry."

I pushed myself up to my feet and used my left hand to rub my behind to try to take the sting away. I yelped when I felt a sudden sharp pain spread out across my head. It took me a second to realise that someone had hold of my hair, and they were pulling at it.

Hell no.

I didn't reach up for the person's hair to pull back, no, I placed my hands on their hands and dug my nails into their flesh. Seconds later, the hands retreated from my head. I swung my head back, located the bitch who attacked me ,and charged.

I dived on the girl, fists flying and legs kicking. It was a blur of punches, slaps, and screeches. It felt like it lasted forever, but in reality, I was lifted off the girl ten or so seconds into the fight.

"That's enough!" a familiar male's voice bellowed into my ear.

A very familiar male's voice.

Uh-oh.

"Sorry," I squeaked and looked up to Skull's blazing eyes.

"Aideen," he sighed, his tone irritated as he set me down on the ground.

I instantly pointed at the girl across from us. "She hit me first. I was only defendin' meself."

Skull looked at the girl who was looking at me like she was going to rip me to shreds the second she got the opportunity.

"Is that true?" Skull asked the she-devil.

"She knocked me to the ground, that's why I hit the fat bitch!"

Fat?

Oh, hell no.

I stepped forward. "Listen to me you STD-ridden little toothpick. Havin' an arse and tits doesn't make me fat, it makes me desirable, just ask your fella. He's been starin' at both since the moment I walked into you, which, by the way, I apologised for."

The girl screamed and tried to come at me with outstretched hands, but Skull stood in front of me and kept the she-devil at bay. I made the situation worse by laughing at her.

"Damn it, Aideen," Skull grunted then barked orders at the other bouncers before he turned, bent down and threw me over his shoulder and walked away from the pubescent teenager who was having the mother of all tantrums.

I didn't struggle against Skull's hold on me. I'd learned from previous experiences that beating on his back and spewing threats didn't work on him. I relaxed as much as I could and simply enjoyed the ride. That was until he brought me somewhere I had never been in Darkness before. He brought me straight through a set of double doors and into a collection of long hallways with multiple rooms.

Where in the hell was I?

"What is this place?" I asked Skull when he placed me on the floor.

Skull closed the doors that led to the nightclub and instantly the noise lessened. You could hear music, but it wasn't loud. Not loud enough to make you think a club was on the other side of the door.

"This is an area for VIPs," Skull replied to me when he turned around.

I raised an eyebrow. "Bullshit, I've been a VIP for years."

He smirked. "I mean the *paid* VIPs. Associates of the boss, if you will."

Oh.

"Ah, dodgy businessmen? Got it."

Skull grinned again. "Go on down to the end of the hallway, take a left and then go into the first room on the right. Lock the door behind you and I'll be down to get you when my shift ends."

I tilted my head and smirked. "I thought we weren't goin' to be havin' sex tonight."

"We aren't," Skull said, but he grinned as he said it.

I laughed as I turned around.

"Take the first left then go into the first room on your right," Skull called after me.

"Yeah, yeah, I heard you the first time." I yawned.

I heard him chuckle then a loud burst of music filled the hallway only to be cut off seconds later. I glanced over my shoulder and saw I was alone in the empty hallway. I was alone in an unfamiliar place.

Keela would *kill* me for walking around an unfamiliar place on my own.

"Shit, Keela," I mumbled.

With the thought of her, I remembered my promise to text her when I was home so she could go to sleep. I took out my phone, thumbed a message that I was safe and going to sleep and then slipped my phone back into my clutch after I hit send.

I turned and continued to walk down the hallway, and just as I came up to the left turn Skull told me to make, I heard a door slam and male voices bellowing at one another from the end of the hallway on my right. I jumped with fright and balled my hands into fists to keep them steady.

The hairs on the back of my neck stood up, and my breathing sped up. I inched my way down the hallway towards the voices, even though every fibre in my body screamed at me to turn and walk in the opposite direction. I rounded a corner and followed the voices taking a left turn, then a right.

I ignored my gut and continued my slow and steady walk down the hallway. I only stopped when I came to a door that wasn't shut all the way. I glanced at the door looking for a number or something to say what the room was for, but there was nothing but dark varnished wood.

There was a space between the door and doorframe and I took it upon myself to look through the gap to see what all the commotion was about. I closed one eye and scanned the section of the brightly lit room that I could see, and when a bloodied man bound to a chair came into my line of sight, I couldn't help but gasp.

I instantly covered my mouth with my hand and ceased to function altogether in fear I would make another unnecessary noise. I remained frozen until a few seconds passed by and nothing happened. I lowered my hand and gently exhaled a relieved breath.

That was close.

I flinched when I looked back into the room just as a tall man rounded into my view and punched the bound man across the face. The poor man's head snapped to the right, and a moan of pain escaped him. Other than that one moan, he made no sound—not one.

"Remainin' silent will only lead to more bad shite happenin' to you, Shane. Do yourself a favour and tell me where my shipment is. I know you tried to jack it, I've eyes everywhere along the docks."

The bound man laughed then spat a mixture of saliva and blood onto the man speaking to him. "If you have eyes all along the docks, why did none of them see where your shipment got to?"

The man, who I assumed was in charge, took out a handkerchief from his jacket pocket and wiped his face. "I don't have time for games; tell me what I want to know or me friend here breaks your legs. Your choice."

There was a lot of shouting, cursing, and screaming that followed in the next twenty seconds and it caused my stomach to churn. I was about to turn away from the room when the door opened wide and the bearded man who was threatening the bound man stood before me, glaring at me.

Oh, fuck.

"I took a wrong turn, I'm so sorry," I blurted and turned around.

I all but sprinted up the hallway and ignored the man shouting after me. I also ignored his calls for someone to 'catch me.' I took a right turn then a left and stopped when I came to an abrupt end to the now small hallway.

How fucking big was this place?

"It's like a bloody maze!" I hissed.

I turned around and mentally prepared myself to retrace my steps so I could find the room Skull told me to go to, but all coherent thoughts left my head when I ran into a hard chest.

"Ow!" I grunted and lifted my hand to my head.

"You should watch where you're going."

I froze.

I knew that voice.

I fucking loathed that voice.

I tilted my head back and looked up at his marred face.

Kane Slater.

"What the hell are *you* doing back here?" he snapped at me.

No hello or stupid comment on his part, just rudeness as usual. I was shitting myself by being here, but I couldn't *not* be a smartarse to him.

"I could ask you the same thing," I said and stumbled to stay upright when he advanced forward.

Kane glared at me. "No, you fucking can't. This is *no* place for someone like you."

I knew that good and well after witnessing a bound man being assaulted, but what in the hell did *he* mean by that?

"Someone like me?" I asked, as I tried to narrow my eyes at him, but found it difficult.

He was mad and I didn't know how to handle mad Kane. Teasing Kane, or annoyed Kane I could deal with, but mad Kane freaked me out quite a bit.

Kane continued to stalk forward, and I continued to back up. "Yeah, someone like you."

I walked backwards until my back hit a wall. "What's *that* supposed to mean?"

I squealed when Kane surged forward and gripped both of my arms with his hands.

"It means," he hissed and leaned in close to my face, "that good girls don't belong here. Understand me, babydoll?"

Babydoll? Was he for real?

"What makes you think I'm a good girl?" I asked trying to get the tremor of fear out of my voice.

Kane looked at me for a long moment as a ghost of a smile curved his lips. "I don't think you're a good girl, babydoll, I know you are."

I didn't know why I felt insulted, but I did.

"That just goes to show you really don't know me, because I *do* belong here... I hang out here all the time. I've actually hung out in Darkness since *before* you moved here. I'm practically an OG of this place."

Kane grinned at me. "Oh, really? Then tell me something, OG, why do you look lost walking down these hallways?"

I opened my mouth to speak, but quickly closed it because I had no idea. Skull said these rooms where for Brandon's business associates, and I was definitely *not* one of those. I honestly never even knew Darkness had back rooms, though I shouldn't be surprised.

Brandon was a shady fucker.

I was too stubborn to admit that to Kane so instead I said, "I don't have to justify meself to you, Slater."

Kane chuckled as he roamed his eyes over my face. "That you don't, babydoll."

I tried to pull free of his hold, but his grip tightened on me.

"Jesus! Let go of me... and what the hell is with this babydoll crap?"

Kane smirked and shrugged his shoulders. "You need babying, and you look like a doll so... babydoll."

Did he just call me childish and fake in one sentence?

"You dick. How dare you call me childish and fake!"

Kane grinned. "I didn't call you childish *or* fake you little weirdo."

Little?

"Now you're callin' me short? You're a real—"

Kane's low laughter cut me off.

It shocked me to silence because I had never heard him laugh like that before. I don't think I have ever heard him laugh at all. I've seen him grin and smirk but never smile like he was doing right now.

He looked so different.

He looked stunning.

Damn him.

"You need to calm down. I'm not insulting you. Firstly, all I'm saying is you need looking after. You being here proves my point so that's what I meant by babying. Secondly, you look gorgeous, fucking unreal, so that is what I meant by a doll. Put them together and you get babydoll, *babydoll*."

His smirk irked me.

I swallowed. "And little?"

Kane grinned. "You're a little bitty thing, what can I say?"

I was oddly flushed with pleasure that he thought I was gorgeous. I was also touched that he wanted to look after me while I was here, but my stubbornness wouldn't allow me to admit that aloud.

"Your observations and sugar sweet words won't get you anywhere with me so you can let go of me arms."

"Make me." Kane grinned.

I glared at him. "I don't have time for this. I just saw somethin' I shouldn't have and I have to leave before they find me—"

"I already found you," Kane cut me off, his eyebrow raised.

I stared at him for a moment then gasped, "*You* were in that room?"

He shrugged.

I shoved his chest. "Get away from me."

Kane held up his hands. "It's not what you think—I was more of an observer than an active participant in that room."

I scoffed, "So you *watched* a helpless man get attacked? How noble of you."

"Shane? A nice man? He is anything but nice." Kane humourlessly laughed. "Darling, you take people at face value too often."

I swallowed. "I clearly do because I thought you weren't into anything bad. Looks like I was wrong."

I rounded on Kane then and turned right, trying to find my way out from the maze of stupid hallways.

"I'm not a bad man, Aideen," Kane said as he followed close behind me.

I grunted. "What are you doin' back here then?"

"Working."

I stopped walking and turned to face him. "What type of work?"

Kane sighed. "It's nothing that concerns you, darling—trust me."

No.

"Bite me, Slater," I growled.

Kane snapped his teeth at me and took a step closer to me. "Tell me where and I'll be happy to oblige."

He was very close to me, a hair away from pressing his body against mine. I could smell his cologne and feel his touch without him actually putting a hand on me.

"Kane," I said then cleared my throat.

He lowered his head. "Aideen?"

"What are you doin'?" I whispered.

Kane smirked. "Call it an act of impulse."

I swallowed. "You... you better not be thinkin' what I think you're thinkin'."

Kane winked at me. "I bet our thoughts are pretty identical right now, babydoll."

Oh.

"Get away from me," I whispered, "and lose the stupid nickname."

Kane jostled me closer to him until our bodies finally touched. "Not a chance in hell on both counts, *babydoll*."

Before I could put him in his place with a well thought-out threat, Kane covered my mouth with his and just like that all bets were off. Okay, maybe not all bets. The stubborn bitch inside me put up a three or four second resistance against Kane's mouth. She really did, but she, and the rest of me, was simply no match for Kane's talented lips and tongue. No match at all.

I caved in to Kane's kiss and touch and latched onto him with a grip so strong it made him hiss as he pushed me back against the wall behind me. I groaned as a slight stinging sensation spread across my back. I gasped when Kane ran his hands down my sides and around to my behind where he squeezed.

I yelped into his mouth when he lifted me up and pressed his torso against mine, pinning me against the wall with his hips. He kept one arm under me and used his free hand to cup my face.

He kissed me so hard that I wanted to scream at him to stop, but I didn't. I did nothing but grab at him with my hands and kissed him harder as I tightened my legs around his waist.

He dropped both of his hands to my behind where he squeezed me and dug his fingers into my flesh. Hard. I hissed into his mouth. He swallowed down my hiss and responded with a nibble on my lower lip.

I felt the moment my back was pulled away from the wall and when Kane started to move. He was blindly walking down the hall while still kissing me. I gasped and pulled back from the kiss and looked around.

"Where are we goin'?" I asked, panicked.

I yelped when he quickly lowered me to the ground and grabbed hold of my hand. He mutely turned and began to all but run down the hallway, pulling me along with him. I didn't speak further because I was trying to keep up with him without tripping and falling on my face. I was in six-inch heels and he was just pulling me along—he wasn't being considerate towards my short legs or feet at all.

"Where are we goin'?" I repeated, still watching the floor as I stumbled along.

Kane grunted, "My house."

His house?

"Why?" I asked. "There are plenty of rooms here we could use."

Kane's quick steps never faltered as we turned two corners and headed down a long stretch of hallway. "I hate this place; the last thing I want to do is fuck you in it."

He was going to fuck me!

When we reached the doors we had been walking towards, Kane reached out and pulled one of them open. I winced when the volume of blaring music attacked my eardrums.

"Fuck!" I shouted and pulled my hand from Kane's hold to slap my hands over my ears.

Kane took a hold of my arm and began to lead me through the club. He was pretty forceful with anyone who got in our way. He had no problem shoving people or shouting at them to 'move the fuck out of the way.'

He was on a mission and I was apparently his main objective.

The thought made me giddy.

The giddy feeling disappeared when we neared the exit to the club. I pulled Kane to a stop. "Skull is expectin' me to be in a room in the back waitin' on him."

Kane looked down at me and snarled, "I don't fucking think so."

He lifted me up and threw me over his shoulder. I screamed and laughed as Kane pushed through the rest of the crowd then through the exit doors. He jogged up the stairs and I moved my hands from his back to my chest.

"Me tits are goin' to pop out!" I snapped.

He laughed, smacked my arse, and ran up the stairs faster.

"Bastard!" I bellowed but then laughed.

Kane zoomed through the bouncers and people who were still trying to gain entry to the club even though it was nearing closing time. I held my breath and waited for Skull's voice to call out my name, but it never came.

I didn't breathe normally until Kane placed me back down on the ground and steadied me by placing his hands on my shoulders. He moved a hand under my chin and used his finger to tip my head up so I could look him in the eye.

"You seem nervous," Kane murmured.

I swallowed. "I *am* nervous."

"Because I'm going to have you or because you're worried Skull will find out?" Kane asked, his voice tight.

"Skull and I aren't together, Kane—we decided that for good tonight. He just put me in the back room because I wanted to go home, but he couldn't leave to bring me home."

Kane snorted. "I'd bet my life that he would have fucked you when he got back to the room."

I narrowed my eyes. "He respects me, you know? He wouldn't take advantage of me if he knew I didn't *want* to have sex with him."

Kane pressed his front against me and forced me to lean against his Jeep.

"Do you *want* to have sex with him?" he growled.

I shoved at his chest. "I don't know what I want."

"I do," Kane whispered. "Me."

He kissed me again and turned my brain to mush.

I reached up and tangled my fingers in his hair, applying heavy pressure to the kiss. I gasped into his mouth when he lifted me up for a second time and pressed his pelvis between my legs. I wrapped my legs around his waist and squeezed him.

Kane growled into my mouth, and then tore his lips from mine. "Get in the car. Now."

He let me down roughly and hurried me around to the passenger side of the car. When I was inside, he slammed the door shut and sped around to the driver's side. When he got into the car he started up the engine, buckled his seatbelt, put the car in reverse and backed out of the spot we were parked in.

"Oh, my God!" I squealed when he switched gears and took off out of the car park. "I want to survive this ride. Slow down."

"The only thing you will be riding tonight, babydoll, is me. Now, sit back, shut the fuck up and let me drive."

I felt my jaw drop open.

I was shocked.

No one spoke to me like that without being verbally or physically attacked. But for some reason, Kane bossing me around in his rude, snippy way was really working for me.

Maybe it was because I had a few drinks prior to us kissing, or maybe it was because I was so horny I couldn't see straight. Whatever the reason, I liked it, but that didn't mean I would play along.

"You know I don't do what I'm told, Kane."

He took a sharp left turn. "You will when I fuck you."

Christ.

I licked my lips and lowered my gaze to the bulge in his jeans.

"That looks really uncomfortable," I murmured.

Kane looked at me and followed my gaze to between his thighs.

"It is, but you can make me more comfortable in less than five minutes, so just shut up and let me get to where I'm going."

I smirked and leaned my head down.

"Aideen!"

Kane groaned when he felt the heat of my mouth on his cock through his jeans. I made motions of kisses, but it was a little difficult to make any kind of contact through the denim.

"Unzip me," Kane breathed. "Fuck, Aideen, unzip my jeans and put your mouth on me."

I grabbed his zipper with my teeth and tugged it down. I used my hand to pull it fully down when it wouldn't budge anymore. "Say please," I murmured and kissed the tip of his erection through his boxers.

"Please!" Kane practically squealed.

I wanted to laugh because I had never heard his voice reach that pitch before, but I didn't because my mouth watered at the thought of what was about to fill it. I reached up to the band of Kane's boxers and pulled them down. The band snapped against Kane's balls and he hissed. I widened my eyes and winced.

"My bad."

He whimpered, "Just blow me, please."

He sounded desperate and because of that I wanted to please him.

I gently kissed the tip of his erection and coated my lips in the clear liquid that seeped from the head of his very impressive cock. I stuck my tongue out and flicked it across the tip, and welcomed the groans of pleasure that filled the car.

"God, *yes*!" Kane moaned as I took him fully in my mouth.

I hoped he kept his eyes open so he could continue to drive—I actually willed it. I bobbed my head up and down ten or so times before I backed off completely and sat upright in my seat.

"Wh-What? Why did you stop?" Kane asked me, breathlessly.

I shrugged. "I figured I'd do a better job once we get into a bed. It's a little awkward givin' head in a fast movin' vehicle knowin' I'm seconds from dyin'. Plus, me seatbelt was diggin' into me side."

Kane was silent for a moment then he cursed and floored the accelerator on the car.

"Kane!" I screeched.

For a couple of minutes, my life flashed before my eyes, my stomach churned, and I just about shit myself when all of a sudden the car came to a sudden screeching halt.

"Out. Now."

I opened my eyes just as Kane fixed his trousers, jumped out of his car, and slammed the door shut. I blinked my eyes a second later and looked at my left as the passenger door was flung open. Kane reached in, unbuckled my seatbelt, and hooked his left arm under my legs and his right around my back.

He lifted me out of the car, turned us around and kicked the door closed with his foot. I laughed and put my arms around his neck and used it as leverage to pulled myself up so I could nuzzle my face into his neck. I kissed along the base of his neck until he shivered. I smirked.

I found his sweet spot.

"Damn it, Aideen," he growled when I latched my lips onto said spot and sucked.

I laughed when he pulled away and set me on the ground outside of his house.

"Out of all the times I've been here, I never thought I'd be stoppin' by for some midnight sex with you."

"Who else would you have sex with here if not me?" Kane asked and he searched for his keys.

I smirked. "Damien could come back here at any time."

Kane glared at me. "You're not sleeping with my little brother."

"Why not?" I teased.

He leaned forward, placed his mouth to my ear and whispered, "Because after tonight, you'll be mine. Only ever mine."

I burst into a fit of giggles.

"Be quiet. Everyone is in bed."

That shut me up.

"Branna and Ryder are home?" I hissed, my voice low.

Kane looked over his shoulder at me and grinned as I took a step backwards. "If you run, I'll chase you and catch you, babydoll."

I both smirked and glared at him. "I'll smack the shite out of you."

"I'm holding you to that." He winked.

I shook my head, smiling.

"Ry and Bran are on the second floor, I'm up top in Dominic's old room. They won't hear us."

I was hesitant.

"Just... just don't say me name."

Kane grunted. "Are you embarrassed?"

Was I?

"No, I just don't want to be the butt of jokes," I mumbled. "You know everyone will tease us if they knew we—well, you know."

Kane opened his front door and stepped inside. I took a few seconds, but I eventually followed him inside and jumped a little when he clicked the door shut and locked it with the key.

There was a sense of finality about it.

"You aren't goin' to let me leave, are you?" I asked, my senses now heightened.

Kane pressed his front to my back and slid his hands around my waist. "For now? No."

"And later?" I whispered.

Kane nipped at my neck and lead me into his house. "Ask me later."

I would.

I definitely would.

I gasped when Kane spun me and flung me over his shoulder for the second time in the space of half an hour.

"I can walk, you know?" I whispered.

Kane slapped my behind. "Not fast enough."

He took the stairs two at a time, and it scared me because I was hanging upside down. I closed my eyes and only opened them when I felt myself fly through the air. It was so sudden I didn't even have time to scream.

I gasped when my back collided with a mattress. I lifted my

head and looked down to my feet when my heels were pulled off my feet. Kane's hands rushed up my thighs, gripped my underwear, and pulled them off my body.

I jumped up to my knees.

"Kane!" I snapped.

I could see the moonlight shining on his face, and he smirked as he threw my knickers behind him. He stepped forward and put his face to mine. I licked my lips and moved in to kiss him, but he pulled back.

"Arms up first."

Huh?

"What—"

"Arms up first, both of them. You can kiss me when you do that."

Okay.

I lifted my arms above my head and squealed when Kane gripped the hem of my dress and pulled it up my body and over my head. I lowered my arms and blinked. Kane had already thrown my dress away and had his hands behind my back where he was unclasping my bra. My bra straps fell down my arms, then like me knickers and dress, it was thrown somewhere in the room.

I should have felt embarrassed to be stark naked but, in all honesty, I was kind of turned on and pissed off at the same time.

"You know, you could have just asked me to strip."

Kane gripped the back of his top and pulled it over his head. "I could have, but where was the fun in that?"

I looked down to his chest and swallowed. I just had the moonlight to work with, but with it I could see jagged marks spread out over Kane's chest and shoulders. I looked up and found him watching me.

"You want me to put my tee back on?" he asked, his voice rough.

What?

"No," I mumbled. "Why would I want you to do that? I'm naked—I want you naked."

I *really* wanted him naked.

Kane didn't move. "My body... it's ruined, babydoll. It's not pretty to look at or to feel. I won't be offended if you want me to stay clothed."

I blinked. "Your body is not ruined, it's unique."

Kane was silent as I reached out and ran my fingers over a lumpy scar that curved from his neck down the centre of his chest. It frightened me to think how he could have gotten this scar. I desperately wanted to ask the question on my mind, but I pushed it aside. That question wouldn't lead to sex—it would lead to being kicked out.

"You're the hottest man I've ever laid me eyes on," I admitted then leaned in close to him. "I'll deny ever sayin' that in the mornin'."

Kane snorted with laughter. "Are you just saying that so you can get in my pants?"

I smirked. "I could say a lot less and get in your pants, but no, I'm being honest. You're perfect the way you are. Your scars don't bother me at all, honey."

Kane growled and it made me jump then smile.

"I *love* when you make that noise."

I jumped again when Kane's hands latched onto my bare behind and squeezed. I held my breath as he leaned forward and placed his mouth by my ear.

"I'm going to fuck you so hard you'll see stars."

Oh.

"Yes," I whispered. "Yes, please."

Kane pulled back and almost glared down at me. "Turn around."

Turn round?

"Okay," I murmured and did as... ordered?

I turned my back to Kane, and it was only then I became fully aware of how naked and vulnerable I was. I flinched when his finger pressed against my neck and slid down my back causing a shiver to run up my spine.

"Bend over," he grunted.

Holy shite.

My already pounding heart kicked up a notch and began to slam into my chest with such force it took my breath away.

"Aideen," Kane growled. "Bend. Over."

Oh. My. God.

This was hot.

So fucking hot.

I bent forward and flattened my palms against the soft mattress beneath me. I began to shake with anticipation of what was about to happen, and it both terrified and thrilled me.

"I'm going to fuck you right here," Kane murmured.

I bit down on my lip when I felt the tip of Kane's finger lazily rotate in circles around my entrance. He never dipped it inside; he stuck to a painfully slow rhythm of gentle finger fucking.

It was torture.

"And if you can take me here," he grunted and moved his finger to my anus, "I'll fuck you here too."

My arse?

I widened my eyes, but I said nothing. I remained calm. Inside I was freaking out though because, in all my sexually active years. I had never once tried anal sex. I wasn't a prude. I thought of myself as adventurous, but anal just never came up.

Until now.

"Aideen?" Kane whispered.

I moaned out loud when two of Kane's fingers dipped inside me without warning.

"Oh, so you *are* awake." Kane chuckled.

Awake?

"You thought I fell asleep positioned like this while you're doin' *that*?" I asked, whilst biting down on my lower lip.

Kane continued to slowly pump his fingers in and out of my body. "Stranger things have happened."

My eyes fluttered closed as a teasing sensation surrounded my core.

"Please," I whispered.

"Please what?"

I groaned, "Please fuck me already."

Kane clicked his tongue. "I don't know... you don't seem to really want me to fuck you."

Seriously?

"Kane," I growled as my clit pulsed to life and began to throb. "I'm *very* ready for you to fuck me."

Kane shook his head. "It doesn't seem like it."

I growled and pushed back against his hand, taking his fingers deep inside me. I yelped when a stinging slap was delivered to my behind.

"That shows your enthusiasm, but not quite enough for me to be bothered enough to take my cock out."

Really?

I was butt ass naked and bent over in front of him while he fingered me at a snail's pace. How did this *not* show enthusiasm? If I didn't know any better, I would say he was purposely trying to piss me off.

"I'll show you enthusiasm," I grunted to myself and turned around, frowning at the loss of Kane's fingers.

I quickly kneeled in front of Kane and then rolled to the left and off the bed. He watched me as I moved, a perplexed look on his face

"What are you—offt!" I cut Kane off when I ran and jumped on him.

He caught me but fell back onto his bed.

I sat upright and glared down at him. "Move up the bed."

Kane looked up at me with wide but amused eyes and did as *I* ordered. He shimmied up the bed and then clasped his hands behind his head. "What now?"

Cheeky fucker.

I didn't reply. Instead, I moved down his thighs and grabbed a hold of his jeans. I unbuttoned them and forcibly yanked his boxers down letting his cock spring free. I didn't ask for permission, nor did I let on to what I was doing. I simply moved back up Kane's body, reached down, grabbed his thick cock in my hand and guided it to my entrance as I sank down.

"Fuck!" he roared.

Yeah, fuck.

I forced myself not to clench as I sunk lower and lower on Kane's cock. It was a battle because I'd never had anyone as big as him before. Skull had a pretty decent sized cock, nothing like Kane's though; he was big in length and width. It almost made me regret taking control because my fast and furious plan was now out the window as I struggled to keep it together enough to take him fully inside of me.

"Christ," I breathed as my pelvis finally touched Kane's.

Kane's hands gripped my thighs. "Don't stop," he begged, his voice pained.

"Give me a second," I pleaded. "It's—you're big, okay. Just... let me adjust."

Kane almost whimpered, "I'm big? You're tight as *fuck*. That inch-by-inch thing you just did is a no-go. Jesus, I'll fuck you into next week if you continue to torture me like that."

He spoke like I did it on purpose.

I swallowed. "Okay," I exhaled and placed my hands on his chest. "Are you ready?"

Kane slapped my arse cheeks. "Ride me, babydoll."

And ride him I did.

I used his chest for leverage to lift myself up and sink back down on him. I closed my eyes and focused on feeling Kane's chest under me rather than the size of his cock. It was so big it almost hurt.

Stop being a pussy.

I growled at my thoughts and picked up my pace until my skin slapped against Kane with each bounce. *There.* That felt better. I could still feel the stretch of Kane's cock, but it no longer felt uncomfortable; the lubricant my body produced made sure of that.

"Just like *that*, babydoll."

I blinked my eyes open when Kane's voice broke through my thoughts. I gazed down at him and was momentarily shocked at how perfect he looked. The moonlight highlighted his face and chest. It was like he almost glowed.

"You look like an angel," I murmured.

Kane began to buck his hips up as I continued to slam my body down on him. "That'd be you, darling."

I cried out and sheer pleasure shot up through me.

"Right there!" I shouted and bore down on Kane as I pushed myself to the peak of my pace. My insides clenched, and my core erupted in fire as tingles spread out all over me while I chased my orgasm down.

I stopped breathing when the first pulse hit me. I screamed when the warm wave of ecstasy slammed into me with enough force to push air back into my body. I felt lightheaded and dizzy, but that was more so because of Kane sitting up, wrapping his arms around me and rolling me under him.

He forcibly slammed the remainder of my orgasm out of me, and I loved every fucking second of it. I lifted my arms and wrapped them around his body. I could feel the lumps and bumps of the many scars that were scattered across his back.

I was a little shocked at how many I felt, and for a second I wished never to see the damage because feeling it was enough to put a lump in my throat.

"Kane," I moaned.

He brought his face down to mine. "I want to watch you come over and over again. You're perfect when you're coming around my cock. Fucking. Perfect."

Oh.

"Please, just don't stop," I pleaded.

My orgasm came and went, but feeling Kane inside me was something I liked, a lot. I didn't want it to ever end.

Kane pulled out of my body then slammed back into me. He repeated the action over and over. I cried out and arched my back in delight. My neck was exposed so Kane buried his face in it and kissed my sensitive flesh.

He found my sweet spot rather quickly, and when I gasped, he bore down and sucked like his life depended on it. I dug my nails into his back and for a moment, he stopped moving altogether, his entire body tensed up.

I was panting as he pulled his head back to look down at me. "What's wrong?"

He pulled out of me and thrust right back inside which sent a shock up my spine.

"Nothing... ju-just be careful with my back. You aren't hurting me, it just reminds me of something I don't like when you dig your nails into me."

I blinked. "I'm so sorry."

It was a bad habit, Skull loved when I dug my nails into his back.

Don't think about Skull right now!

Kane re-captured my attention as he applied a fair amount of his weight down on me. "Don't be sorry, babydoll."

He kissed me lazily and slowed his pace down. He fucked me slowly, but thoroughly. It was delicious torture.

"Kane," I groaned when my insides began to tingle again.

He growled and put his mouth next to my ear. "You're close again. I can feel your pussy tightening around me."

The dual sensations of him fucking me, and his breath on my skin as he growled into my ear caused shivers to break out over my entire body.

"Keep talkin'!" I gasped and bucked my hips when I could feel my second orgasm within reach.

"You like it when I talk to you?" Kane murmured. "Do you like it when I fuck your pretty pussy and make it mine?"

God, yes.

"Kannneeeeee," I hissed.

The pleasure was becoming painful.

"Tell me what you want," he snarled and sucked my earlobe into his mouth.

Fuck!

"Fast. Hard. You. *Please!*"

Kane didn't ask me to beg or repeat what I wanted him to do to me. He instantly obliged me and kept his promise—he fucked me so hard I saw stars.

My eyes rolled back when my orgasm, and Kane, slammed into me. I lifted my hands and tangled them in his hair as my body was swept away in a tide of pleasure. My senses were heightened when I felt the sting of a bite on my neck at the same time Kane's body tensed then twitched. His hips jerked into me at a slower pace.

A few moments of stillness and laboured breathing passed by before I realised I couldn't exactly breathe correctly. I wheezed and shoved at Kane who only laughed and rolled his body off mine.

"Sorry," he panted.

"S'okay."

I looked up at the ceiling of Kane's bedroom and bathed in the relaxation my body was experiencing.

"Give me a few minutes."

I turned my head and looked at Kane. "Huh? For what?"

Kane looked at me and said, "For round two."

Excuse me?

"Round two?" I asked, wide-eyed. "I'm knackered."

Kane smirked. "You don't know the meaning of that word yet, but you will when I'm finished with you."

I gasped then laughed when he dived back on top of me.

"You're supposed to be ill, you can't have too much sex... you might die."

Kane vibrated with laughter, "I don't feel sick when I'm with you. Maybe you're the drug I need to get better."

I glared up at him, but my insides fluttered at his sugar-coated words.

"I'm not a drug."

Kane wiggled himself back between my legs and fisted his, once again, rock hard cock, rubbing it against me.

"I don't know about that, babydoll," Kane murmured then slowly slid back inside my body.

I groaned out loud and reached for him. He leaned down, but instead of kissing me he brought his lips to my ear and whispered, "Feeling you wrapped around me, having you so close to me, breathing in your intoxicating scent, wanting to taste you for as long as I live... I'd definitely say you're my addiction. You're *my* drug."

Oh.

"Kane."

"Aideen," he whispered and nipped at my earlobe, "you're *mine*."

I opened my eyes. Well, I tried to. I found my eyes wouldn't fully open and it was because of my fake eyelashes. I groaned and lifted my hand to my face, peeled them from my eyelids and blinked my eyes open. I dropped my hand down to my abdomen to rub my sore stomach, and when my fingers pressed against my skin I furrowed my eyebrows.

I lifted the blanket that covered me and looked down to my stomach. My bare stomach. I widened my eyes when I quickly realised the rest of me was bare too. I had no clothes on, and I wasn't in my own bed.

Oh, fuck.

I slowly turned my head to the right and almost screamed when the sleeping form of Kane Slater came into my line of sight. I turned my head and looked up at the ceiling. I closed my eyes as images of last night flooded my mind.

I had sex with Kane Slater.

Three times.

Fuck, fuck, FUCK!

I had to leave. I had to get out of there before he woke up.

I carefully, very carefully, slid from under the covers and stepped onto the cool wooden floor. I felt the morning air surround me, and the tenderness between my legs as I moved around.

Kane clearly gave me a right seeing to.

I shook my head clear of last night's sexual adventures and scanned the room for my clothes. I spotted my bra hanging on a knob of Kane's chest of drawers. I tiptoed over to it, yanked it off the knob, and quickly put it on. I scanned the room again and saw that my knickers were on the radiator across the room, which baffled me. I had no clue how they got all the way over there.

I crept over and grabbed them from the radiator. I shimmied them on whilst staring at Kane like he was going to wake up at any moment. Luckily he didn't, which was really in my favour, as I had to sneak around the room looking for my dress and clutch.

I found my clutch on the floor next to the side of the bed I rolled out of, and I found my dress there too. I pulled it over my head, adjusted it to my body, and relaxed. My shoes were over at the window where he threw them last night so when I was near them, I slipped them on and stood upright.

I did it.

I smiled to myself and turned in the direction of the door. I barely moved before I heard him behind me.

"What are you doing?"

Oh, hell.

I froze and momentarily thought about just running out of the room. I thought better of it and slowly turned around because I knew he would chase and catch me if I did run for it. I swallowed when my gaze fell on Kane as he looked at me with his head propped up on his pillows.

"Um, I was tryin' to leave... quietly."

Kane raised an eyebrow at me. "Why? Is a good morning fuck not your thing?"

I silently thanked him for being a prick. I could handle Kane when he was a prick; it was when he acted liked a decent human that I found things difficult.

"Mornin' fuckin' *is* me thing, just not with you," I spat. "Night fuckin', or *any* type of fuckin' with you, is not me thing."

Kane smirked at me. "That's funny since it's *my* bed you just crawled from, and if I remember correctly, it was also *my* cock you were bouncing all over last night. Nice skills by the way. You tired me out, babydoll."

That. Motherfucker.

I balled my hands into fists. "I was intoxicated last night, sweetheart."

Kane slowly rose up from the bed, and I was painfully aware of the bed sheets sliding off his body. I saw the treasure trail on his stomach as the sheet dropped away before I snapped my gaze up to Kane's teasing one.

"You were fully aware of what, and *who*, you were doing last night, *sweetheart*."

I curled my lip in disgust. "Listen, little boy—"

"Little boy?" Kane humourlessly laughed. "You made me stop last night so you could adjust to me, *twice*. When I got you back here, you told me I was 'so big' over and over."

I felt my eye twitch. "I was referrin' to your *age*, you cocky fucker."

Kane grinned. "Hmmm. You're what, one year older than I am? Not bad. You aren't the first teacher I've fucked, and you probably won't be the last... but you're *definitely* the hottest."

He climbed off the bed and began to walk towards me.

I didn't have to look down to know he was naked. My eyes dropped to his chest and my mouth watered. Damn him, and his stupid bloody chest. The hair on a man's chest never did anything for me before, but my God, Kane worked the fuck out of it.

"Stop it!" I snapped and held my hands up. "Stay right where you are."

Kane laughed and continued to advance on me. "You want me to come and drag you back to my bed and fuck you until you scream again? You *know* you do."

I did not!

"You're so wrong. I want to go home," I squeaked.

Kane shot forward, wrapped his arms around me, and tugged me against him. My hands went to his shoulders and I leaned my head back to look up at him. I opened my mouth to tell him off, but I never got the chance because he kissed me before I could get a word out.

I tried not to kiss him back, but it was hard. Kane was hard, too. I could feel his erection against my belly as he pressed his body against mine.

"Tell me no," Kane murmured against my mouth.

"No," I replied, my voice barely a squeak.

Kane devilishly grinned. "Try again."

I cleared my throat. "No, Kane."

He stared down at me, his eyes unblinking. "Do you mean that?"

I hesitated before answering him and he smiled. "There's my answer."

I held my breath as Kane began to lower his mouth to mine once more. I jumped when a bang on his bedroom door interrupted the moment.

Thank God.

"What?" Kane shouted without taking his eyes off me.

"Dominic is downstairs. We're both waiting for your lazy ass. You said you wanted to do a six a.m. run, remember?"

What?

"You *willingly* want to go runnin' at six in the mornin'? That's disgustin'," I whispered.

Kane grinned. "I'll get rid of my brothers—"

"No, Kane," I cut him off. "I'm serious. What happened between us *won't* happen again. Ever. Like you said last night, it was an act of impulse, right?"

Kane stared down at me and set his jaw when he saw I was serious. "Right," he said through gritted teeth.

I swallowed. "So I'm goin' to go. Don't tell anyone about this, okay?"

"Whatever." Kane snarled and took a few steps back away from me.

I nodded my head.

Kane walked over to his wardrobe and took out a black hoodie that he tossed my way. I caught it and quickly pulled it over my torso and pulled the hood up. I shoved my clutch into the large pocket of the hoodie, tucked my hair into the hood and walked over to the door without looking at Kane.

"My door is always open for you," Kane said from behind me.

I halted for a moment but said nothing.

"Bye, Kane."

"Not for good," he grunted, "I'll see you later."

I closed my eyes and fought the urge to turn to him. I shook my head clear and continued walking towards the bedroom door. I opened it just as Alec knocked for a second time.

"Kane—Whoa, you're *not* Kane."

I kept my head lowered. "Excuse me," I said with a raspy tone so Alec wouldn't be able to tell it was me.

I tried to step around Alec, but he stepped to the left when I did. "I'm Alec, Kane's brother, and you are?"

I stepped to the right without answering, but Alec sidestepped with me and once again blocked my path.

I grunted, "I'm leavin', excuse me."

Alec snorted. "Why the quick getaway? Did my little brother not show you a good time?"

I heard Kane snicker behind me and it irked me.

"I had a fine time. Please move."

Alec laughed as he stepped out of my way. I quickly walked down the hallway and turned to the stairs. I kept my head lowered and stared down at my feet as I descended the stairs in the hope that I wouldn't trip and fall.

When I got down to the bottom floor, I made a beeline for the door but, of course, a shirtless Nico walked out of the gym room at that exact time and blocked my path.

"Who are *you*?" he asked, and even though I was looking down at the floor, I could hear the smile in his voice.

I rasped up my voice once more. "I'm no one, excuse me."

Nico snickered. "Are you ashamed of sleeping with my brother? Did he not do you right?"

Excuse me?

"Move before I kick the shite out of you!" I growled.

Nico burst into laughter and stepped aside. "I've heard that threat enough from Irish women to take it seriously. Have a nice day, bed bunny."

I shook my head. "Bloody eejit."

He continued to laugh from behind me.

I walked forward, opened the front door and stepped outside. I reached in, grabbed the door handle and pulled the door shut after me. I shivered from the cold for a moment before I wrapped my arms around myself and walked out of the Slater's garden.

I slept with Kane Slater. I groaned to myself as I started my mile-long walk of shame.

"Stupid, stupid, stupid!" I snapped to myself.

How could I have possibly slept with Kane of all people?

I hated Kane and he hated me.

I really *was* stupid.

I didn't know why I let my guard down. Alcohol. I was blaming it on alcohol. One thing was for sure, what happened last night with Kane—and what almost happened this morning—could *never* happen again.

I'd never live it down otherwise.

CHAPTER NINE

"Oh. My. God," Keela said after a long period of silence.

I sighed, hung my head, and nodded. "You said you wanted every dirty detail."

"I did, but holy fuck. I didn't think it'd be so hot. Can you tell me that again, but this time while I'm takin' notes?"

Excuse me?

I snapped my head up and glared at Keela. "You're not puttin' the events of *that night* in your book. I forbid it."

Keela's small frame slumped. "Why not? It will be me characters, not you and Kane."

Was this bitch fucking with me?

I angrily shook my head. "I don't care. You aren't cashin' in on me fuck up. Me *literal* fuck up."

Keela huffed and grumbled, "Yeah, okay."

Damn right.

When that potential nightmare was crushed, I looked back down to my feet and groaned, "This doesn't feel real."

"Well, it is. You're pregnant for Kane," Keela stated.

Smartarse.

"Stop!" I moaned and covered my face with my hands. "You're makin' me feel ill."

Keela reached out and rubbed my back while she chuckled a little. "Babe, this is an incredible thing. You're goin' to have a *baby*. How amazin' is that?"

Not amazing, just terrifying.

"I can barely take care of meself, Keela. How can I take care of a baby?" I asked, my voice tight with emotion.

"That's what you have me for. I'll help you with everythin' and so will the girls," Keela assured me then snickered. "You're also forgettin' who the baby daddy is—Kane won't let your child want for anythin'."

I didn't know why, but that notion bothered me.

I balled my hands into fists and looked up. "I don't need to rely on *Kane Slater*. I can provide for another person, I just don't know if I'm ready to. I'm not even in a relationship with Kane. We can barely stand the sight of one another. How we had sex is still mind-bogglin' to me."

Keela's hand touched my shoulder. "You aren't the first woman to have a baby whilst being single, and you won't be the last. I love Kane, and you know he will actively help in every way he can, but you can do this with *or* without anyone's help. You helped raise Gavin, you're practically already a mother."

Yeah, Mother Aideen, that's me.

I snorted, "And what a good job I've done with him; workin' for your uncle tryin' to be somethin' he's not."

"Aideen," Keela sighed, her face sullen. "Gavin's choices don't reflect your part in raisin' him. Smart people make dumb decisions every day—we're only human. Gavin will realise his mistake in his own time."

His own time wasn't quick enough for me.

"Even *if* he realises his mistake, he is in Brandon's circle now. He can't be jumped out. Once you're in his circle, the only way you get out is by dyin'. You know that, and so do I."

Keela's hand squeezed my shoulder. "Brandon is me uncle, he loves me. If Gavin wants out, I'll get him out. Trust me on that."

That reassured me a little.

"I can't even think of Gavin right now, me head is a mess," I admitted and sniffled when a sudden lump formed in my throat.

Keela wrapped her arms around me. "It's goin' to be okay, you'll see."

I hugged Keela back. "How can I tell him?"

Keela pulled back and looked at me. I didn't need to verbalise the name, she knew I was talking about Kane.

"I don't know. Kane is a closed book; it's hard to read him."

"Really?" I asked, surprised. "I think it's easy to understand what he is feelin' or thinkin'. You just have to pay attention to him."

Keela raised an eyebrow. "And *you* pay attention to him?"

I deadpanned, "I'm pregnant with his child, what do you think?"

Keela laughed, "He *does* act differently around you. He clearly likes you and more than just sexually. You're the only person he lets give him his insulin when he clearly has a problem with needles."

Kane didn't like me. The only thing he liked to do was piss me off, even when I was helping him. Judging from our past, he possibly liked it when I got naked too.

I gnawed on my inner cheek. "Maybe because he knows I won't take his bullshit and that's why he lets me jab him?"

"Could be." Keela smiled.

I smiled a little until Keela spoke again.

"Have you been takin' care of yourself?" she asked me.

I shook my head when images of nights out over the past three months flashed through my mind. "No, I've been drinkin' and eatin' badly over the past few weeks. What if I've done somethin' wrong and it hurts the baby?"

My heart constricted with pain. I might not be ready to have this baby, but there was no way in Hell I wanted to harm it.

"Calm down," Keela said and placed her hands on my shoulders. "We can go to the Coombe now and find out if everythin' is okay. The emergency room never closes, I heard Branna say it before."

I gasped when I thought of Branna.

"What if Branna sees us?"

"She works in the delivery suite, not the emergency room—we'll be fine."

"Are you sure?"

"Very sure. Let's go."

I swallowed. "Just the two of us?"

Keela nodded. "Just you and I."

The melody of *"Just The Two of Us"* flowed through my mind and it caused me to lightly chuckle and shake my head.

"Okay, let's go before I change me mind," I said and stood up.

Keela jumped to her feet and grabbed her phone and keys. "I'm textin' Alec and tellin' him we're goin' to get petrol and some sweets and that we might be awhile. He won't suspect a thing."

Uh-oh.

I winced. "Do you think lyin' to him is a good idea? Especially after everythin' that happened between you both on movin' day. That's all still very fresh; it was only nine days ago after all."

Keela hesitated as she pressed on her phone then shook her head and gave the screen one final tap. "It's not a good idea, but he will understand why I'm doin' it. Kane should know about the baby *before* his brothers."

I huffed. "When he does find out he is goin' to rip me a new one for tellin' you before him."

Keela rolled her eyes. "Please, you can barely stand him, and I'm your best friend. If he has anythin' to say, I'll kindly tell him to kiss me arse."

I laughed. It felt good—for a moment I was calm and relaxed, then I remembered the situation I was in and where I was about to go.

"You look like you're about to be sick."

I gripped onto my stomach. "I *feel* like I'm about to be sick."

Keela gasped and gripped my arm. "Not on the new floor, it's only just been polished and buffed!"

I didn't get the chance to say I didn't literally mean get sick because Keela proceeded to pull me out of her sitting room, down her hallway, and out of her house. The fast movements and quick turns upset my already unsettled stomach. I bent forward and vomited on her pathway.

"That was close," she breathed when I was finished. "Are you okay?"

I growled as I wiped my mouth with the back of my hand. "I was good until you started swingin' me around. What the hell was that about?"

"You said you felt like you were goin' to be sick!"

"Because I'm in a fucked up situation."

Keela gnawed on her lower lip. "I thought you meant physically sick."

I glanced down at the puddle of vomit and shook my head. "I can see that."

Keela gave me an apologetic smile then ran back into her house only to emerge a minute later with a pot full of water. She poured it over the area where I vomited and cleared it away.

"I'll clean it properly with bleach and boiled water when we get back."

I placed my hands on my stomach. "Let's just go."

Keela returned the pot to her kitchen and emerged with a cold bottle of water for me. I gargled some water and spat it out before taking several gulps.

When I was ready, we headed down the pathway and got into my car that was parked outside the Slater's house. Keela, even though she wasn't insured on my car, got into the driver's seat and buckled up. I got into the passenger side, buckled my seat belt and leaned my head back against the headrest.

"I'm so nervous."

Keela patted my leg. "It'll be okay, you'll see."

When we drove off, Keela began to talk, but I couldn't begin to comprehend what she was saying. My mind was elsewhere.

Ma, please let the baby be okay.

I prayed to my mother and to God, that I wouldn't receive bad news when I arrived at the hospital. I prayed that everything would be okay for the baby's sake. It worried me how scared I was about someone who an hour ago I didn't know existed inside of me.

When my thoughts combined with my worry, I shook my head clear and glanced at Keela. She was still talking. I barely paid attention to her and let her do the majority of the talking during the drive to the Coombe Hospital. If I had to, I couldn't guess what we were conversing about because my mind was elsewhere the entire time.

"Aideen, we're here."

I blinked my eyes and looked at my right. "We are?"

Keela nodded her head. "You were pretty out of it on the way here."

I sighed, "Sorry, just doin' some thinkin'."

Keela smiled. "I understand. Are you ready?"

Was I?

"Yeah," I mumbled. "Let's do this."

Keela parked the car close to the hospital entrance then we exited my vehicle and headed for the hospital.

"Hi, erm, where is the emergency room?" Keela asked the man sitting at the reception desk when we entered the hospital.

He looked bored as hell.

I couldn't look him in the eye. I didn't know why, but I felt like I was somehow in trouble for being pregnant even though I was far from being a teenager with parents to disappoint.

"To your right," the man replied to Keela and gestured with his hand. "Knock on the red door, take a seat, and wait for a nurse to see to you."

Keela and I thanked the man then followed his instructions and walked to the right. I spotted the red door he mentioned and the rows of chairs in front of it.

"Sit down," Keela said to me and walked towards the red door.

I sat down in the third row and watched as she reached the door and knocked three times. She turned then and walked back to me, taking the vacant seat to my right. I didn't know how long we were seated before the red door opened and out stepped an Asian nurse in black trousers, and a white hospital shirt with a pocket watch hanging from the shirt pocket.

"Which one of you ladies wants to check into the emergency room?" she asked in an accent I had never heard before.

I couldn't reply to her so I just raised my hand like one of my students did in class when I asked them a question.

The nurse smiled at me. "Follow me, please. Your friend can come along too."

"Like she could stop me," Keela murmured.

I didn't laugh, but I breathed a little harder through my noise to show I thought what she said was funny.

Keela and I walked after the nurse into the emergency room. I stood idly by the red door Keela closed until the nurse gestured me to take a seat in front of her desk. Her desk was off to the right of the room. On the left was a hospital bed, a bunch of monitors and other hospital equipment. I sat down and breathed easy when I felt Keela's presence behind me.

"Name, please?" the nurse asked me.

I cleared my throat. "Aideen Collins."

The nurse got out a pink folder, and clipped freshly printed out forms into the folder. She clicked her pen and began writing. She asked for my home address and wrote it down when I called it out to her.

"Date of birth?"

I licked my lips. "February 5th, 1987."

"Is this your first pregnancy?"

I blinked. "Yes, ma'am."

"Planned?"

Was that really a required question?

"Well, no," I answered, honestly.

The nurse looked up at me and smiled. "Sorry, standard questions."

Why?

"It's fine."

The nurse nodded her head and looked back down at the pink folder. "Any known allergies to medication or food?"

I shook my head. "Nope."

She went on to ask a bunch of questions about the medical history of my family and myself. I froze up when she asked if there have ever been pregnancy complications with the women in my family.

"Not durin' pregnancy, but me mother died while givin' birth to me brother. She lost a lot of blood and didn't receive a blood transfusion in time."

"Sorry for your loss."

I swallowed. "Thank you."

After a moment, the nurse launched back into the questions she needed to ask and I was grateful because I really didn't want to think about my mother dying during childbirth when I was in an emergency room for a pregnancy I just found out about.

"When was your last menstrual period?"

"I can't remember," I replied honestly. "Mine are very irregular so I was never good at keepin' track."

The nurse nodded her head and made note of what I said.

"Do you have a date for possible conception?"

I grunted, "Yeah, the 1st of April."

"The 1st of April... are you sure?" the nurse asked, not sure if I was lying or not.

"Pretty sure," I replied.

Like I could forget the day I fell into stupidity or the day I let stupidity fall into me... three times.

Keela snorted behind me.

"I'm sure you have already taken a test, but I have to ask if you have or not."

I nodded my head. "Yes, I took one today. It was one of those digital ones; it said I was over three weeks pregnant."

The nurse wrote that down.

"I'm going to need you to go into the bathroom through the door behind you and urinate into this jar," she put a little clear jar with a silver twist cap on the desk in front of me, "and then bring it back out to me."

I did as the nurse asked; peed into the little jar, wrapped it in tissue and returned back to my seat.

"Here you go," I said and handed her the tissue-wrapped wee jar.

The nurse put on latex gloves, took the jar, and stood up from her seated position. She walked over to the left side of the room, binned my tissue, and removed the cap from the jar. She dipped a little stick into the jar and pulled it back out. The tip of the stick was a bright hot pink.

"Yep, you're with child," the nurse said and chuckled to herself.

I wanted to smile at her, but I was so freaked out that I could do nothing more than stare at her. Luckily the nurse didn't seem to notice my anxiety and gestured me over to the hospital bed next to her.

"As your conception date is a few weeks back I won't have to perform a vaginal ultrasound. If you would lie down on the bed and pull up your t-shirt, I can check and see how the baby is doing by using a probe on your stomach."

Oh, fuck.

"Okay," I whispered.

I did everything the nurse said. I laid down on the hospital bed, pulled up my top until my bare stomach was showing, and then I waited. The nurse stepped closer to me and looked down at me.

"Can you unbutton your jeans and shimmy them, and your underwear, down a little?" she asked. "The baby will be positioned very low right now."

I began to sweat. "Sure."

Again, I did as she asked. I unbuttoned my jeans and pulled them down a little, along with my underwear. "Is this enough?" I asked.

"Yep, that's perfect."

I looked left when Keela sat on the spare chair that was positioned there. "You okay, boss?" she asked, smiling.

She looked so happy.

I shook my head. "I'm so scared."

"It's all goin' to be okay, you'll see."

I nodded my head and looked back to the nurse when she cleared her throat.

"I'm going to squirt some gel on your lower stomach and use this probe." She held up a device that looked like a microphone. "We'll take a look at your baby. Okay?"

Okay.

I nodded my head and said nothing. I was afraid I would throw up again if I opened my mouth and spoke.

"This will be a little cold," the nurse said and squirted the gel.

I flinched when it made contact with my skin. "Shite."

Keela and the nurse laughed.

"It really *is* cold," I murmured to Keela, who was still laughing at me.

"Okay, let's find the baby," the nurse chirped and placed the probe on top of the gel and began to swirl it about.

She pulled a monitor closer to us, and stared at the screen as she moved the probe around. I stared at the screen too, but all I could see was black, white, and some grey. It looked like a shitty station on a television that had a poor connection.

I thought it would have taken the nurse awhile to find anything, but less than a minute later I heard a little chirp come from her mouth. I looked at the nurse and saw her smile.

"This little one was hiding from me," she mused and began to take what I thought was measurements of the baby. I couldn't really tell though because I still couldn't see anything but the fuzzy screen.

"Can you see it?" I asked Keela.

She was silent as she stared at the screen so I looked back at the nurse. "I can't see it."

The nurse smiled and pointed to the screen. "Do you see this little bean shaped blob right here?"

"Honey, that's it. That's your baby. Just the one baby, too."

It was?

I widened my eyes. "Really?"

I squinted my eyes then gasped when the nurse enlarged the picture.

"I see it!" I whispered.

I could see my baby; the little shape before it was zoomed in looked like a little bean, but now it was definitely a baby.

The nurse pointed at the screen. "That's the head; the little stumps there are the arms and legs. Still quite small, but forming beautifully."

"Really? So everythin' is okay?" I asked then held my breath.

"From what I can see everything is progressing perfectly."

The relief that filled me was whole.

Thank you, Ma.

The nurse then zoomed in more on the screen and I froze when I saw a little flutter within the centre of the baby.

"The flicker right here is your baby's heartbeat." The nurse smiled and leaned over to the machine where she twisted a knob. A loud and quick paced thudding filled the room.

"And *that* is the sound of your baby's heartbeat. It's nice and strong."

I felt Keela's hand grip mine. "Aideen," she whispered.

I swallowed down the lump in my throat and fought back the tears that suddenly wanted to burst free. "I know."

"Baby is measured at twelve weeks exactly, expected due date is January 1st."

I widened my eyes. "January 1st?"

The nurse nodded her head.

"Oh, my God," I whispered and used both of my hands to cover my mouth.

Keela grabbed hold of my hand and smiled with me. Her eyes

began to well up with tears.

"Does that date mean something to you?" the nurse asked, curiously.

I nodded. "It's me ma's birthday."

The nurse smiled. "That's a clear sign she is watching over you. That's lovely."

I smiled wide as pride filled me. "Thank you so much."

"It's my pleasure. I'll print out some scan pictures for you to show family and friends." She placed some tissue on my stomach and said, "You can clean away the gel now."

I did just that. I swiped away the cold gel, folded the tissue over and repeated the action until my lower stomach was dry and gel free. I gave the tissue to Keela who binned it for me. I tugged my jeans back up, buttoned them up, then got up off the bed.

"Here you go," the nurse said and handed me a large white envelope.

I peeked inside and saw a few scan pictures.

I gave the envelope to Keela and I said to the nurse, "What happens now?"

The nurse smiled. "We will pick a follow-up appointment date for you and you will receive a letter in the post within the next week. It won't be until you're twenty weeks. The appointments are spaced out so you don't have to come in as often, but don't confuse it with not coming in if you need to. This room is always open; a nurse is always on duty for the emergency room."

I nodded my head in understanding.

"You can also attend your local medical centre for weekly check-ups. We have a nurse there who will listen to the baby's heartbeat and give your tummy a feel. We have classes here at the hospital for parents or mothers-to-be and friends who you can sign up and attend whenever you like. They get you prepared for birth and for the arrival of the baby. I'll give you some pamphlets that you can read up on, and if you decide on a class just go to our website, login, and sign up. Your patient number is your username and your date of birth is your password. Please allow twenty-four hours for you to be registered."

I took the pamphlets she held out to me—which had a sticker with my name, address and patient number on it—and thanked her.

"My pleasure. Congratulations."

I smiled for the umpteenth time and thanked her.

Ten minutes later I found myself back in my car. Keela and I didn't speak when we got inside. We were silent for a few minutes until I said what I was thinking.

"I'm keepin' her."

Keela smiled. "Her?"

I shrugged. "I dunno, feels right sayin' her."

Keela reached over and gave my hand a squeeze. "Our family just got bigger."

My eyes welled up. "I'm really havin' a baby! I'm goin' to be a mammy!"

"Oh, my God!"

I burst into laughter and began crying at the same time. I reached over and hugged Keela as tightly as I could. This was huge for me. Huge. I was having a baby. A real baby.

Holy fuck.

The entire journey home we talked about the baby, my being pregnant and how everyone would react. It was only when we walked into Branna's house that we shut our mouths.

"Where have you two been?" Alec asked us as we walked into the kitchen.

Keela and I shared a look then looked around the room and found Alec, Ryder, Nico, Branna, and Bronagh staring at us. It was very late, past eleven pm, and it was weird that they were all sitting around the table together.

What was going on here?

"The garage to get sweets and petrol for me car," I replied.

Alec cocked an eyebrow. "For three and a half hours?"

Were we gone that long?

"We went on a drive after it... Havin' some best friend time... you know?"

Alec didn't believe me when I spoke. I could tell by the frown that he gave me.

"What's goin' on here?" Keela asked as she sat down next to Alec.

I chose to remain standing.

"We're bein' questioned," Bronagh said, rolling her eyes.

"Questioned?" I asked. "About what?"

Bronagh sighed, "Dominic wants to know—"

"I want to know which fucking one of you is pregnant!"

Oh... Crap.

CHAPTER TEN

"I'm sorry, what?" I asked, pretending I didn't hear Nico's question.

He glared at me, his eyes burning holes into me. "I *said*, which one of you is pregnant? No bullshit, each of you better answer the question."

Bronagh held up her hands. "You *know* it's not me. You made me drink two litres of water then piss on ten bloody tests."

I snorted, but then quickly covered my face when Nico snapped his head in my direction and gave me a warning look.

When he was sure I wasn't going to make another sound, he refocused and said, "Bronagh's right—she's not pregnant. Alannah isn't here because she *swore* it wasn't her so Branna, Keela, and Aideen that leaves you three."

Branna sighed. "It's not me either. Ryder knows this."

Nico looked at Ryder who nodded his head in confirmation.

"Okay, the sisters are off the list, which leaves you two."

Keela and myself.

Fuck.

"This is stupid," I mumbled.

"Why is it stupid?" Bronagh asked.

I shrugged. "I feel like whoever says they're pregnant is goin' to be interrogated or somethin'."

Bronagh frowned. "That won't happen."

I nodded at Nico. "Tell that to Drill Bit Taylor then."

Bronagh looked at Nico. "You *do* need to back off; you're comin' on a little too strong."

"Me?" Nico snapped. "I'm trying to find out who is pregnant. I wanna know if I'm going to be an uncle or not. So come on Keela, is it you?"

Oh, damn.

"Bronagh's right, you know," Branna intervened. "It's not up to you to find out who is pregnant. She'll tell us when she is ready. Your pressure won't help matters."

"Ah-ha!" Alec suddenly shouted. "At least we know it's a *she*."

I couldn't help but laugh at his stupid but brilliant sense of humour.

"Please Bran, you're just saying that because you know it's not your sister. If Bee didn't take a test yet, you'd demand she find out just so you'd know," Ryder quipped ignoring Alec's joke completely.

Branna turned her head and locked her gaze onto her fiancé. "Not if she wasn't comfortable with doin' it of her own accord."

"Yeah, right," Ryder snorted.

"What the fuck is your problem?" Branna snapped.

"Why are you shouting at him?" Nico demanded of Branna. "He's right."

"Are you serious?" Bronagh screeched. "He is *wrong*!"

The four of them engaged in a battle of words then and it hurt my head. Each person tried to shout louder than the person they were talking to and it grated on my already shot nerves.

"Please, just stop."

Everyone ignored me apart from Alec and Keela who shot me a sympathetic look. I shook my head and looked back to the four screeching cats who were all but tearing at one another's throats. It made me feel sick that they were fighting over me without knowing it.

I wanted to make it right.

"It's me," I sighed.

Keela looked at me with wide eyes, but she was the only one. I knew what she was thinking from her alarmed look too. She was mentally telling me to shut up because Kane needed to know first, but drastic times called for drastic measures.

"It's me," I said a little louder, attracting Alec's attention, but none of his brothers.

Bloody hell.

"It's me!" I screamed. "I'm the one who is pregnant. *Me!*"

The silence that flooded the room was even louder than the shouting that filled it only seconds ago. All eyes were trained on me and a few mouths were agape.

Great.

"*You're* pregnant?" Bronagh asked, her eyes wide.

I nodded my head, but said nothing. I wanted the ground to open up and swallow me whole at that moment.

"Really?" she asked as she slumped back into the kitchen chair she was sat on.

Again, I nodded my head.

"For who?" Branna asked, her face a picture of shock.

I lifted my hand to my neck and rubbed it. "Well, you see, that part... it's a little complicated."

Alec raised an eyebrow at me. "Why? Do you not know who he is?"

I felt my jaw drop open.

"Yes, I know who he is!" I angrily snapped. "I'm not a slut who opens her legs for every Tom, Dick, or Harry she meets, Alec!"

Keela shot daggers at Alec, who winced and gnawed on his lower lip. "My bad, Ado. I didn't mean it like *that*."

I didn't even want to know what way he *did* mean it.

I waved him off. "It doesn't matter. What matters is that he should have known before all of you, but I couldn't take the arguin' anymore. The way you talk to one another is *not* okay—you're couples, you shouldn't behave like that with the person you love."

Everyone frowned, even Keela and Alec who didn't even argue.

"Sorry, babe," Dominic said to Bronagh who apologised to him also.

"Sorry, Ry," Branna mumbled to Ryder.

"Me too," he replied, not looking at her.

I glared at the pair of them, but they avoided my burning gaze. They couldn't even warm up to one another to apologise, or to even look at one another? Pathetic.

Alec cleared his throat and it got my attention. "So, who *is* yo baby daddy?"

I pulled a face at his fake ghetto accent. "Please, don't phrase it like that."

He snorted.

"And I can't tell you until he gets here."

The sisters gasped. "He is comin' here? *Tonight*?"

Well, he lives here.

"Yeah, eventually," I murmured and glanced up at the clock.

Everyone was silent.

"Where is Kane?" Keela asked after a moment.

I tried not to tense up at the mention of his name.

"He went out about two hours ago," Nico said. "Not sure where though."

Keela nodded her head.

"How long have you known?" Alec asked me.

I counted on my fingers. "About three or more hours now. I took a test in your bathroom."

Bronagh blinked at me. "You didn't go to the garage with Keela, did you?"

I shook my head. "We went to the Coombe to confirm it. The nurse checked me and the baby out, and everythin' looks great so far."

Keela let out a squeal. "We heard the heartbeat and even saw it flicker about on the monitor. It was just brilliant."

If Alec was annoyed with Keela for lying to him he didn't show it because he threw an arm around her shoulder and gave her a squeeze.

"So you just found out today?" Branna questioned with a raised eyebrow.

I nodded.

"Then how come Ryder found a positive pregnancy test in our bathroom last week?" she asked, her gaze narrowed.

I scratched my neck. "I took that test because I had to know if I was the pregnant one, but before I could look at the results Keela called me about Kane. I've been puttin' it off since then—I've just been scared I guess."

No one said anything, but I saw they understood where I was coming from, which relieved me greatly.

"Did you get scan pictures?" Bronagh asked, her voice high with excitement.

I smiled. "I did, but I'm goin' to show the father them first, since I told you lot about the baby's existence before I told him."

Everyone huffed, but understood my decision.

"I'm puttin' the kettle on," Branna said and broke the silence that coated the room. "Who wants a cuppa while we wait for the baby's father to arrive?"

"Me."

Everyone answered Branna, even the lads.

It appeared all their nerves were shot... at least I wasn't the only one scared shitless to tell the baby's father that he was indeed becoming a father.

A cup of tea didn't seem strong enough for *that* conversation.

God, help me.

"What is everyone in here for?"

I looked at the kitchen door and frowned when I saw him. He was slumped and had his shoulder pressed against the doorframe. It looked like it was holding him up. I could see from across the room that his eyes were bloodshot and his face was pale grey.

He looked like shite.

"Have you been drinkin'?" I asked.

Kane shrugged uncaringly. "What's it to you if I have?"

He didn't slur, or sway from side to side... but his eyes looked empty.

"You shouldn't be drinkin'," I replied, and stood up from my seat. "You never even got your second injection today. The sugar and calories from alcohol will require more of it. Damn it, Kane."

Kane waved me off. "I'll survive."

I growled, "No, not without the bloody injections you won't."

I didn't threaten Kane in the least; I could tell by the way that he smiled at me. "Come here," he said.

I felt everyone in the room glance between us.

I ignored them and focused on Kane as I got up and walked towards him. I stopped just short of knocking into his body. I tilted my head back and glared up at him. "What?"

He laughed down at me and pressed his forehead against mine. The action shocked me. "You're the only person who I know that isn't afraid of me."

I lifted my hands and placed them on his biceps. "How much did you have to drink?" I asked.

He shrugged. "Didn't count the pints as they were pulled. Sorry, *Mom*."

"Damn it, Kane," Ryder grunted from behind us.

Kane lifted his head, looked over my head, and shot him an evil grin. "You mad, big brother?"

He was looking for a fight—I could sense it.

"Don't tempt me to start some shit with you, Kane," Ryder growled.

Kane tried to step around me, but I wouldn't let him. There was no way in hell that I was allowing him to take whatever was up his arse out on Ryder.

"Hey!" I snapped and reached up, linking both my hands behind Kane's neck and forced him to look down at me. "Come outside and talk to me, okay?"

Kane's eyes burned into mine, and for a moment they flicked to my lips before he nodded his head and broke away from me. Without a word or look in Ryder's direction, he turned and walked out of the kitchen and down the hallway. I followed him, closing the door behind me as I went.

I found Kane sat on the bottom of the stairs—his elbows resting on his knees, his hands clasped together and his eyes focused right ahead at the front door. I stood in front of him causing him to sigh and lean back so he could look up at me. When he did, he smiled lazily at me.

"You're beautiful."

I snorted, "That's the drinks talkin'."

"No," Kane replied, "it's me."

Oh.

I tilted my head to the side and hunkered down so I was eye level with him. "Honey, what's wrong with you? Why did you go off drinkin' on your own? It's not like you."

Kane shrugged. "Just felt like it."

I felt my eye twitch. "I want a better answer than that."

"Or what? You'll spank me, Miss Collins?"

I hated that I snorted.

"Made you laugh." Kane grinned and closed his eyes.

I observed his face. I ran my eyes over his scars, the curve of his jaw, the shape of his straight nose, the thickness of his eyebrows and the length of his eyelashes.

"It's not fair to the rest of the male population that you're so good lookin'."

Kane opened his eyes. "It's not, is it?"

"You make up for it by being a huge prick though so it balances out."

Kane laughed and closed his eyes again. "Babydoll?" he murmured.

"What?"

His lip quirked as he reopened his eyes and looked at me. "Just wanted to see if you'd answer to babydoll."

I glared at him. "You've called me it so many times that it's stuck, you arsehole."

Kane blinked at me. "I feel sad, Aideen."

That gutted me.

That sudden admission twisted something inside me.

"Why, sweetie?"

He shrugged his shoulders. "I don't know, and that's what's pissing me off. I just feel... alone." He lifted his hands and rubbed his face. "God, I'm such a bitch. Don't tell my brothers what I just said."

I chuckled. "Your secret is safe with me, big lad, but know that you aren't alone. You have your brothers and the girls, and you have me."

Kane looked at me. "Do I have you?"

It felt like there was an underlying meaning to his question.

I mentally shook it off and smiled. "Of course, you do, silly. I'll always be here for you. Me and you?"

Kane never broke eye contact with me as he said, "Me and you."

A little voice in me wanted to tell him that 'me and you' would become a me and you and a mini you, but I bottled it and decided I couldn't tell him until he was in a better place mentally. The only problem was that everyone else knew, and if he found out from them he would instantly know the baby was his and he would be really mad that I wasn't the one to tell him.

"Come and let me give you your insulin. I'm goin' to have to give you a higher dose because you were drinkin'."

Kane smirked. "If you want to punish me, Miss Collins, just let me know."

I realised then just how close my face was to his at that moment. The sudden urge to close the space even further freaked me out so I took a step back and held out my hand.

"Come on, you big baby. Let's go get this done."

"On one condition."

I folded my arms across my chest. "What's the condition?"

"That you stay a few more hours and watch some *Sons of Anarchy* with me."

Did he not realise how late it was?

"You haven't started the second season yet?" I asked, curiously.

He shook his head. "No. I watched the first one with you so I want to watch the rest with you, too."

"You plan on watchin' them all?"

"Yes."

I burst into laughter, "I told you, the *Sons* have hold of you—there's no escapin' now."

Kane stood up and looked down at me. "I can think of worse ways to be tied up."

I didn't know if that was a sexual jab or an admission from past experiences.

I pretended to think about it so Kane lifted his hands to my sides and began to tickle me. I gasped and jumped backwards. "Okay, okay. I'll watch the Sons with you, just don't tickle me."

Kane smirked. "Let's go then."

"Nuh-uh, your insulin first... and then I've to share somethin' with you before we go and watch some Netflix."

Kane raised an eyebrow. "Share what?"

"Come and get your insulin first then you'll find out."

"Witch."

I followed Kane when he turned and walked back down the hallway and into the kitchen. No one looked at us when we entered the room and I suspected it was because one of the girls pressed their ear to the door and listened to my conversation with Kane.

Kane got his insulin kit from the top shelf in the press and handed it to me. He looked at the others and so did I. None of them looked at us though; they were all conversing with one another, but I could tell it was forced.

"Did you check your glucose levels today?" I asked Kane, returning my attention fully to him.

He deadpanned, "That would require me sticking a needle in myself so no."

Smartarse.

I pocketed the insulin pen, and took out Kane's glucose meter from the side pouch on the insulin kit to check his blood glucose levels. I also took out a device I dubbed 'the finger pricker.' I had put a new testing strip into the glucose meter and a fresh needle into the finger pricker before I looked at Kane.

He reluctantly gave me his hand and looked away while I used the gadget to prick his finger. I squeezed his finger and when a little bubble of blood rose, I pressed the testing strip in the glucose meter against his finger and let it soak up the blood.

I waited for a few seconds as the meter determined Kane's glucose levels. I widened my eyes when I saw the results. "Kane, look how high your blood sugar is. It's almost two hundred!"

Kane looked at the results of his test and shrugged. "Big deal."

"It *is* a big deal. You're lucky you aren't doubling over and we don't have to bring you to the hospital!"

"Just give me my normal insulin dose; that will be fine. It'll set my blood sugar right."

He was pissing me off.

"It won't. I've to up your units now to make up for it!"

Kane sighed, "So turn the dial and up the units—problem solved."

Oh, my God.

"You know what? If it's not such a big fuckin' deal, then *you* do—"

"I'm sorry," he cut me off.

I opened my mouth then closed it.

I glared at him. "Why did you cave so quickly?"

He frowned down at me. "'Cause I need you. I can't inject it myself... You're the one who does it. Only you."

God damn his big sad eyes.

"Be considerate then," I snippily replied. "It's your body so look after it or I'm goin' to kick the shite out of it. Your decision."

Kane looked away from me as he tried not to smile.

I rolled my eyes and took out the insulin pen, and rolled it between my fingers like Doctor Chance showed me, to make sure the insulin was properly combined. Kane's insulin was mixed so I had to make sure the colour was all as one and there were no swirls or air pockets inside the cartridge before I injected it into his body.

I held the pen tightly and then picked up an alcohol wipe; I opened the little packet and used the wipe to sanitize the little stopper that the needle slid into. Next, I grabbed a fresh needle from the kit and screwed it onto the area I just cleaned.

The whole device was pretty safe; my setup usually only took a minute, but because I felt Kane's eyes on me I did things a little slower just to make sure I did it correctly. I focused on my job at hand and began to prime the pen. I selected two units to prime the pen and pushed on the end of the pen twice until I spotted a little insulin squirt from the needle. Once any trapped air was gone, and the pen was primed, I upped his insulin units and removed the cap.

Kane recognised the noise of the cap being removed and grunted as he undid his jeans and pushed them down his thighs. "Close your eyes," I said and went in.

I pinched a fatty part of his thigh, inserted the needle into his leg at a ninety-degree angle and pushed the insulin into his body. Ten seconds later I released my pinching grip and removed the needle.

"All done," I said with a sigh.

Kane grabbed hold of my arm and pulled me up to my feet, which I was grateful for because my knees were starting to hurt.

"Can we go watch Netflix now?" he asked, looking down at me with hopeful eyes.

I looked over my shoulder and found everyone looking at me; it reminded me of what they all knew. I turned back to Kane.

"Can I talk to you?" I asked him.

He shrugged. "Shoot."

"Pull your trousers up first, perv."

Kane smirked when his brothers snorted from behind me.

"Spoilsport," he mused as he pulled up his trousers and buttoned them. "Okay, done, now shoot."

Just say it.

"It's me."

Kane looked at me with furrowed eyebrows. "It's you what?"

Here goes nothing.

"I'm pregnant."

He raised an eyebrow. "No, Branna is pregnant, we heard Ryder—"

"I got it wrong, bro," Ryder cut Kane off.

Kane looked at his brother then to Branna, who nodded her head in confirmation. He looked back to me with wide eyes.

"You?"

"Me."

"Does that mean—?"

"Yes."

"Are you sure?"

"Yes."

"Holy. Fuck."

I nervously laughed, "My thoughts exactly."

Kane shook his head. "*Aideen.*"

"I know."

I reached into my side bag and pulled out the ultrasound pictures of the baby. "I got these from the hospital about an hour ago."

Kane took the pictures and stared at them, hard. I wasn't sure if he was shocked, or if he just couldn't see the baby.

"That's not fair," Nico whined. "You said you were going to show the pictures to the baby daddy first!"

I looked at Nico. "And I've done that. You can all see now, too."

No one moved except Nico, who jumped up and shot over to Kane's side and looked at the ultrasound pictures.

Alec glared at me. "Shut the fuck up."

I laughed, "Okay."

"Aideen!" Bronagh and Branna said in unison.

I laughed again. "Yes?"

"Don't fuck with me, Ado," Branna warned.

"Or me," Bronagh added.

I raised my hands and nodded in Kane's direction. "I'm not, I swear. Ask him."

"Ask him what?" Nico asked. "What are you all talking about?"

"Kane?" Ryder questioned with wide eyes. "*Seriously?*"

I shrugged my shoulders. "Seriously."

"Fuck me!" Alec whispered.

I looked at Nico who was looking around the room, and after a few seconds it clicked in his mind what we were all talking about.

"*Kane* is the father?" he asked, his eyes wide with shock.

I nodded. "Kane is the father."

"Is Kane *really* the father?" Bronagh asked.

"Yes, Kane is *really* the father," I said, shaking my head.

"I feel like we're in an episode of *Maury*," Alec murmured to himself.

I snickered as I looked around the room, then finally to Kane who was still staring down at the ultrasound pictures in his hands.

"Are you okay?" I asked him.

"I'm going to be a father." It wasn't a question. It was a statement.

I stepped closer to him. "Is that okay?"

He looked up at me, his eyes shining. "Are you kidding? Of course it's okay! I'm going to be a father!"

The relief that filled me was instant and warm. I burst into laughter when Kane surged forward, wrapped his arms around me and lifted me up then spun me around. I held onto him when he stopped spinning me and groaned a little.

"I'm nauseous all the time; don't do that again," I said and held my hand over my mouth just in case I suddenly vomited.

"Shit, sorry," Kane rushed out and pressed his hand on my back.

When nothing happened I removed my hand from my mouth and waved him off. "I'm good."

"I can't believe this," Bronagh said when she came over to look at the ultrasound photos.

I couldn't believe it, either. I wasn't expecting Kane to take the news so... well.

"We're going to be uncles!" Alec shouted and dived on Keela, kissing her face and hugging her with so much force I think he cut off her air supply.

I smiled and watched the brothers embrace their girlfriends, then moved on to Kane who was back to staring at the ultrasound pictures in his hand. He looked up when they approached him and smiled as he began to walk backwards. He yelped then jumped a little when they grabbed hold of him and then burst into laughter when they started to hit him. He grunted here and there, but his laughter was vibrant and loud.

"You told me you haven't had sex in *six* months. You said the girl who came from your room three months ago fell asleep before any fucking could happen. You lying jackass!" Nico said as he jumped on Kane's back.

I jumped back and laughed when Ryder socked Kane in the stomach. "You told me you didn't like Aideen in *that* way. You fucking bullshitter."

Alec then tripped him up and laughed as Kane fell and took Nico down with him. "And you told me that you didn't like her at *all*. You *fucking* liar!"

I snorted as each of the brothers called Kane out on his pile of lies by piling on top of him.

They only got off him when he tapped his hand on the floor in submission to their attack. He stayed on the floor, groaned in pain, and yelped like a little girl when Alec kicked his leg.

"That's not necessary!" he snapped but made no move to get up off the floor.

Alec stuck his middle finger up. "You lied to us so you deserve all the hits you get and you'll take them like a man or we'll beat the shit out of you."

I shook my head.

Brothers.

"You won't hurt him," I intervened, "because he is still *ill*, remember?"

Kane got up to his feet and moved over to me where he stood behind me. "Yeah, I have diabetes, you bastards."

"He is smiling, Ado," Nico growled. "He is just using his diabetes as an excuse to get out of an ass whooping for lying to us."

I gasped and turned, "You wouldn't!"

Kane held up his hands as he looked down at me. "Of course, I wouldn't. You think I'd make a joke out of my diabetes? Aideen, it's not something you play around with. It's *very* serious."

Exactly.

"You're right, sorry." I turned around and glared at the brothers. "Diabetes isn't a joke."

"Yeah," Kane said from behind me.

Alec growled, "He is sticking his finger up at us right now."

Kane placed his hands on my shoulders. "They're lying; you can't trust them, Aideen."

I groaned, "I haven't even had me child yet and already I'm separatin' the good child from the bad ones."

Nico gasped, "If one of us is the good one, it's me or Damien—Kane is a bastard."

"Hey!" I snapped. "No name callin'."

Branna burst into laughter. "And so it begins."

I groaned and placed my face in my hands and ignored everyone when they started laughing at me. Kane wrapped his arms around my chest from behind and pressed his head into mine. The bastard was laughing too.

I was fighting off a smile when he turned me in his arms and leaned down pressing his forehead against mine. "This means we have to start liking each other... at least enough not to kill the other person anyway."

I snorted, "You better get very good at not pissin' me off then."

Kane snorted and pulled me into his chest. He slid his arms down to my arms and rested his head on mine. I put my arms around his and hugged him back, which was weird as hell. I never hugged Kane.

Ever.

That was kind of sad considering I had sex with him, yet I'd never hugged him.

"Have you ever seen them so civil?" I heard Keela murmur to everyone.

"Nope," Ryder replied back. "Twenty euros it only lasts till morning."

"Hey," I said and pulled back from Kane and turned to face my family, "don't jinx this. This is a rare event."

Everyone chuckled.

"Okay, so you and Kane are havin' a baby. Do your brothers know?" Bronagh asked me.

My good mood was instantly squashed. I surprisingly didn't think of telling my family about the baby... and I wished Bronagh had never brought them up.

I shook my head and groaned out loud, "I don't want to think about tellin' them."

Branna widened her eyes. "Your brothers don't know... Does your *da* know?"

I winced. "No... I was *hopin'* I wouldn't have to tell any of them either."

Kane came to my side and frowned. "Why not? You're twenty-eight."

I said nothing so Branna filled him in for me. "Being pregnant isn't the problem; it's who her baby daddy is that will be the problem."

"Why would they have a problem with me? They don't even know me," Kane asked, his tone confused.

Keela snorted and said, "That's not exactly true."

All the brothers looked at Keela and in unison they said, "Explain."

Keela looked at me for permission and I shrugged my shoulders. "Go ahead, they'll find out sooner or later."

"A year or so after Nico and Bronagh started datin', at one of Nico's fights in some club in town, Aideen's eldest brother beat the shite out of Ryder for accidentally knocking a drink out of his hand. You three proceeded to beat the shite out of him and his brothers which had to be broken up by her da, who tagged along to watch the fight. Her family is really into UFC."

Kane snapped his head my way. "Your older brothers are James, Harley, and Dante Collins?"

I shrugged my shoulders. "Yep."

All the brothers glared at their girlfriends.

"Why did you never mention that?" Nico snapped at Bronagh.

Bronagh shrugged. "After they almost bested you four that night, you told us never to talk about them or even mention the fight again, so we didn't. What good would it have done to know we were friends with the sister of the brothers you hate?"

Kane put his face in his hands and groaned.

I placed a hand on his shoulder. "It won't be that bad."

"Yeah, it will," Nico sighed and shook his head. "If your brothers don't kill him for getting you pregnant, your dad will."

CHAPTER ELEVEN

"Are you okay?" Kane asked me the next morning as I sat in the passenger seat of his car.

Was I okay?

I was on my way to tell my father and brothers that I was pregnant and that the baby's father belonged to a group of brothers they hated with a passion.

Why would I be okay with any of that?

I gently shook my head. "I was up all night thinkin' about this and I'm pretty sure I'm currently havin' a silent panic attack. Outside I'm calm, but inside I'm freakin' the fuck out."

Kane snorted, "It's goin' to be okay."

I glanced over my shoulder and groaned, "If it's goin' to be okay, why are your brothers in the car behind us?"

Kane shrugged and glanced in his rear view mirror. "They don't trust your brothers."

I growled, "I do. They will be pissed at first, but they'll get over it... eventually."

"Well, let's call them worried shadows just until this *meeting* is over."

The word 'meeting' translated to 'death sentence.'

I shook my head. "Their presence will only make things worse."

"It will be fine."

That phrase was starting to piss me off.

"Stop sayin' that to me. Everyone keeps sayin' that to me."

Kane opened his mouth but closed it before any words escaped.

I thought of my brothers during the silence and I figured it would be best to ring and call them around to my father's house for a family meeting. I dug my phone out of my bag, unlocked it, found Harley's number and pressed it.

"Who are you calling?" Kane inquisitively asked.

I looked straight ahead as I answered, "Me brother."

Out of my peripheral vision, I saw Kane nod his head in understanding. I refocused on my phone when I heard a voice say, "Hello."

"Hey, are you with James and Dante by any chance?" I asked my brother, Harley, when he answered his phone.

Harley chortled, "Good morning to you too, little sister."

I rolled my eyes. "Are you with them or not, Harley?"

He clicked his tongue at me. "Temper, sister. They're both round in mine. Why?"

I exhaled a nervous breath, "Meet me at Da's house in ten minutes, I need to tell you all somethin'."

Silence.

"Are you okay?" Harley asked apprehensively.

I glanced at Kane, who was driving and swallowed. "Yes, I'm fine."

Kind of.

"Okay, see you in ten," Harley quipped.

I put my phone back into my bag when my brother hung up. I busied myself with closing my bag just so I wouldn't have to look up. I didn't want my eyes to drift to Kane because I still couldn't believe the situation we were both in.

"Before we tell your family about the baby... can we talk about it first? After you had told me last night, we talked a little but not much."

That caught me off guard.

"Sure... wh-what do you want to talk about exactly?"

"Okay." Kane nodded more to himself than me. "Be honest with me... are you happy you're pregnant?"

I blinked. "Why are you askin' me that?"

Kane sighed, "Because I don't want you to carry on with the pregnancy if you don't want to."

I stared at Kane. Hard.

"I'm not havin' an abortion Kane, not even if you want me to. I will *not* murder an innocent child because we were too stupid to use protection!"

"Hey!" Kane snapped. "I am *not* suggesting that at all. I swear I'm not. I was just putting the option on the table in case you felt pressured into having the baby. Honestly, I'm fucking thrilled you feel the way you do because I feel the exact same way."

I swallowed. "You do? Really? You aren't just sayin' that?"

"Really, sweetheart. I never thought I'd have kids, but surprisingly I'm really excited about it. I can't begin to explain why. I'm scared shitless, but I'm very happy at the same time and I want you to be happy about it too."

I blew out a big breath. "I'm happy now. At first I wasn't because I thought of the worst possible things like how you would react, would I be able to be a good mother, things like that, but now that I've had a little time to think about it, I'm happy. I haven't fully processed it all yet, but I'm excited."

"I don't feel as sick now," Kane chuckled.

I laughed and rested my head back against the headrest.

"I'm not going to flake on you, you know that, right?" he said a few moments later.

I had to look up because his question confused me.

"Huh?"

Kane glanced at me and nodded to my stomach before returning his eyes to the road. "You and the baby. I won't flake—I'll be there every step of the way. I won't be a deadbeat dad, I promise."

The comfort that gave me shocked me and I tried to play it off like it was nothing.

"Oh, yeah, sure. I know you'll be a good father."

It was my ability to be a good mother that was still worrying me.

"It's all going to be okay. I know the girls have been repeating that to you, but it really will be okay. I'll look after you. The both of you."

That made me curious.

"How?" I asked.

Kane glanced at me for a moment. "What?"

"How are you goin' to look after me and the baby?" I clarified.

I sounded snippy and rude. I didn't mean to, I was generally interested in this discussion.

"By supporting you—"

"In what way?" I cut in and probed.

Kane's hands tightened on the steering wheel. "Financially, emotionally... whatever way you need my support, you've got it."

I blinked. "You don't have a job, and we aren't in a relationship so how can you support me financially and emotionally?"

Kane shook his head. "I don't need to be dating you to be there for you... and you let me worry about my money, okay?"

"No," I answered. "I'll give on the emotional aspect, but if this is goin' to work, if you want to raise this baby together then I want to know where the financial support is comin' from."

"Aideen," Kane said, his tone firm.

I straightened up. "Kane."

"Do we have to do this right now?" he asked, irritated.

"Yes," I replied. "You may think we have all the time in the world to have this conversation, but this baby will be here before we know it and babies require a lot of things *before* they even get here. I'm three months gone, so that leaves me six months to find somewhere else to live because me current apartment is too small for a party bigger than one. I'll need to go out and buy a cot, a pram, a changin' table, a whole wardrobe of clothes, nappies—a *lot* of nappies—wet wipes, creams, lotions, powders, linen, blankets, a car seat—"

"Aideen!" Kane cut me off with a shout. "I get it! I know there is a lot of things that *we* will need to buy and a lot of things that need to be done, but I'll make sure it gets done. Okay? Just trust that I can take care of you."

I wasn't convinced. I shook my head and turned to look out the window of the car.

"Why are you shaking your head?"

I huffed, "Because you sayin' 'trust me, I've got this' doesn't make me feel better at all. I work a full-time job five days a week, and I live in a tiny apartment. Granted it's bigger than Keela's old place, but it's not ideal for everythin' I'm goin' to need. I'm worried, okay? I've never had another being dependin' solely on me before."

Kane was silent for a moment before he said, "You could move in with me. That's an option."

I hurt my neck when I snapped my head to look at Kane. "That was a joke, right?"

Kane set his jaw. "No."

I couldn't help but laugh, "We aren't in a relationship and you think livin' together is the way to go?"

He ground his teeth together before saying, "Living in the same space doesn't mean anything *has* to happen, or that anything *will* happen between us. Believe it or not, my focus is one hundred percent on our baby inside of you. I can't even think of sex or anything else right now."

I snorted, "Yeah, well that makes two of us."

Kane sighed, "I don't want to fight, not about this. When you—I mean when *we* have time to process things we can talk about this further, okay?"

I saw no point in arguing against that right now, so I nodded my head and remained silent for the final few minutes of the drive. We got to my father's house quicker than I would have liked. Before I knew it, I was standing outside staring at the front door, hesitant to knock.

"Do you want me to—"

"No," I cut Kane off. "I can do this. You just tell your brothers to stay across the road."

Kane mumbled something. I didn't know what it was, but I took it as an okay. I stepped towards the front door of my father's house and just as I lifted my hand to knock, the door swung open.

"Hey, what took you so long? We got here five minutes ago."

Five minutes ago?

"What the hell do you drive? A rocket?"

My eldest brother, James, laughed at me, but when his eyes drifted past me and landed on the soul to the right of me, they instantly narrowed.

"Slater," James snarled.

I jumped in front of Kane.

"Please, don't," I begged my brother. "What I've to say is too important."

James stepped forward then backwards as veins bulged in his arms and neck. He took a final step back as he fully stepped inside our father's house.

"Thank you," I breathed.

James looked past me. "Step foot in here and I'll knock you out."

With that said, James turned and stormed off down the hallway and into the kitchen.

I groaned, "That couldn't have gone worse."

Kane snickered, "Actually it could have."

I ignored him as I entered. "I'll be five minutes. Do you mind waitin' here?" I asked without turning around. I wanted to keep an eye on the kitchen door in case my brothers suddenly burst through it in a bid to kill Kane.

"Are you sure you want to tell them on your own?" Kane asked.

"I told everyone else on me own, this will be easy... the tellin' part at least. It's the reactions about you that I'm worried about."

"It will be—"

"Don't say okay."

"Fine," Kane finished.

I stepped inside. "I won't be long."

I closed the front door with the heel of my right foot and slowly walked down the hallway. I paused in front of the kitchen then entered it with my head held high and my chin stuck out.

Showing fear would only cause them to attack.

"I can't believe you brought a *Slater* here!" the voice of my second eldest brother, Harley, bellowed.

I gently closed the kitchen door behind me.

"Nice to see you too, big brother."

"Cut the bullshit," Dante, my third eldest brother, hissed. "Why is he here?"

I avoided eye contact. "He is here because he is involved in what I have to tell you all."

"If you say you're goin' out with him, I'll kill him and lock you upstairs," Harley said to me, his tone venomous.

Who was I? Rapunzel?

"Can you just sit down, please?" I asked as nicely as I could.

Harley silently regarded me but did as I asked.

"What's goin' on, baby?" my father, who was already seated at the kitchen table, asked me.

I opened my mouth, and then closed it when I noticed one of my brothers was missing. "Where is Gavin?"

Dante held up a finger then turned his head and shouted, "Gavin! Get your arse down here?"

I winced at the volume of Dante's shout.

"One second!" Gavin hollered down the stairs.

"What's so important that you called us here?" Harley asked, curiously.

His patience was wearing thin, but I wasn't breaking. I wanted all my brothers in the room before I let on any information.

"Hush for a minute and wait for Gavin."

"Gav!" my father and brothers bellowed in unison.

No patience.

"I'm bloody comin'!" Gavin snapped back.

I heard his footsteps on the stairs as he descended them. He entered the kitchen a few moments later wearing just a pair of boxer shorts.

I rolled my eyes. "Really? You couldn't have put trousers on?"

"They called for me, here I am. You're lucky I put boxers on." He shrugged and sat on a chair next to our father. "What's up?"

I looked at James. "Sit down."

He didn't move from the counter. "I'd rather stand."

I glared at him. "James."

He didn't bat an eyelid. "Aideen."

I growled, "Why are you being difficult?"

James shrugged. "I know I'm not goin' to like whatever it is you have to say, so I'd rather be standin' up when I hear it. Deal with it."

Arsehole.

"Fine. Okay," I grunted.

I heard a rap on the front door and I groaned. "One more minute, Kane!" I shouted.

"Kane?" Gavin questioned. "As in Slater? What is *he* doin' here?"

James snorted, "See? Even little brother knows he shouldn't be here."

I rubbed my temples. "He is here with me so I think that gives him a pass."

Harley snarled, "I knew it, I'm goin' to—"

"You aren't goin' to do anythin' because we aren't together. I'm not in a relationship with anyone, okay? He is just *here* with me."

Harley relaxed. "Why is he *here* then?"

Oh, God.

My palms began to sweat. "Promise me you won't do somethin' stupid when I tell you?"

"Is this about me?" Gavin asked, his face paled with worry.

He wants to be in a gang, but he can't man up and tell our brothers about it?

The little bitch.

I glared at him. "No. That is a conversation for a different day."

All my brothers, my father included, looked at Gavin.

"What's *that* about?" Harley asked our brother.

Gavin waved him off. "Nothin' important, I want to know what Aideen has us all around the table for. It must be *really* important."

The little fucker, he switched the heat from him to me.

"Aideen."

I jumped at my father's voice.

"Promise first," I pressed.

"I promise," Gavin, Dante, and my father said in unison.

James and Harley remained mute though.

"You two?"

"I'm not promisin' anythin' because I might break it, so get on with what you have to say before I get pissed off. I'm serious, Aideen."

I glared at James but nodded my head.

"Okay, so... I'm pregnant."

Silence.

"With a baby."

More silence.

"And Kane... he is the father."

An even longer stretch of silence.

"But we aren't together. It was one night of stupidity, and we're both prepared to raise a baby—James!"

My heart jumped when James suddenly shot out of the kitchen and down the hallway towards the front door. I took off after him screaming for him to stop while chairs scraped against the tiled floor in the kitchen as my other brothers quickly followed.

James flung open the front door and headed for Kane, who was down the end of the garden talking to Nico. When he heard all the commotion he turned, and instantly took a defensive stance when he saw James heading for him.

He had his hands raised in front of his chest. "Bro, we can talk about this—"

James cut Kane off with a well-placed punch to the jaw.

"Stop!" I screamed and placed my hands on the side of my head.

I watched in slow motion as Kane bent low and speared my brother to the ground. Nico jumped over the fence and delivered an incredible jumping punch to Dante, who instantly ran for him when he came into the garden.

I could see Ryder and Alec running from across the road where their car was parked, and I saw Gavin and Harley move around me to fight against them. I screamed for everyone to stop, and I didn't realise I was crying until I began to gulp for air when the sobbing started.

I didn't think of myself when I moved forward and placed my hands on Kane's shoulders and pulled at him. He was hitting my brother's face so hard I thought it would bust open.

"KANE!" I screamed. "You'll kill him. *Stop!*"

"Aideen!" James bellowed. "Get... back!"

James held his own against Kane and gave as good as he got, but Kane... He was like an animal and watching him in action made me sick to my stomach. I smacked at his back and kicked him as hard as I could in the side in hopes to knock him off my brother and put a stop to this madness.

It didn't work.

It was like Kane felt no pain. I thought Nico was a ruthless fighter, but Kane was on another level. He dished out punches and took hard hits like they were nothing. I was screaming at him, but he didn't acknowledge me in any way. It was like he blacked everything and everyone out except James.

His target.

I didn't give up though. I shoved at Kane and tried my hardest to pull him off James, but all that came with me when I pulled was his t-shirt. I ripped it right off his body and revealed his back, which

KANE

was covered in scars, the ones I felt three months ago in the dark of night. Some big, some small. Some purple, some light pink.

"What in God's name?" I whispered.

What on Earth could have caused such damage to his back?

I pushed that question aside, dropped the fabric in my hand and slapped the back of Kane's head. "Get the hell off me broth—" I was cut off when Kane lifted his arm and tried to swing it at James, but the angle of his swing caused it to rear back into my face and it knocked me backwards onto the ground.

"That's ENOUGH!"

I cowered on the ground for only a moment, before I pushed myself up to my feet and looked at my father who walked out of his house with a steel baseball bat in his hands. He walked directly over to James and Kane—James had the upper hand and was on Kane now—and he grabbed my brother by the scruff of the neck and pulled him off Kane with one tug.

James flew backwards onto the ground, and Kane was quick to try and follow, but my father pointed the bat at Kane's face and got his attention. Kane shook his head and blinked his eyes and after a moment he lifted his hands. "I'm done."

"Too fuckin' right you're done," my father snarled and moved past him and smacked Alec in the back of the head and pushed him off my little brother with his foot.

Gavin was bloody all over, Alec had a cut or two on his face showing my baby brother at least got some hits in on the big lad. Next up were Dante and Ryder—Dante and Harley obviously switched brothers—who were locked into a war of punches. It was hard to say who was beating up whom because both of them were messed up. It took a lot more effort to break up Harley and Nico, but eventually my father got the upper hand.

When he got everyone separated, he pointed to the cars across the road. "You four, get in your cars and leave. Do *not* come back here."

After my father's dismissal, he turned to me. "Are you okay?"

he asked me, his tone soft.

I held my face with both hands but nodded my head.

Kane looked at me then. "Wh-what?"

"You back-handed her you son of a bitch," my father snarled over his shoulder. "Now leave before I put this bat to good use."

Kane stumbled a little, the skin on his face that wasn't cut or swollen, visibly paled. "Oh, Christ. Aideen, I would never—I'm so sorry, babydoll."

I turned from him. "Leave, Kane."

"But the baby—"

"Will still be in me stomach for another few months. For today, just leave. I can't even look at you."

Kane didn't move. "He hit me first."

I dropped my hand from my throbbing cheek and looked at him. "Me students come at me with excuses like that and don't get away with them so don't you dare think you will either."

Ryder intervened, "Kane wanted to talk it out, Aideen. Your brother was hell bent on fighting—not Kane."

I looked at Ryder. "Did you stop for a second from hittin' me other brother to look at Kane? I screamed at him and hit him to try to stop him but he blanked me out. He was like an animal, and if me da didn't stop it, he would have killed me brother."

James grunted against my argument. I wasn't thinking about his pride for the moment, I was thinking about his safety, and the safety of my other brothers.

"I'm sorry," Kane said to me, not to my brother.

I shook my head. "I don't want to hear it. I want you to leave."

Again, he stood firm.

"If she has to ask you again, boy, I'll make you sorry," my father growled.

Ryder stepped into the garden, glaring at Harley, who followed him.

"Bro," he said to Kane, his tone softened, "let's go."

"I can't leave her," Kane said to Ryder without looking away from me.

I pressed my hand back to my cheek. "Just go home, Kane."

I turned and walked into my father's house ignoring Kane calling my name, and my brothers shouting for them to leave. I walked up the stairs to the bathroom and closed the door behind me, turning the lock to make sure no one could come in without my say so.

I rolled my eyes as I put the toilet seat down and sat on it—I never could get my father and Gavin to break the habit of leaving the seat up after my other three brothers moved out. I leaned forward, placed my face in my hands, and sighed. I rubbed my eyes but winced when a pulsing pain in my cheek demanded attention.

"Damn it," I mumbled to myself and stood up.

I turned and took two steps towards the sink. I turned on the taps and washed my shaking hands. It took a few seconds of inner pep talk and deep breaths in order for me to look up, but when I did, I wished I hadn't.

"Oh, no," I grumbled.

My eye wasn't swollen, but my cheekbone was. It was already bruised as well, a light electric blue spread out over my upper cheek. I thought back to nearly two years ago in Playhouse Nightclub when I last had a bruised face. That was Kane's fault too, or was it Alec's? Whatever, it was one of the brother's fault. A lay of theirs got pissed and hit me because she thought I was trying to take her face down arse up position.

Please.

I shook my head clear of my thoughts and refocused on my reflection.

"How am I goin' to hide this?" I thought aloud.

The last time I had a bruised face was before school term started so I didn't have to worry about work. I had to worry about it this time around since term was already in session.

Make up.

I hoped the bruise wouldn't darken up too much over the coming hours. I would be able to cover it up if it stayed light. Otherwise, it would draw unwanted attention at school from students and fellow colleagues.

"Me stupid brothers," I muttered as I examined my face in the mirror. "Stupid Kane!"

I lowered my hands and tightly gripped the sides of the sink and took a few breaths to relax myself. I had enough to worry about without adding the Slater feud with my brothers and their stupid fight to my ever-growing list.

I refused to work myself up over them. I wasn't taking bullshit from anyone, not even my family. That was final. I didn't need the stress.

I nodded to myself in the mirror, turned and exited the bathroom. I descended the stairs and marched into the kitchen where I found my father scolding my brothers.

I felt my anger dip when I saw Gavin and how beat up he was. I didn't have a favourite brother, but I did feel a little closer to him because I helped my father with him after my mother died giving birth to him. Granted I was only six when Gavin was born and couldn't do a lot, but I stepped up as much as a little girl could. I knew not to complain, hog my father's attention, or be an all-around problem. I accepted I wasn't the baby anymore and that there was a serious change in our family.

I took it on the chin.

By the time I was ten, and Gavin was four, I would make food for him, wash and clean him, dress and play with him. He came everywhere with me. I would drop him to pre-school on my way to school and collect him from after-school on my way home. One of our older brothers would always tail us to make sure we both got to class on time, and to make sure we were safe. I think they just let me believe I was bringing Gavin to and from school because it made me feel like I had a great deal of responsibility with him.

I never told them I knew they followed us all those years—they were just doing what I was doing with Gavin in making sure we were safe. I couldn't fault them for that, and I still couldn't... except when they do really unnecessary things like fight other people over me.

"I'll clean them up," I said to my father and got the First-Aid kit from under the kitchen sink.

My father grunted, "You don't deserve to be fussed over, you little pricks."

James groaned, "Jesus, Da. What did you expect us to do? It's the *Slaters*!"

"I don't give a fuck who they are; you should have more respect for your sister than to treat her like a child who cannot handle her own situation. She is twenty-eight years of age."

Go on, Da!

I stepped around my father when he paused his pacing to kick James in the leg. "And *that* is for makin' the baby's father hit Aideen in the face."

"Da!" James hissed, leaned forward, and rapidly rubbed at the spot where our father kicked him.

I felt my lip quirk.

James glowered at my father but said nothing to him. He was thirty-four, but he knew age didn't mean a thing when it came to our father. If he back-talked or stepped out of place, he would still get a hiding. All my brothers would. Even if they were bigger than our father, he'd cut them down to size real quick.

I audibly snorted, and it caused James to shoot daggers my way.

"Don't look at me like that; you're the one who just made me life ten times harder."

"You're blamin' *me*?" James asked, angrily.

"Yeah, she is," my father snapped, "and so am I."

James threw his hands up in the air. "I defend me baby sister and I get backlash for it? Fuckin' terrific."

I glared at James. "You hit Kane for your *own* bloody reasons, don't pretend you were doin' it to defend me honour. I'm twenty-eight. I shouldn't have to deal with this bullshit from me family."

I turned away from James and walked over to Gavin who was

holding his bloody face. I opened the First-Aid kit and then went and got a bowl of water. I put some ice in it from the ice dispenser in the fridge and grabbed a clean cloth.

"Look at me," I asked Gavin when I reached him once more.

Gavin did as asked. He barely even winced when I dipped my cloth into the ice water and began to clean his face. I was angry with him, and not exactly for fighting. He was only helping our brothers, but I was pissed he went for Alec. Alec can be sweet as pie, but he can fight viciously when need be. Gavin's face was proof of that.

"Big tough lad now... aren't you?" I muttered to Gavin.

Gavin's eyes shot to our brothers and father, his demeanour relaxed when he saw they paid us no attention.

"Why are you so nervous? They're gonna find out sooner or later."

Gavin grunted, "You'll tell them?"

I shrugged. "Depends."

"On what?" my stupid brother asked.

I moved my head down to his. "On whether you leave Brandon's circle willingly or if I've to drag you from it."

Gavin pulled away from me. "Bloody hell, Aideen."

I stowed my itching palm and instead placed it gently on Gavin's shoulder.

"I love you, and makin' sure you have no part of that life is my job as your—"

"Sister!" Gavin cut me off on a growl. "You're me sister, *not* me ma."

I swallowed down the hurt that Gavin's statement made me feel and played it off with a shrug. "You're right, I'm not Ma, but I'm the closest thing you've ever had. You would want to start remindin' yourself of that."

I pressed a cotton ball hard against a cut over his eyebrow and it caused Gavin to hiss. I cleaned up the rest of his face and pushed the kit over to my other brothers as they began to clean themselves up.

"So," James mumbled from across the table, "when are you goin' to have... the baby?"

Fuck, that sounded so strange.

I cleared my throat. "In six months. I'm three months gone so it will be a short while yet before I start to show."

"What's that mean?" Dante asked me.

I snorted as I moved away from Gavin. "It means before I start to show a bump. A pregnant belly."

"Oh. Right," Dante said and pressed a pack of frozen peas to his jaw.

"Six months' time will be in January," Gavin commented.

I smiled. "Yep, and you won't believe when my due date is?"

My brothers all smiled. "Ma's birthday?"

"The very one. Can you believe it? Out of all the days for me to be due a baby, it falls on Ma's birthday."

"I told you she is watchin' over you—all over you." I looked at my father when he stepped next to me. I smiled when he folded his arms around me. "Congratulations, babygirl."

I squeezed my father tightly. "Thanks, Da."

"Yeah, congrats sis," Harley's voice rang out.

I smiled as I pulled away from my father and found all my brothers up on their feet and moving towards me. I laughed when they surrounded me and we had us a big group hug.

"We're goin' to be uncles!" Gavin said, his voice sounding like a child's.

I laughed and moved away from my brothers and over to the sink where I got a drink of water. "Yep, you will be uncles but so will the Slater brothers, so I'd appreciate you four not attackin' them when you see them in the future."

James smirked at me. "No promises."

I shook my head. "Everythin' is crazy right now for me and Kane. Please be considerate. He only got out of hospital ten days ago."

"For what?" Harley questioned.

"He has diabetes," I explained.

My father shook his head and glared at James.

"I didn't know he was ill!" my brother snapped in his defence.

I exhaled.

"Besides, he didn't hit like he was weakened in any way."

I couldn't help but laugh at that. My brothers and father followed suit.

A few hours passed by with just myself, my father, and my brothers talking to one another. We went down memory lane and discussed our futures with smiles and laughter. Around nine pm I began to feel really tired. Harley offered to drive me home, which I happily accepted. I hugged everyone goodbye, let them know I thought they were dicks for fighting, but that I loved them anyway.

Harley drove me home and walked me up to my apartment door. He bailed on my invite for a cup of tea because he knew I was tired. He left when I was safely inside my apartment with the door locked.

For a few moments inside my apartment I was calm and collected but all of a sudden, I couldn't help it when tears welled in my eyes and spilled down my cheeks. I wasn't much of a crier—I grew up with four brothers and a single father, it toughened me up—but with everything on my mind, I couldn't keep it together.

I was going to have a baby, and my family *hated* the father of the baby.

I looked up to the ceiling and whimpered, "Whatever game you're playin', Ma, I don't find it one bit funny."

I could hear my mother's rich laughter in my head and for a moment, it soothed me. I walked into my kitchen, flipped on the lights, and put my bag on the kitchen table. I filled my kettle with water and set it to boil.

I needed a cup of tea.

I actually needed something stronger, but seeing as I was pregnant, tea would have to be my go-to stress reliever drink from now on, and I could see *a lot* of cups of tea being made in my future.

CHAPTER TWELVE

"Aideen? Open up, it's me."

I blinked my eyes open and couldn't help but smile a little as I got up from my sofa and lazily walked over to my apartment door and opened it wide for my best friend.

"I'm so sorry, babe," Keela said as she stepped into my apartment and wrapped her arms around me. "I would have come over this mornin' had I known."

I hugged her back. "It's fine."

"It's fuckin' not!" she stated and pulled back.

She closed my door and led me into my sitting room where we sat on my sofa. I tucked my legs under my bum, and Keela did the same.

"Your face!" she gasped.

I waved her off. "It was an accident."

"I promise I would have been over this mornin', but the lads went back to Nico and Bronagh's house to clean up and they stayed away until twenty minutes ago. They thought it would be better for us to hear what happened without seein' them covered in blood."

Flashes of the lads fighting this morning flooded my mind.

I shivered and wrapped my arms around myself. "It was horrible, Kay. They beat the shite out of one another. All of me brothers will have black eyes."

"The lads have sore jaws and bruises, that's for sure. Kane and Ryder's jaws are swollen to hell, the bruises are up on their cheekbones and jawbones. Nico's nose bled for ages he said, his eye is darkening and Alec... well, Alec only had two cuts—he was perfect compared to the others."

I couldn't help but snort. "That's because Gavin stepped up to him, the little eejit."

"He was helpin' his brothers, which is what Alec was doin'. They're both as bad as each other."

"Men."

"Yeah."

We sat in silence then until Keela said, "From all the violence, I take it your brothers didn't take Kane being the baby's father well then?"

I burst out into unexpected laughter. "You could say that."

Keela smiled at me. "Who was more pissed?"

"James," I sighed. "He hates the brothers, so do the other three, and now me da definitely does. He threatened to kill Kane with a baseball bat."

Keela gasped, "The steel one?"

"That's the one."

"Fuck me."

"Yep."

Keela shook her head. "I don't understand why this shite happens to the lads, they can never just talk stuff out."

"The day they talk somethin' out, is the day pigs fly."

"I second that."

I smiled, but it was forced and I couldn't hold it for long.

"Are you goin' to stay here for rest of the weekend?"

I nodded my head. "No offence to you, but I just want to be on my own to wrap me head around everythin'. I still can't quite believe I'm pregnant. It's just so crazy."

Keela let out a little squeal, "I'm so excited."

I genuinely smiled at her. "This might be the start of a baby boom in the Slater family."

Keela nodded her head. "I think it will be. I'm perfectly content with Alec and meself goin' at a slow pace, but I bet when the baby is born it will be *me* wantin' to speed things up this time and not Alec."

I chuckled, "Once you're happy, that's all that matters."

"I'm gettin' there," Keela said. "The four sessions I've had this week with me shrink are helpin'. We're discussin' things and it's makin' me feel better. Much better. Last night was the fourth night in a row that I didn't have the nightmare. I'm takin' it as a good sign."

I reached over and squeezed Keela's knee.

"It will get even better. Before you know it that horrible nightmare will be a thing of the past, just like its content."

Keela smiled then waved her hand. "Enough about me, let's get back to you."

I groaned, "Let's not."

"Come on, you're pregnant. This is huge."

I grunted, "I know that, trust me."

Keela was silent for a moment then she said, "Are you really goin' to keep it?"

"The baby?" I asked, surprised. "Of course, I already told you that last night."

Keela beamed. "I know, but I just wanted to make sure. I would support you no matter what you decided to do, but I'm glad to hear you say you're really keepin' it. I can't wait to be an auntie."

I blinked. "Givin' the baby up never even entered me mind, neither did an abortion. I was just thinking about livin' space, and money... and tellin' Kane and me family."

Keela chortled, "That's normal. You wouldn't be human if you didn't worry about being able to finance a child, but you can. You have a solid job with good pay. You can do this."

I was still unsure.

"I guess, besides, it doesn't look like I could get rid of Kane even if I tried. I've a strong feelin' he came here with you and you just made him wait downstairs."

Keela stared at me, unblinking. "Are you a Jedi?"

"Yes."

"Seriously, how did you know he was downstairs?"

I shrugged. "I told him to leave me alone, so he will do the exact opposite of that. He is like his brothers—he doesn't listen to a word we say."

"I'm seriously freaked out right now," Keela said and stared at me like I was Obi Wan.

I snorted. "Were you goin' to tell me he came with you?"

She shrugged. "I wanted to judge how you were feelin' first. I thought you'd be pissed, but you just seem... sad?"

I frowned. "I'm not sad, I'm just overwhelmed. It's been one hell of a twenty-four hours. I'm ready for it to be over."

A light knock sounded on the door then and Keela growled.

"I told him to wait in the car."

I winked. "Told you, he doesn't listen. Just like his brothers."

Keela sighed and stood up from the sofa. "Will I drag him along with me?"

"Go for it. I want to see how long it takes for him to get past you."

Keela silently laughed as she stood up and headed towards my front door. She opened it and instantly pressed her hands against Kane's chest when he tried to step foot inside my apartment.

"She doesn't want to see you."

Kane growled, "Tough shit. She is going to see me whether she likes it or not."

Stubborn arsehole.

"Don't have me call me brothers, Kane," I called out from my sofa.

"Because that worked out so well the first time around?" he hissed back.

Keela screeched, "Don't even think of comin' over here and takin' your bullshit out on her. She has been through enough already.

She's stressed to the max and your presence is not helpin' things. Can you not just do as she asks and leave?"

"No."

I couldn't help it, I laughed.

"What's so damn funny?" Kane snapped.

"You," I said still laughing. "You're such a prick and so very predictable that it's funny."

"You should really—Hey! Kane! Let go of—"

I widened my eyes when my front door slammed and Kane was the one who shut it... in Keela's face. He was going to die when she got her hands on him.

"You're dead Kane Slater, do you hear me? D.E.A.D!"

Kane snorted as he flipped the lock on my door. "Whatever you say, short stuff."

Keela screeched and smacked at my front door with her hands. "I'm gettin' Alec and Nico and comin' right back here to get you!"

"Good luck."

I shook my head. "What was the point of that? I'll just ignore you and when Keela gets her hands on you, she'll kill you."

"I'm not worried about Keela Daley, babydoll."

You should be.

"Kane, I've been a wreck all day thinkin' about this mornin'. I'm tired. I just want to go to bed and not wake up until Monday."

I stood up and made a move to walk towards the narrow hallway that lead to my bedroom, but Kane stood at his full height in front of me and showed no signs of moving.

"Will you at least look at me?"

I grunted, "No, just get out of me way."

"No."

I growled, "Kane."

"Aideen," he calmly replied.

I balled my hands into fists. "You're makin' me mad on purpose. Just move."

"Not until you hear me out."

I threw my hands up in the air and turned my back to him. "There is nothin' to hear out. You're a pig just like your brothers, and just like me own brothers. You don't respect me—"

"Bull-fucking-shit. I respect the hell out of you."

I humourlessly laughed, "Is that why we always argue and fight with one another? Your respect for me requires that?"

"We argue because it's just what we do. It's our foreplay."

I gasped, "Foreplay? You have *got* to be jokin' me."

I held my breath when Kane gripped my arm and turned me to face him. "I'm not kidding. You know good and well why we fight so much."

"Nope, you'll have to enlighten me."

Kane growled, "It's because you want me just as much as I want you."

Sex.

It was *always* about sex.

"Sex with you just results in pregnancy. I'd rather be celibate, thank you very much."

Kane placed his fingers under my chin and lifted my head until I looked at his face. My eyes zeroed in on his bruised jaw and black eye.

"Sex with me doesn't usually result in pregnancy. I lost focus that night. There is just something about you. I couldn't think about anything but being inside you."

How often was he going to bring that bloody night up?

I gritted my teeth when I felt my cheeks heat up. "It was a moment of stupidity."

Kane glared at me. "It was a long ass moment that was repeated three times in the space of a few hours."

I turned my head away from him. "We talked about this, it is *not* happenin' again. We have bigger problems than arguin', sex, or even fightin'. I'm pregnant with *your* baby, Kane. This is serious."

His face hardened. "I know damn well this is serious. Do you think I'd be here if I didn't know that?"

I shook my head. "You're here because you hit me this mornin' and you feel bad about it."

Kane's eyes flicked down to my still swollen cheek that now had an array of dark colours on it. He lifted his hand and gently brushed his fingers over the tender area. I winced a little and it caused him to frown.

He lifted his other arm, cupped my face with both of his hands, and lowered his head down to mine. I froze because I wasn't sure what he was doing.

"Kane?"

He swallowed. "I'm so sorry."

I blinked. "It's okay."

"It's not," he instantly replied. "I've never laid a hand on a woman in my life, and to hurt the woman carrying my baby... it makes me sick with myself."

Oh, God.

"Look, I'm more pissed about the fight you got in with me brother than gettin' a knock from you. You didn't mean to hit me. It was me own fault for tryin' to stop you and James."

Kane lowered his hands away from my face and lifted his head. "That still doesn't make me feel any better."

"If you're goin' to feel like shite, then feel like it because you almost killed me brother."

Kane rolled his bright blue eyes. "He hit me first."

"So? You couldn't be the bigger man and back off?"

Kane grunted, "He was gunning to hurt me, Aideen."

"He doesn't like you, and he found out you fathered me unborn child, it's not like it was *completely* unreasonable."

"I don't like him either, but do you see me attacking him or any of your other brothers when I see them?"

It was a rhetorical question so I stayed mute.

"You're silent because you know I'm right," he huffed.

"Maybe so, but it still doesn't change anythin'. You really hurt James, Kane."

"He hurt me too, Aideen. Do I not matter?" Kane snapped.

"That's not fair." I frowned. "You do matter; you're the father of—"

"I only matter because I'm the kid's father?"

Uh.

"Please, I don't want to do this."

"Tough shit," Kane snarled, "because I do."

Here we go.

"Before yesterday I was just a woman you could barely tolerate. Stop tryin' to make it out to be more just because I'm growin' your kid. You pretty much hate me, Kane."

Kane lifted his hands up to his head, ran them through his hair, then turned and walked over to the window in my sitting room. He placed his hands on the windowsill and stared through the pane of glass. "Before yesterday you were a woman I could barely tolerate, and today you're a woman I can *still* barely tolerate, but that's not all. You're also a woman who gives me daily life-saving injections. Do you think I would let someone who I hate jab me?"

I didn't know what to say, so I said nothing.

"What?" Kane asked as he turned to face me. "No smartass reply?"

I narrowed my eyes at him. "Give me a second, I'll think of somethin'."

Kane lightly shook his head. "I don't hate you, and I know you don't hate me. We aren't friends, not even close, but we *are* closer than we were before I found out I had diabetes. That has to count for somethin', right?"

"Yeah, it does," I said then widened my eyes when I thought of his diabetes. "Your second injection!"

I had given him his first injection this morning before we went to my father's house, but I never gave him his second.

Kane held up his hands. "It's okay, I have my kit with me."

I noticed then that he was paler than I would have liked and it made me mad at myself. I took on giving his injection to him as a responsibility and I flaked on him.

"I'm so sorry, I forgot—"

"Hey," Kane cut me off. "You have a lot on your mind—don't worry about me."

"I can't help it," I murmured, then widened my eyes because I didn't mean to say it out loud.

He raised an eyebrow at me. "You can't help but worry about me?"

I shrugged my shoulders. "I sometimes wonder what will happen if you don't get your injections on time or if you have to wait a day or two for them."

Kane blinked at me. "That's kind of nice."

I raised my eyebrows. "Freakin' meself out is nice?"

He snorted, "No, but that you freak out over something to do with me is nice. You never usually worry about me."

I pointed at my stomach. "That all changed yesterday."

Kane's eyes dropped to my belly. "Everything changed yesterday."

"Yep."

He looked up at me then looked around my apartment. "It's small here."

I narrowed my eyes. "I'm aware of that. It's one bedroom because it's just me, but now that it's not going to be just me, I'll have to figure somethin' out. I'll find somewhere bigger that's within me budget."

Kane stretched his neck. "Or you could just move into my place. That's still an option. We have three bedrooms that no one is using now that Dominic, Damien, and Alec don't live there anymore."

I shook my head. "We're civil today, Kane. That could change tomorrow. I don't think makin' such a huge decision right now is a wise choice."

Kane shrugged his shoulders. "Well, the offer is on the table. Take me up on it whenever you want."

I wouldn't.

"I'll keep that in mind."

Kane nodded his head then reached down and took out a black pouch from his pocket. I walked over to him and held my hand out. He gave me his insulin kit and got to work at unbuttoning his trousers.

I gasped, "Wait!"

Kane's fingers froze on his zipper. "What?"

I grunted. "I'm on the second floor; people can *see* in me windows."

Kane looked at both of my windows and snorted, "They probably would be happy to see me with my pants down."

I rolled my eyes. "Then get one of *them* to be up close and personal to you in all your trouserless glory."

Kane laughed as I walked over to my window and drew my curtains. Before I closed them, I noticed there were no cars in front of my building and it made me smile.

"Keela went to get Alec and Nico like she promised."

I turned to face Kane when he laughed. "Come on, babydoll. My brothers knew I wouldn't leave here without seeing you. They're prepared to deal with Keela."

"Even a pissed off Keela?" I asked.

Kane smirked. "*Especially* a pissed off Keela."

I shook my head. "You're sentencin' yourself to death."

"I can deal with Keela Daley, trust me."

What a stupid lad.

"Whatever you say, Kane," I chuckled and opened up the insulin kit in my hand. I tested his blood sugar first with the glucose meter and when I got the result, I adjusted the pen with the correct dosage of insulin. I then kneeled before Kane and looked up at him and said, "Close your eyes."

He shook his head. "I'll just keep my eyes on you and *not* your hands."

"Um, okay," I murmured feeling unsure why he wanted to watch me. Whatever, it kept him calm and at ease and made this task go by quicker.

I uncapped the insulin pen, reached in and pinched a fatty part of Kane's inner thigh and went in. I pushed the needle tip into his skin then pressed the injector button on the pen and delivered the insulin into his body.

After ten seconds I withdrew the needle, recapped the pen and popped it back into the insulin kit. "Give the kit to Branna when you get back home. Tell her to change the needle and to put it into the yellow bucket. Fresh needles are in the top press and she just has to click it into the pen. Easy peasy."

When Kane said nothing, I looked up at him and flinched a little when I found him looking at me.

"What?"

He licked his lips. "I always want to kiss you after you do this for me."

Oh.

I got to my feet and busied myself with zipping up the insulin kit. "Don't forget to tell Branna what I just told you."

"Aideen."

I walked over to my front door. "Make sure she knows to change out the needle. It's *very* important."

"Aideen."

I opened the door. "I don't want a used needle to give you an infection—"

"Aideen!"

I jumped. "What?"

Kane buttoned up his trousers as he walked towards me. "I'm sorry; I didn't mean to make you uncomfortable."

I looked away from him. "I know, but I just don't think any talk of kissin' or sex is good around us. We have more important things to focus on, right?"

I wasn't looking at Kane's face, but I could imagine his jaw set as he said, "Whatever you say, babydoll."

I sighed, "Okay, so... just come by tomorrow for your injections.

I've a bunch of things to figure out before I go back to work on Monday."

"Fine."

I heard a rapid pace of footsteps storm down the hallway outside my apartment just as Kane stepped outside. I jumped back when, out of nowhere, Keela dived onto his back.

"I told you I'd be back!" she bellowed.

Kane swung around and wheezed when Keela's arm locked around his neck. "Can't... breathe."

More footsteps sounded then.

"Damn it, Keela!" Alec's voice snapped. "Get off him."

"Since when can she run so fast?" Nico's voice rasped. "She is like a fucking bullet."

I stood and watched Kane swing around with Keela still on his back. Alec pulled at Keela but she didn't break her hold. Nico shook his head and put his hands under her armpits and tickled her. I think she was off Kane and in Nico's arms in less than a second.

"You fucker!" Keela snapped at Nico then shivered and locked her arms at her sides so he couldn't tickle her again.

"I was leaving!" Kane snapped and rubbed at his neck.

Keela looked at me when Nico sat her on the ground. "Are you okay?"

I nodded my head. "Yeah... b-but can you stay tonight? I don't really want to be on me own."

"Of course. I have me overnight bag in the car," she said and looked at Alec. "Will you grab it for me, please?"

"Apologise to Kane first."

Keela snarled at Kane, "Trick me again and I'll kill you for real."

Alec rolled his eyes. "Close enough, I'll be right back."

I couldn't help but snort as Alec walked down the hallway. I looked to Nico and found him looking at my cheek. I waved him off. "It's fine."

"It's bruised and a little swollen."

"So is your face, and Kane's."

"We're fine though."

"So am I."

I felt Kane look at me then so I again waved Nico off. "Honestly, it's okay. It was an accident."

Nico smiled at me. "You can tell him that all you like but he will still feel like crap for causing it."

I frowned. "And you know that because?"

"Because I accidentally hit Bronagh during a fight with Jason Bane a few days after I first met her. And even though I didn't mean to do it, I still feel like shit when I think about it, and it's been years since it happened. I won't ever forgive myself for hurting her."

I didn't know why, but I thought that was really sweet.

I looked from Nico to Kane. "I'm really okay. Trust me on that, please?"

He nodded his head, but I could see he still felt bad about the bruise.

I looked back at Nico when he laughed, "Told you so."

I rolled my eyes. "When he sees me in labour it will overshadow some stupid bruise. When I'm screaming in pain, you can feel bad and be fully aware that you're the cause of it."

"Jesus, Aideen," Kane groaned. "You were on top of me the majority of the time so technically speaking you brought this upon yourself—"

"Don't finish that sentence, you won't live to see the birth of your child if you do," Keela said and held her hands up in warning.

We all laughed at her.

"Have a boy," Nico said to me, his tone dead serious.

I laughed, "It doesn't work like that, sweetie."

"Just keep thinking of the baby being a boy and he will be."

I laughed, "Okay, I'll do that for you."

Nico smiled happily.

Keela nudged him. "When Bronagh eventually gets pregnant, you both might have twin girls since you're a twin."

Nico grabbed his chest. "Don't wish that upon me, I can't have one girl let alone *two*."

"Why not?" I giggled and leaned against my door frame.

Nico gave me a *duh* look. "You've seen Bronagh, she's stunningly beautiful. Any girls she'd have would take after her and I cannot live my life fighting off every stupid boy that sniffs around my girls. I feel sick just thinking about it."

I smiled. "Not *all* teenage boys are creepers."

"No, but I know what all teenage boys think about. It's all *I* could think about when I first met Bronagh. It's all I *still* think about and I'm a grown man so yeah, I want boys, not girls. All boys. Ten of them."

Kane groaned and looked up at the ceiling. "Please God, I don't want any of what Dominic just said. Please bless me with a boy. *Please.*"

Myself and Keela fell around laughing.

"I want a girl just to torture you," I said to Kane.

He growled at me, "She-devil."

I laughed so hard I gave myself a stitch.

"Stop," I wheezed. "I'll wet meself."

Kane smiled at me. "I'll see you tomorrow, okay? Please don't worry about things—it really will be okay. I promise."

I felt the other two look at me, but I focused on Kane and said, "I'm holdin' you to that promise."

And I did.

CHAPTER THIRTEEN

8 weeks later...

"Make sure you get the DVD, Aideen. Pregnant or not, I'll kick your arse if you don't. I want to see me niece in all her 4D glory."

I saluted my oddly aggressive best friend. "I've got this, Kay. Trust me."

Keela nodded her head to me once and then switched her gaze to Kane. That was when her eyes narrowed and her hands balled into fists.

Uh-oh.

"Don't look at me like that," Kane said to her, his tone firm. "You went to the first big appointment, the rest are mine."

He sounded manly, but really he was being a bitch because he wouldn't look at Keela directly in the eye when he spoke to her.

"Don't talk to me, *you*," she growled.

I wanted to smile, but I knew better so I didn't.

I simply leaned over to the passenger door of Kane's SUV, or now the family SUV, opened it and proceeded to get into the car. Keela, Alec, and Kane, however, thought sliding into the passenger seat was more like climbing Mount Everest for me. The three of them reached for me and held onto some part of my body and tried to ease my already easy transition into the car.

"Oh, my God," I grumbled. "I'm not a doll, I won't break."

Alec snapped his fingers at me. "Don't jinx yourself."

I snorted, "Stop it. You're all being way overboard with me. I'm pregnant, not disabled. I can do things meself and not cause any bodily harm, you know?"

"We know, Ado, but you can't blame us for wantin' to keep you extra safe."

I grinned. "If your over-protectiveness causes me to lose the plot and go crazy, I'll blame all of your for drivin' me to the point of being coo-coo."

Alec raised his eyebrow at me and said, "You'll be fine."

I chortled, "Please, for all you know I could suffer from a mental illness. That means I could kill you, plead insanity, and get away with it. I'd think about that if I was you."

Silence.

"Keela, why are you friends with her?" Alec murmured to his fiancée without taking his eyes away from me.

My best friend turned, looked him dead in the eye and said, "I honestly have no idea."

I gleefully laughed, "I do. It's because I'm the glue that holds this fucked up group together."

"Or you're just the incubator to my nephew and that's the only reason I, and everyone else, puts up with you," Alec countered.

"Kiss me arse, Slater!" I snapped.

Kane sighed, closed my door and gestured Keela and Alec away from the car. He shook his head and walked around to the driver's side of the car and got in. I glared at Alec through the window and then stuck my middle finger up at him. Keela burst into laughter while Alec shook his head at me while grinning.

I glanced at Kane as he leaned over to me and grabbed a hold of my seatbelt. He pulled on it, positioned it over my body then buckled the belt. He lowered the bottom half of the belt under my belly and fixed the upper strap across my shoulder. He looked up on the Internet the proper way for a pregnant woman to wear a seatbelt and he was pretty hands on in making sure it was always adjusted correctly every time I was in his car.

I waved to Keela until she and Alec left my sight. I relaxed into my seat and rested my head back against the headrest. I closed my eyes and hummed as the vibrations of the engine slithered up my seat and reverberated against my back.

I opened my eyes and glanced at Kane after a few minutes of music filling the car.

"Are you excited?"

He nodded his head as he drove. "I'm nervous, too."

I raised my eyebrow. "Why nervous?"

He shrugged and for a moment I thought the shrug was his reply until he grunted and said, "I'm worried I might cry."

I burst into unexpected laughter.

"It's *not* funny," he hissed. "I can't cry—it will be the ultimate bitch thing to do."

I continued to laugh.

"You aren't helping, you know?" he snarled.

I crossed my legs when my bladder objected to my laughter.

"Sorry," I wheezed a little and forced myself to calm down.

"Are you really?" Kane questioned.

I bit my lip and nodded my head.

"Bullshit."

I laughed again then waved my hands. "Stop. I'm goin' to wee meself."

"It'd serve you right for laughing at me."

I calmed myself down—it took two minutes—until I was only chuckling here and there.

"I'm only teasin'. You'll be fine," I said and fanned myself with my hands.

Kane grunted, "We'll see."

"If you *do* cry, we can blame it on your diabetes somehow," I said, grinning.

"I hate you," Kane murmured.

I smiled to myself. I was enjoying this conversation far more than I should have. It was like every other conversation we'd had over the past few weeks; it resulted in me feeling giddy with happiness. All. The. Time.

I glanced at Kane then looked down to his thighs.

"I haven't asked you this in a while, but how are you feelin'? You have had a steady routine over the past few weeks with your injections. Are you startin' to feel like yourself again?"

Kane didn't look at me as he spoke, "Yes and no. I feel stronger and overall really good because I don't feel sick anymore. But I don't feel one hundred percent myself because I have to rely on you for my injections. It makes me feel a little... inadequate."

"Inadequate? That's silly, you could haven chosen not to let anyone give you your insulin, but *you* made the choice to let me do it. You have the control, not me. You *allow* me to give you an injection, that's all on you. I'm just the helper."

Kane mulled this over in his mind, but I could see that my response made him feel a little better so I didn't push for further conversation, I let it lie.

"I'm glad we're getting along better."

I snorted, "We fought over baby names yesterday and I threw a cup at you."

"That's true," Kane nodded, "but we spoke five hours later which is way quicker than usual."

When he put it like that, we sounded so weird.

"You're right, that's major progress," I said, sarcasm dripping from every word.

Kane shook his head. "That's just me and you, Aideen."

"Yeah," I chuckled. "Me and you."

"We still aren't naming the baby Jenna if it's a girl."

I growled, "But it's cute!"

"Not happening. I *hate* that name."

"Why?" I complained.

Kane shrugged. "I just do, okay?"

I groaned, "Fine, whatever."

Kane laughed at me when I folded my arms over my chest and it pissed me off. "Don't poke the bear, Kane. I said fine. Accept that and don't bathe in your smugness or I'll knock it out of you."

"Damn," he murmured, "hormones are in full swing today."

"Excuse me?"

"Nothing, I just said you look so beautiful today."

Bullshit.

"I'm wearin' leggin's, an over sized shirt, and a cardigan."

"Yep. Beautiful."

I rolled my eyes. "You're so full of it."

"I've meant to ask—you don't wear jeans anymore, it's just been leggings the past two weeks. Why is that?"

I frowned. "I'm twenty weeks and a day pregnant, Kane. You can see my belly has gotten bigger, but so have my thighs and arse. Me old jeans don't fit anymore."

It hurt saying that. It really did.

"So why not buy the next size up?"

I felt sick. "Because the next size up for me is a twelve! I've never been a twelve. Always a ten."

Kane glanced at me before returning his eyes to the road. "I forget the difference between Irish and US sizes. What is a twelve in the States?"

I pouted, "A sixteen."

"Really, you're a sixteen now?" Kane asked, his eyes wide with surprise.

"No, I'm a *twelve*, it's just a sixteen in the States."

"Yeah, but you just said it was the same—"

"I'm a twelve, Kane. A *twelve*."

"Gotcha."

I huffed, "By the time I have your bloody kid I'll probably be a size thirty!"

Kane gnawed on his lower lip. "My baby has an appetite, what can I say?"

"I could say a lot of things, but I'm not goin' to," I snarled.

"If you're so worried about gaining weight, why don't you work out with me?"

"Because I don't like workin' out. It gives me hives."

Kane laughed, "Bullshit excuses give me hives."

"Well, excuse me," I retorted.

Kane sighed, "Come on, baby mama. Let me work you out."

I looked at Kane with narrowed eyes.

He snickered, "You know I mean a legit work out. *But...* sex with me *would* be one hell of a workout for you."

Yeah, right.

"So would sex with any man."

Kane's joking attitude fled. "You won't be having sex with any man that isn't me while you're pregnant."

"And why not?" I asked, curiously.

I wouldn't have sex with any man while pregnant with Kane's baby, but being told I *couldn't* ticked me off.

"Because you're pregnant with *my* baby," Kane said, his tone firm. "Put it this way—if you did fuck someone I'd be really hurt and I'd kill the bastard who you did it with. Is that a good enough reason?"

The threats didn't surprise me, but the mention of him being hurt did.

"You'd be hurt if I was with another man while pregnant?"

Kane nodded once. "Yes, I would. Right now your body has a part of me inside it and it's changing and growing each day. I just want you to belong to me, no one else. I'm being very serious right now, Aideen. I don't know what I'd do if someone touched you."

I swallowed down a lump that suddenly formed in my throat. "Kane... that's... that's actually really sweet."

He shrugged. "Thanks, I guess."

"I don't want you to be hurt, or to kill anyone, so you have me word. I'll suppress me sexual urges."

Kane smirked. "I wouldn't go *that* far. Have all the sexual urges you want, just make me your go-to guy when you want to act those urges out."

The moment was over.

"You're such a pig."

"I know."

I bobbed my knee up and down. "Are we nearly there yet? I have to go to the toilet."

"You *always* have to pee. You go fifty times a day."

I punched his shoulder. "It's one of the joys of being pregnant, *Daddy*."

"Call me daddy one more time. Better yet, call me big daddy."

I laughed and so did Kane.

That is something we did a lot lately when we were together. We teased each other, sometimes fought with one another, but we mostly laughed together. It was a nice change to not want to beat him to death all the time.

Twenty minutes passed by and we parked and entered the Coombe hospital. We checked in and sat in the waiting area to wait for my name to be called. We were amidst a bunch of pregnant ladies and their husbands, friends, or boyfriends.

Kane threw his arm around the back of my chair when we sat down and for some stupid reason I liked it. I don't know why, I just did. Kane didn't though. I could tell he was crazy uncomfortable with being around this many people even if the majority of them were pregnant.

"What is the procedure here like?" he asked as he scoped the room out. "Do you have to do anything special or just go into the room and lay down?"

I shrugged my shoulders. "I was only here once and it was in the emergency room. I don't know what a proper appointment is like."

Kane nodded his head then looked at the right when a woman dressed in white scrubs called my name. "Keela Daley, room three for blood works."

I groaned, "I've to get a needle, do you want to wait here?"

I only asked because I knew he had some sort of fear of them.

"How many needles will they use on you?" he asked me, his eyes wild.

I frowned. "Just the one, honey. Just the one."

He swallowed. "I'll go with you, just in case you need me."

Aww.

I smiled. "Let's go then."

We stood up and walked towards the nurse who pointed at the floor. "Follow the red strip until you come to room three." With that said she was on to calling out another woman's name for her blood, too.

I took hold of Kane's hand when he reached out for me and felt butterflies in my stomach because of it. "Stay close to me, it's very busy in here. I don't want to have to start some shit if someone knocks into you."

Wow.

"You aren't startin' trouble in a maternity hospital."

"I know I'm not because you're going to stay behind me."

Smartarse.

"Fine," I sighed. "Lead the way, germinator."

Kane growled and it made me smile.

He really hated that nickname.

We followed the red line on the floor until we came to room number three. Kane knocked on the door and opened it without waiting. "Aideen Collins," he said.

"Yes, send her in."

Kane turned to the side and gestured me in. I walked past him and stopped short in front of a middle-aged nurse who was sitting on a chair next to a hospital bed.

"Hop on up, honey."

It was too high for me to hop, but I could scoot my way up perfectly fine. I handed Kane my pink file that was given to me when we checked in and walked towards the bed. I shimmied my way onto the bed and frowned at my thighs. They became the size of Australia when I sat down, and I hated it.

"How are you today?" the nurse asked me, a smile on her face.

"I'm fine, thanks. You?"

I watched as she put a strap on my arm. "I'm great, honey. Can you make a fist with your hand and relax it for me?"

I did as she asked.

"Perfect. Can you repeat that action a few times?"

I nodded and repeated the action over and over. The nurse had tapped on the inside of my forearm before she cleaned it with an alcoholic wipe. I watched as she picked up a needle and stuck in into my arm.

Fuck. Fuck. Fuck.

It hurt—it hurt a bloody lot.

"Are you okay?" Kane asked me.

I hadn't realised I closed my eyes. "Yep," I replied and tried not to sound like I wanted to cry even though I did.

I gave him injections every day. I had to be brave for him. I hissed though when the nurse wiggled the needle around in my arm.

"Sorry, honey. Your veins were hidin', but I got one."

Brilliant.

I opened my eyes when I felt a hand touch my back. Kane was next to me and he looked very worried. "Can you use a smaller needle, ma'am? I don't want you to hurt her, she's important."

I melted.

My heart literally melted into a puddle.

"I'm fine," I murmured to him and looked away because my cheeks flushed with colour.

The nurse looked between us and smiled. "It's in the vein now. A few more steps and we're done. Okay, sir?"

Kane reluctantly nodded his head, but he didn't move away from me. He kept his hand on my back and leaned down to kiss the crown of my head when I pressed it against his chest.

I was absolutely beaming on the inside, and I thought myself such a fool for being so giddy.

I tried not to dwell on my growing feelings for Kane—yeah, I admit it, I was stupidly starting to fall in like with the dickhead—and focused on the nurse instead.

I watched as she withdrew a few vials of blood from me, and then removed the needle and put a cotton ball where the needle had been and some sticky tape over it to hold it in place on my arm.

"Okay, honey, you can go back out to the waiting area. Leave your file with me and by the time you're called in for your scan, the nurse attending you will have your file. It will be updated with all the results from the tests that will be performed today with your blood."

I nodded my head. "Thank you."

Kane stepped close to me and held my hands as I got off the bed. I was a little surprised that my legs suddenly felt a little weak. It caused me to slump a little.

"Whoa."

"I've got you," Kane said and lifted me back up onto the bed.

"Poor dear. Has she eaten today?" the nurse asked Kane.

I was leaning against his chest so I couldn't tell if he shook his head or not.

"No, she throws up in the mornings. Her morning sickness hasn't gone away yet."

The nurse sighed, "I'll go get her some Lucozade for her blood sugar. After she drinks it go bring her to the deli in the café area and get some food into her."

"Yes, ma'am."

A few seconds of silence went by then I felt Kane kiss the crown of my head again. "You okay?"

I nodded against his chest.

He sighed, "I was losing my mind watching her take so much blood from you. I had to stop myself from interfering and telling her to stop."

I shyly smiled. "Aww, you care about me."

"I care about you more than anyone."

I blinked my eyes and looked up at him. "I'm tellin' your brothers you said that."

Kane chuckled and placed his hand on my back and rubbed up and down. I could get used to this side of him, I thought as I closed my eyes until my dizzy spell went away. I opened them when the nurse walked back into the room holding a white plastic cup.

"This is Lucozade, drink it," she said and handed me the cup filled with orange liquid. "It will make you feel better until you get some food into you."

I thanked the nurse as I took the cup from her hands and brought it to my lips. I took a little sip of the drink then finished it in three gulps.

I hummed, "That was nice."

Kane chuckled, "Food time."

Yes. Food.

Kane took my hand and lead me out of the blood room and if I wasn't so lightheaded, I would have blushed like a little schoolgirl. I shook my head at myself and followed Kane as we headed to the café within the hospital. I sat down at an empty table while Kane went about and got some sandwiches and crisps.

"Excuse me, ma'am, do you have the correct time?"

I looked up to who spoke, and for a second, I got a fright. The man was a burn victim—half of his face was just one big scar. I tried my very best not to stare at it.

I glanced at my phone for the time and when I got it, I looked back to the man and said, "Just after nine, sir."

"Thank you." He winked.

I smiled. "You're welcome."

He glanced at my stomach. "Good luck."

Huh?

I looked down to my stomach and laughed.

He meant good luck with my pregnancy.

I think.

"Oh, thank you. I'm only twenty weeks away. It's not long now."

The man stared at me for a moment. "Yeah, not long at all."

What?

I was about to say what I was thinking to him, but he turned and walked away without waiting for my reply or saying goodbye. He didn't look back, just walked out of the cafe and towards the exit of the hospital.

That was weird.

I thought about it for a minute, but then my stomach grumbled and I forgot about everything except about how hungry I was.

When Kane came back, I wanted to burst into song. He put food items on the table and pushed them towards me. I blinked down at the items and looked up to Kane, who was staring at me like he was willing me to open up a sandwich and eat it.

I chuckled, "This can't all be for just me?"

Kane shrugged. "I don't want you to be hungry, we might be here for a while."

"Kane," I laughed and pushed a sandwich towards him, "eat this. I can't eat with you just sat there starin' at me like I'm a doll on display in a museum."

Kane grinned. "You are a doll though. You're my *babydoll*."

I narrowed my eyes at him. "Stop being cute and eat the bloody sandwich."

He did as I asked with a ghost of a smile on his face. I finished a double chicken and stuffing sandwich within five minutes. Kane was only halfway through his BLT sandwich by the time I was done.

I groaned, "I feel so much better after that."

"The girls were right; you *do* eat like Bear Grylls."

Oh, for the love of God.

"Get over it. It's your child that is the cause of it."

Kane snorted, "I know, he's gonna be an awesome kid."

I growled.

"Do you want to sit here for a bit or go back to the waiting area?" Kane asked, grinning at me.

"The waitin' area," I replied. "I don't wanna miss me name being called."

We got up and went back to the waiting area and found all the seats were taken. This irritated Kane.

"I'm telling one of the husbands of those women over there to get up."

I grabbed his arm. "You'll do no such thing."

"You aren't standing around for God knows how long—"

"Aideen Collins?"

I looked from Kane to a nurse I recognised. It was the nurse I met in the emergency room eight weeks ago. She had a pink folder in her hand that I assumed was mine.

"I'm here." I smiled and walked over to her with Kane in tow.

"That was just lucky," he mumbled.

I ignored him and smiled to the nurse. "Hello again."

The nurse smiled then flicked her eyes past me and tensed up a little. It caused me to frown so I looked back to Kane then to the nurse.

What was her problem?

"Is everythin' okay?" I asked.

She nodded her head and kept her eyes on me. "Everything is fine. I'd like you to follow me up to the second floor so I can carry out your appointment."

"Lead the way."

The nurse smiled, turned and began to walk. Kane and myself followed her, but I was no longer smiling. I was scowling.

"Hey," Kane murmured, "what's that face for?"

"I don't like how she looked at you," I replied lowly to him.

"What way did she look at me?" he asked.

I set my jaw. "Like she was frightened."

Kane sighed, "I get that a lot, darling. I don't blame her though—I do look scary."

Hearing him say that made me really mad.

"No. You. Don't," I hissed. "You look perfectly fuckin' fine, and fuck anyone who thinks differently."

Kane grabbed hold of my arm and brought us to a stop. He rounded on me and looked down at my face. "Babydoll."

I shook my head. "I'm fine. I... I just don't like people thinkin' you're somethin' to fear. You aren't. They don't know you like I do."

Kane smiled at me. "Have I ever told you how amazing you are?"

I flushed. "No, but it'd be nice to hear it often."

Kane laughed and wrapped his arms around me. "I love that you want to defend me, but you really don't have to. I'm a big boy, I can handle myself."

"You shouldn't have to," I mumbled.

Kane put his arm around my shoulder and smiled with glee. "Come on, gorgeous. Let's go see our baby."

If our nurse hadn't annoyed me enough, the teenage girl that was openly drooling over Kane as we waited in the new waiting room on the second floor, brought me to boiling point. I was fuming mad and this kid wasn't helping simmer my rage.

"What is your name?" the girl asked Kane after minutes of uninterrupted staring in his direction.

He glanced at her and said, "Kane."

"Kane," she repeated. "I *love* that. It sounds dangerous."

Oh, please.

"Are you waitin' on someone, *Kane*? Your sister perhaps?"

Was she blind?

Kane had a ghost of a smile on his face when he glanced at me and saw me openly glare at the girl.

"No, I'm here with—"

"His girlfriend. That'd be me," I finished for him.

I saw Kane look at me, and I was just as surprised as him that I said it, but I couldn't go back and unsay it, so I just went with the flow.

"Oh, I didn't realise," the girl murmured.

Didn't realise my arse.

"It's okay, harmless mistake," I said and leaned into Kane who was smiling a little too wide for my liking.

He put his arm around me and dropped it down to my hip and began rubbing my side.

"Are you expectin'?" I asked the girl and glanced at her stomach, which was tanned, toned, and on display for everyone in the waiting room to see.

She definitely wasn't pregnant—I was just being a bitch.

Colour flushed her perfectly positioned cheekbones. "No, me sister is. I'm just here for moral support."

I faked a smile. "Oh, sorry. I thought you were waitin' for an ultrasound."

She caught onto my cattiness and looked me up and down. "It's fine, a harmless mistake. Are you expectin' triplets?"

That. Little. Bitch.

"Nope, just one big baby," I said and pointed at Kane. "He is the daddy, you can only imagine how big *our* child will be."

I had no idea why I was being so defensive. Usually, I wouldn't care about Kane and any possible lay he could have, but we were about to see our baby together for the first time, and I just wanted him to myself right now. If the chick wanted him after the appointment, she could damn well have him.

No, she couldn't. I take it back. If I couldn't sleep with any men whilst being pregnant, then Kane couldn't sleep with any women. That was fair.

"What is going on with you?" Kane murmured.

I didn't know the answer to that question so I made something up.

"I just can't wait to get home."

"Why?"

"So I can take me bra off."

Kane snorted at me, "It's uncomfortable?"

I nodded my head. "The straps are startin' to dig into my skin and I'm about to pop out of this one. I need to go and get some maternity bras, me old ones aren't cuttin' it anymore."

Kane glanced down to my chest and licked his lips. "They look fine to me."

I looked down also and grunted. My bra was tight, which made my newly enlarged breasts push up and almost spill out of my bra. Pre-pregnancy I was already big chested at a thirty-two double D. God only knew what I was now.

"They look too big. It makes them look fake and nasty."

Kane gasped, "Don't you ever say something so disgusting again. There is no such thing as boobs that are too big. Do you understand me?"

I laughed, "If you like them so much, you have them."

Kane lifted his hands to my boobs and tried to touch them only for me to smack his hands away.

"I mean you have them on your chest. I didn't mean *touch* them!"

Kane shook away the sting on his hands. "You have to be more specific."

Clearly.

"You're such a pervert."

Kane smirked. "You love it."

I hated that I smiled.

"Whatever," I mumbled, trying to appear annoyed.

"Aideen Collins?"

Finally.

"Yes?" I replied to the voice calling my name.

The nurse from before popped her head around the corner and

smiled. "I'm ready for you."

I felt hands on my hips.

"Come on, Daddy, you can come too," the nurse chirped to Kane then turned and disappeared around the corner.

I laughed at Kane's facial expression as he looked down at me. "She called me Daddy," he murmured.

I shook my head, smiling. "I'm sure she calls all the fathers-to-be, Daddy."

Kane waggled his eyebrows. "Or maybe she wants—"

"Finish that sentence and I'll hurt you," I warned, my hand raised and my index finger pointing at him dangerously. "I'm not havin' me midwife seduced by you today or any other day. She is here for *me* so keep it in your boxers or else."

Kane laughed at me and placed both his hands on my shoulders when I turned and began to walk in the direction the nurse went. I spotted her outside a room and she gestured us in with her hand when we neared her.

We entered the large room filled with medical equipment. I recognised two things: The bed and the monitor used to see a baby inside its mother's tummy.

"Pop up onto the bed, Aideen, and we'll get started."

I eyed the nurse, but did as she said. She seemed a lot happier than earlier and not at all wary of Kane like she was before. Maybe Kane was right and people can't help but instinctively fear him when they first lay eyes on him.

I just didn't get it—I didn't have that problem when I first met him two years ago. I thought he was gorgeous; scars included.

"How have you been feeling over the past few weeks?" the nurse asked me.

"Good," I replied and got up onto the bed with the help of Kane, who then sat next to me on a vacant chair. "I've been goin' to my medical centre every week for little check-ups. It's all there in my file, or it should be."

The nurse flipped open my pink folder. "Yep, I see all your

logged visits. Everything is looking great. Has your tummy settled down? I see a note here that you are still quite ill."

I grunted, "It's calmed down, but I still throw up mostly in the mornin's."

The nurse nodded her head and wrote something down on my file.

"Are you excited for your visit today?" the nurse asked with a smile. "You're halfway there, only twenty weeks to go."

I felt a huge smile stretch across my face. "I'm so excited, I can't wait to see the baby again. They don't have a machine in the clinic that lets you see the baby, only the one to hear it."

"Well, you'll be in for a treat. Baby will be a lot bigger than when you were here last time. You get to see 4D images today also."

"I can't wait."

The nurse looked at Kane. "This is your first time seeing your baby, are you excited?"

"Very excited," Kane replied.

The nurse smiled and looked to me. "You can lift your top and lower your leggings down just like before."

I nodded my head and reached down and pulled up my t-shirt until it was tucked under my breasts. I tried to wiggle my leggings down, but it just wasn't happening so I looked at Kane. "Pull my leggin's and knickers down a little, will you?"

Kane stood up and gripped the hem of my leggings and underwear. "How far down?" he asked with a smirk on his face and a wiggle of his eyebrows.

I laughed, "Only a little bit."

He pouted and tugged them down ever so slightly before sitting back down to look like a sad puppy. Smiling, I shook my head at him.

"The gel is cold, Aideen. I'm sure you remember."

I lightly giggled then yelped a little when the nurse squirted the gel over my belly. "I don't think I'll ever get used to that sensation."

The nurse smiled and used her microphone looking probe to

swirl the gel about on my stomach. She moved the probe around a couple of times and smiled. "Found baby fast this time."

I looked at the screen.

"Here is baby's torso," she moved the probe, "and here are baby's legs. They're crossed right now."

"Oh, she's gotten so much bigger!" I squealed and clapped my hands together.

"He," Kane said absentmindedly as he stared at the screen on the wall in front of us.

I wasn't getting into the same repetitive debate again so I ignored Kane and stared at my baby. At *our* baby.

"*She* has gotten so much bigger since the last time I was here."

The nurse chuckled, "Yep, it's amazing the differences you see in a foetus within such a short period of time. Even in yourself—you're very different from when you walked into the emergency room eight weeks ago."

I looked down at my rounded stomach and smiled. "Yeah, it's crazy how quickly me body has changed."

The nurse looked at Kane. "Have you noticed the changes in Aideen's body as she grows the baby?"

Kane snapped his attention from the monitor that displayed our bun to the nurse's pretty face.

"What?" he asked.

I laughed as she repeated her question.

"Oh, yeah." Kane smiled. "I've noticed *all* the changes in her body."

He has?

"Like what?" I asked, quizzically.

Kane smirked. "Your stomach, ass and bust has... enlarged."

I rolled my eyes while the nurse snorted. "He has good observation skills."

"He failed to mention my thighs, hips, and waist have expanded too."

Kane waved me off. "I haven't noticed."

Of course, he hadn't, he was too busy constantly looking at my 'enlarged' arse and chest.

"He's smart," the nurse chuckled. "He knows what to notice and what to stay mute on."

Kane winked at the nurse and it made her blush.

I narrowed my eyes at Kane. "Really? First the girl in the waitin' room and now me midwife. Are you shittin' me?"

Kane held up his hands. "I didn't do anything."

"Make sure you don't. I'll cut your balls off if you do."

The nurse stared back and forth between Kane and myself with wide eyes so I smiled and used Kane's words against him. "This is our foreplay."

"Cool," she said and nervously smiled, making sure to avoid looking at Kane.

She spent a lot of time then taking new measurements of the baby, and pressing on certain areas of my stomach before measuring it with a measuring tape.

"So, let's re-cap. I've recorded ten minutes of four-dimensional movement plus the foetal heartbeat for sound. You're measured at twenty weeks and one day exactly. Your weight is pegged at a three to four-pound weight gain per week, and your bloods and blood pressure is perfect. What about your movements? Have you being getting your ten kicks a day?"

I nodded my head. "Yeah, but it's literally just a little move or kick, they don't last very long. I barely notice them if I'm being honest. I haven't experienced a real big one yet. Is that somethin' I should worry about?"

"Nope," the nurse chirped. "Give it another few weeks and you will feel stronger kicks as well as be able to see your stomach moving. Dad, that means you can get a good feel of them so you can experience your baby moving too."

"Can't wait," Kane commented lowly.

Uh huh.

"Would you like to know the gender of your baby?"

I shook my head firmly. "Nope."

"Dad, are you okay on that matter?" the nurse asked Kane.

"You can tell what the gender of the baby is from just looking at the screen right there?" Kane asked the nurse and pointed at the monitor.

She nodded her head.

"So you know right now?"

Again, she nodded her head.

"You know if it's a boy or a girl?"

She laughed and nodded her head once more.

"Are you going to put it in Aideen's file?" he asked with his eyebrow arched.

The nurse snickered, "No because you both don't want to know... right?"

"Right," I answered instantly.

Both the nurse and myself looked at Kane when he remained silent.

"It's killing me, babydoll. How can you *not* want to know?" he asked me with a pained groan.

I couldn't help but smile at his tortured face. "Because seein' you tormented like this brings me so much joy."

"Evil!" he snapped. "You're pure evil."

I laughed, "I want it to be a surprise. As long as the baby is healthy, it doesn't matter to me what the sex is."

Kane sighed, "I guess... but it's still going to kill me."

I snorted, "You'll get over it."

"Okay, Satan," Kane grumbled.

I smirked. "If I'm Satan, what does that make the baby?"

"The *spawn* of Satan," Kane grunted and shook his head. "I've fathered the spawn of Satan. No amount of private talks with the man upstairs is going to get me off the 'doomed for an entirety in hell' list now. I'm fucked."

Tears formed in my eyes when laughter racked through my body. I placed a hand on the top of my stomach and the other on my chest. Both sections of my body were hurting so bad.

"Stop," I wheezed and flagged Kane with my hands.

He tried to glare at me, he really did. I saw him fight the smile that tugged at the corner of his mouth. He couldn't help but succumb to the laughter floating around the room though. He couldn't not smile when he looked at me for some weird reason.

"You'll start premature labour if you don't calm down," the nurse joked.

It took me a minute, but I calmed down enough not to laugh out loud. A big smile stayed put on my face though. We finished up the rest of the appointment smiling and laughing, and Kane and myself continued it when we left the hospital.

Kane dropped me off at work and wished me a good day. I got in at ten and luckily the three hours until lunch went by pretty quickly. All of my students were well behaved and caused no problems throughout the day. Even though everything went by smoothly, I was still pooped by the time I sat down in the staff room next to my friend, and fellow co-worker, Kiera McKesson.

We discussed how my appointment went and fawned over my new scan pictures of the baby. I told her how I was showing everyone the DVD later and I mentioned how excited Bronagh was to see it and that made Kiera smile.

"How are Bronagh and Dominic doin'?" she asked me.

I took a gulp from my water bottle, swallowed it down then said, "Great, they're still goin' strong. They're both mad, but they're pretty cool people. I love them, they're like me family now."

Kiera smiled. "I'm glad, even though I'm very surprised they are together still."

I raised my eyebrow. "You are? Why?"

She sighed. "They hated each other in school, and when I say hate I *really* mean hate. I could tell Dominic fancied Bronagh though and he didn't know what to do with her cold shoulder. The poor lad was sent into a three-sixty the moment she walked late into class that morning. I'll never forget the look on his face the moment he first saw her—it was perfection. He sat up straight and stared at her when she walked towards her desk. I'm pretty sure he was about to say somethin' sweet to her until she told him he was seated at her desk in a snarky tone."

I laughed, "I wish I could have been there. He worships her now. I wonder if it was instant for him."

"Instant attraction? Yeah, I'm sure it was. He thought winnin' her affections was a game, and one he would easily win. She made it very hard for him though, bless her."

"He adores her." I smiled. "He gets her little gifts all the time just to shower her with them. He is a sucker for gettin' her flowers."

We laughed together for a few moments until Kiera gasped.

"What?" I asked, alarmed.

She face palmed herself. "I completely forgot to tell you about a delivery you got this mornin'."

"A delivery for me?" I questioned.

Kiera nodded. "I signed for it and told the delivery man your classroom number. Class was in session so he left the delivery with the caretaker who said he would bring it to your room during break time. Whatever it was, he left it in there for you."

I yawned. "Good thing I didn't go home right away today. Usually, I do durin' the week to get to Kane early for his injections."

"I'll say." Kiera smiled. "Enjoy your weekend. Don't hurt Kane... too much."

I stood up and saluted her. "Yes, Miss. Mckesson."

Kiera snorted at me and waved me on as I left the staff room. I cracked my back as I left the room and groaned out loud. I was tired, my back hurt, my feet were sore and no matter what I ate, I still felt hungry.

I felt my phone vibrate in my pocket so I took it out and answered it. "Hello?"

"Do you want me to come get you?"

I rolled my eyes at his rudeness. "Hey, Kane. How are you on this fine Friday afternoon?"

I heard him sigh. "Hello, babydoll. Do you want me to come pick you up?"

I grinned. "Hiya and no, I'm fine. I have me own car, Keela dropped it off for me two hours ago."

"Oh, right." Kane was silent for a moment. "Are you swinging by my house or going home after work?"

I yawned. "I'm going to yours to give you your injection, then home. I'm knackered."

"Oh."

I sighed. "Oh, what?"

"Well, I thought we were going to show everyone the DVD of the baby today?"

I groaned, "I forgot about that. I was just talkin' about it and I still forgot. I'm not with it today."

"It's okay we can—"

"No, it's fine," I cut Kane off. "I'll just go to your house and stay there for the day. I'll nap on the sofa or somethin'."

"Or something," Kane grumbled.

"What?"

He cleared his throat. "Nothing, I'll see you soon."

"'Kay, bye."

I hung up my phone, pocketed it, and continued to walk down the never-ending hallway to my classroom. Kiera kindly swapped rooms with me for the reminder of the year because it was closer to the staff room than what my old room was. I didn't see the logic of her offer when I was thirteen weeks pregnant, but now that I was showing and feeling a little strained, I was glad I didn't have to walk as far.

My students liked it as well because they got to see more of the older students. The school I worked in was huge; it was both a primary and secondary school in one, which meant there were students of all ages roaming around.

I made it to my temporary classroom, but just as I walked inside I halted all movements. "Oh, my God," I whispered as I walked closer to the huge bouquet of flowers on my desk. There were so many flowers and colours packed into a single glass vase. I was stunned to silence. I didn't know what to think or do—I just stood and stared.

I didn't know how much time had passed by before I slowly began to make my way over to the breathtaking arrangement on my desk. When I was close enough to do so I leaned in, closed my eyes and inhaled a deep breath.

The scent was divine.

I smiled as I opened my eyes and roamed them over the stems, petals and then to the white envelope that was placed neatly on the side of the bouquet. I reached in and picked the envelope up, then gently opened it. I pulled out the card from inside and read what was written: *Halfway there, Mama Bear.*

Who could have sent these?

Kane.

I don't know why, but he was the first person that came to mind and it made me a little giddy. It only took a few seconds for that giddiness to quickly turn to annoyance. I was annoyed at myself, not necessarily at Kane. He was being very sweet to me lately. He gave me no ammo for arguments so they have been few and far between, but not arguing with him made me mad.

The fact that I *knew* I was starting to *really* like him really bothered me as well. I didn't want to get invested in him in case things went badly between us. I would only end up being hurt.

I just didn't know what else do to or how to act with both of us constantly being civil towards one another. Falling in like with him seemed to be unavoidable.

"You're havin' his baby, you shouldn't want arguments!" I snapped to myself.

I didn't know what the hell was happening to me, but I knew that I didn't like it. I liked Kane's sweet side, and yet I didn't at the same time. I knew how to handle annoyed Kane. I could probably even stand a chance against mad Kane, but sweet Kane, are you kidding me? That was a losing battle.

Was I losing my mind?

Going crazy was the only explanation because any part of me that liked something Kane said or did was just obscene. I couldn't fathom a reality where I could possibly like anything about him or in relation to him. Then again I would have never pegged myself to be knocked up with his child either.

It was official.

I was losing my damn mind.

"Hello?" I called out as I entered the Slater household.

I heard movement upstairs then footsteps as someone descended the stairs.

"Hey, gorgeous."

I rolled my eyes. "Don't bullshit me right now. I'm tired, hungry, and want to sleep."

Kane snorted as he neared me. "You want me to tell everyone to fuck off?"

"No," I laughed. "They're all excited to see the DVD of the baby. If we deprived them of watchin' it, the girls might kill you."

"Why me?"

I smirked. "They can't hurt me, I'm the pregnant one."

"Technicality."

I grinned. "Whatever. I've to wee first, give me five minutes?"

"Why five?"

"If you must know it takes me a minute or two to heave meself up from the toilet."

Kane burst into laughter, "How long will it be before you're calling me to help you up?"

"Never. I'm not weak, I can lift meself up from a bloody toilet… it just takes me a minute or two."

Kane laughed as I walked past him. I adjusted the strap of my bag over my shoulder and sighed as I began to climb the stairs. I hated that there were so many flights of stairs in this house. I hated it even more that Kane's room was on the top bloody floor.

"You could just use the bathroom on the second floor instead of going all the way to the top, you know?"

I rolled my eyes. "I know, but I want to put my slippers on and I left them in your room."

Everyone had slippers belonging to me in their house so I could wear them when I was over. I loved how thoughtful it was and my feet really appreciated it.

"Do you want me to come with you?" Kane asked.

I shook my head. "I'm fine. I'll be back down in a few minutes."

"Okay, shout if you need me."

He went into the sitting room on the second floor while I continued up two more flights of stairs to get to the fourth floor. I noticed that this many stairs would be a hazard to a child and that the entire house would have to be baby proofed.

"More work," I grumbled to myself.

I sighed when I got to the fourth floor and headed into Kane's room. I walked into his en-suite and relieved myself on the toilet. When I was finished, I washed and dried my hands and headed back into his bedroom.

I kicked off my shoes and slid my feet into my fluffy bunny slippers and groaned in pleasure as I did so. They felt like a million tiny kisses on my feet with each step I took in them. They were simply Heaven.

I turned to exit Kane's room, but the sound of a phone ringing halted my movements. I scanned the room and spotted Kane's phone charging on his locker on his side of the bed. I blinked dumbly when I realised my mind automatically put him on the right-hand side of the bed, and made it his spot while I claimed the left.

Brain, we don't live here!

I shook my head clear and walked over to the phone. I glanced at the screen and saw *Damien* flash across the screen. I smiled and picked the phone up. I tapped the screen of the phone and brought it to my ear.

"Welcome to your voicemail inbox, you have one new message. Press one to hear this message."

I went to put Kane's phone down, I really did, but I was curious as to why Damien would leave a voicemail when he could have just rang the other brothers if he wanted to talk. He clearly had something to say for Kane's ears, and the nosey bitch in me wanted to know what it was.

I pressed one on the screen and brought the phone back to my ear.

"Hey, it's me. Look, I don't want you or the others to worry, but I've been keeping tabs on Big Phil and his boys. Before Ryder says anything, I've been keeping them from a *distance*. I was just curious who was running the compound now that Marco is gone. Turns out Big Phil has made himself at home there."

Damien paused when a noise sounded in the background then resumed speaking a moment later.

"Anyway, I swung by when everyone was out and found Manny on watch. Can you believe it? That dude is *still* the worst drunk I've ever come across and he is on guard duty. Fucking idiots."

Damien paused when another noise sounded in the background. I snorted when he said, "Fucking broken window."

He either left the room he was in or moved away from the window; wherever he was now it was quiet. Real quiet.

"So I asked Manny how things have been. He didn't know it was me because I had a hat on and a scarf covering my face. He was kind enough to let on that the new boss was heading to Ireland because Dominic's name resurfaced in the underground. Brandon runs his end in the underground legally now so word has spread that Dominic is his fighter, and if anyone wants to challenge him, it's fifty grand a head. Fifty. Grand. Dominic better be getting a nice pay cheque for that price. Tell him to hit training hard. No doubt those ball busters in the underground will want that purse."

Fucking hell, people had to *pay* to get their arse kicked by Dominic?

I mean, *really*?

Why on earth would anyone want that type of hurt for *free,* let alone pay for it?

People baffled me!

"Be on the lookout and keep lying low. Especially you Kane. Manny said he has some unfinished business with you. I gotta go, my shitty apartment is falling apart. I'll call again later. Bye."

I lowered Kane's phone from my ear and looked at the screen. I didn't move for a couple of minutes as I tried to process what I just heard.

"Hey, what's taking you so long?"

I turned my head to face Kane when he entered his room. He looked at my hand as I lowered my arm to my lap. He had focused on the phone for a few moments before he looked up to my face.

"Who was that?" he asked, taking a step closer to me.

I blinked. "I missed the call, but accidentally entered your voicemail."

Another step forward.

"Who left me a voicemail?"

I licked my lips. "Damien. He was warnin' you and your brothers that he heard someone was comin' to Ireland."

Kane kept his eyes on mine. "Can I have my phone?"

I lifted my arm and held the phone out for him to freely take.

"I've a question."

Kane swallowed as he took his phone from me. "Shoot."

"Who is Big Phil and what business do you have with him?

CHAPTER FOURTEEN

"I don't understand the question."

I stared at Kane. "It's a pretty direct question. Who is Big Phil and what business do you have with him?"

Kane opened his mouth to speak but closed it when no words were spoken.

"Kane?" I pressed. "Why can't you just answer the question?"

He continued to stare at me and after a further silence he parted his lips and said, "Because I don't want you to know who Big Phil is."

I blinked. "Why not?"

"Because you're pure to me and Big Phil taints everything he has involvement in. I don't want to discuss him with anyone, *especially* you. I can't give you a direct answer, so this will have to be good enough."

I hated that his reply made me more curious to know who this Big Phil was. But instead of arguing, I raised my eyebrows and said, "Okay."

Kane licked his lips. "I'm sorry. Please don't be mad at me."

"I'm not," I replied, honestly.

He eyed me, unsure if I was telling him the truth or not. "Really?"

I shrugged. "Kane, you don't have to share every aspect of your life with me. We are just havin' a baby together. We don't need to know one another on a deep personal level."

My reply made him frown, but he said nothing.

"Are you ready to show everyone the DVD?" I asked, hoping to get out of his room and away from the sudden awkwardness and lingering silence.

Kane nodded his head and held his hand out to me and pulled me up to my feet.

"They're all in the living room waiting."

I snorted, "It's so weird you have your sittin' room on the second floor."

He raised his eyebrows at me. "The two most important rooms have to be next to one another, the kitchen and the gym."

I snorted. "*My* two favourite rooms right now are me bedroom and the bathroom. Luckily they're next to each other in me apartment."

"That's only because you pee more than you eat right now."

My stomach rumbled and it caused me to grunt, "Damn you for mentionin' the kitchen."

Kane lightly smiled. "Come on, we'll get you something to eat before we play the DVD."

I was down for that.

"I'll give you your injection, too."

"Great," Kane grumbled.

I walked by Kane and tried to ignore how different he was being. He looked deep in thought, a million miles away even though he was right next to me.

"Are you okay?" I asked as we walked down the stairs.

Kane glanced at me. "Huh? Oh, yeah. I'm fine, babydoll."

I didn't believe him.

Mentioning this Big Phil person changed him.

"Okay," I said, not wanting to the press the issue.

We walked down the stairs side by side, but Kane let me go first into the kitchen. I checked his blood sugar level then gave him his second and final injection of the day. When that was done, I made myself a bowl of cereal because I didn't want to wait around for something to cook. Kane sat and played around with his phone while I ate my food.

I didn't exactly feel awkward, but I did feel a little uneasy. Something was bothering Kane, I could tell. He was avoiding eye contact with me and playing with his phone, his shoulders slumped and his head bowed. He looked like one of my students when they were hiding something from me.

I thought of something to talk about, and my flowers at school quickly entered my mind.

"Thank you for my flowers."

Kane looked at me. "What flowers?"

I frowned. "The flowers I received at school today... you sent them, right?"

Kane shook his head. "No."

I furrowed my eyebrows. "Who sent them then?"

"I have no idea, but it wasn't me."

Huh.

That was weird.

I stood up when I finished my cereal and Kane followed suit. He walked over to the kitchen door and waited for me to put my bowl in the sink. I walked out ahead of him and sighed when I got to the stairs. "I wish there was a lift in this house."

Kane snorted behind me and placed his hands on my hips. "Let's go, babydoll."

I huffed and puffed up the stairs and sighed in relief when I got to the second floor and headed for the sitting room. Kane was still behind me, but his hands were no longer on my hips. I kind of missed his touch, but I forced myself to believe that was because he gave me a boost and made moving around easier.

That was my story and I was sticking to it.

"Finally!" Bronagh stated when Kane and I entered the room.

I held up my hands. "Sorry, I was hungry."

Bronagh waved me off. "Play the DVD. I wanna see me niece."

"Nephew," Nico mumbled.

I rolled my eyes at him and picked up the remote to the television. "Is the disc loaded?"

"*Duh*," Bronagh and Alannah said in unison before they high-fived.

I snorted and hit play. I walked over to the largest settee in the room and sat down next to Kane, who apparently had the spot saved for me.

"It's a boy!" Nico stated proudly six or seven minutes into the DVD.

I rolled my eyes. "We don't know the gender so pipe down, you."

"I can *see* that the baby is Slater boy," Nico cheered, ignoring me.

I pulled a face and looked at the television and instantly laughed when I saw what he saw. "That is a *leg*, not a penis, you freak."

"Whatever. It's a boy. I can tell."

Everyone laughed at Nico.

Bronagh looked at her sister. "Do you know what the gender is?"

Branna tilted her head as she looked at the screen. "Not from this video. The legs are crossed so it's too hard for me to tell. Then again, I'm a midwife, not an ultrasound technician."

I was glad she couldn't tell because I really wanted the gender to be a surprise at the birth. It made everything more exciting for me, and hopefully for Kane.

"How cool would it be if you were on a shift when I go into labour." I smiled to Branna.

Branna squealed, "I'll swap patients to make sure I have you in me care."

I leaned over and high-fived her. "I'm holdin' you to that."

We sat back then and watched the rest of the DVD, which was just the most amazing thing ever. The girls awed when the baby's four-dimensional face came on screen, and the lads smiled when the heartbeat played.

"This child is goin' to be *so* spoiled," Alannah commented as she stared at the screen.

I snorted, "You're tellin' me. Me brothers are already fightin' over which football team she will support."

"He," Kane murmured.

I looked at him and glared. "Stop that."

He smiled. "Can't help it, feels like 'he' is the right thing to say."

"Bro. Yes. We're on the same wavelength." Nico beamed.

I rolled my eyes at the brothers and smiled as I looked around the room. I felt happy and content with how everything was turning out for me. I was no longer terrified of having this baby. Sure I was scared, but I was also excited now, and so was everyone else.

I jumped when Dominic's phone rang. I glanced at him when he dug his phone from his pocket and looked at the screen. He smiled wide.

"Damien is FaceTiming me."

I squealed, "Answer it so he can see the video too."

Dominic tapped on the screen of his phone.

"Dominic," Damien's voice chirped. "What's up, man?"

I loved how Damien spoke like he hadn't spoken to Dominic in a long time even though they spoke every day. He always got really excited, just like Dominic did—it was beautiful to watch.

"Watching the DVD of Kane's baby. Look," Dominic said and stood up from his seated position. He tapped on the screen of his phone and aimed it at the sixty-inch plasma screen in front of us.

"Can you see?" Dominic asked.

How could he not?

The screen was sixty bloody inches wide.

Not a second later Damien said, "It's a boy!"

Us females groaned, while the males cheered.

"He's right," Kane smirked. "Us men know what we're talking

about."

I rolled my eyes. "*She* will not like being called a lad you know."

"Let me see Aideen," Damien asked Dominic.

Dominic pointed his phone at me so I smiled and waved. "Heya, cutie."

Kane put his arm around my shoulder and tugged me into him. "Really?"

I laughed and so did the girls.

"Do you remember on movin' day you said Damien could be your f—"

"Friend," I cut Bronagh off. "Me best *friend*."

Keela snickered to herself and it caused me to glare at her.

"Right," Bronagh laughed. "Your *friend*."

I shook my head at her and looked at Kane when I felt his eyes on me.

"Don't look at me like that, I didn't say anythin' about him. I swear."

Kane didn't believe me, I could tell by the look on his face.

"Stand up, *friend*," Damien laughed. "I want to see you. Do you have a baby bump yet?"

I nodded and leaned onto Kane's arm as I got up off the chair. I flattened my t-shirt to my stomach, but it was black so didn't really look like I had a bump from the front. I lifted my t-shirt up, tucked it under my breasts and turned to the side.

"Can you see?" I asked Damien.

He whistled. "You've gotten so much bigger since a few weeks ago."

I frowned. "I know. I gain like four pounds a week. You and your brothers apparently produce hungry children."

The brothers high-fived which just caused me to shake my head.

"Okay, he's seen your stomach. You can you pull your t-shirt down now," Kane's voice grunted.

I looked at the girls before I looked at him and saw all of them smirk and grin to themselves like a bunch of weirdos. I looked at Kane who was glaring at his brothers who were all openly looking at me with sneaky smiles that I knew were just to piss Kane off.

"I want to feel it," Dominic said and stepped forward, flattening his hand over my bare belly. "Wow. It's really hard, now."

I nodded and pulled a face at Dominic's phone because it was directly in my face. Damien laughed as he got an up close and personal view of my face.

I laughed when Kane got to his feet and Dominic jumped back. "I'm just playing," he swore.

Kane glared at him, the muscles in his jaw working.

I sighed, "You really aren't going to let them feel *their niece* as she grows?"

Kane didn't look at me, as he said, "No, that's just for me."

The girls awed while the brothers cursed and argued they would feel my belly whenever they wanted because it was their right as uncles. That made me chuckle.

"Just pull your tee down, babydoll."

To avoid an argument, and because I strangely liked him wanting me covered up in front of people, I pulled my top down and sat back down in my seat. I leaned into him when he sat down.

"Are you two dating?" Damien asked.

I looked at the phone, even though Kane's gaze was on me. "We're friends."

"Friends or *friends*?" Damien asked making Dominic snort.

I blinked. "Is there a difference?"

"Yes," everyone in the room said in unison.

I looked around at them, and then looked at Kane. "Are we friends or *friends*?" I asked.

He smirked. "I'm aiming for *friends*."

Why did they keep saying it so weird?

"Okay, we're *friends* then."

Bronagh hooted while everyone else laughed.

I frowned and looked at Kane. "What is so funny? What am I

missin'?"

He smiled and kissed my cheek. "I'll tell you later."

"This is weird," Damien muttered. "I'm not used to seeing them so... civil."

"It's been like this for a while now," Alannah said then shrunk into Bronagh's side when Dominic turned his phone in her direction so Damien could see her.

"Hey, Lana," he said, his voice a little tight.

Alannah cleared her throat and nodded. "Damien."

I could feel the sudden awkwardness in the room.

"How are you?" Damien asked.

Alannah flushed a little. "I'm good, thanks. You?"

Damien was silent for a moment and said, "I'm okay."

Things were silent again until Alannah stood up and said, "I've got to get goin'. Call you later, Bronagh."

Bronagh sighed, "Alannah."

Alannah was already out of the sitting room and halfway down the stairs of the house though. From the sounds of things, she was running down the steps at full speed.

"Damien," Dominic murmured.

"It's fine," Damien replied. "I deserve it."

I frowned. "Deserve what?" I whispered to Kane.

"I'll tell you later," he whispered back.

I nodded my head and looked back to Dominic's phone.

"She looks incredible," Damien murmured.

Bronagh sat up straight. "She's single, too. Come home and rectify that."

Damien's laugh was genuine, "I'll be home soon."

We all held our breath.

"*Our* soon, or *your* soon?" Dominic asked.

Damien laughed again. "*Your* soon. I have to finish three more months on my current contract here at work to get a big bonus at Christmas. It'll be triple my current salary so I'll stay for that, then I'll be back. The bonus will hold me over until I get a job somewhere in Dublin."

We were all silent, except for Dominic.

"If you're joking, I'm going to fly over there and fucking kill you."

Damien chuckled, "I'm not, bro. I've been staying away to figure out the shit inside my head. I've made peace with most of it, but I have to come back to fix the rest of it."

Alannah.

I didn't know their history, but I was sure he was talking about Alannah.

"When did you decide this?" Ryder asked his little brother.

"I've been thinking about it for a long time, but decided to do it about two minutes ago."

Yep, definitely Alannah.

I blinked. "You'll be here to see the baby born!"

Kane leaned against me. "I'm so happy you'll be here for it, bro."

"Me too," Damien replied.

Bronagh burst into tears and that instantly set me off.

"You bastard," Alec snapped. "You're making them cry."

"You're just mad because you know Keela will question why she is with you when she sees me in person."

Dominic burst into laughter while Alec glared at the phone with a smirk on his face.

"Trust me, blondie, my girl is going nowhere."

Damien snorted, "We'll see."

I turned to Kane and placed my face right against his neck. He instantly wrapped me up in his arms and pulled me onto his lap. I closed my eyes and rested against him. I was so happy Damien was coming home, and I knew how happy Kane and the others were too. This meant everything to the brothers.

"Kane is taking full advantage of this emotional news," Ryder commented, dryly.

Kane lifted a hand off me; the lads laughed a few seconds later, then his hand returned back to me. He stroked up and down my back. It calmed me, but also made me ridiculously tired.

"I'm goin' to fall asleep," I murmured after a few minutes of his back rub.

Kane's body vibrated as he chuckled. "Come up to my room."

I growled.

He laughed, "Just to nap. Promise."

Damn right it was just to nap.

"Okay," I sighed and pushed myself to my feet. "Bye Damien."

"Bye, gorgeous. Bye, bro... Have fun being *friends*."

I didn't know what he was talking about, but I was sure it was a sexual reference so I gave Damien the finger as I walked away, making Kane laugh as he placed his hands on my hips and followed me. He continued to laugh as he pushed against me in order to get me up the stairs. I had one eye open just to watch the steps I took. I was tired before we sat down to watch the DVD, but now that I had a little cry and closed my eyes on Kane, I was absolutely drained.

We made it into Kane's room and I kicked off my slippers as he pulled back the covers for me. I fell sideways onto the bed and sighed.

"I want your bed," I murmured as I snuggled deeper into the pillow and massive mattress I was lying on.

Kane chuckled as he climbed onto the bed and lay next to me. He was on top of the covers while I was underneath them. "What's mine is yours."

I snorted, "That only works if we were married."

"You're having my kid, you own my balls for the next few years. We might as well be married."

I kept my eyes closed as I snickered.

"Don't let me fall asleep," I said after a yawn.

Kane was silent for a moment then said, "Why not?"

I wanted to say because it was wrong for us to sleep in the same bed, but somehow saying it would feel like a lie. In all honestly, I would happily sleep in the same bed as Kane. It was my willingness to do so that was the cause of my hesitation. My willingness for all things Kane was becoming a big bloody problem for me.

"Because I don't want to ruin a night's sleep for you," I eventually said. "I'm restless durin' the night now."

Kane scoffed, "Babydoll, go to sleep. We're having a sleepover tonight."

My belly burst into butterflies.

I opened my eyes. "Are you sure?"

Kane was already on his side looking at me. "Yes, I'm sure. Why wouldn't I be sure?"

I shrugged. "I thought it might be weird, us sleeping in this bed together when the last time that happened I got pregnant."

"Huh. I never thought about that." Kane blinked then smirked. "Think of it this way then—if we fuck this time, we don't have to worry about you getting pregnant because you're already knocked up."

I forced myself to keep a straight face and not laugh.

"If I wasn't so tired, I'd smack you."

Kane grinned. "I'm glad you're tired then."

I closed my eyes and smiled. "I'll get you tomorrow."

Kane hummed, "Go to sleep, my babydoll."

His babydoll.

His.

The last thing I remembered before falling into darkness was that being Kane's wouldn't be the worst thing in the world. Not being his would be.

CHAPTER FIFTEEN

"Aideen?"

I looked to my right and smiled to Ryder as he entered the kitchen. "Mornin'."

He returned a smile. "*Early* morning, it's six in the morning. Why are you awake?"

I chuckled, "I fell asleep real early yesterday and didn't budge all night. I woke up at four and was wide-awake so I came down here for some tea. Do you want a cuppa?"

Ryder nodded his head. "Sure, light on the milk and one sugar, please."

I got up from my seat and moved over to the kettle. It was already refilled so I pressed the button on the base to re-start the boiling process.

"So, you slept in Kane's bed last night?" Ryder mused. "How was that?"

I turned around. "Very comfortable."

Ryder laughed.

I looked down my feet then back up to Ryder. "I've been down here awhile and I've done some thinkin'."

Ryder bit his lower lip. "Uh-oh. Should I be worried?"

I snorted. "No... well, maybe."

He sighed, "Lay it on me, mama."

I grinned. "So you know I live in a small apartment, and that Kane has been askin' me to move in here, right?"

Ryder nodded his head. "Are you thinking of accepting his offer? We'd be more than happy to have you here, sweetie."

I smiled. "I know you would, but no, I'm not goin' to move in here. But I *am* goin' to move someplace else. Some place bigger than my current apartment."

Ryder blew out a breath. "Kane won't like that."

Which is why I was worried.

"I know," I admitted, "it's why I need your help."

"*My* help?" Ryder asked. "Why would you need my help?"

I shrugged. "I need you to help me brainstorm. Kane thinks we're gettin' on famously right now, and we are, but Ry, we *did* hate each other at one point. I don't want to move in and have everythin' fall apart. Am I crazy for wanting stability?"

"No," Ryder instantly replied. "You're right on all counts, but I also understand where Kane is coming from. Out of the five of us, he really doesn't understand people. He steers clear of them if he can, but now that he has you in his life, he wants to steer you away from them too. Living with him gives him the control he wants, but since you *aren't* together, it's probably best that you find a different place other than here. He is getting too comfortable with you... or rather the idea of you."

I nodded my head. "I think I should involve him somehow though just so he feels like he is part of the decision. What do you think?"

Ryder mulled it over for a few seconds. "I like it, it will give him peace of mind."

"I agree," I said then blew out a big breath. "I'll bring him apartment huntin' with me."

"Sounds like a plan."

I nodded my head. "Let's just hope it's a good one."

Ryder smiled. "Trust me, Kane will be good at apartment hunting. Everything will be fine."

"This comin' from the man who is on anythin' but fine terms with his missus."

Ryder's face hardened. "We're just going through a rough patch, it'll get better."

He didn't sound like he believed his own statement though.

I raised my eyebrows. "Your rough patch has been goin' on awhile. Are you sure everythin' is okay with you and Branna?"

Ryder stared at me for a long moment then in a lowered voice he said, "No, I'm not sure everything is okay with Branna."

Fuck.

"Don't tell me you're both gonna break up?" I asked and held my breath.

Ryder lifted his hand and rubbed his face before dropping it back down. "I don't know, Aideen. I'm not sure about anything right now when it comes to us. All I know is we're fighting a hell of a lot. It's more than childish arguments, it's just... anger. Pure anger. We can't be in the same room longer than ten minutes without someone blowing up."

I swallowed. "You're both stressed with Kane bein' ill—"

"It's been going on for months now."

Oh.

"I didn't think it was this serious."

Ryder nodded his head. "It's bad. We don't even have sex anymore, and I can't remember the last time I kissed her just because I wanted to."

Shite.

"There... there isn't anyone else, is there?" I asked, my stomach rolling as the words left my mouth.

Please say no.

"No," Ryder replied. "Nothing like that. We're just growing apart I think."

I felt a lump rise in my throat.

"You have to talk to her about this."

He nodded his head. "I know. I'm just going to wait awhile to see if things change."

"It won't change if you both don't make changes—it needs to be discussed. Now."

Ryder held up his hands. "I will, eventually, I promise. I just have a lot going on right now."

He did?

"Like what?" I asked.

Ryder smirked. "Never you mind."

Oh, he was up to something.

"Why are you up and dressed this early in the mornin'?" I asked, narrowing my eyes at him suspiciously.

He snickered, "I've got to go and take care of some business, nosey."

I feigned offence. "I'm not nosey."

"Sure you aren't."

I grunted and Ryder smiled.

"Promise me you'll keep our conversation between us, okay?"

I groaned, "You're askin' me to withhold information from me oldest friend?"

"Yes, to keep her from unnecessary hurt."

Bastard.

"Okay, fine," I sighed. "I'll keep me mouth shut."

Ryder winked. "Later, mama."

The kettle boiled just as Ryder walked out of the kitchen. I told Ryder I wasn't nosey, but I really was. I followed him down the hallway and looked out the small window next to the door to see where he was going. I raised my eyebrows when I saw him climb into a Jeep. Nico's Jeep. I could see Nico in the driver's seat, he laughed at something Ryder said then drove off seconds later.

Where the hell were they going at six in the morning?

I turned around and walked back into the kitchen feeling puzzled. I didn't like when people kept secrets, especially when I wasn't in on what the secret was. Kane was hiding something about a person called Big Phil, and Ryder and Nico were going places at six in the morning in normal clothes, not workout gear.

Hmmmm.

I shook my head and walked over to the kettle and made myself another cup of tea and chuckled to myself.

Maybe Ryder was right; I *was* nosey.

I woke Kane when I climbed into bed next to him three hours later. I was sat upright eating some cereal from a bowl that I balanced on my belly. He opened one eye, smiled at me, and rolled onto his back.

"That's a pretty sight to wake up to in the morning."

I glanced at him and snorted, "Yeah, I'm a real catch."

I flicked on Kane's television and turned on Netflix. "More of the *Sons*?"

Kane stretched, sat upright and nodded his head.

He had that just-awake-fuck-me-now bedhead that did things to my vagina and I just wasn't happy about it.

"Have you been awake long?"

I shrugged. "About five hours."

"Five *hours*?" Kane asked with wide eyes. "Why didn't you wake me?"

I glanced at him then back to the television. "Because I woke up at four in the mornin'."

"So?" Kane clicked his tongue. "You should have woke me."

I rolled my eyes. "I was fine. I went downstairs, had a lot of tea, some food, then more tea and some more food. Then I came up here. No big deal."

Kane grunted, "Just wake me in the future."

"In the future?" I laughed. "How frequent do you think these sleepovers will be?"

Kane moved closer to me. "I'm hoping frequently."

I swallowed. "Kane..."

"I feel better with you here, so humour me and stay with me awhile."

I looked at him and raised my eyebrow. "How long is awhile?"

He smirked. "How long have you got?"

"All day. It's Saturday."

"All day then."

I raised my eyebrow. "Is this like a bondin' exercise?"

"Yes." Kane replied, his lip twitching.

I laughed, "Okay. As long as I don't have to move I'm cool with bondin' time."

Kane grinned at me then turned his attention to the television. Five minutes later I finished off my cereal. I placed my now empty bowl on Kane's locker next to me and shimmied lower while pulling the blankets over my body. I groaned when I discovered it wasn't a comfortable position to watch the telly in.

"What's wrong?" Kane asked.

I didn't reply. Instead, I tested out a few different positions and settled on lying on my side. My pillow was too soft to prop my head up to so I looked at Kane and said, "Can I lie my head on your chest so I can see the telly?"

Kane gestured to himself. "Use my body as you see fit, baby-doll."

I snorted as I placed my head on his bare chest and cocked my leg over his. There. That was better. *Much* better.

"Are you comfortable?" Kane asked.

"Uh huh."

"Good... but just so you're aware, you *are* lying on me, and your leg is pressed against my dick. I can't control it if it gets hard, okay?"

I laughed, "Okay."

"I'm serious, I don't want you to freak out on me."

I placed my hand on his faint, but still visible abs—they were becoming more visible now that he was working out again.

"I'm too comfortable to freak out, sweetie."

Kane's body relaxed. "That's good to know."

I shushed him, "Jax is on the telly. Close your mouth."

Kane grumbled to himself about Jax Teller, but did as I asked and shut up. We stayed quiet and wrapped around one another for two episodes. Kane had to move when the urge to go to the toilet became too much for him.

"I'll be right back."

I waved him on. "Go get yourself food and what not. I'm not goin' anywhere, Kane."

"Promise?"

Damn it.

"I promise."

He left the room looking like a happy camper, but I knew that would change when I would eventually tell him that I was going to look for a new apartment instead of moving in with him. I just hoped including him in my search for a new apartment would appease him, because if it didn't, things would get bad between us real fast.

I didn't want to take two steps back into the past with Kane—we were getting along so well now. I wanted to look into the future because, whether I wanted it or not, that future now included him.

CHAPTER SIXTEEN

"Whatever it is that you have to say, say it already. Your constant glances my way are starting to bug me."

I stared at Kane wide-eyed. I didn't think he caught my not so subtle glances every thirty-seconds. After he went to the toilet and got some food, I gave him his morning injection of insulin. Since we came back up to his room, I would nervously look at him every few seconds. Each time I looked at him I planned to tell him my housing plan, but I bottled it at the last second because I was a big chicken shit.

I quickly looked straight ahead when he called me out and pretended I didn't hear him.

He laughed, "Aideen?"

Play it cool.

"Hmmm?"

He reached over, put his fingers against my cheek and turned my head until I was looking at him.

I gave Kane a big toothy smile as I said, "Hi."

"Hello," he chuckled.

"What's up?" I questioned.

He lifted his hands to his face and rubbed his eyes. "Please stop, I don't want to laugh right now. I want to talk."

I forced a giggle, "About boys, nails, or make-up?"

Kane belly laughed, and it made me beam.

I loved his laugh... and I hated myself because of it. I truly liked him now, and there was nothing I could do about it. I had to try my best to get rid of those feelings and stop them from developing into something like *love* because it could have disastrous results for us—or me—if it went badly.

"Be serious, babydoll. Say whatever it is that's on your mind."

I sighed when I realised he wasn't going to drop the subject.

"I'm tryin' to figure out how to tell you, either way you won't be happy with what I have to say."

Kane sat upright. "You're okay? The baby?"

"Yes." I blinked. "Nothin' is wrong with anyone, we're all good."

Kane relaxed. "What's the problem then?"

I groaned. "Promise you won't be mad."

"How can I promise when I don't know what you're going to—"

"Just promise."

Kane grunted in annoyance. "Fine. I promise. Now, tell me."

I looked away from him, closed my eyes and in one big breath I said, "I'm movin' out of me apartment, and findin' somewhere bigger. Somewhere close by."

I pushed aside the urge to cover my face when I was met with silence. I sighed and opened my eyes. I looked at Kane and found him staring at me.

"I thought we were getting along so well."

"We are," I assured him with a bobbing nod. "That's *exactly* why I shouldn't move in here. I don't want to jinx the friendship we're buildin'. Things are so good between us right now... I don't want to ruin that."

Kane looked away from and nodded his head in understanding. "Okay, Aideen."

Crap.

"Please don't be mad at me, I really want you on board with

this. I need your help."

That regained his attention. "My help with *what*?"

"Findin' an apartment, of course. I want your input since *your* child will be livin' there."

Please feel involved.

Kane raised an eyebrow. "You want my input on an apartment?"

I nodded my head. "Of course."

Kane was silent as he studied my face. "Okay, fine. I'll help you search for an apartment, but on one condition."

I didn't like the sound of that.

"What's the condition?"

"If we both don't agree on an apartment that is suitable for you *and* the baby, then you move in here."

I narrowed my eyes. "You're tryin' to trick me."

"I am not."

"You are too!"

Kane raised his hands in the air. "I'm offended you'd even suggest I would trick you. Moving apartments is a huge deal. I wouldn't play around."

I growled, "You can't bullshit a bullshitter, Kane. I know you like the back of me hand; you'll just say no to every apartment we view so that I'll *have* to move in here."

"That's completely false," Kane chirped. "I don't have any ill will towards you. You're my *friend* so I will help you just like you want me to."

I was *so* onto him.

He looked as innocent as a child with their hand in a cookie jar, and even though he *did* sound like he was on point with not trying to trick me, his little speech didn't fool me. Something was cooking in his twisted mind, something evil. I knew him well enough to know he wasn't giving in to my decision without a fight.

I held out my pinky finger, and the action caused Kane to beam at me.

"You *swear* you won't say no to an apartment just to see me move in here?"

"A pinky promise, are you kidding?"

"No."

"Damn, I could eat you up, babydoll. You're too cute."

I growled, "Swear."

Kane smirked as he latched his pinky finger around mine. "I swear."

I held his gaze. "You pinky swore, and you can't go back on a pinky promise... it's the law."

Kane winked at me. "I wouldn't dream of it, babydoll."

I gnawed on the inside of my cheek so that I wouldn't curse at him.

"So," Kane smiled, "when are we going apartment hunting? I'll arrange everything, just give me a day."

He suddenly seemed delighted with the idea of apartment hunting which only fuelled my suspicions that he was up to no good. He really wasn't doing himself any favours.

"Monday. Me class is out on a school trip all week and because it's to do with hikin', I don't have to attend. We can go check out places then. Is that okay?"

Kane thought for a moment then he said, "Yeah, I can do Monday."

I snorted, "You said that like you would be switchin' somethin' else out so you could come with me."

"I will be."

"What were you goin' to be doin' on Monday?" I asked, quizzically.

Kane shrugged his large shoulders. "I had a little business to attend to at the club in town, but I'll push it to Tuesday."

The club?

I sat upright and narrowed my eyes. "If you're talkin' about doing bad things in Darkness, I'm goin' to be unbelievably mad at you."

Kane scrunched up his face. "What are you talking about?"

I grunted, "I'm not stupid, Kane. I remember good and well what I saw in Darkness the night we had sex. I just haven't brought it up since then because it was your business and not mine."

Kane tilted his head. "Is it not still my business?"

His playfulness was gone, and serious Kane was rearing his angry head.

"Yeah, it is, but I'm a lot closer to you now so—"

"So nothing, Aideen," he cut me off, his tone firm. "My business is my own. If I want your opinion on something, I'll ask for it."

I reared back at little, not liking being talked down to by him.

"You wanna take your own bloody advice then because you've been stickin' *your* nose into *my* business since you found out I was pregnant."

"So?"

So?

"What the fuck do you mean so?"

"I mean so." Kane shrugged, uncaringly. "You're the one who is pregnant, not me. If I butt into your life, it's because I want to make sure you're okay. You're carrying my child. Call me crazy for caring about you."

I felt my temperature begin rise.

"You do realise the double standards you're settin' right now, don't you?"

Kane laid back and sighed, "No, but I'm sure you're going to explain them to me anyway."

Right, he was.

"What gives you the right to pick apart everythin' I do, but when I bring up some shady shite you do, I get shut down by big, bad Kane."

"Big, bad Kane?" Kane repeated the corner of his lip quirked.

"It was that or pig-headed, arsehole Kane. Take your pick."

Kane humourlessly laughed, "Don't stop now, babydoll. Tell me how you really feel."

I itched to smack the stupid smug look off his face, and I would have only I didn't want to get arsehole all over my hand.

"You know what you can do?" I bellowed.

"I'm going to guess something unpleasant."

Oh, my God!

"Go and fuck yourself, you fuckin' wanker."

Kane laughed, "That doesn't sound unpleasant all, hit me with something else."

As you wish.

I turned and grabbed the battery-operated alarm clock on the locker next to me, then turned and smacked Kane right in the chest with it.

"Take that, you tick tockin' prick!"

Kane grunted and hissed for about a second, then he laughed. And he laughed hard. It infuriated me. I angrily pushed his bed covers off me and got off the bed. I didn't get up as swiftly as I wanted too, but I got up, and that was the important thing.

"Where are you going?" Kane asked through his stupid laughter.

I stuck my middle finger up at him then turned and stormed out of his room. I briskly walked down the hallway towards the stairs and speed it up to a light jog when I heard Kane's footsteps coming after me.

"Slow down, Aideen," he said as I began to descend the stairs.

He wasn't laughing anymore.

"Don't tell me what to do!" I snapped and continued to storm down the stairs.

Kane grunted from behind me. "You'll fall—"

"I won't fall!" I snapped. "I can still fuckin' *see* where I'm goin'!"

I got to the second floor but before I could walk down to the first floor Kane jumped in front of me. His hands were raised in front of his chest, and he had no trace of a smile on his face.

"Just calm down."

I shook with anger.

"I *am* calm," I spat. "I'm perfectly bloody calm; now fuck off away from me."

Kane lowered his hands to my shoulders, but I slapped them away.

"Ow!"

I growled, "Good. I hope it hurts."

That brought back Kane's silly smile.

"Stop smilin' at me; I'm *not* playin'."

I moved around him then and walked down the rest of the stairs.

"What's all the shouting about?" Nico's voice shouted from the gym room.

He came home about after hour after he left with Ryder. I asked where he went, but he told me to mind my own business.

The fucker.

I walked into the gym room and walked directly over to Nico, who was lifting weights that were bigger than my head. "I'll give you fifty Euros if you punch Kane in the face for me."

Nico laughed at me then looked over my shoulder. "What did you do? Bitch about not getting laid?"

"The only bitching that occurred was entirely done by Aideen—not me... And the last time I had sex, I got her pregnant, so I'm taking a well-deserved break."

Nico laughed at Kane, but I didn't.

"I'm a nice person so if I'm a bitch to you, you need to ask yourself why."

"Because I'm an easy target?"

I looked at the red mark on his chest and smirked. "Clearly."

"What happened to your chest?" Nico asked his older brother when he saw me staring at it.

Kane shrugged. "She threw a clock at me."

Nico looked at me with raised eyebrows and I suddenly felt the need to defend myself.

"He told me to hit him."

"I meant with your words, you little smartass."

Little smartass? The fucking nerve of him!

"I'm leavin'. I'll smash a weight over your head if I stay here any longer."

Kane moved away from the doorframe and zeroed in on me. In the blink of an eye, he was in front of me and all up in my personal space. He was so close to me that his belly touched mine.

"Like you could lift one of those weights." He smirked.

My left eye twitched as my mind accepted his challenge.

"Watch me!"

I turned and stomped over to Nico, who was standing in front of the rack that carried all the weights.

"Step aside, son, Mama's gotta put an arsehole in his place."

Nico smiled wide at me, his dimples creasing his cheeks. "No can do, *Mama*, you'll hurt yourself."

Oh, no, not Nico, too.

"But I'm strong!"

Nico held my gaze. "Damn right you are, but these weights are pretty heavy, and I don't want to put any extra strain on you... what if your back starts to hurt more than it already does or you pull an abdominal muscle?"

I gasped.

I didn't think of my back or my belly.

"Well... my back already hurts at night, I wouldn't wanna make it hurt durin' the day either."

Nico nodded his head. "Exactly, why hurt yourself just to prove a bitch wrong?"

"Hey!"

I smirked at said bitch's objection.

"You're right. You are *so* right."

Nico opened his arms. "Give me a squeeze."

I snorted and stepped into his embrace then screeched. "You're soakin'!"

"My bad," Nico laughed and released me but not before giving me a big wet kiss on the cheek and, of course, a quick belly rub.

He had a thing for my pregnant belly; every time he passed me by, he would give my stomach a quick rub. It was like his own little way of saying hello to the baby. It was adorable. And the fact that it bothered Kane made me love it more.

"Are you done?" Kane asked from behind me.

"With you?" I questioned as I turned to face him. "Yes."

Kane tensed. "What does that mean?"

"It means that I've seen enough of your face today and have had more than enough of your dicky attitude. I wanna go home."

I hated that Kane frowned, and I hated that a stupid frown made me instantly feel guilty.

"Don't look at me like that."

Kane flicked his eyes over my shoulder then looked back to me and frowned deeper.

"Kane."

He batted his eyes at me.

"Mother of God!" I gasped. "Don't you dare try to woo me with your eyes. I know wooin' when I see it."

I had my eyes narrowed, and when Kane's eyes flicked over my shoulder, I quickly turned around and caught Nico frowning and pouting. He stopped both when he saw I caught him.

"Sup?" he nodded and smiled.

I looked over my shoulder to Kane, who was shaking his head and smiling before I looked back to Nico and pointed my finger at him. "Am I the subject of a Man Bible lesson right now?"

"I have no idea what you're talking about," Nico said and lifted his chin.

Yeah, right.

"Don't bullshit me, kid."

Nico grinned at me but said nothing.

I put my face in my hands and groaned, "I'm not able to deal with both of you today."

I felt hands on my hips. "So come back to bed and just deal with me."

"My man," Nico whooped.

I growled, and it shut his happy arse up.

"Come on, babydoll. I promise we won't argue anymore, at least until you have the strength for it."

I laughed even though I didn't want to. I wanted to remain mad at him because I knew he was up to something that was bad.

What I saw Kane partake in Darkness all those weeks ago shook me up. I wanted to believe he was a good person, but I just didn't fully trust that he was. I knew he cared about me and the baby, but outside of our little circle he was clearly involved in things that I wanted no part in. I was connected to him so whatever he was into, I had a connection to it too, whether he liked it or not.

I hoped I was just paranoid, and it's why I let Kane lead me back up to his room. I told myself that whatever he was into really was his own business and that he wouldn't be involved in it if it would put me, or our baby, in danger. I just hoped trusting in that didn't prove futile.

I heard male voices laugh from downstairs as I entered Kane's room, and I smiled to myself. Alec and Ryder were here. I was smiling to myself as Kane jumped onto his bed and patted the spot next to him. I stopped short of the bed and said, "I'm hungry."

Kane deadpanned, "You couldn't have said that when we were next to the kitchen?"

I made a motion to stick my finger up at Kane, but I moved my hand too fast and hit it off his bedpost. It sent pain shooting up my finger and caused me to scream bloody murder.

"Oh God! I broke a nail!"

"No!" Kane cried.

Multiple footsteps pounded up the stairs, down the hallway and then three bodies burst into Kane's bedroom. "What?" all of his brothers hollered as they piled through the doorway.

Kane pointed a trembling hand at me. "Her nail! She broke her *nail!*"

With a perplexed look, I looked at Kane then to the brothers who all gasped and flung their hands over their mouths. They all gripped onto furniture, or onto one another to stay upright.

I was so confused. I had no fucking idea what was going on. None.

"Your *nail*?" Alec screeched.

Nico placed his hands on the side of his head and shook it from side to side. "Anything but your *nail*!"

Ryder rushed over to me and grabbed the hand I was cradling and thoroughly examined it, and when he saw confirmation that my nail was gone, he whimpered. "It's gone. Gone *forever*!"

"No!" Kane wailed, fell back to his bed, and flung his arms over his face. "Why did it have to be her nail? Why, God? *Why?!*"

I glared at Kane, then his brothers when I realised what was happening. The bastards were taking the piss out of my broken nail.

"I hate you all," I said then turned walked out of the room and headed for the kitchen because even though I was still in *a lot* of pain, I was also very hungry.

I had made it halfway down the stairs before I heard the eruption of belly rumbling male laughter. Even though it pleased me greatly that they were smiling together, I hated that it was at my expense.

"Bloody brothers."

CHAPTER SEVENTEEN

"**A**re you excited?"

I looked at Kane when he asked the same question for the tenth time in two hours. I shrugged my shoulders and looked out his car window. "I guess so, I'm just nervous. I mean... this woman you contacted *is* a legit realtor, right?"

It was Monday, and Kane and myself were on our way to view a few apartments. We had a total of five to check out. Kane contacted a friend of his on Saturday and got the number to a realtor that would help us on such short notice.

"Of course," Kane said, offended. "You think I'd hire someone to show us crappy apartments?"

Yes.

"I *would* think that. It wouldn't be above you to stoop that low in order for me to live with you."

"I haven't stooped to any level. This chick is the real deal. She works for Upton Realtors, and Upton is a... wealthy area, so they would only produce the best. "

I didn't know why, but Kane's enthusiasm didn't give me much encouragement.

"Okay, I just want to find somewhere that's good for me and the baby. You told her two bedroom apartments, right? Oh, and that my budget was fourteen hundred a month?"

Kane lifted a hand off the steering wheel and scratched his neck before returning it to the wheel. "I gave her a budget of twenty-five hundred a month."

I must have heard that wrong.

"Twenty-five hundred," I repeated.

"Well, yeah."

"Twenty-five fuckin' hundred?"

"Don't hit me, I'm driving!" Kane quickly said and glanced at me—well, at my hands.

I wasn't planning on hitting the idiot, but it was nice to see he thought I was some crazy lady who would smack him going eight kilometres an hour down the bypass.

Dickhead.

"You're *lucky* you're drivin'!" I angrily spat. "Why on earth would you say twenty-five hundred? That is me monthly salary, Kane! How can I afford me utility bills, food, and all the things I'll need for the baby if me entire paycheque goes on fuckin' rent?"

Kane sighed, "Because I'm paying half of your rent."

Come again?

I stared at him. "Excuse me?"

"I knew you wouldn't let me pay for it all, so I decided I would pay half."

"You decided, huh?" I hissed. "You just *decided* that you would pay half me rent without even *askin'* me?"

"Consider it half of my monthly child support payment, the other half will be to help you buy things the baby needs."

I placed my fingers against my temples as a profound pounding began to pulse away.

"Come on, Aideen," Kane sighed. "A two bedroom apartment for anything less that twenty-five hundred around our area will be shitty and we both know it. You said you wanted to be close by, and since I live in Upton, we needed to up the price."

I knew what he was saying was true, but I was deeply bothered that he just decided something that directly involved my life without even consulting me. It wasn't okay.

"Fine," I muttered and looked out the window once more.

Kane's sigh was deep, and long.

"You're mad."

"You're a genius."

Kane grunted and closed his mouth for the remaining ten-minute journey to the first apartment location. It was fifteen minutes away from Upton in a bigger estate area called Ballycash. It was a rough area and I already knew it would be a no from me when I stepped out of Kane's Jeep.

There was a dead cat on the path across from us and it turned my stomach. I glared at Kane as he walked around the car to me. "This estate, really?"

Kane held up his hands. "With the notice I gave her, Cala said she could round up five apartments to show us. I just told her I wanted it to be close to Upton. I didn't pick this area."

Ballycash was the complete opposite of Upton so I didn't doubt Kane had involvement with the location. He wouldn't live here even if you paid him to, so no way in hell would he want his child living here.

"Who is Cala?" I asked as I made sure to keep my eyes averted from the cat.

"The realtor."

I raised my eyebrow. "You're on first name basis with the realtor?"

Kane shrugged. "I called her Miss Harding, but she told me to call her Cala... so I did.

"Uh-huh."

"Uh-huh, what?"

"Nothin'."

Kane stood in front of me. "'Nothing' is something; I don't need the Man Bible to know that."

I scoffed, "I'm fine."

"No, you aren't. Just tell me now what's bothering you. I don't want you giving me the silent treatment for the next ten hours."

I rolled my eyes. "I could explain what you did wrong, but you still wouldn't understand."

"What is that supposed to mean?"

I was going to have to spell it out for him.

"You're the reason there are instructions on shampoo bottles."

"Are you insinuating I'm stupid?"

"No, I'm flat out sayin' you're stupid."

"Rude!" Kane snapped. "You're so rude!"

I couldn't help but laugh.

"Sorry, flower."

"Dealing with you and your stupid hormones would drive a man to drink," Kane grumbled, not even trying to muffle his words.

I snorted. "Told you we shouldn't have had sex. Totally your fault for kissin' me in Darkness."

"*My* fault? You're the one who was dressed in that barely-there dress and sent me fuck-me-now glares. You wanted my cock, baby-doll, you just didn't want to accept that you wanted it."

What he was saying was true and it infuriated me.

"Please," I laughed, "I could've had me pick of men that night."

Lie.

Kane smirked. "Then why did you come home with me?"

I opened my mouth, but quickly closed it when I couldn't think of a snippy reply.

Kane laughed at me. "I'll answer for you, it's because you wanted me, not Skull or anyone else, just me."

I grunted, "Yeah, well, you wanted me, too."

"Want not wanted."

I flushed and slapped Kane's shoulder. "I'm not havin' sex with you."

"I'll wear you down eventually, Mama."

I growled, "I'll bite you."

"Please do," Kane countered, his eyes gleaming.

I laughed and shook my head. "You never let me get the last

word in."

"Because it pisses you off," Kane snickered. "It amuses me when you get all red-faced in anger with me."

"You *enjoy* making me angry?"

Kane shrugged. "I just like that I have an effect on you, even if it's just to annoy you."

"You're unbelievable."

"I know."

"Kane!" I snapped and then laughed.

He threw his arm around my shoulder, smiling as he did so. We both walked over to the entrance of the apartment building *Cala* told Kane to meet her at. Kane opened the door for me and gestured me into the building.

I snickered, "What a gentleman."

I walked past Kane and yelped when his smacked my arse.

"There's nothing gentle about me, babydoll."

I'll say.

I shook my head, chuckling but instantly stopped when I looked at the goddess walking towards Kane and myself with a bright, white smile. She was taller than me, but might have been the same height if she didn't have rose red stilettos on her tanned feet.

Her attire was very business-like, but fashionable at the same time. She was wearing a well-fitted grey pencil skirt and a matching blazer. Her wine coloured hair was pulled back into a tight bun that looked like it was professionally done. There wasn't a hair out of place on her pristine head.

It made me feel like a fat slob when I compared myself to her.

I knew I was pregnant so having a belly was nothing to compare, but everything else I had no excuse for. I was in a pair of black leggings, and oversized white t-shirt that had '*I believe in unicorns*' in black bold letters across the front of it. I also had a blazer on, but mine definitely wasn't fitted. It was just a cheap blazer I picked up when I was in Penny's a few months ago with Keela.

It was one of the only things from my old wardrobe that I could still wear because it didn't have to be buttoned closed. I didn't even want to look at my footwear because I knew I opted for open toe sandals and that was never a good idea unless there was sand and a big blue ocean involved.

"Mr. Slater, wonderful to meet you, sir, and you, Miss Collins." Cala smiled, her hand outstretched to Kane then to me. We both shook it, and I frowned when I let my hand fall back to my side.

She had a really good and firm handshake. Her voice was perfect, too. It was soft, soothing, and what I imagine an angel would sound like if I ever heard one.

Was I hot for this chick?

I scowled at my thoughts and stepped closer to Kane trying to use his large body to overshadow mine. I felt like a geeky teenager who was in the presence of a real woman. It made me feel very insecure, and I didn't like it.

"The first apartment to view is on the fourth floor. If you would follow me please, the elevators are this way."

Cala spun on her heel and walked away. I automatically turned my head and looked at Kane. I shook my head when I found his eyes glued to Cala's arse.

"I'm standin' right here, you fuckin' arsehole!" I hissed and punched him in the arm.

I turned and walked after Cala with Kane quickly following me. "I wasn't looking at her ass," he whispered.

"I never said you were lookin' at her arse."

Kane stuttered. "I... uh... are you sure?"

He didn't even hear me because he was lost in perfect arse heaven, again.

I doubt he even felt me when I hit him.

"Bite me, Slater."

Kane sighed from behind me but kept his mouth shut as we both entered the elevator Cala was stood inside. She hit the button for the fourth floor once we were all inside. She looked down at my stomach and smiled. "Do you know what you're having?"

I shook my head. "No, but I'm hopin' for a girl. A boy might turn out like his pig of a father."

Cala blinked her eyes a couple of times, then flicked them between myself and Kane before clearing her throat when the elevator came to a stop and the doors opened wide.

"Follow me, please."

She all but ran out of the elevator ahead of Kane and myself. It made me snort.

Kane growled from behind me, "I'm glad your rude ass attitude amuses you."

"So am I," I snarky replied.

I walked down the hall and followed Cala into an apartment that was bigger than my current one, but absolutely freezing and dusty as hell. I coughed and put my hand over my mouth.

"It will be cleaned before you move in if you decide on this apartment."

I nodded to Cala then asked, "Can I look around?"

"Of course, take as much time as you need."

It wasn't going to take long—my answer was already no.

I walked through the apartment and frowned when I spotted not only dirt, but mould on the bathroom walls. I stepped into the bathroom to get a closer look and screeched when I looked into the bathroom and saw the biggest spider I had ever seen in my entire life. It was the size of my bloody head.

"No!" I shouted and all but ran out of the apartment. "Not this one."

"What? You didn't even—"

"There is a tarantula in the fuckin' bathtub. This place is a *no!*"

"Uh, this place is a no, Cala, sorry."

"No worries, the next apartment is up on the sixth floor. Up we go."

The second apartment was in *this* building?

Ugh.

We re-entered the elevator and I was twitching and itchy because I felt like the spider was crawling all over me.

"Aideen?"

I didn't look at Kane as I said, "What?"

"Don't move. There is something in your hair."

I instantly began to scream as I whipped my head back and fourth in a way that would have made Willow Smith proud.

"Get it off. Get it off. Get if off."

"That is the opposite of *not* moving!"

I squealed and buried my face in Kane's chest when he grabbed hold of me. He locked his arms around my body and it halted my movements.

"Stay. Still," he ordered.

I whimpered into his chest and cringed when I felt his hand on my head.

"There," he said seconds later. "It's gone."

I stood rooted to the spot. "What was it?"

"Just a little bit of cobweb."

I bet it was really big—he wouldn't have spotted it otherwise. He just said it was small to make me feel better.

"I don't like it here."

Kane sighed, "Let's just check out this apartment, okay?"

No.

"Fine."

"Come on, Cala is holding the doors open for us."

I moved away from Kane and walked by Cala without looking at her. I waited for her to walk around me so I could follow her to the next apartment. Kane was behind me as we walked, but he was a lot taller and I was curious to know what—or who—he was looking at. I would have put money on Cala's arse, but when I glanced over my shoulder, I was surprised to find his eyes locked onto my arse.

"What are you doin'?" I asked, irritated.

I really wanted to smile though.

Kane flicked his eyes to mine and said, "Enjoying the view, do you mind?"

I turned my head forward and shook my head, a smile stretched across my face.

"Number six-zero-eight, this is apartment number two." Cala smiled as she stopped outside said apartment.

I swallowed as she opened the door and gestured me into the apartment. I was hesitant, but when Kane snorted from behind me I grunted and walked into the apartment. It was the same layout as the apartment downstairs, but it was clean.

Very clean.

"This is better," I murmured to myself.

"Again, take all the time you need."

I heard Kane say something Cala, but I didn't know what it was because I was already walking down the narrow hallway to the bathroom.

Please, no spiders.

I slowly opened the bathroom door and observed it from the hallway for a few seconds. I planned on walking inside and making sure there were no spiders, but I panicked and backed away.

"Kane," I called out. "I can't look; you do it for me, please."

Kane walked down the hallway, snickering and shaking his head at me. He walked right into the bathroom and slowly spun around checking out the entire room. He looked at me and shrugged. "It's clean.

"Check the bathtub."

"Aideen—"

"Check it."

Kane grumbled, but did as I asked and checked the tub.

"It's clean."

I blew out a relieved breath.

"Okay, you check the sittin' room and kitchen, I'll see to the bedrooms."

Kane saluted me. "Yes, ma'am."

I smacked his arse when he passed me and he found it hilarious. Feeling pretty pleased with myself I turned and walked down the hallway and checked out the bedrooms. Both of them were the same size, a double.

It wasn't huge, but it was bigger than my current apartment, the extra room was ideal for the baby's room, too. I smiled as I glanced around. I liked it.

"Kane, this place is—"

The sudden blaring music cut me off and caused me to press my hands over my ears.

What the fuck?

"Kane!"

Kane entered the bedroom—he had his hands on his ears also.

"What is *that*?" I shouted in dismay.

He pointed at the wall. "I think it's the neighbours."

I widened my eyes. "We're havin' a *baby*. I can't have music blarin' through the walls!"

He nodded his head in agreement. "Let's tell Cala it's a no for here, too."

"Damn fuckin' right!"

I stormed out of the bedroom and out of the apartment where I found Cala. She flushed a little when she looked at me.

"I apologise."

I shook my head. "It's a no for the two apartments in this building. Can we go to the next one, please?"

Cala nodded then looked over my shoulder at Kane. "Next location is closer to Upton, it's Old Isle Green and is fifteen minutes away, sir."

Bronagh and Dominic lived in Old Isle Green.

"Okay, let's go."

I flushed when Kane threaded his fingers through mine and tightly held onto my hand as we walked down the hallway and into the elevator. I mentally chastised myself for being so giddy because it was just hand holding, but I didn't care. I liked it.

We exited the building and got back into Kane's Jeep. We followed behind Cala then until we got to Old Isle Green roughly fifteen minutes later. I was relieved upon exiting the car when I saw no dead animals.

"Dominic and Bee live close by," Kane murmured to me as we followed behind Cala into a tall apartment complex."

I nodded my head indicating I heard him.

"You ready?" Kane asked.

I gnawed on my inner cheek and said, "As I'll ever be."

We entered the building and went straight up to the third floor. Cala was explaining all the high points of the apartment to Kane and myself. I let him do the listening while I silently prayed this apartment would be better than the last two. When we made it to the apartment, both Kane and myself checked it out. I found nothing wrong with it. The rooms were big and clean, and when I pressed my ear to the bedroom wall I couldn't hear a sound.

Score.

"I like this one."

Kane smiled at me but said nothing.

I moved past him and Cala, who were in the hallway of the apartment. I stepped outside the apartment and walked up and down the hallway outside just to see if I could hear any signs of noisy neighbours.

I heard nothing, which pleased me.

My pleasure was short lived because as I walked back to my possible new apartment with a spring in my step, I walked into the apartment directly next to me just as the door opened. I jumped when a cloud of smoke and a foul smell escaped.

My mind screamed fire, but when a bunch of young lads stumbled into the hallway all laughing and shoving one another I knew better. The little fuckers were all stoned.

"Yo, lady," one of them slurred at me. "You wanna hit?"

A hit of what?

"Kane!" I shouted.

Seconds later I was pushed behind his large body.

"Go back into your apartment or you won't live long enough to take another hit."

The lads burst into fits of laughter, but when Kane didn't move they quieted down. One of them even said, "I don't wanna get Hulk smashed, let's go get food instead."

The rest of them cheered and piled back into the smoke filled apartment. Kane turned to face me, and I saw he was trying not to laugh. I wasn't in the mood for laughing though.

"A dope house... *really*?"

This day was a fucking disaster.

"The next one will be good, I have a good feeling about it," Kane said, trying to assure me.

I grunted, "Let's just go, it can't be any worse than here."

I didn't even look at Cala as I got back into the elevator.

She fucking sucked at her job.

We left disaster number three and headed for the fourth one, which was only five minutes away. I got out of Kane's Jeep and looked around.

"We're in Upton," I murmured.

Kane snorted. "Yeah, this is where the next apartment is."

"You live two minutes away from here. Keela, too," I suddenly squealed in excitement.

Kane smiled. "Fingers crossed it's the one."

I quickly crossed my fingers together and whispered, "Please be the one, please be the one."

We entered a building that looked brand spanking new. The lobby was huge and spotless. It even had security! Huge plus.

Oh, please be the one!

"Fourth floor," Cala said and gestured us to the elevator.

We got inside and rode to the fourth floor. When I stepped out of the elevator, I was in awe. The hallway outside of the apartments looked like something out of a five-star hotel.

"Wow," I murmured to myself.

Kane led me down the stunning hallway after Cala, then he led me into Heaven.

"Oh, Kane," I breathed. "This is gorgeous!"

We entered the apartment and had a look around. I was instantly in awe. I stared wide-eyed around the spacious rooms. The sitting room and kitchen were two separate rooms! My old apartment had a combination of the two in the one room and it was so small it would fit into the new sitting room. The hallway was long and wound to the left where the bedrooms and bathroom were located.

Without a word, I walked out of the huge sitting room and ventured down the hallway and into the kitchen. I gasped when I took in the newly refurbished kitchen that was accompanied with cream gloss cabinets and black marble countertops. The appliances were stainless steel and brand new. Everything seemed brand new.

I was speechless.

I backed out of the kitchen then turned and walked down the hallway to check out the bedrooms and bathroom. I squealed when I peeked inside the bathroom. Everything was black and white. It had a tub *and* a shower. The room reminded me of one of the bathrooms in Keela's house. It was stunning. And clean. Very clean.

"I can't believe this place," I whispered to myself then left the bathroom.

I checked out both of the bedrooms and found they were both master sized with large windows that allowed a lot of natural light to fill the rooms. None of the rooms came with en-suite bathrooms, but that didn't bother me because I had the mother of all bathrooms next door.

I screeched when I walked into what would be my new bedroom and looked to the right of the room. There was a fitted wardrobe that was the length of the bloody wall. It was huge. I opened one of the varnished doors and gasped when the door automatically folded to the side and kept folding revealing the full wardrobe.

I heard quick paced footsteps come from down the hall, then a squeak as they came to a stop. "You scared the shit out of me!" Kane's voice huffed from behind me.

I brought my hands to my face and sniffled. "Look at the wardrobe," I whispered.

Kane laughed, "You like it?"

"Love," I corrected and turned to face Kane with tears in my eyes. "I *love* it so much. It's perfect."

Kane's shoulders relaxed and a smile took over his handsome face. "Then it's yours, let's go and fill out the paperwork. We can get you the keys right now—Cala has the keys to all the apartments. They're all immediate move in too."

I shook my head in disbelief. "How is this place only twenty-five hundred a month?"

Kane shrugged his shoulders. "It's a buyer and renters market."

"I guess, but this looks like somewhere Tony Stark would happily live. It's amazin'."

Kane snorted, "Let's go make this amazing place yours."

I couldn't form a single word, so I just nodded my head and took Kane's outstretched hand as we walked down the hallway and back to the sitting room where Cala was.

"She wants it," Kane declared to Cala who smiled.

"I thought you might. This place is beautiful."

I still couldn't speak so I just nodded my head and tried my best not to cry.

I was leasing the apartment.

Holy. Fuck.

I stared at Cala as she explained the lease to me. I filled out my bank information on a form so my rent could be taken out each month, then Cala went through the ins and outs of the terms and conditions. When I understood them, she gave me a black ballpoint pen, placed the lease on the table and pointed to the bottom line on the page.

"Sign here, please."

I looked at Kane, who was smiling at me then I looked down, held my breath and signed my name on the dotted line. I did it quickly in case Cala changed her mind.

"Congratulations, Miss Collins, this apartment is leased in your name. Here are the keys, you can move in right away. I will inform the utility companies that you're the addressee. All mains are turned on already—heating, water, electricity. Everything."

Holy. Fuck.

I was so excited that I squealed, "Thank You."

Cala laughed and shook our hands. "You're welcome."

Cala said goodbye and left Kane and me alone. I instantly hugged him and he laughed and hugged me back. "You're happy?"

"Very!"

Kane chuckled then hissed, "Crap, I forgot to pay Cala. Give me a minute."

He jogged out of the apartment after Cala, and because I wanted to see the stunning hallway outside once more, I followed him. I stopped in the doorway when I heard voices conversing.

"It worked like a charm. She picked this apartment just like you said she would, *sir.*"

What?

Kane snorted, "Well done, you did a good job today."

"Anything for my boss."

Again, what?

I stepped out into the hallway.

"Kane."

His eyes locked on mine as he took a step backwards from Cala. "Aideen."

I narrowed my eyes. "What does Cala mean by 'it worked'?"

He blinked. "God, you're so gorgeous, baby—"

"Don't," I cut him off. "Don't dodge the question, answer it."

He closed his mouth.

I flicked my eyes to Cala. "What did you mean by 'it worked'?"

Cala's eyes were wild and they flicked back and forth between Kane and myself. I took at step towards her and Kane broke his innocent act.

"Run, Cala!" he shouted. "Save yourself!"

I then witnessed a fully-grown woman sprint away from me in

six-inch heels like a fucking boss. I didn't move or even shout after her, I was too impressed to distract her.

Kane was a different story though.

"What did you do?"

Kane nervously scratched his neck. "A really sweet and thoughtful thing."

I deadpanned, "I seriously doubt that."

"I sort of... sabotaged the viewings today."

I stared at him.

"That's bullshit, how could you sabotage the apartment viewin's? You were standin' next to me in all of them."

He looked anywhere but at my face.

"I may have paid some people to be loud, the realtors to dirty up some apartments and have some kids I know from the club pretend to be druggies who wanted to get you high."

I didn't know whether to laugh or cry.

"Please tell me you're jokin'."

Kane shrugged. "I wanted you to have an amazing home, this was the only way I could do that without openly saying, 'here, enjoy this rent free apartment.'"

I reared back and stared at him.

"What the fuck do you mean rent free? And what did Cala mean by callin' you boss?"

He gnawed on his lower lip. "I own the building, Aideen."

"You *what*?"

"Upton Realtors... this building and the five others situated throughout Dublin—I own them."

I stared blankly at him.

"I don't believe you."

Kane tilted his head. "Yes, you do."

I didn't... did I?

Ugh.

"You're fuckin' with me head."

"I don't mean to."

"Are you tellin' me the truth?" I asked. "Be honest."

Kane nodded his head. "I'm telling you the truth, I swear."

I was quiet for a few moments trying to take in this new information.

"Who knows about all your... properties?"

"My brothers know, but I don't like my business being common knowledge so they didn't tell it to their girlfriends. They didn't need to know."

"I can't believe this."

Kane frowned. "I'm sorry I tricked you. I was afraid you would think an apartment was payment for being pregnant with my child."

"What?" I asked, dumbfounded.

"I don't know," Kane sighed. "I was just afraid of explaining this to you and then giving you an apartment would seem like charity."

"So you decided giving me an apartment by trickin' me would be the better option?"

Kane ran both of his hands through his hair. "It was stupid, I know... but to be fair, you wouldn't have found out if you didn't overhear Cala."

Cala.

"So you're her boss, right?"

He shrugged and nodded.

"Did you sleep with her?"

I had no clue why I was even asking the question.

Kane blinked. "What?"

"Did you sleep with Cala?"

Kane raised his eyebrows. "Yes, but it was a long time ago—"

"Oh, my God!"

I turned and walked towards the elevators of *Kane's* apartment building.

"Aideen," Kane snapped from behind me. "Hold the fuck on!"

I gasped when Kane shot around me and blocked my way.

"Move!"

"No!" Kane snapped back at me. "She happened before I even knew you. It was one time. Why the hell are you pissed off over *Cala*?"

I realised the answer just as Kane asked the question.

I was jealous.

I was jealous that Cala had slept with Kane.

Fuck.

"I'm not," I replied and tried to move around him.

Kane wouldn't let me by. "Try answering me with an honest answer this time."

I shoved at his chest. "Move, Kane."

"Make me."

I screeched in annoyance, "I'll scream and have someone call the guards."

Kane smirked down at me. "Scream all you want, there are no tenants in this building."

I stared at him. "What?"

"Technically speaking, you're the only person who lives in this building."

What the fuck?

"I don't live here."

Kane smiled at me. "The signed lease in my back pocket says differently."

Oh, my- motherfucker!

"It's invalid. I didn't know—"

"You signed a contracted lease for twelve months, babydoll. I have it in black and white."

I was being hustled.

"Kane... you can't force me to live here."

"Sure I can."

I placed my face in my hands. "This can't be real."

"Sure it is," Kane chuckled. "You get a brand new, fully furnished apartment for free. You don't have to worry about noisy neighbours, or for your safety because I have security working twenty-four-seven in the lobby of all my complexes. Also, your utility bills are covered by your very generous, landlord. He is a really nice guy and quite the looker, or so I've been told."

I hated him.

"I want to hurt you so much right now," I whispered. "I can't believe you have done this—it's crazy."

"The only crazy thing here would be if you fought me on this."

"How can I not?" I asked. "You're givin' me a home, and takin' away all me financial worries. You expect me to just be happy?"

"As a matter of fact, babydoll, I do."

I shook my head. "It's too much."

"It's not enough," Kane countered. "Please just let me treat you like the queen you are to me. I don't think you understand just how important you are to me."

"Me, or the baby?"

He closed the space between us. "Both of you. You're my family, and I take care of my family."

I couldn't think.

"I don't know what to say," I cried.

Kane leaned down and pressed his forehead to mine. "Say you won't be a trouble tenant for me. I'm a no bullshit kind of landlord."

I huffed, "You leased the wrong girl in that case, buddy."

He laughed and put his arms around me.

"I'm sorry for lying to you."

I put my arms tightly around him. "You should be. I feel so mindfucked right now I don't know what to do with meself. Me brain is a fart right now."

Kane laughed as he placed a hand against my lower back and rubbed it around in lazy circles.

"Do you feel a little better though? Knowing your whole paycheque can go towards food, the baby, and yourself?"

My mind was a mess.

"I'm overwhelmed. I've never not had bills to pay or extra cash lyin' around for impulsive buys. I'm in unknown territory here."

Kane kissed my head. "Keela adjusted to Alec having money, you will adjust to me having it, too."

I frowned. "Keela put her foot down with Alec though, she didn't want to spend money she didn't earn."

"You *have* earned this, babydoll," Kane assured me. "Putting up with me on a daily basis means you deserve all this and more."

I thought about it for a second then said, "That's true."

Kane guffawed, "You're as modest as ever."

I snorted and hugged him tighter.

"Thank you," I murmured.

I could hear the smile in his voice as he said, "You're more than welcome, babydoll."

I couldn't believe that I had a brand new apartment, but what I simply couldn't wrapped my head around was that Kane own said apartment. He owned an entire building full of them, *five* of them.

"I can't believe you've been runnin' a business without any of us catchin' on. I'm annoyed actually, I pride meself in findin' stuff out, but I had no clue."

Kane chuckled and pulled back from our hug.

"It happened by accident, actually. I came across Upton Realtors for sale and three buildings they owned for a steal of a price. I bought them a few years ago, then this building last year and remodeled them. I have a hundred tenants, you'll make one hundred and one. I have plenty of apartments left to fill, too."

I arched an eyebrow. "It's all legal, right?"

Kane laughed, "Yeah, it's all legal. I own everything fair and square."

That made me feel a little better, but I was still feeling mindfucked.

"I can't believe this, I thought you were unemployed!"

"I know," he replied, "and I was going to tell you. I just wanted you to know me before you knew about all this."

I frowned. "You were worried that I'd act differently if I knew you had money?"

He shrugged. "I wasn't sure of anything, so I kept it to myself."

I was silent for a moment then I said, "I understand. Thank you for telling me even if only you did because I overheard Cala."

"Aideen," Kane sighed, "I was going to tell you when you got settled into the apartment, I swear."

I believed him.

I nodded my head. "I know, this whole situation is just insane."

Kane scratched his neck. "While I'm telling you about properties I own, you know the old community centre in the middle of town?"

The centre he was talking about had been empty for years.

I eyed him. "Yes?"

"I own that too," he admitted. "I plan on turning it into a youth centre to help get kids off the street and away from gangs and trouble."

I blinked. "Oh, my God. Kane."

"What?" he murmured.

"That is… wonderful. I could kiss you for telling me that, I work with kids so that means a lot to me. Thank you so much."

Kane smiled. "Kiss me if you want to."

I pulled a face at him but got on my tippy toes and kissed the corner of his mouth.

"Tease," he breathed.

I smiled up at him. "I remember you sayin' years ago you wanted to do somethin' with the centre, I just didn't think this was it."

He shrugged. "It's just something I want to do. If I can help one child, It'll all be worth it."

My heart!

"Can I help?" I asked. "I mean, with the kids, when the centre is open?"

Kane's eyes lit up. "I'd love nothing more than you to help me, babydoll."

I beamed. "It'll be amazin', I know loads of ways to keep a child's attention even into adolescents. We can do up plans, and get in volunteers to help—" I paused my rambling when I found Kane smiling at me.

"What?" I asked.

He shook his head. "You just make me happy."

Oh.

"Yeah? Well, you make me happy, too."

Kane's eye heated and I knew I needed to change the subject or this beautiful hallway would be destroyed in bodily fluids.

I shook my head and glanced around the hallway. "I can't believe you own this place. It's gorgeous."

Kane smiled knowingly at me. "Thanks, it's officially not open yet because the bigger apartments upstairs aren't ready yet, but the will be soon."

I looked up and down the hallway. "I wonder who my neighbours will be."

Kane snorted, "You won't have neighbours, you'll be the only person on this floor."

"What? Why?"

Kane deadpanned, "Because I said so. The elevator will only open on this floor to those with a special keycard."

"That's stupid, there are other apartments here that should be used."

Kane shrugged. "I'd rather you had everything to yourself."

I blew out a breath. "I really don't know what to say."

"Say thank you, landlord and master."

I growled, "Thank you, master dickhead."

Kane laughed and put his arms back around me and said, "Close enough."

I smiled.

He was too perfect.

I pulled back from Kane when my phone rang. I dug it out of my pocket and answered it without looking at the screen.

"Hello?"

"Did you find an apartment?" Keela asked, expectantly.

I rolled my eyes. "Hello, Keela."

"Don't hello me. Did you find somewhere?"

I chuckled, "Maybe."

"Aideen!" she growled.

I looked at Kane and snorted, "I found me new apartment."

Kane winked at me while Keela screamed in my ear. I pulled the phone away and hissed, "Me ear, you bitch!"

"Sorry," Keela said. "Where is it? What's like?"

"It's literally two minutes from your house, and it's gorgeous."

Keela screamed. Again.

"Damn it, Keela!"

Kane laughed.

"I'm so fuckin' excited."

I smiled. "Me too, I can move in right away, too.

"Tomorrow we can all help you move in, but tonight?" Keela cackled, "Tonight we celebrate."

Uh-oh.

CHAPTER EIGHTEEN

This was a horrible idea.

I was sat in a newly opened pub, fifteen minutes down the road from Upton, with all my friends and family surrounding me, and all I wanted to do was go home and go to bed. As much as I wanted to, I couldn't leave because everyone was out celebrating my pregnancy and new apartment. It was a night for me, and for Kane. I had to suck it up and pretend like I wasn't seconds away from face planting on the table.

"Aideen?" James called out.

Yes, my brothers were here.

My father too.

They were also sat at the same table as us, which included the Slater brothers. When they first arrived, I envisioned world war erupting in the pub but everyone was surprisingly civil. James even apologised to Kane. Yeah, he *apologised*.

I stared at him when the words let his mouth. I didn't trust that it wasn't a trick to catch Kane off guard, but when I looked at James's face, I saw he was being genuine.

He didn't like apologising, I could sense that, but he was being the bigger man, and I think it was because of me. He was putting asides his differences with the Slater brothers for my sake, and for my baby's sake. I was so grateful that I hugged my brothers long and hard, which they each thought was hilarious.

"What?" I replied to my brother's call.

He grinned. "Are you okay?"

I nodded my head. "I'm fine, why?"

"Because," Alec cut in, "you look like you're about to fall asleep sitting up."

I lightly chuckled, "I'm okay, just a little tired."

I shivered when I felt *his* hand pressed against the base of my spine.

"We can leave now if you want?"

I wanted to groan when Kane spoke into my ear. It felt good and relaxed me, which only made me feel that bit more tired. I turned and looked at him, our faces inches apart.

I shook my head. "I'm fine."

Kane's eyes were a little bloodshot. "You sure?"

There was a faint smell of whiskey on his breath, and it made me want to nibble on him.

"I'm sure." I nodded then swallowed. "But do me a favour?"

"Anything," he murmured and looked at my mouth.

Stop it, Kane.

"Don't drink anymore. I gave you a high dose of insulin before we left but don't abuse that, please."

Kane winked. "I'm done."

I arched an eyebrow making him chuckle.

"I promise, I just had one beer and a whiskey."

That was it?

"Your eyes tell a different story."

Kane grunted, "I've never been a big drinker, it doesn't take a lot for me to feel the effects from it."

I nodded my head. "Okay then, thank you."

He grinned at me and exhaled again.

Whiskey breath apparently got me going.

"Take a mint or somethin'," I whispered. "I'll nibble you if you don't."

Kane licked his lips. "You like whiskey?"

My brother Dante overheard Kane's question and it made him laugh.

"She loves whiskey, probably the smell more than the taste. If there was such thing as a whiskey scented candle, Aideen would buy hundreds."

I glared at my brother, but couldn't correct him because what he said was completely true. I *loved* the smell of whiskey.

"That's good to know." Kane grinned.

I growled at him. "Don't think it will get you into me knickers."

Kane lowered his voice and said, "I'll just keep talking and wait for *you* to beg me to get into your knickers."

I burst into laughter and it got the attention of my girlfriends.

"What's so funny?" Bronagh asked, smiling.

I chuckled, "When one of the brothers say the word 'knickers' I think it's the funniest thing ever. Their accents just butcher the word."

Nico snorted. "Which is why we say 'panties' instead."

"*No!*" every female at the table bellowed.

Nico jumped and quickly raised his hands up in the air. "I'm sorry."

His brothers, and mine, laughed their arses off about how terrified Nico looked of us. It amused us girls, too.

I yawned and it caused my friends to smile at me.

"It's nearin' eleven, Ado, go home."

I groaned to Keela, "I'm ready for bed at eleven? A few months ago I didn't go *out* till eleven! This is so messed up."

Everyone laughed.

"This is the easy part, baby." My father smirked. "You don't sleep for the first eighteen years."

I almost cried. "Thanks for tellin' me that, Da."

My father winked and smiled at me. I did too until the sudden urge to go to the bathroom hit. I groaned and stood up. "Be right back."

"Where are you goin'?" Harley asked me.

I grunted, "The toilet."

I glared at the table when snickers were heard.

"It's not funny, you try havin' the spawn of Satan sittin' your bladder twenty-four-seven!"

I turned and walked around the edge of the dance floor that was packed with people. I rolled my eyes at the laughter from my friends and family that followed me. I made it to the bathroom and was happy to find a vacant stall.

I quickly relieved myself and sighed while doing so. I hated going to the toilet so often, but I had to admit that peeing was the only relief I felt lately. I was now twenty-one weeks and four days pregnant, and all the little things I used to take for granted were starting to catch up with me.

My feet, for example. I never had any problems with my feet. I never went jogging, but I did walk a lot and I never felt any pain, but now they were swelled up at the end of each day and hurt like a motherfucker. I didn't know how much weight I gained so far, but I was sure it was a lot more than experts would say was healthy. I knew that much.

I also knew, thanks to Google images, that I had a big bump for almost twenty-two weeks. This scared me because I didn't want to have a big baby—my vagina wouldn't be able to handle it.

It was like my body had an allergic reaction to being pregnant. My feet swelled, my back hurt, my boobs hurt, I couldn't sleep very well at night, and I was always hungry. It fucking sucked.

I finished up in the toilet, then washed my hands and dried them at the sinks. I exited the bathroom and walked back into the pub, but when I opened the door I walked into a tall man and stumbled backwards. The man grabbed my arms and stopped my impending fall.

"Whoa, there!" the man said, his tone panicked.

I blew out a big breath. "Omigod! Thank you."

"No problem, honey. Jesus, you're pregnant, are you okay?" he asked with an alarmed look.

I looked up and noticed he was the man I met in the hospital a few days ago. He didn't seem to recognise me, and I was little embarrassed to remind him that we already met just in case I was mistaken. I was sure I knew him though, I remember his facial scar.

He was an older man with a thick head of black hair. He looked near the same age as my father, which would put him in his fifties. I smiled when he let go of me and pushed the glasses he wore up his nose.

I nodded my head. "I'm really fine..."

"Philip."

I smiled. "Philip. I'm Aideen."

Philip winked. "You take *very* good care of yourself, Aideen. Watch where you put your feet."

I chuckled. "Nice advice, I'll remember it."

Philip tipped his head forward, glanced over his shoulder then turned and walked towards the bar. I blew out a breath and shook my head at myself.

Watch where you put your feet.

That *was* really good advice for me, it was advice I'd have to put into immediate use because I couldn't afford to be as clumsy as I usually was whilst being pregnant. It was too dangerous. I glanced around the pub I was stood in and decided I need to go home. I knew everyone was out celebrating my pregnancy and new apartment, but a pub was no place for a pregnant woman. It was a hazard, a pending accident waiting to happen.

It was also hot as hell with all the bodies packed in here and the heat made it difficult to catch my breath.

I needed to leave.

Without a single thought, I turned and walked towards the exit of the pub. When I walked through the doors and made it outside and cold air wrapped around me like a blanket. I deeply inhaled.

That felt better.

"Well, well, well, if it isn't me forever disappearin' ex-girlfriend."

I cringed when I heard his voice, but plastered on a smile as I slowly turned myself around. "Heeeeey, you. What'd up, homie?" I asked Skull as he stood before me with his large arms fold across his chest, and a grin stretched across his mouth.

Skull laughed, "What'd up, homie? Really? Where the hell have you been? I've been tryin' to get in touch with you for ages. Did you change your number?"

"No, I've just been busy."

Skull winked. "I thought you might've be avoidin' me."

I frowned. "Avoidin' you? What for?"

"The last time we were together we decided that we were done for real, so I figured you wanted me out of your life when I couldn't get in touch with you."

My face fell. "That's the furthest thing from the truth, Trevor. I love you, you know I do."

I never used Skull's real name unless I was serious, and I was being deadly serious right now. I wanted him to know I would never try to cut him out of my life. Ever. He was a huge part of my life.

Skull's face softened. "I love you, too."

I smiled and relaxed my features. "What are you doin' here?"

"I work weekends so my drinkin' nights are weekdays, I'm here with some lads from the club."

I nodded my head but said nothing else.

"Are you okay?"

I snorted, "Depends on what you mean by okay."

Skull stared at me, hard as he waited for me to explain.

I sighed, "I'm fine, things are just a mental for me right now."

"Let's go back inside, and I'll buy you a drink, we can talk about it."

"I would, but I can't drink."

"Why not?" Skull asked, perplexed.

I didn't know how to tell my ex-boyfriend, who at one point was my world, that I was pregnant with another man's child. So I decided to make a joke out of it. I placed my hand on my stomach, rubbed it around in circles and smiled wide.

Skull looked down my hands and then back up to my face. "Why are you smilin' and touchin' your stomach like that? You hungry? Wanna get some food?"

I burst into laughter. "Not hungry. I've a human being to think about in there now so no more drinkin'. Not for another few months anyway."

Skull chuckled but stopped when I made no motion of telling him I was joking. He stared into my eyes and when he saw no traces of a lie he gasped, "I don't believe you!"

I shrugged. "It's true."

"Shut the fuck up!"

I again burst into laughter, "Now that's just rude."

"You're *pregnant*?" Skull asked, his eye bugging out his head. "For real?"

Could he not see my big belly?

I nodded my head. "Yep."

"For who?" he asked worriedly.

I chuckled, "It's not you, don't worry."

Skull relaxed. "Sorry, it's not that I don't want kids, I do, but you know. Wow."

I nodded my head. "I understand, I was pretty shocked when I first found out, too."

"I can't believe it," Skull said dumbfounded. "You're really havin' a kid?"

"I am." I beamed.

"Fuckin' hell, me little baby is havin' a baby," he laughed. "Congratulations, sweetheart!"

I squealed when Skull stepped forward, wrapped his arms around me and lifted me up off the ground. I latched my hands onto his shoulders, closed my eyes and laughed.

"When are you havin' the brat?" Skull asked when he set me back on the ground a few seconds later.

I held onto him because I didn't fully feel steady on my feet.

"January," I said, smiling up at him. "I'm due on me ma's birthday."

"No!" Skull gasped and beamed. "That's incredible."

He gave me a big kiss on the cheek that made me laugh. I was about to step back away from him now that I had my bearings, but I remained put when I heard the commotion from my right.

"Kane. No!" I heard Nico's voice bellow.

Kane?

I looked at my right and widened my eyes when I spotted him storming towards myself and Skull, his face was twisted in rage, and I had no clue why. All I knew was he was pissed, and his focus was completely on Skull.

Fuck.

Time slowed down then as I stepped backwards just as Kane collided into Skull, taking him up off his feet and spearing him to the ground. The noise of Skull hitting the ground struck me like a physical slap, and I heard my ear-piercing scream before I realised the sound even left my mouth.

"Stop!"

I stupidly rushed forward to try and stop Kane from hurting Skull, but Nico was on me in a second. "I don't fucking think so!" he snapped at me. "You're *pregnant*, stay back!"

I blinked my eyes and nodded at him.

He was right, and I hated that it took another person to remind me not to rush into a fight. I should have already known that—I was the one who was pregnant after all.

"Eejit," I hissed at myself.

I lifted my hands to my face and covered my ears with my palms to block out the sounds of all the chaos around me. I could hear Skull trying to get through to Kane, as well as Nico. I widened my eyes when Nico jumped on Kane's back and wrapped his arm around his neck. For a few seconds nothing happened, Kane continued to hit Skull, but then ever so slightly Kane's movements slowed and I realised why.

Nico was suffocating him.

"Stop!" I screamed. "You'll kill him."

Kane rolled off Skull with Nico still attached to his back like a monkey, and it was only when his eyes closed that Nico released him and pushed himself up off the ground. Kane wheezed a little on the ground as he caught his breath back and blinked his eyes open. He stared up at the night sky and laughed.

I stared at Kane then Nico.

"You fuckin' eejit!" I bellowed and stalked forward, shoving Nico in the chest. "Don't ever do that to him again. You were suffocatin' him!"

Nico grunted as he slightly stumbled. "It's the only way I can get him to stop when he starts."

"Starts what?" I asked.

Nico looked me in the eye. "When he starts fighting... he blacks out and doesn't stop until he is forced to."

Like when he was fighting James a couple of months ago.

I swallowed and looked away. "Bring him home. I have to make sure me friend is okay."

"He had a few drinks more drinks when you went to the bathroom. Your brothers challenged him to a shot contest. He is drunk and saw Skull kiss you on the cheek, he got the wrong idea," Nico said when he grabbed my arm to keep me put in front of him.

"Why're you tellin' me this?" I asked.

Nico shrugged. "So you go easy on him when he is sober."

"Fat chance of that," I replied.

Nico smiled. "Come with me, I'll bring you home."

I looked over my shoulder for Skull, but he was gone, and the crowd that gathered outside the pub was already breaking up.

I sighed, "Comin' here was a stupid idea."

"Tell me about it."

"I have to tell everyone goodbye—"

"I'll text Bronagh to make something up, she'll say goodbye for you and Kane."

I sighed but nodded my head.

He turned away from me then and helped his stupid older brother up to his feet then slung an arm around his waist as he guided Kane to their parked Jeep in the car park. I silently followed behind them.

Nico settled Kane in the back of the Jeep, buckled his seatbelt and muttered curse words when Kane fell to the left and instantly began snoring. "Heavy bastard," he grunted.

I smiled to myself as I rounded on the passenger side of the car and climbed into the front seat, buckling myself up. When Nico was settled in the driver's seat, he started the fifteen-minute journey to get us home. For the first few minutes, we were silent until Nico began to talk.

"He likes you. You know that right?"

I didn't reply because I didn't know what to say.

"He does. He just has a funny way of showing it, but he likes you."

My heart thudded lightly against my chest.

"He can't stand me, Nico."

Nico laughed, "Get real, Aideen. He only argues with you because he doesn't know how else to approach you."

That was stupid.

"So he's just a dick to me because he likes me? That's the dumbest thing I've ever heard."

"I never said he was smart."

I grinned a little at that then frowned when Kane snored behind us.

"I... I don't know if I can spend time with someone like him. His temper... it scares me. I like him too, but I don't know if it's enough."

"He would never hurt you," Nico assured me.

I nodded my head. "I believe that, but his ability to hurt other people frightens me just as much."

Nico set his jaw. "It's not his fault, he is the way he is."

I blinked. "Whose fault is it then?"

Nico's hands tightened on the steering wheel of the car. "People from our past."

"Ah," I said and snapped my fingers. "Marco? He made you a fighter and Alec an escort, right?"

Nico mutely nodded his head.

"What were Ryder and Kane's jobs for him?"

Nico glanced at me. "You don't know?"

I huffed, "No. The girls are all about 'respectin' their men's privacy' or some bullshit like that."

Nico laughed, "I bet that kills you."

"You could say that," I admitted.

With a smile Nico said, "You aren't missing a lot by being in the dark, trust me, Ado. Being in the dark when it comes to my family is a kindness."

I groaned, "Not when I'm havin' a baby with a man who is lost in that darkness."

"I don't know what you want me to say, Ado. Kane is my brother, but even I don't fully understand or know the things he was put through. He doesn't talk about it. Ever."

I began to feel sick.

"You mean the cause of his scars?" I asked, my voice low.

Nico nodded and kept his eyes on the road. "He doesn't talk about how he got them, and we don't push him on it."

I leaned back. "Why not? If you understood what he went through, you could help him now."

"He is fine," Nico assured me. "He rarely gets into fights... it's only since... well, since—"

"Since I got pregnant?"

Nico glanced at me then back to the road as he nodded his head.

"I know you're adjusting to your life suddenly changing, Ado, but you have no idea how huge this is for Kane."

I remained silent as Nico gave me more insight into Kane.

"He has a low tolerance for people. He accepted Bronagh,

Branna, Keela and even Alannah because my brothers and me love them, and luckily he grew to love them too. He is a funny and kind person... but he is fucked up, Aideen. I'm not going to sugar coat it—things won't be easy with him. But just... just remember how difficult this is for him."

I lifted my hands to my face and rubbed. "I need to know what made him the way he is. It's not right that he blacks out when he fights—it's dangerous as hell. He is like a machine."

Nico was quiet for a few minutes until he said, "Ask him why. Just pick the right moment."

Until we fully trusted one another to open up and really talk, I just wasn't sure if the 'right moment' would ever happen. Kane had a lot of layers to him, I didn't know if he would ever let me get to his centre.

CHAPTER NINETEEN

"I can't believe you paid people to move everythin' for me into me new apartment. Me old apartment is empty, I just have me bed, a few clothes and that's it."

I was currently sat on my bed looking around my bare bedroom. I would be moving out of it for good tomorrow, and I wasn't even sad about it. I was ready to be moving on to a new chapter in my life.

Keela snorted through the receiver of my phone. "It was all Alec's idea, but yeah, I was totally on board with it because there was *no way* in hell we were havin' a repeat of movin' day. No, thank you."

I shivered. "Amen, sister."

Keela was a little quiet before she said, "Did you ring your landlord yet?"

I nodded my head even though she couldn't see me. "Yeah, I rang him this mornin'. He knows I'm leavin' here tomorrow. He was a little surprised I wouldn't be renewin' me lease, but he was fine with lettin' me out of my current lease two months early if he could keep me deposit I paid him when I first moved in."

"I'm glad that's sorted for you. I'm even happier you'll be livin' in Upton. Two minutes away, too!"

I squealed in delight. "I know! I can't believe me apartment, it's stunnin'."

"I can't wait for a sleepover."

I laughed, "Neither can Kane from the way he carries on."

Keela murmured, "Nico told us what happened with him last night. Are you mad at him?"

Was I?

I exhaled. "Yes and no. I'm mad he hurt Skull—who I still have to call, by the way—and how he behaved, but I understand that he got the wrong end of the stick. He thought Skull kissed me."

"Well, he does have a right to be angry if he thought it was a real kiss."

"What?" I gasped. "You know we aren't together."

"Officially yes," Keela replied. "But you have both been actin' like a couple for weeks now—you just don't kiss and have sex."

"I don't think—"

"*I* think just get with him already. You're torturin' the poor lad," Keela griped as she cut me off.

"Keela!" I snapped. "You're supposed to be on *my* side."

"I *told* you I'm on the side of love."

I groaned, "What does that even mean?"

"It means," she guffawed, "that you two clearly like each other but are either too stupid to realise it or too stubborn to admit it. It's one or the other."

I growled, "Are you callin' me stupid?"

"Yes!" Keela cackled.

I seethed in silence until she stopped laughing at me.

"I'm sorry," she said through her muffled laughter. "I just love that you're in this position."

"*Why?*" I asked, appalled.

"Because," she sassed, "being with Kane is what you want deep down, and how he acts around you is forcin' it out of you and you hate it. It's interestin' to watch it unfold."

"You're un-fuckin'-believable."

"I know."

I pressed my free hand to my face. "I'd smack you if I could."

Keela snickered, "I don't doubt it."

I thought about what she said for a couple of seconds and frowned. "I'm not goin' to lie, I do like him. I like him so much, but say we get together... what if we fuck things up? I can't risk it with the baby comin'."

"That's a big 'what if', babe."

"You're not helpin' me see sense here," I whined.

"I am," Keela countered, "you're just tryin' to convince yourself what I'm sayin' is bullshit. You know it's not. I wouldn't suggest givin' things a go with Kane if I didn't think you'd both be great together."

I knew what she was saying was true. Keela always had my back.

"I guess so."

"Does that mean you'll give you and Kane a chance?"

I thought hard about it.

I knew I liked Kane. He gave me butterflies by just looking at me, and he made me so happy. We still argued, but we were so close now that not being with him would eventually become a problem. My feelings for him were developing fast, and the longer I didn't give into him, the harder I was making things for myself.

I grunted to Keela, "I suppose."

"Good, because he left to go over to talk to you ten minutes ago."

"You fuckin' bitch!"

I heard Keela's laughter just before she hung up.

Evil.

She was pure evil.

I shook my head and threw my phone onto my bed. I laid back and sighed as I looked up at the ceiling. I couldn't get comfortable, the person who rang my doorbell made sure of that.

Kane.

I sat upright, got up from my bed, and walked out of my bedroom and down the hallway to the door. I opened my door without looking through the peephole because I knew who it would be.

"What are you doin' here?" I asked as he walked into my apartment.

"I needed to see you."

I closed my door then folded my arms across my chest. "Why?"

Kane stuffed his hands into his jean pockets. "I've to get my insulin shot... and I wanted to tell you that I'm sorry."

I ignored his diabetes for a minute.

I raised my eyebrow. "Are you really sorry?"

He set his jaw. "Why did you let him kiss you?"

That was a no then.

"He kissed me *cheek* because he is a *friend* who was congratulatin' me on me pregnancy."

Kane blinked. "Oh."

"Yeah, oh."

He avoided looking me in the eye then. "I thought it was your lips he kissed."

I shook my head. "You know you and I aren't together, right? That means other men could kiss me if I allowed it."

Kane growled, "Stop it. You're just trying to make me mad."

"No, I'm not. I'm tryin' to make you understand that you can't just attack people, Kane."

He blinked. "I don't usually. I usually keep to myself, but then you happened."

I scowled. "What does *that* mean?"

He shrugged. "I don't know what it means. I just know I don't want you with other people. Men, women... anyone. I can't explain it, I'm used to keeping to myself, so now that we're tied together with the baby, I want to keep you away from people, too. I know it's stupid and crazy, but I can't help it. It's just how I am. I don't trust people, Aideen, especially not with you and our baby."

Just remember how difficult this is for him.

Nico's voice sounded in my mind and caused me to sigh out loud.

"So, what?" I asked. "You don't want me to talk to anybody? You know I'm a teacher, right?"

He frowned. "I know that, I mean outside work... Who else do you want to talk to besides my brothers and the girls?"

I shrugged. "Skull."

Kane gritted his teeth.

I pointed my finger at him. "He is me *friend* and, to be honest, I'm closer to him than I am to you. I've known him for years, Kane."

The muscle in his jaw rolled back and forward as he ground his teeth together.

"I don't like him."

That pissed me off.

"You don't even know him."

"I know that he knows you... all of you. I don't like that, so therefore I don't like him."

"Oh, my God," I groaned and rubbed my eyes. "You're confusin' the hell out of me."

"I'm sorry."

I looked at Kane and saw he really was sorry, even though he didn't truly know what he was doing wrong.

"What do you want?" I asked. "I want to make us both happy. Just tell me what you want."

Kane raised his eyebrows. "It's not obvious what I want?"

"Not to me."

He blinked. "You, Aideen. I want *you*."

What?

"What do you mean you want me?" I asked, dumbfounded.

"You aren't stupid, you know what I mean."

I did, but my mind refused to believe it unless he said it.

"We *just* became real friends," I protested.

I didn't know why I was protesting—I told Keela I'd give things a go with Kane. I wanted to give things a go with him, I was just getting caught up in a stupid argument and straying from what needed to happen for my sanity as well as Kane's.

Kane shrugged. "I just want to try being with you. I'll probably be a shitty boyfriend, but what if we don't put a title on us and just... hang out?"

I tilted my head. "Let me get this straight. You want us to be together in a relationship without callin' it a relationship?"

"Exactly."

"Why?"

"Less pressure?" he sighed. "I don't know. I'm trying to figure this out as I talk, babydoll."

I stared at Kane for a long moment. "Is this just because I'm pregnant?"

"No," Kane instantly replied. "Look, I talked to Dominic and he made me make sense of why I think of you a lot and enjoy arguing with you so much. It's because I like you but don't know what to do about it. I don't like people, Aideen. Ever. I sometimes can't stand to be around my brothers, but I want to be around you all the time. Do you understand that? I *want* to be around you. I *need* you, babydoll. You keep me sane, by driving me insane."

I blinked and tried to avoid the heavy part of what Kane was saying with a joke. "Did he give you a run down on his Man Bible as well?" I asked.

I could have sworn he blushed.

"Yeah," he mumbled. "He's learned a few things from being with Bronagh."

I couldn't help but snort.

"I don't know what to say, Kane," I admitted and shifted my stance. "I'm twenty-eight years old, and I'm pregnant with your baby. Startin' a relationship with you seems to be the logical thing to do, but if I'm honest, I'm really scared. What if it goes badly and we hate each other more than before?"

Kane stepped forward. "We won't let that happen."

"We *can't* let it happen," I corrected. "Do you understand me? We can't hate one another whether we get together or not, I don't want our child to grow up in a hostile environment."

Kane's face softened. "Trust me, babydoll, that's that last thing I want, too."

I inhaled and exhaled. "I'm very unsure about this, but if we don't put a title on it, and just continue the way we are, I'll become more trustin'. Is that okay?" I asked. "It's the best I can do right now. I can't jump into a relationship with or without a title without trustin' you."

Kane nodded his head. "That's fine by me, babydoll. I'm just relieved you want to try."

"I do. I like you so much. I'd be lyin' to you and meself if I said I wasn't feelin' for you lately."

Kane waggled his eyebrow. "What things have you been feeling for me exactly? Be descriptive."

"How descriptive?" I grinned.

Kane gasped, "Aideen Collins, are you flirting with me?"

"Flirtin'? You mean me awkwardness is seducin' you?

Kane laughed, "Just give me a come-hither look and you'll seduce me plenty."

I burst into laughter. "Bloody pervert," I said as Kane invaded my space and folded his arms around me, pulling me against his body.

I wrapped my arms around his body and sighed with a smile on my face. This felt right. I didn't know if it was right, but it felt right, and right now that was good enough for me.

"I've never been someone's boyfriend before. Sorry if I'm shit at it."

I laughed against Kane's chest. "I'll ease you into things."

"That sounds good to me, babydoll."

I rolled my eyes but smiled wide.

I felt happy.

Truly happy.

I just hated that there was a voice in the back of my head that whispered, *but for how long?*

CHAPTER TWENTY

"Aideen?"

I looked at my little brother when he called my name. Gavin and my other brothers were in my new apartment putting up new shelves and bookcases that Kane bought for the apartment. He was out with Nico so he couldn't put them up for me, but I didn't mind because it gave me a chance to hang out with my family.

I was officially fully moved out of my old apartment and settled into my new one. It didn't take long for the movers Alec hired to shift everything because Kane already took care of buying new, expensive furniture for the new apartment so it was just things like my clothes and such that needed to be moved in.

"Aideen?" Gavin repeated.

"Hmmm?"

"What's the difference between a girlfriend and a girl friend?" he randomly asked me.

I gave him my full attention.

"Why?" I asked.

Gavin shrugged his shoulders. "I text this girl I've been hangin' around with and asked her what she was to me and she said me girl friend with a gap between the words. I don't get the difference."

I looked at the text when he showed it to me then shrugged my shoulders and said, "The difference, little brother, is the space between girl and friend that everyone calls the friend zone."

My older brothers burst out laughing while Gavin glared at me and said, "Pregnancy has made you evil."

I evilly smirked. "So I've heard."

Gavin grunted, "I feel sorry for Kane, he has to put up with you twenty-four-seven."

I rolled my eyes at him.

Kane and I had been dating, without putting a title on it, for just over a week and things had been great with us. We're getting on better than ever. The only thing I had done with him so far was kissing though. Intense kissing. He wanted to have sex, bad, but I was nervous about it because it was different now that we're together.

Gavin leaned over to me then and got my attention when he put his hand on my stomach. He grinned when the baby moved under his touch. "He loves me already."

I grunted, "She... and you're just lucky."

Gavin snorted and pulled his hand away. "He always moves when I talk, or when I touch your stomach. He can sense me."

"The poor kid is probably sick of hearin' your voice and turns over to get away from you... did you ever think of that?"

Gavin gave our oldest brother the finger and it caused me to snicker.

"He loves me," Gavin repeated, firmly.

I smiled. "Course *she* does."

Gavin laughed, "No more girls are allowed in this family, only boys."

I snickered to myself, "Whatever you say."

Gavin grinned at me then looked at his phone when it beeped. He got a text message and whatever it read caused him to stand up. "I'll call you later, sis."

My stomach churned.

"Where are you goin'?" I questioned.

Gavin gave me a stern look. "Out."

"Don't be smart, Gavin," James grunted as he glanced at our little brother.

Gavin raised an eyebrow. "I'm twenty-two; I don't need to check in when I go someplace."

"Why?" Harley questioned. "Is it too cool to let your family know where you'll be at?"

"No, it's just none of your business."

I narrowed my eyes. "Gavin."

He looked at me and widened his eyes. "Don't you dare."

He knew what I was about to do.

"Are you goin' where I think you're goin'?"

He shrugged and it made my blood boil.

"Tell our big brothers about your new *friends*."

Dante walked over to my front door and leaned against it with his arms folded over his chest when Gavin turned and walked towards it with the intent of leaving.

"Move."

Dante grinned. "Make me."

Gavin's hands balled into fists, and his entire body tensed, but he didn't attempt to make Dante do anything, which I knew he wouldn't.

"Thought so," Dante smirked.

Gavin growled, "Dante, just move."

"No," Dante responded. "Who are these 'friends' Aideen is talkin' about?"

Gavin looked at me. "You're a nosey fuckin' bitch. Why can't you just keep it to yourself?!"

He hissed was Dante forcefully smacked him across the head. "Don't you *ever* talk to her like that, you disrespectful little shite. Do you hear me?"

Gavin rubbed his head. "Tell her to mind her business then!"

I shook my head. "Forgive me for fuckin' carin' about you!"

"I'm fine!" Gavin bellowed. "I don't need lookin' after."

James looked at me. "Tell us who these people are he is hangin' around with. I don't have the patience to wait for him to grow a pair and tell us."

"Oh, my fuckin' God!" Gavin shouted and walked over to my lounge chair, falling onto it. "I can't believe you all treat me like a little kid!"

Because you act like one.

I ignored him and looked at James. "Brandon Daley's crowd."

James stared at me for a second then turned his attention to Gavin. Dante and Harley did the same thing and Gavin yelped when the three of them rushed at him. Dante reached him first and pushed him back onto the lounge chair, holding him there.

"Don't hit me!" Gavin shouted at our brothers.

He wasn't scared of them, he just knew how hard they could hit, and he didn't want to feel any pain.

"You're goin' to explain what you have gotten yourself into. Now!"

I blinked.

James. Was. Pissed.

"I don't need to do a fuckin' thing- Harley!" Gavin roared when Harley reached down and grabbed hold of what looked to be Gavin's dick and his balls.

Ouch.

I pulled a face and tried to cross my own legs as if I could feel Gavin's pain, but my ever-growing belly got in the way.

"So help me God," Harley growled, "I'll rip your pride and joy off in ten seconds if you don't answer the question."

"Wait- just give me a SECOND!"

Harley pulled or twisted something, and it definitely hurt because Gavin's voice rose an octave or two.

Harley evilly chuckled, "Talk, little brother. Now."

"Okay!" Gavin bellowed.

Harley released his privates and stood up straight, he stared down at Gavin, who pressed his hands between his legs and groaned in pain.

"Gav." James pressed.

Gavin looked up at my brothers through hard eyes. "You don't need me to say it; you know I'm jumped in."

Dante reached down, and for the second time, he whacked Gavin across the head. "You just up and made a decision to join a fuckin' gang? *Brandon Daley's* gang? You stupid little eejit!"

Gavin growled, "It's was *my* fuckin' choice. I didn't need permission from you or anyone else."

James was lightning fast when he hit Gavin. He landed a punch directly across his jaw and it caused me to jump up to my feet.

"James!" I bellowed.

Without turning around my brother said, "Sit back down, Aideen."

How did he know I was standing?

"Don't hurt him!" I snapped. "He is stupid beyond measure, but he is our brother. Our *little* brother!"

"Which is exactly why I'm goin' to knock some fuckin' sense into him. Now, sit back down. *Please.*"

Bossy bastard.

I grunted but did as asked and sat back down on my settee.

"Hit me all you want, nothin' will change."

All three of my brothers glared down at Gavin.

"Why?" Dante asked.

"Why what?"

"Don't play stupid, boy," James growled.

"Why join a gang? Why do somethin' so out of character for you? Why do somethin' plain fuckin' stupid?"

Gavin set his jaw. "Because I wanted too, okay?"

"That's your answer?" Harley asked, his voice firm. "Because you wanted too, are you fuckin' jokin' me?"

"Just leave me alone. I don't do anythin', Brandon just has me hang around, and that's it. I don't do anythin' wrong."

Bullshit.

"Not yet," I muttered.

Gavin switched his gaze to me and glared. "Shut up, Aideen."

Yeah, like that would happen.

"*You* shut up and listen to sense," I countered. "Being in a gang is dangerous, it's run by scumbags and you aren't a scumbag. You're tryin' hard to be somethin' you're not."

Gavin pushed himself to his feet and shoulder past Dante and Harley.

"Where are you goin'?" I snapped.

"Away from you four, I don't fuckin' need this bullshit," he threw over his shoulder then slammed my apartment door.

"I'll go get him," James growled.

I began to tear up. "Leave him. The more we force him to do somethin' he doesn't want to, the more it'll push him away."

"So we're just supposed to accept he is in a gang now?" Harley asked me.

I shook my head as tears slipped down my cheeks. "No, I'm handlin' it."

"You're pregnant," Dante frowned. "You shouldn't be handlin' anythin'."

I sighed. "Just trust me. Keela can convince her uncle to do almost anythin'; she said she will get Gavin out without a scratch on his head."

"When?" James questioned.

"Soon," I replied.

He nodded.

Harley frowned at me. "Don't cry, sis. It'll be okay."

I nodded my head and sniffled.

Damn, Gavin.

My brothers continued to frown at me, and then we all looked at sitting room door as the sound of the front door opened and closed.

"Hello?"

"Sittin' room," Harley called out without looking away from me.

Kane, Nico, and Alec walked into my sitting room and each of them raised their eyebrows.

"Everything okay?" Nico asked when he saw me wipe my eyes.

I nodded my head. "Everythin' is fine."

I walked by them, out of the sitting room and directly towards the bathroom. I heard the lads murmur some things as I walked down the hallway, then just as I entered the bathroom, I heard footsteps come down the hallway.

I picked up some tissue and blew my nose. I wiped under my eyes as a large body filled up the doorway.

"Are you okay?"

I nodded my head. "Yes."

"Look at me."

I didn't want to so I kept my back turned to Kane and sniffled. Kane sighed and walked into the bathroom. He put his arms around me and hugged me from behind.

"What happened?" he murmured, "James mentioned Gavin."

I turned in his arms and pressed my face against his chest.

"He is so stupid and stubborn. How can he not see I just want to protect him?"

Kane rested his cheek on the crown of my head. "Like you said, he is stupid and stubborn. He'll realise in time that you and your brothers are doing the right thing."

I sniffled. "What if somethin' bad happens to him?"

"It won't, I can talk to Brandy—"

"No!" I stated and pulled back from Kane's hold. "I don't want you involved with him, I know Brandon, I'll sort this out meself."

Kane's lip twitched. "What happened to everything being me and you?"

My lower lip wobbled. "On this, it's just me. I can't protect both of you at the same time."

Kane smiled. "I'm the protector, babydoll—"

"No, I already called dibs. Sorry."

Kane laughed. "We can protect each other."

"Deal," I murmured.

"Please don't cry anymore," Kane murmured. "It makes me want to beat the shit out of your brother for upsetting you."

I surprisingly laughed, "Me brothers beat you to it."

"I figured as much."

I sighed. "I've missed you."

Kane snorted, "I've only been gone a couple of hours."

"So? I still missed you."

Kane tilted my head up so he could lean down and press his lips against mine. Our kiss started slow, but it quickly became one filled with hunger. Kane kissed me hard and hissed when I bit on his lower lip making me smile.

"I can't wait to have you," he whispered.

I smiled. "You do have me."

"I mean I can't wait to have you naked."

I playfully swatted him. "We *just* started datin', what kind of girl do you think I am? I have morals."

"I hate your morals," he whimpered.

I laughed. "Let me get really comfortable with being with you first. I don't want this to just be physical."

Kane rubbed his nose against mine. "I can wait. It will kill me, but I can do it."

I knew he could, and it made waiting harder.

Literally.

I was in pain.

My back was sore, and I was a grouch because of it.

"Do you want a foot rub?" Kane asked me.

I rolled my eyes. "I want you to piss off and leave me alone."

"Damn, Aideen," he mumbled. "You're cranky today."

I shrugged my shoulders. "You'll get over it."

"You should go fuck yourself."

I looked at Kane with raised eyebrows. "*Excuse* me?"

He held his hands up. "Masturbation is a proven stress reliever. If you won't let *me* fuck you, then fuck *yourself* and calm your pregnant ass down."

I hate that my lip quirked, and I hated that Kane, and his brothers, saw it. My brothers left my apartment hours ago; I was just left with Kane, Nico, and Alec.

"Ah-ha!" He pointed at me. "I made you smile!"

I rolled my eyes. "So?"

"So!" Kane beamed. "I'm not that much of a bastard if I can make you smile."

I forced myself not to laugh. "*You* are a bastard. A huge one."

"I want to throw a lamp at you."

"What? Why?" I asked, wide-eyed.

"Because you need to lighten the fuck up!" Kane grunted and folded his arms across his chest.

I stared at him for a moment, and then burst into laughter.

"What? *Now* you laugh?"

I laughed harder.

"I'll never understand women, never!"

"I'm here to guide you, brother."

"Fuck off, Dominic."

I was wheezing so hard that I thought I might pass out.

"Stop!" I begged and fell sideways into Kane, who was laughing at me laugh.

I quickly got up and waddled out of the room and down the hallway to the toilet. I barely made it to the toilet before I relieved myself. Laughing whilst being pregnant sucked—wetting myself was always a possibility.

When I finished up in the bathroom, I headed back down to the sitting room. I passed the kitchen and saw all three of the brothers were inside making sandwiches. I didn't feel hungry—for once—so I walked back into the sitting room and sat down.

As soon as I sat down, she woke up and it made me smile.

"Kane," I called out.

He walked into the sitting room a few seconds later, a sandwich in his hand.

"Yeah?"

"She's awake; ask your brothers if they want to feel her move."

Kane smiled and walked over to me. He put his sandwich on the coffee table and kneeled before me, pushing my t-shirt up and placing his hands on my belly.

"Dominic, Alec," he called. "Come here."

They both walked into the room, sandwiches in their hands.

"What?" Alec asked.

"Come here, the baby is awake."

They put their sandwiches down then flanked Kane on both sides and kneeled down next to him. Like Kane, they just stared at my stomach.

"Put a hand on her stomach," Kane whispered, a big smile still in place on his handsome face transforming it into a thing of beauty.

Nico and Alec glanced at one another over Kane's head, but did as told and carefully reached a hand out and hesitantly placed them on my bare stomach. I smiled at them both and moved my hands from Kane's to theirs. I laughed when the baby gave a gigantic kick and Nico screeched a little.

"That's definitely a boy!" he declared, proudly.

Alec nodded his head in agreement but then frowned. "Although, Ado can kick pretty hard herself. So can our girls, they can even outdo us some days... Damn, it may be a girl after all."

I snorted, "It *is* a girl, I'm sure of it."

Kane snorted but said nothing.

He beamed when both of his brothers patted him on the back.

"That's a baby Slater in there." Nico smiled.

Alec beamed. "The first of many! I can't wait to make babies with Keela."

I was in awe of the three of them.

They were some of the fiercest men I have ever met in my entire life. They had each severely harmed or killed people—so I'd heard... and yet here they were, kneeling before me and like putty in my hands, over a baby who wasn't even here yet.

"You're goin' to be great uncles," I said to Nico and Alec.

They looked up at me and smiled then leaned up and kissed my cheeks at the same time making me giggle. They refocused on feeling the baby kick. They didn't even move when the door to my apartment opened.

"It's me," Keela shouted.

"And me, and Branna," Bronagh's voice chimed in.

I snorted.

They entered the sitting room and once they saw what the lads were doing, they shot over and leaned over the lads, placing their hands on my stomach.

"I love this," Bronagh squealed.

I frowned. "I'm sad that me stomach is gettin' so big all of your bloody hands fit on it now."

Everyone laughed.

Alec stood up and picked up his sandwich. "We have to go, so you ladies can have more room to feel away."

I frowned and looked at Kane. "Where are you goin'?"

He leaned in and kissed me. "To help Dominic figure some stuff out."

Brandon Daley and Darkness popped into my mind and I grunted.

"My thoughts exactly," Bronagh murmured.

Nico looked at Bronagh then leaned up and kissed her cheek. "It's just a fixture list for fights; I get to choose which ones I want, that's all."

Bronagh nodded her head so Nico kissed her cheek again making her slightly smile. He stood up then and so did Kane.

"Bye," I mumbled.

Kane frowned. "No, I'll see you later."

I rolled my eyes.

He always said that.

"What is with this whole 'see you later' thing?" I asked Kane. "What don't you ever say good-bye?"

Kane focused his eyes on me. "Good-bye is final to me so I never say it to people unless I mean it. I especially don't say good-bye to people I care about so, babydoll... I'll. See. You. Later," he said then turned and walked out of the sitting room and then out of the apartment with Alec and Nico in tow.

Things were silent for a minute or two until Keela opened her big mouth. "I *told* you he deeply cared for you. Didn't I tell you?"

I looked down to the ground and smiled, then looked back up with the same smile playing on my lips as I turned to face my friends.

"Yeah, you told me so."

The girls gasped.

"And you care about him! You're a real couple, not just tryin' it out!" Bronagh squealed then aww'd.

Branna clapped her hands together. "You both make the most beautiful couple!"

"This was the first time he left a room and I didn't feel like I wanted to kill him, let's just take a breather and calm down your big tits down."

All the girls simply smiled at me and after a minute, I cracked and laughed.

"Okay, we make the most beautiful couple."

"And you're both goin' to have the most beautiful baby. Say it!"

I laughed at Bronagh, "We're goin' to have the most beautiful baby, too."

"Atta girl." Keela beamed then stood up and hugged me.

I shook my head, snickering, "It's weird that we're all friends and we're each datin' a brother from the same family."

Bronagh blinked at me. "I've actually never thought about it like that."

"We'll have to fix Damien up with Lana when he comes home to complete the circle," Keela grinned.

Bronagh and Branna shared a look.

"What was that look for?" I questioned.

Bronagh sighed, "It's a long story."

"We've got tea and time," Keela replied. "I've always wanted to know the full story behind Alannah and Damien."

I raised my hand. "I'm kind of tired so can you tell us the short version, but with all the major details?"

Bronagh snorted at me and looked at Branna. "Do you wanna tell them?"

"Nah, you're a good storyteller. You do it."

I aww'd, "You're so nice for sisters."

Bronagh snorted, "She's me sister—I'm supposed to like her."

I snickered when Branna shoved her younger sister with a smirk on her face.

"Okay," Bronagh chuckled. "The short version is Alannah had a crush on Damien from the day she first saw him, but because he slept with so many pretty girls, she didn't fall into his line of sight. That's what she believed anyway."

I clicked my tongue. "Let me guess, he had it bad for her?"

"For her face and body?" Bronagh question. "Yeah."

I widened my eyes. "That's a pig-headed move."

Bronagh shrugged. "Damien was a player back then; he had issues with connectin' to people. He just slept around and didn't care about the trail of broken hearts he left behind him. Granted, he never set out to hurt anyone; he made it clear he just wanted a physical relationship. It didn't change the fact that he was a bit of prick... but a really nice one."

I frowned. "Don't tell me he shagged Lana and left her high and dry."

Bronagh snapped her fingers at me. "Bingo."

I slumped down in my seat. "Poor Lana."

"Yeah, she was crushed," Branna mumbled. "Bronagh had

words with Damien though and it completely knocked him back... she was a little harsh."

Bronagh grunted, "I've said sorry for it, but he needed to hear it. I wasn't standin' for him hurtin' Lana."

"So when Damien left, they were on bad terms?"

Bronagh nodded her head. "Yeah. It's not any better now either. They don't speak, and if they do, it's curt hellos when she is in the room and he is on the phone."

I blinked. "What do you think will happen when Damien comes home?"

"Honestly?" Bronagh asked.

I nodded my head.

She shook her head. "I have *no* fuckin' idea what will happen between them, but whatever *does* go down, no doubt it'll be fuckin' insane. I expect nothin' less from Damien Slater."

CHAPTER TWENTY-ONE

Five weeks later...

"Yeah, I get that, but what I don't understand is how women can bleed for days... and *not* die? That blows my mind."

Alec?

I walked into the kitchen, leaned against the doorway, and folded my arms across my chest.

"We've been over this," Branna groaned and rubbed her hand over her tired face. "*That* blood supply is not pumped from your heart. It doesn't come from a veins or arteries—"

"Then *where* does it come from?" Alec cut Branna off in an ah-ha tone like he caught her on something.

What in the hell did I walk in on?

Branna stared at Alec. "I'm too sober to have this conversation with you."

I snorted and it got both Alec and Branna's attention.

"Preggers!" Alec beamed when he saw me and jumped to his feet.

He walked over to me and leaned his head down to my stomach, kissed it, and rubbed it with his hand. "Hello, baby." He stood up straight and rubbed my head, kissed my cheek, then said, "Hello, Mama."

I smiled and rubbed his chest. "Hello, Uncle."

"Is this a new thing?" Branna asked from the table. "Rubbin' and kissin' body parts when we greet one another."

"Yes!" Alec instantly replied. "Yes, it is, and for future greetings, my preferred body part to be rubbed and kissed is between my thighs."

"Pervert," I said laughing as I playfully swatted at him before walking over to the table where I sat down across from Branna.

I groaned as my feet pulsed with delight when my weight was taking off them.

"Tired?" Branna asked me, smiling.

I nodded my head. "I'm exhausted, and me feet are killin' me. I feel like I gained fifty stone this week alone. I can't stop eatin' pizza. It's a curse."

Branna snickered at me. "You'll be fine; it's just your cravings."

I frowned. "Why can't I crave fruit or vegetables though? Why does it *have* to be pizza? I have no willpower to stay away from it."

Alec laughed from the sink as he filled himself up a glass of water. "Blame Kane, pizza was all he ate back on the compound."

"What are we blaming me on?"

Speak of the Devil.

I didn't look at Kane as he entered the room; I was too tired to even move my head.

"Aideen has pizza cravings, and pizza is all you ate when we were kids so I told her to blame you for her weight gain," Alec snickered.

Kane mumbled curse words at him then moved across the room to me where he hunkered down next me and nudged my arm with his head. "What weight gain? You look hotter than ever."

I growled. "Don't. I'm too tired to hit you for lyin'."

Kane chuckled and leaned in, pecking my lips. He rubbed his nose against mine, and it only caused me to lean into him further.

I sighed against his mouth. "Did I give you your second injection yet? I can't remember."

Kane licked my lower lip before he pulled back and said, "No, we can go do it now... then watch a movie?"

That sounded perfect.

"Okay. Help me up."

Kane stood up, took hold of my hands, and pulled.

My back clicked and I groaned. "That felt brilliant."

Branna laughed at me. "It's goin' to be interestin' to see how you are in a few months when you're bigger."

Bigger?

"If I get any bigger, I'll split in two," I said to Branna, my eyes narrowed.

She burst into laughter. "You're twenty-seven weeks gone, and though you *are* big for that time scale, wait till you're four weeks out from your due date. That is when hell happens. You will balloon out, you'll be constantly uncomfortable, you'll never sleep, you'll cry a lot... all the good stuff."

I stared at Branna, my eyes wide.

"I hate you."

She laughed as I left the room with Kane in tow.

"Bye, preggers!" Alec shouted after me.

I grunted but didn't reply.

I walked up the first flight of stairs without much effort, but halfway up the second flight, it almost killed me. "I can't make it up to your room," I groaned.

This was ridiculous, I was pregnant, not disabled, and yet I could barely walk. Pregnancy was hard, *so* fucking hard.

Kane placed his hands on my hips. "You're nearly there; you can nap when you get to my room."

"Okay," I breathed.

Kane kept his hands on my hips and I felt him push me upwards as I took the stairs one step at a time. I appreciated it; he was giving me a much-needed boost.

"What can I do to make you comfortable?" Kane asked me when I laid down on his bed.

I glanced at him, feeling a little embarrassed though I wasn't sure why. He was my boyfriend after all... but I was wary around him because we still hadn't had sex yet. I wanted to. God, I really wanted to. But I wasn't comfortable enough with my body right now to even attempt it.

"You can rub me back because it's hurtin' a lot lately."

"Okay, turn on your side," Kane murmured.

I did as he asked, but stilled when he moved very close to me. I quickly relaxed and groaned when he pressed his fingers into the base of my spine and rotated them in a circle. "Here?" he asked.

It felt nice, but not nice enough.

I gnawed on my lower lip. "Pull up me top, the material is botherin' me when you rub."

Kane mutely pulled up my top and exposed my skin. I felt a little insecure with what I knew he was looking at so I cleared my throat and said, "Sorry about the stretch marks. I tried a few different creams to keep them at bay, but they don't seem to work on me."

Kane stilled. "Don't apologise for what your body is going through because you're growing my baby. Not ever."

I flushed when he placed his palm on my soft hip and slid it around to my front where he rubbed over my belly in lazy circles. "Your body is perfect, babydoll, even more so now that you're swollen with my baby. I love that you look like this because of me."

Oh.

I needed to break the sudden rise in temperature in the room.

"Come back to me in a few months when me body is enormous, and I have stretch marks so purple they look like a roadmap to Hell."

Kane vibrated with laughter then placed a kiss on my still covered shoulder. "Relax, be quiet, and let me rub your pain away."

The growing, aching, pain between my thighs or the one in my back?

I grinned to myself as I exhaled and snuggled deeper into the pillow under my head. I licked my lips when Kane brought his hand back to the base of my spine and rubbed.

"Harder," I groaned.

Kane brought his head to my shoulder and growled. He dug his fingers into my back and I felt myself go cross-eyed as an amazing but unexpected sensation crashed into my body.

"Yes," I breathed. "Right there. Harder."

Kane moved he fingers faster against my skin, and I gasped when hot heat spread throughout my body. I closed my eyes and hummed in delight at the relaxation that spread throughout my body in hot tingles. I was silent and dazed for a few moments until I opened my eyes, and then widened them to the point of pain when I realised what just happened.

Did I just... Did I just?

"Omigod," I breathed and flung hand over my face. "Oh, my God. I'm *so* sorry."

Kane was silent for a moment then he said, "For what?"

Like he didn't know.

"I'm mortified right now. I didn't realise I would be able to... to..."

"Come from a back rub?" Kane finished my sentence for me. "Your body is super sensitive, I'm not surprised. Besides I am *the man*, so you shouldn't be surprised either."

Well, I bloody was. I had an orgasm and all he did was knead my back, for Christ's sakes. I was *never* going to live this down.

"Babydoll, don't be embarrassed. Not about this. Not with me."

I huffed, "How can I not? You just rubbed me back and I had an orgasm. A really good one, too."

Kane nipped my shoulder with his teeth. "This is a pretty proud moment for me. I feel like the king of the world for making you come from just rubbing your back. I took your back pain away and made you feel drunk on an orgasm. Pat on the back for Kane," he teased.

I groaned as he rolled me onto my back and froze when he nuzzled his face against the side of mine. "Besides," he murmured, "it was sexy."

It was?

"Really?" I whispered.

"Oh, yeah," he purred. "I *felt* the moment you let go, babydoll."

Oh damn, the ache from before was back, and it was pulsing hard between my thighs.

"Stop talkin' like this," I pleaded, my voice low.

Kane looked down at my legs and saw the moment I clenched my thighs together. A devilish smirk curved his lips as he looked back to me.

"Why?" he asked, licking his lips. "I can make you feel *so* good, babydoll. I can rub, and thrust, your pain away. You know I can."

Oh, God.

"I wanna fuck you during the daylight. I want to see you. Every single inch."

"Stop it."

"I'd bet you'd look adorable grasping the sheets of my bed."

He did not.

"Kane!"

"Oh, a preview." He beamed.

That bastard.

I was going to beg him to touch me if he didn't stop.

"Kane," I whispered. "*Please.*"

"Say yes," he murmured and brought his lips down to mine, brushing a kiss over them. "Say yes, and I'll love your body until you can't see straight. Let me fuck you good, babydoll."

Oh, damn.

"Yes," I breathed. "Yes, please."

Kane growled and took my mouth in his. The kiss was slow, seductive, and perfect. *So* perfect. I lifted my hands up so I could slide them around his neck, but Kane reached up and caught them both before I could touch him.

"No touching," he breathed against my mouth.

What?

"Kane, please," I pleaded. "I *need* you."

Kane smiled, and the action transformed his entire face.

"You have me, babydoll. All of me," he said then disappeared from my sight.

He moved down the bed, gripped onto the band of my leggings and my underwear, slid them down my legs, and pulled them off my body in one fluid motion. I yelped with surprise and tried to close my legs, but Kane was already between them and stopped my hide-my-vagina reflex from kicking in.

I looked down, but could only see his hair.

It made me laugh.

"What's funny?" Kane asked.

"Me belly. It's blockin' me view of you," I cackled.

And Branna said I wasn't even big yet, I called bullshit on that.

"You don't need to see me, babydoll. Just feel me."

And feel him, I did.

I fisted the bed sheets around me when he spread me with his fingers, put his tongue on my clit, and sucked. My hips bucked, so he gripped my hips with his strong hands and held me down as he danced around my clit with his talented tongue.

Fuck.

Breathe, just breathe and you will be- "Oh, fuck! Kane!" I cried out and cut my thoughts off when he rubbed his lips back and forth over my clit, and then moved his head from side to side. I bit down on my lower lip and fisted the bed sheets around me.

I felt my eyes roll back when Kane bore down on my clit and sucked like his life depended on it. I felt my orgasm build, and just before it hit, everything when numb then I stopped breathing as the first pulse hit me.

"Yes!" I cried out.

With each pulse Kane sucked out of me, my back arched. As soon as the pleasure stopped and all that was left was the sensitive tingle between my thighs, I wiggled away from Kane's mouth. He chuckled low in his throat when I pushed my way up the bed.

"Are you trying to get away from me?"

"Sensitive," I panted as flattened my back on the bed.

Kane crawled up my body and hovered over me. I looked down and found his stomach touching mine, and it made me laugh.

"This is so awkward."

Kane glanced at my belly then back to my face and smirked. "You could always be on top if this position bothers you."

I swallowed. "What if I look horrible from that angle though?"

Kane deadpanned, "Nothing about you is horrible. I love your pregnant body. Do you understand that? I love it."

He did?

"Oh."

"Yeah." He grinned. "Oh."

"I'll get on top then," I murmured.

Kane rolled onto his back, quickly rid himself of his trousers and boxers, and reached over to help me sit up. I kneeled next to him and bit the bullet by gripping the hem of my shirt and pulling it over my head.

"Fuck me," Kane breathed as his drank in the view of me.

He sat up and reached his hands around to my back. He unclasped my bra and I sighed in relief as it fell from my body.

Kane placed his hands on my back where the straps were and massaged the area in circles.

I groaned in pleasure.

"Does that feel better?" Kane murmured.

I nodded my head and looked down at him. He was looking up at me with a mixture of lust admiration on his gorgeous face. I leaned my mouth down to his and kissed him.

He moaned into my mouth, slid his hands down to my behind, and squeezed. I growled into his mouth and latched onto his lower lip, nibbling on it.

Kane slapped my behind and it caused me to yelp.

"Ride me, babydoll." Kane grunted into my mouth.

I blinked at him. "Deja vu."

Kane grinned. "I'll change it up. How does... fuck me, babydoll sound?"

I smiled as I leaned up and allowed Kane to grip his cock so I could sink down on it. My eyes fluttered closed as Kane rubbed himself against my clit before lining his cock up with my entrance. I squeezed his shoulders with my hands as I lowered myself down onto him.

"Yes," he hissed. "Fuck, Aideen. You're so tight."

Enjoy the tightness while it lasts.

I swallowed down a moan and leaned my head down to Kane's as I began to move up and down. I gasped and bit down on my lower lip when jolts of pleasure shot up throw my body.

"What is it?" Kane breathed.

I licked my lips. "The sensation is heightened. I feel *everythin'*."

Kane watched me as I lifted up and lowered myself back down onto his cock.

"Is that a good thing?" he asked.

I nodded my head. "Yes, it's *so* good."

Kane grinned and lay back on his bed. He ran his hands over my pregnant belly, and then lifted them to my breasts. I hissed when he rubbed them a little too roughly.

"Gently," I chastised.

Kane smirked but did as asked.

He ran his fingertips in lightly circle patterns around my nipples, and it caused shivers to run up and down my spine.

My breathing became laboured when I picked up my speed and slammed down on Kane's cock like there was no tomorrow.

"Fuck!" Kane roared and bucked his hips up into me.

"Yes," I panted. "Oh, please, yes!"

"Come on, babydoll," Kane growled and smacked my thighs. "Come all over me."

I cried out as I bore down on him and slammed down onto him until my body exploded into sensation. I felt Kane's hand grab hold of my arms to stop me from falling off his body sideways.

My insides pulsed, my skin tingled, and my head was swimming. I blinked my eyes opened as Kane lay me down on the bed. I could see he was about to crawl between my legs, but I shook my head.

"Doggie style," I breathed and rolled onto my side.

I used every ounce of strength in my body to push myself up on all fours, but I did it, and Kane wasted no time entering my body from behind.

Fuck.

"I'm so into you, babydoll," Kane said then placed a kiss on my back.

I glanced over my shoulder. "Yeah, well, I'm into you... a little."

Kane grinned at me. "I am most definitely *in* to you, too. A lot. Quite literally, actually."

I rolled my eyes. "You're such a lad; you never miss an opportunity to make a sexually related pun."

"We're having sex... I'm *inside* of you right now," Kane growled. "Do you expect anything differently of me?"

"No," I instantly replied, "I don't, and that's really sad. You aren't very high up on my expectations list."

Kane closed his eyes. "I'm hearing your words, I really am, but I'm balls deep inside you right now, so I just don't give a fuck what the hell you're saying."

I opened my mouth to tell him off, but he slid out of my body and thrust back in with such force that it made me choke on my own words.

"Harder?" Kane asked.

I was about pass out, and a harder pounding might make that happened, but what the hell?

"Harder."

Kane dug his fingers into my hips and squeezed my flesh as his thrust deep inside me.

"Yes!" I cried out.

Kane slapped my arse. "Fuck, babydoll, you feel so good

wrapped around my cock."

My eyes fluttered shut. "Kane, please."

"Say you're mine." He growled.

"Kane," I panted.

"Say." Thrust. "You're." Thrust. "Mine." Thrust.

"I'm yours," I cried out.

Kane let out a low rumbling growl as he got a huge spurt of energy and repeatedly slammed into my body causing me to go cross-eyed.

I stopped breathing as he banged an unexpected third orgasm out of me. I lost control of my arms and fell forward. I twisted so I landed on my side.

Kane fell in front of me onto his back.

"That was—"

"Brilliant," I finished on a laboured breath. "Pregnant sex is just fuckin' *brilliant*."

Kane turned on his side, pressed his face against my cheek, and threw his arm over my chest. He kissed my cheek and it made me lazily smile. He nuzzled against me and cocked his leg over mine. It caused me to giggle.

"I can only do one round, big boy. Leave me be."

Kane laughed, "I'm not trying. I'm too tried to move."

I cracked up, "At least you're honest."

Kane lightly chortled then sighed in content.

I lifted my hands and ran my fingers back and forth over his arm. I leaned my head to the side then gasp when I felt her... move in my stomach. She really moved. I'd felt her move about during work, and sometimes during the night, but never when Kane was next to me.

I swallowed.

"Kane," I murmured as she gave me a swift kick causing me to gasp.

Kane sat up. "What is it?" he asked, panicked.

I looked at him with tears in my eyes and gestured him over to me.

"Quickly," I whispered. "She's movin'."

Kane's eyes widened and for a moment, he just sat staring at me, then he suddenly snapped out of it and moved closer.

"What do I do?" he asked me as he stared at my abdomen.

He looked lost.

I reached out and took his hands in mine, and placed them flat on my stomach. I covered them with mine and waited, for a few seconds nothing happened, and then... and then magic happened.

"Oh, my God," I said and looked at Kane. "Can you feel that?"

Kane gazed at my stomach and then up at me. "I can feel him. I can *really* feel him."

I burst into tears and nodded my head.

Kane kept his hands on my stomach and a huge smile on his face. He leaned down and kissed my stomach then he whispered, "I'm your daddy."

Oh, God.

I couldn't take it.

The tears were fast and furious as the streamed down my face. I forced myself to calm down because I didn't want the baby to stop moving so I took in a few breaths until I wasn't a blubbering mess.

"Finally, she moves a lot when you're around," I laughed as my tears of joy fell down my face.

Kane smiled and looked down to my stomach. "I can really feel him."

"Her," I corrected through my tears.

Kane shook his head, smiling.

"Our relationship is based on this argument."

"This isn't a relationship."

"What is it then?"

"A debate team."

Kane laughed at me then bent his head and kissed my belly. "I love you already."

My heart!

"I can't wait to meet her," I murmured.

Kane looked at me and smiled. "Me too, babydoll. Me too."

I simpered, "You looked like a new person right now. I love it."

Kane blinked his eyes then lowered them. "You mean because I'm smiling? I know—it changes my face. I've heard that before."

I frowned. "No, I meant you as a person, not your looks."

Kane swallowed. "Oh."

I tilted my head to the side. "I love *your* body the way it is; I just want to make that clear."

"You love my body?" Kane asked, moving back to my side now that our little one settled into a peaceful slumber.

I nodded my head. "What's not to love?"

"My scars," Kane instantly replied.

"Your scars are beautiful. *You* are beautiful," I said as I tenderly traced the many scars on his arm with my fingertips.

Kane looked into my eyes. "Beautiful?" he repeated, his voice low.

"Beautiful." I nodded and placed my hands flat on his marred but stunning skin. "Your wounds are closed, and your pain is over. What's left behind is a design, a picture that shows you were stronger than your hurt. That's what I see when I look at them, I see how strong you were. How strong you *are*."

Kane fully turned to me and stared at me with a gaze that caused my breathing to quicken.

"The scars... they physically healed a long time ago, but I've relived receiving them a million times in my head, and then... then you happened and made everything better. You've kept my demons at bay by just being you." Kane reached and placed his trembling hands on my thighs. "You healed me, babydoll."

Oh.

"Kane," I whispered breathlessly.

He licked his lips. "Yes?"

"Kiss me," I panted, "now."

I didn't need to ask him twice.

He covered my mouth with his and pressed me back down against his mattress. I tried my best to kiss him back with the same intensity he gave to me, but I was exhausted.

"You're tired." He smiled.

I hated that my stamina was fucking up our moment.

"I'm sorry," I panted.

Kane kissed my head. "Don't be sorry, just rest."

"Let me feel you. All of you."

Kane swallowed. "O-Okay."

I sat up and traced my fingers over all of his scars. I paused a couple of times to kiss them too. I wanted to shower Kane's body with love so he never doubted my thoughts towards it again. I was about to lie back down on the bed when I brushed my fingers over the hair that covered his neck and felt really thick lumps.

I tilted my head to the side and I pushed Kane's hair out of the way. When I did so, I froze.

"Kane," I whispered, "it says 'Marco'."

Kane moved away from me. He stood up from the bed and pulled on a pair of tracksuit trousers. "I know what it says."

"That's not a tattoo," I continued. "It's a scar."

Kane wouldn't look at me as I stated the obvious.

"Yes, it's a scar, Aideen."

I shook my head. He said it like it wasn't a big deal when it was. It really was.

"Was it carved into you? Who done it? Why—"

"Aideen!"

I jumped with fright when Kane bellowed my name. I shrunk back against the pillows behind me and tightly closed my lips together.

"Leave it alone."

I couldn't.

"Marco made you do your jobs, right? They were the cause of the scars, weren't they?"

"Aideen."

Oh, fuck.

He was infuriated.

"Okay," I whispered and looked away from him.

Kane was silent for a few moments before he said, "I'm going for a run. I'll be back later."

I looked at his bedroom door when he exited through it and to his back I thought, *I won't be here when you get back.*

CHAPTER TWENTY-TWO

"What's wrong with you?"

I was sitting in my new apartment with my girlfriends surrounding me, but I didn't feel present in the room with them. My mind was elsewhere.

I looked at Bronagh when she spoke to me.

"What?"

Bronagh deadpanned, "Don't play dumb, somethin' is botherin' you. You ask us round for some tea and a chat, but you have barely spoken and we got here hours ago. Spill."

I didn't want to spill. I didn't want to do anything.

"Did you and Kane have a fight?" This came from Branna when I remained silent.

I shrugged my shoulders. "Kind of."

"You can't *kind of* have a fight with a Slater brother," Keela interjected. "You either did or you didn't."

I rolled my eyes. "I did then."

"Why?" Bronagh asked, her voice soft.

I exhaled. "I asked him about his scars."

"Oh, fuck," Branna mumbled.

Yeah. Oh, fuck.

"My sentiments exactly," I grunted.

Keela whistled. "A shitstorm happened?"

I nodded my head. "There was no cursin' or even much shoutin'... he just shut me down with the look in his eyes and the way he said me name. He went out runnin' so I came home."

Bronagh leaned her head back against my settee. "We can be expectin' him soon then." It was a statement, not a question.

I shrugged. "He might not come over, he wasn't happy with my pryin'."

"You could hold a gun to his head and he would still come to you," Keela snorted and the girls agreed.

I frowned. "This time was different... I asked about a scar with a name on his neck and he just... blew up."

"What name on his neck?" Bronagh asked, surprised.

I looked at her. "You've never seen it?"

She shook her head and so did the others.

"Huh. His hair must have hidden it from sight. It's right on the back of his neck."

"Whose name is on his neck?" Keela asked, her voice tight.

I looked away as I said, "Marco."

"*What*?!"

I swallowed. "It's carved onto his neck. It's horrible lookin'. I can only imagine how much it hurt him."

"Oh, my God," Keela whispered.

"Poor Kane," Branna whimpered.

Oh, no.

"Don't cry, you'll set me off and if I start I won't stop."

"Sorry," Branna sniffled and wiped under her eyes.

I clasped my hands together over my stomach. "I didn't only ask about his scars..."

"I don't like how you left that open," Branna sighed.

Bronagh sat forward. "I asked about his job for Marco because I know whatever it was caused the scars."

"Bollocks," this came from Keela.

I nodded my head. "Yep, it's a right shit storm."

"Why did you ask the questions?" Bronagh questioned.

"Because I felt like I only know half of a person, I just want to understand him... Nico said—"

"Oh, Jesus Christ," Bronagh cut me off. "What did that bastard of mine tell you?"

I couldn't help but laugh. "He told me a few weeks ago to ask Kane these questions, but I had to wait for the right time. Earlier on felt like the right time."

Bronagh rubbed her hands over her face. "Knowin' the answers to your questions is this important?"

I nodded. "I wish I could overlook the scars. I wish I could be that woman who didn't have to know what made him the way he is today, but I'm not. I need to know, so I can fully understand him. Does that make me sound crazy?"

"No, honey," Branna said and moved closer to me. "It makes you human."

I nodded my head. "I'm just afraid... I don't want to lose him. This feelin', it's exactly what I was terrified of. It's the reason I didn't want to get with him. I didn't want to develop deep feelin's and I have. I love him so much, and it breaks me heart that someone hurt him and that it's still hurting him. I want to help him, but I don't know how."

"You love Kane?"

I blinked. "What?"

"You said you loved him."

I did?

I closed my eyes as realisation struck me. "I love him. Fuck!"

"Aideen," Keela murmured, her voice soothing.

I turned to her and wrapped my arms around her body.

"You won't lose Kane," she said firmly in my ear.

I hiccupped, "How do you know that?"

"Because," Bronagh chuckled, "he loves you, too."

What?

I pulled back from Keela and looked at Bronagh. "He loves me?"

Bronagh was beaming at me. "Of course, only an eejit would miss it."

The girls nodded in unison.

I dumbly blinked.

I guess I was a massive eejit then because I had no clue. The more I thought about Kane, the deeper my own feelings became. It caused a sick feeling to fill my stomach and a pain to develop in my chest.

I must have been coming down with something.

The flu probably.

"I know he really cares—"

"Ado," Branna interrupted, "he loves you, he probably won't say it for a while, if ever, but he does."

Oh.

"That's... a lot to take in."

"I know, but *do* take it in," Keela said. "Don't ignore it."

I looked down. "It doesn't change that I want to know about his past and it's a huge problem for him."

The girls sighed but said nothing.

I looked down for a few more minutes then said, "I'm really tired."

Keela frowned. "Go to bed, we'll tidy up here and lock up after we leave."

I didn't need to be told twice.

I hugged all my friends and ventured out of the sitting room and down the hallway to my bedroom. I didn't even change for a nap, I just kicked off my shoes and climbed into bed. I closed my eyes and let my exhaustion take over.

I was out in seconds.

I woke up some time later and found it was dark outside. I pushed myself up as I swung my legs over the side of my bed and just sat there for a few seconds. I groaned when my bladder demanded to be emptied. I rubbed my eyes then stood up and walked out of my room and down the hallway to my bathroom.

After I had relieved myself, I washed my hands in the bathroom sink and dried them with one of the new, soft hand towels I purchased. I left the bathroom and walked back out into the hallway. I listened for any noises—usually Kane would be watching the television or something while I napped, but it didn't sound like he was here.

He was still mad at me.

I shook my head and walked down to my kitchen. I stepped inside the room and quickly jumped back into the hallway. The cold of the tile floor in the kitchen was a little too much for me so I walked back down to my bedroom and switch the light on so I could find my slippers. I couldn't see them lying around so I walked over to my wardrobe and pushed open the door then stood back as the rest automatically folded open.

I looked inside for my slippers and spotted them next to a bag.

I glanced at Kane's gym bag. He brought it with him when he stopped by a few nights ago, but he forgot to bring it with him when he left the next day, so I put it into my wardrobe for safe keeping. I forgot all about it because he never mentioned it. But now that I see it, I realised he has worked out in his house and has gone running with Nico and his other brothers plenty since then. Wouldn't he need his stuff from inside the bag? His runners and such?

Curiosity got the best of me, so I kneeled down on the floor and pulled the bag towards me. I gripped onto the zip and pulled it open. I puffed the sides of the bag out so I could look inside and see the contents. I leaned back a little expecting a foul smell—it was a gym bag after all—but there was no stench. There was no smell at all.

That was weird.

I leaned forward and looked into the bag, but I couldn't see anything thanks to the shadows from my wardrobe. I scooted back a little and slid the bag along the floor with me. I leaned forward again, and this time when I looked into the bag, I clearly saw the contents. I gasped when saw bundles of money with elastic bands wrapped around them. Not small bills either, it was bundles of five-hundred Euro notes. Hundreds of them.

"Oh, my God," I whispered.

I didn't flinch when I heard my front door open and close. Nor did I flinch when I heard him call out my name.

"Aideen?"

I continued to stare down at the money and called out, "In me bedroom."

I heard his footsteps then—each one brought him closer to me and my discovery.

"Hey baby, I just wanted to say I'm—" Kane cut himself off when he entered my room, and I knew it was because of what he saw.

He was silent for a few moments then he said, "I have an explanation for that."

I looked up at him, my eyes burning into his.

"Really? Because I can't wait to hear it."

Chapter Twenty-Three

"Well?" I prompted Kane after a minute of silent staring.

He swallowed. "I'm trying to think of the right way to word what I'm going to say."

"Please, take your time," I sarcastically hissed.

Kane narrowed his eyes. "I want to explain myself correctly. Just give me a second to figure out how."

"You mean you want a second to figure out a way to weasel your way out of tellin' me where the fuck you got all this money from?"

Kane set his jaw. "I'm not going to lie to you, so don't insinuate that I will."

Was there a silent 'or else' at the end of that sentence?

I ignored Kane's brewing temper.

"I'm waitin' on your explanation as to why thousands of Euros is sittin' in me fuckin' wardrobe like it's nothin' more than a pair of cheap shoes."

"And I'll give you the explanation if you would give me a fucking second to speak."

I struggled to my feet and slapped Kane's hand when he came to my aid.

"I can do it meself," I snapped and pushed myself upright. "You just talk."

The muscles in Kane's jaw rolled back and forth.

"It's my money. I earned it. End of story."

Like fuck it was.

"Don't you fuckin' *dare* try to brush this off. Do you see how much money is in that bag?" I bellowed.

Kane's hands balled into fists. "It's my money, I know how much is there."

"Why're you actin' like this is normal? It's not fuckin' normal!"

He placed his face in his hands. "I don't want to argue, please."

Seriously?

"If there was ever a reason to argue it's because of this, Kane!"

He turned and punched my bedroom door, instantly denting the wood.

"What the fuck do you want from me?!"

I didn't hesitate.

"The truth," I demanded. "For once just tell me the fuckin' truth!"

"Why?" Kane screamed causing me to stumble backwards away from him. "Why do you have to know everything about me? Why can't I have some secrets left that are just for me?"

I pushed the wardrobe door closed and pressed my hand against it. I just needed something to hold onto. "Because I just found a bag of cash in the back of me wardrobe and I want to know where the hell you got it from."

Kane lifted his hands to his head and ran his fingers through his hair. "It's *my* money, okay? Apart from the income from my apartments, I don't do bank accounts with my money. I never have. I don't like paper trails. I only deal in cash."

I blinked. "That doesn't answer me question."

"Aideen."

"Where did the money come from Kane?"

Kane stared at me, hard. "I've been freelancing my... talents to some shitty people, okay?!"

A knot twisted in my stomach.

"Why does *that* mean?"

Kane set his jaw. "It means if someone requires a beat down, people pay me to do it. I hurt shitty people for other shitty people."

I reared back like I was slapped across the face.

"You... you *hurt* people?"

Kane said nothing, he didn't even blink.

"Get out."

"No."

No?

"You don't get a say in this. Get the fuck out of me apartment. Now."

"I own the building."

I knew he would eventually throw that in my face!

"You may own the building, but I lease this fuckin' apartment so *get out!*"

Kane stood rooted to the spot. "You wanted to talk about this, so now we're going to talk about it."

"After what you just admitted? I don't think so!" I snapped.

I got my phone from my pocket and dialled Nico's number. I put it to my ear and looked Kane dead in his eyes as his brother answered his phone.

"Come and get Kane from me apartment right now."

Nico's voice was hard when he asked, "What's wrong?"

"He is a lyin' son of bitch who hurts people for a livin'. I want him out of me apartment right now. I'm serious, Nico, come get him or I'm callin' me brothers."

I screeched when Kane came at me.

"Don't you touch me!" I screamed and dashed to the right.

Kane punched my wardrobe door, and because the wood wasn't thick like my door, his fist went through it.

"Tell my brother everything is okay and hang up the phone."

I couldn't help but laugh. "Not a chance in hell- Kane!"

I gasped when Kane shot forward, grabbed my phone and threw it against my bedroom wall. My iPhone shattered into pieces before it even touched the ground. I stared at the fragments on the floor for a moment then without looking at Kane I turned and walked out of my bedroom.

"Wait, I'm sorry," Kane said from behind me. "I didn't mean to do that, you just—"

"Made you angry?" I shouted and spun around to face him. "Every time you get angry you seem to lose it. You shout at people, punch stuff, and now you've upgraded to breakin' stuff? How long will it be before you black out and hit the real source of your anger, huh? How long until you take out your anger on *me*?"

Kane widened his eyes. "I would never, hear me clearly on this, *ever* hit you."

"I can't trust that and that's the fuckin' problem."

Kane looked like I punched him.

"You can't believe I would hurt you. You just can't."

I swallowed. "I don't know, Kane. This is all becomin' too much for me. You aren't honest with me, you lash out at me when I ask questions, and you borderline obsessed with me when it comes to other men."

"Because you're mine!" Kane snapped.

I jumped a little, but quickly composed myself.

"I understand that," I stated, my voice surprisingly calm. "I really do. I'm your girlfriend—"

"No, you don't get it. You're mine. Everything about you is mine."

I blinked. "You don't own me, Kane."

"Yes. I. Do."

I took a step backwards. "I'm not property."

"I know you're not," Kane grunted and took a step towards me, "but being mine doesn't make you an object, it makes you my life. You are my life, Aideen. I love you."

I stopped breathing.

"What?" I whispered.

"I love you," Kane repeated louder and firmer.

My stomach began to hurt, my chest tightened, and my head spun.

"What?" I repeated, again.

Kane closed the remaining distance between us. "I. Love. You."

Fuck, Bronagh was right.

That was the only thing I could think of during Kane's declaration of love for me.

"I can't deal with this," I eventually said.

Kane didn't move. "What are you saying?"

"I'm sayin' that was the wrong moment to tell me you love me. You shouldn't have said it."

"I shouldn't have said it? It's what I'm feeling."

I swallowed. "You harm people, Kane."

"*Bad* people, Aideen. We're talking about the scum of the earth here."

I shook my head. "I don't care, it doesn't justify what you do."

Kane turned and began to pace up and down the hallway.

"You own apartments, a real-estate agency. You have more money than you need, why do you continue to... freelance?"

He had his back to me when he stopped moving. I saw the muscles in his back tense as I asked my question.

"I donate all the money I get from freelancing to different charities. I don't do it for the money, it was never about money."

I closed my eyes. "Then why do you do it?"

"Because I have to."

"*Why?*"

He turned to face me, a sadistic smirk on his face.

"Don't dare look at me like that. Don't think being cold and mean is going to get you out of this conversation."

"Cold and mean," Kane repeated then humourlessly laughed. "That pretty much describes what people think of me. One look at me and they're scared. Are you scared of me, babydoll?"

Only of the way you make me feel.

"A puppy has more chance of scarin' me that you do, Slater," I deadpanned.

A smile light up Kane's face, but only for a moment before his sullen look took over once more. "Everyone is scared of me. They think I'm a monster, and you know what? Maybe I am. I didn't get this way by being an angel, that's for damn sure."

I frowned. "I don't understand."

"Good," Kane replied, "I don't want you to understand me."

"Well, I want to!" I shouted. "I *want* to know you."

That admission shocked me as well as Kane.

Kane shook his head. "If you get answers to the questions on your mind you will leave me. You won't let me get within five feet of you and our baby. I know you won't."

I swallowed. "Sweetheart, if you tell me what I need to know nothin' will happen. I'm not goin' to leave you."

Kane blinked his eyes. "Everybody leaves me, Aideen. Everybody."

What?

"Who has left you?" I asked, my hands trembling.

"You want the list?" Kane snorted. "My parents—they left me long before they died because they were shitty fucking people. My brothers mean everything to me, but they don't have the time of day for me anymore since their girls came into the picture. Damien up and left and went back to the States four years ago and hasn't been back since. When you aren't with me, I'm on my own. Everybody leaves, even if they don't mean too."

I was surprised when hot tears filled my eyes. "You should let your brothers know how you feel, you know they would re-evaluate everything they do if they thought for a second you felt alone and pushed aside by them."

Kane shook his head. "It's fine. I'm fine."

"Don't lie to me," I stated. "You're not fine, and you need to talk to your family about this."

"I am," he murmured, "I'm talking to you."

He considered me his family?

"Kane," I whispered.

He shook his head. "Enough with the heavy emotional bullshit, let's talk about something else."

I glared at him. "No, the heavy emotional bullshit needs to be discussed."

Kane blinked. "Please, babydoll, I don't want to lose you too and a conversation about *my* heavy shit will make that happen."

I stood my ground. "Talk about your heavy shit or I *will* leave you."

I didn't like saying that, but I had too.

Kane stared at me for a long moment. "You won't be mine anymore once you know the things I have done. I know you won't."

I placed my hand in his. "Me and you?"

Kane swallowed and squeezed his eyes shut. "Me and you."

I waited patiently then for him to speak. He silently led me into the sitting room and sat us down on the settee. I turned to face him, but Kane kept his body straight and stared at the television in from to us.

"Do you know why my brothers and I were involved with Marco?"

I swallowed. "I know that he ran a business with your father and after your father had died he took over. That's about it. The girls don't like talkin' about it so I'm short on information."

"Okay, that's true, but there is a lot more to it than that." He sighed and prepared himself to say words he didn't want to say. "Marco and my father ran a business that earned them the title of gangsters. Nothing they did was straight up—even the legal shit was corrupt. Everything from drugs, to weapons and prostitution, was fair game."

Wow.

"I, along with my brothers, was raised in a compound back in New York. We were homeschooled so we never got out much. The compound was huge and there was always something to do so we weren't bored... until we were old enough to be put to work."

I didn't like the sound of that.

"The twins were still kids when Ryder, Alec, and myself started out. We did small time shit like moving product, delivering it, breaking in new recruits. Bullshit like that. Marco always said my dad had big plans for us, but I don't think he ever did. I think it was Marco who had plans for us, and when my dad double-crossed him, killing him and my mom gave him access to us. Granted the three of us were old enough to leave if we wanted to—and we did—but we couldn't get out with the twins fast enough."

"What do you mean?" I murmured.

Kane leaned his head back against the sofa cushion. "Damien had this girlfriend called Nala. She was a cute Asian kid and he adored her. That was little brother's problem—he cared too much about people. He was messed up when our parents died. He understood we couldn't cross Marco though. We were brought up around an empire that preached loyalty. It was instilled in us from a very young age. We were loyal to the core to one another, to our parents, and even to Marco, even though the three of them didn't deserve it. What our father did was wrong, he betrayed someone he swore to be loyal to, and to us and that's not right. You don't turn your back on your own, but my parents did."

I listened to Kane as he spoke, and the more I listened, the more scared I became.

"Even though Damien understood our father was a traitor, he wouldn't let anyone talk smack about him. One of Marco's nephews, Trent, did just that. He said our father deserved to be shot and buried, and it was no more than he deserved. That set Damien off, they fought, but Trent pulled a gun—"

I cut Kane off on a gasp, but he pressed on.

"Long story short, Damien somehow got the gun and shot Trent. We were told he died, and in order to protect Damien for betraying one of our own, we began to work for Marco. Different work for each of us. He thrust us into different environments—Dominic into fighting, Alec into being an escort, Ryder into dealing, and me... I became a monster."

I shook my head.

"Slow down, you said you were told this Trent kid died?"

Kane growled, "Yeah, up until few years ago when the little prick resurfaced. We found out *Marco* betrayed *us*, so we bounced. We were paying a debt that wasn't valid in the first place. Damien never killed Trent... not the first time anyway."

I blinked. "I don't want to know what that means."

"Good," Kane grunted.

I flicked my eyes over his body.

"Okay, so you got a job to hurt people... how did you get your scars?"

Kane swallowed and looked away from me. "Punishment."

"Punishment?" I repeated.

Kane nodded his head, still looking away.

"When I didn't do a job... correctly, I was punished. Severely."

I didn't like how that sounded, not one bit.

"I'm confused, Kane," I murmured. "*What* job? *What* punishment?"

"Aideen, you *have* to have an inkling of the people I am involved with. Even before I explained shit, you had to know deep down that I don't deal with straight people."

Why wasn't that phrased in the past tense?

"I... I guess so," I admitted. "I know Marco was like Keela's uncle Brandon, a crooked prick... but that is it. Keela doesn't talk about Marco or anything that went down with him. He had me knocked out before he shot Storm and took Keela, Alec, and Bronagh to Darkness, remember?"

Kane balled his hands into fists. "I found you unconscious on the floor of Keela's apartment. Of course I fucking remember. It haunts me."

It did?

I was taken back by his sudden anger. "I'm sorry, I didn't mean—"

"Don't apologise," Kane sighed. "I'm not angry with you, none of that was your fault. I just get pissed with I remember what happened to you."

I knew he found me before anyone else last year when Marco trashed Keela's place and took her, Alec, and Bronagh captive. It was like something out of a film. They knocked me out, hurt Storm, and just took the others. It was surreal to even think it happened let alone realise I was part of it. Kane found me that night, then he left me with Branna while he and the rest of his brothers went to get Brandon so they could rid themselves of Marco for once and for all.

Ridding themselves of Marco hurt my friend though. Marco was no longer on this Earth, not amongst the living anyway, and yet he still had a hold of Keela through her nightmares. I was beyond delighted to hear her mind was fighting back and was slowly, but surely, ridding her if Marco too.

Fucking Marco.

"Can I ask you something that has been on my mind since the day you woke up in the hospital?"

Kane shrugged. "Shoot."

"What is your problems with needles?"

Kane stilled. "It's not the needle, it's the stabbing."

I swallowed. "What stabbin'?"

He scrubbed his face with his hands. "When I was punished, to keep me from fighting back, my wrists were bound with rope and strung up above my head." He paused to touch the scars that look like circular burns around his wrists.

Rope burns.

"When I was bound, the boss would take a needle so thin you could barely see it. It wasn't long enough to pierce any organs, so he would stab me in the back over and over until I screamed. He said if I was stabbing him in the back by not working, then he would stab me in mine. Literally."

My stomach twisted.

My eyes flicked to his neck then. "And the name on your neck?"

Kane looked down. "I refused to hurt a woman. She was a horrible person who drugged women who were trafficked into the compound. Her name was Jenna, she crossed Marco and he wanted me to hurt her, but I refused. Marco had me tied up with ropes and he carved his name into my neck, he branded me as his. It was to be a constant reminder that I was owned by him."

That was why he hated the name Jenna.

I wanted to cry my eyes out.

I hated Marco Miles, and I was glad the son of a bitch was dead.

"Why would Marco do that?" I whispered. "What would he stab you and hurt you so badly?"

Kane tensed for a moment. "You think Marco was the one who stabbed me?"

What?

"Wasn't he only man involved with you and your family?" I asked, confused.

Kane laughed, "I wish. I wish Marco was all I had to worry about, but no, Marco was the big boss of me, but he wasn't the one who gave me jobs."

Plural?

"So... who else gave you... *jobs*?"

Kane growled, "You already know who."

I did?

"What? Who?"

Kane voice was not his own when he snarled, "Big Phil. *He* was my old boss. He caused the scars. He caused the hurt." He locked his eyes on mine and said, "He created me."

CHAPTER TWENTY-FOUR

"Big Phil?" I questioned. "The man Damien mentioned was comin' to Ireland?"

Kane nodded his head. "Yeah. Him."

"Wh-what did he make you do?"

Kane looked away from me then. "Horrible things."

"I don't want to make you relive doing anything, but can you tell me a little?"

Kane rubbed his eyes. "Big Phil was a clean up guy. Marco ran everything and made the deals, but if deals were never fulfilled, Big Phil was the one to go and find out why. That means if someone never paid Marco money he was owed, the clean up crew went it to rectify that. It wasn't just money, if someone did anything wrong to Marco, the clean up crew went in. I was just under Big Phil in a chain of command with the clean-up crew. He said jump, I asked 'how high'."

Kane laughed, but it wasn't humorous.

"I had to hurt people... pain was an easy way to get people to pay up."

I stared at him, horrified at the life he lived. Kane looked at me and saw the mixture of sadness and disgust on my face, and he panicked.

"Please understand we all had a role to play, and this was mine.

I was protecting my little brother, Aideen. I was afraid if I pulled back too much and didn't do what I was supposed to do then Marco would kill Damien."

"I understand," I whispered.

I surprised Kane with my reply, but I surprised myself even more. I understood Kane did what he did, and it was because I truly understood that he was doing horrible things to protect his brother. If I were put in a position to save one of my brother's life, I'd do it no matter what the cost.

To protect those we love, we'd do anything, regardless of the consequences.

"There were stubborn people though, people who didn't want to pay back what they owed," Kane said, then swallowed. "I had to hurt them in a different way."

He stopped talking and I decided I didn't need to know what way he meant. I could imagine the horrible things and I didn't even fully know the extent of what he was forced to do, so I didn't need a detailed description.

I then jumped to a question that was boggling my mind. "Why were you punished if you did your job? That doesn't make sense to me."

"Because I didn't always do it."

He didn't?

"Why not?"

Kane looked at me, his eyes empty. "Because I hated every single second of it. I hated hurting people. I *hated* it."

"Okay, baby," I breathed and moved closer, hoping I offered him some comfort to him. "I know you wouldn't do any of what you told me out of your own free will."

Kane's eyes went dark, and the muscles in his jaw tensed.

"I do it out of free will now, but only if they're scum."

I blinked when he said that. He didn't have to hurt people, yet he did it anyway, but this time they were bad people? To me, that sounded like he was trying to make up for all the bad he had done by trying to right a wrong in the only way he knew how.

I placed my hands on Kane's tense face and forced him to look at me. "You do *not* need to do anythin'. You don't need to hurt bad people to make up for hurting any innocent people. You've paid your debt, you don't need to burden yourself with it anymore."

"I just wanted to prove to myself that I'm not the monster everyone thinks I am," he whispered. "If I stop even one scumbag, it'll be enough."

Oh, Kane.

"You did, honey," I murmured as tears welled in my eyes. "You helped stop Marco. He was a horrible human being, and you stopped him. Who knows how much hurt, and how many lives, you saved by doin' that."

Kane blinked up at me. "I-I never considered that."

I pressed my forehead against his. "You're free from those evil people. Your past doesn't make you who you are. All the horrible things you were *forced* to do doesn't reflect your character. You *know* you're a good man, and so does everyone else."

"You really believe that?" he murmured as he looked at me with his ocean blue eyes.

I nodded my head and said, "I do."

He swallowed and licked his lips. "Hearing that... it means everything."

"Bad things happen to good people every day, Kane," I assured. "You just got caught up in somethin' you had no control over."

He wrapped his arms around me. "I love you so much, Aideen. I'm sorry for anything I've ever said or done that has hurt you."

That admission caused the tears in my eyes to fall.

"Do you really love me?"

"More than anything in this world," Kane instantly replied. "You're everything to me."

My lower lip trembled. "I'm nothin' to fuss over, Kane."

"You haven't seen yourself through my eyes. You're definitely something to fuss over, babydoll. Trust me."

I did.
I trusted Kane.
"I do," I whispered, "with me life."
He closed his eyes. "I need to tell you everything inside my head so you get a clear picture of how much I need you in my life. By my side."
He didn't have to, I had already known.
"Kane—"
"When we don't speak, I don't sleep. I'm a mess without you, and I'm not afraid of admitting it. I *am* afraid that if you don't come back to me that I'll exist just always feeling this empty inside."
"Kane."
His grip on me tightened. "I'll do whatever you want, I swear it."
I knew he would.
"I still believe in us, babydoll, and I hope you do too."
His words hit me harder than I'll ever admit.
"I know damn well that you can do a million times better than me, and you deserve that, Aideen. You deserve everything the world has to offer you, but I'm a selfish bastard who wants you for nothing more than his own happiness."
"Babe," I whispered as my heart pounded against my chest.
He lifted his hand to my face and brushed his thumb over my lips. "I'll spend every day showing you how much I love and adore you, babydoll. You can trust me with your heart. I can't give you a lot of things, but I'll be damned if I can't give you your happily ever after."
Oh, my God.
"What we have, babydoll... it's better than words."
He was my undoing.
"I love you, too," I breathed.
Kane froze. "I didn't say all that to make you feel like you had to say it back—"
"I'm sayin' it because love is exactly what I feel for you. It's

been growing for like weeks and weeks now. I was just afraid to admit it to myself. I want to be with you. I swear I do."

Kane blinked a couple of times then showcased his perfect smile. "A relationship without a title, like before?"

"No," I replied, happily.

Kane raised an eyebrow so I said, "Skull... he was me Mr. Almost, but you? You're what I like to call me Mr. Pain In The Arse and that translates to me Mr. Right."

Kane blinked he eyes. "So... we're really dating?"

Men.

"Yes," I giggled, "we're really datin'. We're officially boyfriend and girlfriend."

Kane smiled. "Yay."

I felt my mouth drop open. "You should never say 'yay'. You're big, scary, and manly to the core. Big scary men do *not* say 'yay'."

Kane's eyes gleamed and he leaned into me and whispered, "This one does."

Okay, so big, scary, and manly men to the core *could* say 'yay' and make it work, or at least *my* man could.

CHAPTER TWENTY-FIVE

"**M**iss Collins?"

I closed my eyes as I wrote up homework for my class on the blackboard. School was out in five minutes, and hearing 'Miss Collins' was something I could have desperately done without. I was tired, cranky, and hungry. I just wanted to go home and be with Kane.

Who knew admitting you love someone could make you want to be around them twenty-four-fucking-seven?

Not me, that's for sure. My sudden clinginess to Kane was embarrassing, but I couldn't help it. We said those three important words just one week ago and I felt like I needed to be with him all the time because my heart hurt when I wasn't. I didn't know if this was love in general or if my hormones multiplied it by infinity. Whatever it was, it turned me into a complete love-sick puppy.

"Yes?" I replied sweetly to the *darling* who called out my name.

"Your belly is rubbin' off the writin' on the bottom of the blackboard."

The giggles that followed that statement caused my eye to twitch.

I looked down and groaned when I saw my pregnant belly did, in fact, rub off the writing on the lower half of the chalkboard. It made me a little teary because I had to bend down when I fucking wrote it!

"I'm not rewritin' it," I announced. "No homework tonight. Consider yourselves lucky."

The cheers that filled my classroom made me laugh. I turned to face my class and smiled at them. They were a good group of kids, and I loved teaching them.

"You can all pack up, and line up by the door. The bell will ring in a few minutes."

The talking that quickly ensued was so loud it gave me an instant headache.

"Pack up *quietly*, please," I said, loudly, a stern look in place on my face.

This hushed everyone up, and my head was grateful for it.

"Miss Collins?"

I looked at Niamh, a blonde girl who sat in the front row of my class, when she spoke. "Yeah, darlin'?" I asked, smiling at her.

She was so cute that I wanted to squeeze her cheeks.

She nodded to my stomach. "Are you excited to have your baby?"

One of my male students groaned and it caused me to giggle. The girls in my class loved talking about my baby and asking all kinds of questions about pregnancy. A few weeks ago the boys got fed up with it and zoned out whenever the girls asked me about being pregnant. They used the time to close their eyes or stare off into space.

I found it hilarious.

"I'm very excited."

Niamh smiled at me. "I bet, me ma is havin' a baby too and I'm *super* excited."

I beamed. "That is brilliant, you're goin' to be a great big sister."

"Thanks," Niamh blushed. "I can't wait to help me ma take care of the baby. She said I have a huge job to help her because me daddy got a new job and he has to work hard so we can buy new things for the baby."

At that moment, my love for Kane grew even more. He took away my worries about money—he also gave me precious time that could be spent as a family. If I had to worry about money, or a babysitter so I could work, I didn't know how I would I have coped.

"You're a very good girl for helpin' your ma, and you're goin' to have *so* much fun with your new brother or sister. You'll be the one to teach him or her all the fun things." I winked.

Niamh giggled, and so did her friends.

I could only imagine what 'fun things' they thought of.

A few seconds later the bell indicating school was over rang loud. It did nothing for my sore head, but it did relieve me knowing I could go home and stay there for the day.

I *loved* Fridays.

I walked out behind my students as they filed out of the classroom, and headed out to the yard where they each lined up until their parents made themselves known. Luckily it only took ten minutes for me to say goodbye to my students and their parents. I went back to my classroom and began to pack up my things.

I grabbed my phone, and its charger and put them in my bag along with my lip balm and mints. I clipped my bag shut, hooked the strap over my shoulder and walked out of the classroom, locking the door with my keys behind me.

The hallways were clearing fast of older students as they always did on a Friday because it was a half-day. I made my way down the hallway and headed for the staff room so I could hang the keys to my room up on the key rack. When I entered the room, it was just as scarce as the hallway. Staff members wanted to get out of the school just as much as the students did.

I hung the keys to my room up on the key rack and left the staff room, smiling to myself.

I was halfway down the main hallway, headed for the exit of the school when I looked up and saw a man leaning against the wall outside the school doors.

He was just standing there, waiting for something... or someone.
Who was that?

"Aideen?" I looked over my shoulder when I heard Kiera's voice call my name. I saw Kiera coming towards me so I stopped walking and waited for her to reach me. While I waited, I turned my head and looked back down the hallway. I was surprised when I found the area outside the school doors were empty.

No man.

"I'm going crazy," I mumbled and turned back in Kiera's direction.

"Hey," Kiera breathed, "I'm glad I caught you.

I pushed stray hairs back out of my face. "Is everythin' okay?"

"Yep, everythin' is *perfect*."

Perfect?

I smirked. "Who is he?"

Kiera laughed, "How did you know it was a man?"

I shrugged. "You got that big goofy smile on your face."

"You've had the same smile for a while now, don't rag on me."

I laughed, "I happily admit mine is for Kane, who is yours for?"

"His name is Trevor Moore. I met him in Tesco, of all places."

I froze. "Trevor Moore?"

Skull?

Kiera frowned. "Do you know him?"

I swallowed. "Trevor is Skull, babe."

Kiera's face dropped. "Oh."

I pointed my finger at her. "Don't you even think about what you're thinkin'. Skull and I are old news. I love him to death, but only as a friend. He feels the same way about me."

Kiera groaned, "But he was your lad for years, it'll be weird if I—"

"It's only weird if you make it weird. Skull is amazin', and I'm being honest when I say you won't find a better lad than him. He is a gem, Kiera, and how rare are gems?"

She gnawed on her lower lip. "You really don't mind if I go on a date with him?"

"I really don't mind," I assured her.

She eyed me. "Are you tellin' the truth?"

I nodded my head. "Honestly, if I could pick someone for Skull, it'd be you."

She flushed. "It's only a date."

"Then why're you so giddy about it?"

"Because he is perfect," she gushed.

I burst into laughter.

Kiera playfully swatted at my shoulder. "Stop laughin', I haven't been on a date in years. I'm in me mid-thirties, I shouldn't be this giddy over a man."

"Skull is the man, though. He is brilliant, you have every reason to be excited."

Kiera beamed. "I really am."

I was so happy for her, and for Skull. Kiera was perfect for him.

"When is your date?" I asked.

Kiera slumped. "It's tonight."

I frowned. "Aren't you on detention duty tonight?"

She always did Friday evening detention.

"I am," she groaned. "I forgot all about detention."

"What are you goin' to do?" I asked.

She scratched her neck. "I was goin' to ask you to take over detention for me tonight?"

My answer was already a yes.

"Like you even have to ask, of course I'll cover."

Kiera screeched and threw her arms around my body, hugging me tightly to her chest. I laughed and hugged her back.

"Thank you so much, this is exactly why I love you. You're brilliant."

I sighed, "It's true."

Kiera laughed, "Okay, so detention is in my old room, which is your new room. It starts at half four and ends at six. You don't have to do anythin', the kids bring their own things to work on. You just sign off that they attended."

She handed me a sheet of paper with only one name on it.

"Detention for one kid? I questioned.

Kiera held up her hands. "Don't blame me, blame the board."

The board were arseholes.

Kiera and I turned and walked down the hallway and through the school doors.

"Don't worry about it, I've got this covered. How hard can running detention with one kid be? I'll be home by half six with my feet up."

"Atta girl," Kiera chuckled. "I'll tell you everythin' on Monday."

I gave her a thumbs up. "I can't wait. Have fun!"

We headed our separate ways then. Kiera went home, and I drove to Kane's house. He stayed in my apartment every night, but he didn't officially live there. I think keeping it like that for a few months was best. I didn't want to bring too much upon ourselves since everything was still so fresh for us.

"Kane?" I called out when I entered his house.

"In the kitchen, babe."

I yawned as I walked down the hallway and into the kitchen. I found Kane sitting at the kitchen table next to Nico, both of them watching something on a laptop.

"What're you both watchin'?" I asked as I opened the fridge door and began to root around inside for food.

Things were silent for a moment until I felt arms slide around my waist and to my belly. I jumped a little and it made him chuckle in my ear.

"Scared you," he murmured and lightly bit on my ear.

My eyes fluttered closed for a second but quickly reopened.

"Please, don't," I groaned. "Lunch time sex will kill me with tiredness and I have to go back to work in a few hours. Kiera asked me to cover evenin' detention because she has a date and I said okay."

Kane chuckled, "I'm only teasing. Well, kind of."

I growled, "Evil man."

He continued to bite on my earlobe to I turned and shrugged him off me.

"I may look completely calm and at ease, but in me head I've killed you twice already. Stop it."

Kane grinned. "You have a short fuse."

I snapped my fingers. "No, I've a quick reaction to your bullshit."

"Woo," Nico said from the kitchen table and snap his own fingers in Z formation accompanied with his head bobbing from side to side. "You go girlfriend."

I tried not to laugh, I really did, but it was too difficult not to.

"You're such an eejit."

"I own that shit," Nico said then looked back to the laptop.

I walked over and tried to see what he was watching, but he closed the laptop before I could see what was on the screen.

"What was that?"

"Porn."

Liar.

I stared at Nico until he began to fidget under my glare.

"It's a guy I'm fighting tonight in Darkness. I was just studying his fighting style."

I frowned and touched Nico's face. "You're too pretty to receive punches in the face."

Nico laughed and said, "Bro, your girl thinks I have a pretty face."

"So? She thinks I have a pretty cock, I know which one I'm happier with."

Nico cracked up laughing while I rolled my eyes.

Men.

"I wish I could stay here all day," I sighed.

"So do," Nico said with a shrug of his shoulder.

I rolled my eyes. "I can't. I told Kiera I'd cover for her. Were you not listenin' to me? I just said it a few minutes ago."

Nico looked at me, a thoughtful on his face. "Who is Kiera?"

I smirked. "She is a friend, but you know her as Miss McKesson."

"No!" Nico gasped. "She still teaches at the school?"

I nodded. "Yep."

"Is she still hot?"

I deadpanned, "Really?"

"What? If Bronagh never walked into class that first day of school, I would have made it my mission to bang Miss McKesson. She is *too* hot to be a teacher."

I stared at Nico, long and hard.

"She wouldn't have touched you."

Nico smirked. "I disagree."

I shivered in disgust. "You're nasty."

"I'm a guy."

That was no excuse.

I move away from Nico then and over to Kane. I tested his blood sugar, then gave him his final injection for the day. It relaxed me know he was loaded up on insulin and good to go until tomorrow. When I put his kit away, I made a sandwich for myself as he went back and watched the fight video with Nico. I was leaning against the counter eating my food as I listened to the brothers talk.

"Right there, his counter strikes are weak. He gets a ten-second burst for fast punches, then he needs twenty to thirty to cool down. He is dancing around there avoid the big hits. After he does that tonight, you counter and don't stop until he drops."

I shook my head. "So violent."

Neither of the lads paid me any attention.

"I don't think that will be enough," Nico replied to Kane. "He is huge, he'll take my hits and keep coming."

"Not if you get his shoulder on the right side," Kane argued. "Look at how protects it. I bet it's a recurring injury. When you take him to the mat, apply enough pressure to the joint and the bone should break easily if it's an old injury."

"Jesus Christ," I gasped. "Is that really necessary?"

Again, the lads ignored me.

I huffed, "Yeah, Aideen, it is necessary, but we're barbarians and this was we do."

Kane looked at me then. "Did you say something?"

I growled, "I was talkin' to meself."

"Why?"

"If I don't talk to meself, who will?"

"Uh, me?"

I rolled my eyes. "Please, you don't listen to me half the time so I might as well be talkin' to meself."

Nico snorted but didn't look up from the laptop.

Kane stood up and walked over to me and pulled me into his body when he was close enough to do so. He looked down at my stomach, then up to me and grinned, "I feel like there is something between us."

I laughed, "Yeah, a belly that is gonna keep on growin'."

"The bigger, the better."

"Bigger is not better when it comes to my belly."

Kane chuckled and kissed me before returning to Nico's side. I had a drink of water and glanced out of the kitchen and down the hallway that lead to the front door when I heard a car door close.

"Ryder or Branna is home," I murmured.

"It'll be Ry. Bran doesn't finish work till later tonight."

Hmmm.

Ryder.

"Have either of you notice how weird Ryder has been lately?"

Kane and Nico shared a look then looked my way.

What was that about?

"What do you mean?"

I shrugged. "He's been out of the house a lot lately, like... a lot. He doesn't have a job so I'm just wonderin' what he's been up to."

Kane frowned at me. "It's his own business."

I rolled my eyes. "That means nothin' to me. It's like you don't even know me."

Nico laughed but covered his mouth when Kane elbowed him.

"Don't hurt him, he has a fight tonight."

"Yeah," Nico argued, "you bastard."

I snorted then.

Kane shook his head and focused on me. "Don't rag on Ryder, please? I don't want you involved in whatever problems he is having with Branna, okay?"

Oh, for God's sake.

"Aideen?"

Bloody hell.

"Okay," I grunted and looked down the hallway when the front door opened.

Ryder looked up and saw me. He closed the door after him and smiled as he walked down the hallway and into the kitchen.

"Hey gorgeous." He winked and gave me a kiss on the cheek in greeting.

Kane grunted, "Calling her by her name isn't an option for you?"

Ryder smirked as he puts his arms around me. "Nope."

"Ryder," Kane snarled.

Ryder moved away from me and to the fridge, laughing to himself. I snorted too because it was too easy to wind Kane up when it came to me. He easily got jealous, but I had to admit that I liked it.

A lot.

I looked at Ryder as he dug out a bunch of food from the fridge and put it on the counter. I laughed and asked, "Hungry?"

"Starving," he replied as he worked on making a huge sandwich.

I was just about to look away from him when I spotted some white powder on his jacket. I reached out and swiped some powder onto my fingers.

"You have white stuff all over you," I mused.

Ryder looked over his shoulder to me, then to my fingers. I saw his eyes widen as I brought my fingers to my nose so I could sniff my fingers and see if I could identify the powder that covered them. But just as I brought my hand to my nose, Ryder stuck his arm out and smacked my hand away from my face.

I screamed with fright, and the sudden pain that radiated from my hand.

"Don't sniff it!" Ryder bellowed and quickly grabbed my hand.

He pulled me to the sink and thrust my hand under the tap he'd turned on. He pumped some handwash on his hand and spread it all over my hand and scrubbed. He finished washing my hand until there was no trace of powder stuck to my skin.

"What the fuck is your problem?!" I shouted at Ryder and pulled my hand from his, cradling it against my chest.

I felt hands on my shoulders then a growl, "Explain that. Now, Ryder."

Kane was angry.

Ryder looked at Kane, then to Nico. "I couldn't let her sniff it, she's pregnant. God only knows what would have happened to her."

Kane's grip on me loosened. "It's okay," he breathed.

It was okay?

"Excuse me?" I questioned and turned to face Kane. "Did he smack you and pulled your around by the hand?"

Kane licked his lower lip. "It was for your own safety."

What?

"How is hittin' me for me own safety?" I asked.

"I'm so sorry if I hurt you, Ado. I panicked."

Why would he panic?

I turned to Ryder. "Why? I just wanted to see if I knew the scent of the powder, that's all."

"You wouldn't have known," Ryder replied.

"How do you know?"

"Have you done coke before?"

I reared back. "No, I haven't. What type of fuckin' question is that?"

"A valid one."

What was going on here?

I furrowed my eyebrows together. "Are you tryin' to say that powder on your jacket is cocaine?"

Ryder was silent.

"Ryder."

Still, he said nothing, and that, in turn, gave me my answer.

"Oh, my God!" I breathed. "Why do you have cocaine on your jacket?"

Ryder rubbed his face. "Kane."

"I'll talk to her—"

"I'm standin' right here! Don't talk about me like I'm not!"

"Aideen," Ryder sighed, "for once, I'm going to need you to mind your own damn business."

Oh, hell no.

"Fuck you, Ryder!" I snapped.

Nico tried to change the subject, but I was too hyped to allow it.

"I fuckin' *told* you he was up to somethin'!" I snapped to Kane and Nico. I looked at Ryder then and bellowed, "I have no idea what the fuck you're up too, but I know it's connected to your old life. That powder is a drug! I swear to God, Ryder, if you hurt me friend with your bullshit I'll *never* speak to you again, and you will *never* be around me child."

"Aideen!" Kane snapped. "Don't threaten him with the baby. It's my kid too and my brothers *will* be around him."

I glared at Kane. "You wanna bet?"

Kane drilled his eyes into mine. "Yeah, I do."

Wanker.

"Take me to court then."

Kane's face hardened. "I would if it came to that."

"Go for it. I'm sure a judge will favour a mother with a good, steady job over a father who batters people to a pulp for a livin'."

I hated myself the instant the words left my mouth. The look of hurt that settled on Kane's face broke my heart.

"Guys, please," Ryder pleaded. "Don't fight over me."

I was about to cry, and I didn't want to do it in front of the lads so I turned and exited the kitchen. I got the fright of my life when I shut the front door behind me with no attempts from Kane to try and stop me from leaving.

He never let me leave so easily... but this time he just seemed to let me go.

CHAPTER TWENTY-SIX

"Miss Collins?"

I looked up when Caleb Marks called me. He was a sixth-year student and was also the only student in detention this evening. I didn't particular like the kid that had me sitting in my classroom at five pm on a cold winter's evening.

Couldn't he have been a brat on another day?

Preferably one when I *wasn't* pregnant and feeling like utter crap.

"Yes, Caleb?" I sighed. "What is it?"

"I think the school should invest in new tables. This one is really old and has a bunch of names carved into it."

I inwardly rolled my eyes. "I'll be sure to bring that up at the next staff meetin', Caleb."

He snorted as he read something on the desk his was sat at. "They're degradin' to women, too."

That piqued my interest.

"Go on then, read out what it says."

Caleb snickered, "It says, 'Bronagh Murphy has a phat ass'. Spelled with a 'ph' instead of 'f', is that correct?"

I burst into laughter, but quickly had to cover my mouth.

Nico.

This was Kiera's classroom, and she was both Nico and

Bronagh's tutor when they were in sixth year. That must have been one of their old desks.

"Miss, why're you laughin'?"

I looked at Caleb, still smiling. "I know the lad who wrote that. He goes out with the Bronagh written on the desk. They've been together since they were in sixth year."

Caleb blinked. "If he goes out with her, why did he call her fat?"

See?! It wasn't a compliment.

"He is from New York, and apparently in America if the word fat is spelled with a 'ph' at the start it means it's a good big. He really likes her big arse."

Caleb laughed, "Okay, that makes sense."

No, it didn't!

I shook my head and stood up from my seated position. I walked over to the desk and looked at the writing Caleb was talking about. *Bronagh Murphy* was written in capital letters while the rest was in lower case letters.

I'd bet my life that Bronagh carved her name into the desk over the years in school, and Nico added the rest to it when he moved here.

What a fucker.

I snickered to myself as I took out my phone, took a picture of it, and sent it to Nico and Bronagh with the caption: *Vandalising school property. I'm ashamed to know both of you.*

Nico instantly replied with a tonne of laughing emoji faces and it made me snort.

"Why did you take a picture of it?" Caleb asked me.

"So I could send to them. Chances are, Bronagh will kill Nico for writin' it in the first place."

Caleb snorted, "You're a shit-stirrer."

Usually, I'd scowled at a kid for using bad language, but in this instance, Caleb was spot on correct.

"I know, it amuses me."

Caleb laughed as I returned to my desk and sat down with a

sigh.

"When is your baby due?" he asked.

I counted on my fingers. "Nearly ten weeks left."

"Ah, that'll fly in."

I grunted, "Not when you're the pregnant one."

Caleb laughed but said nothing.

"So," I began, "what did you do to get stuck here on a Friday evenin'?"

Caleb smirked. "Got caught in the girls dressin' room will Charlotte Price."

I narrowed my eyes. "Please don't tell me you were doin' what I think you were doin'."

Caleb held up his hands. "The teacher who caught me didn't see anythin' because I pulled- I mean walked out before they could see any hanky-panky. You can't get in trouble when there is no proof. I just got detention for being inside the girls room, not for shaggin' Charlotte."

The dirty little bastard.

"Condoms are left in the school reception for a reason, I hope you *know* that."

Caleb continued to smirk. "I do."

I shook my head.

Men were all the same.

"Are you really gonna keep me here until six, miss?"

I looked at the clock on the wall and saw it was only twenty to six. I wanted to leave just as much as Caleb did. I caught his gaze and gave him a stern look. "If anyone asks, you didn't walk out of this school until after six. Understood?"

Caleb stood up and saluted. "You're brilliant, miss."

"I know."

Caleb laughed as he swung his bag over his shoulder and headed for the door.

"Are you walking or do you have a parent to collect you?" I asked for my own piece of mind.

"Me da is in the car park."

I nodded. "Okay, off you go."

"See ya, miss."

I smiled then looked down at my own bag when Caleb all but ran from the room. When I no longer heard his footsteps patter down the hallway, I gathered up all of my things. I was moving at a snails pace because I was tired. I was ready for this day to be over. When I got my things together, I hooked my bag strap over my shoulder, groaning under the weight. With a sigh, I moved away from my desk and towards the classroom door.

I looked up to where I was going and gasped when I realised I wasn't alone. There was a man standing in the doorway of the classroom. A familiar man.

"Oh, hello."

The man smiled. "Hello, Aideen."

I stared at the man, and suddenly a sick feeling consumed my stomach. I recognised him as the man who I spoke to briefly in the hospital and later in the pub a few weeks ago.

What on earth was he doing here?

"Can I help you..."

"Philip."

Right, he already told me that before.

"Sorry, Philip." I smiled, forcing sincerity onto my face. "Can I help you?"

He nodded his head. "Yes, you can help me a great deal, actually."

I could?

I furrowed my eyebrows together. "Okay, what can I help you with?"

"You can sit down so we can have a little... chat?"

No.

That was the first thing my mind and gut screamed.

"I'm sorry, sir, it's after hours and as you have no child that is under my care during school hours, you will have to set up a formal meeting."

Philip chuckled, "Sorry, I phrased that as a question, when it should have been a demand."

A demand?

"I beg your pardon?" I asked with a shake of my head.

Philip looked at my desk then, and he smiled. "Ah, I see you got my flowers."

I stared at the flowers I got delivered to my classroom weeks ago. A lot of the flowers had died, but because I liked the arrangement so much, I bought new flower and kept it looking pretty.

"*You* got me them?" I asked, wide-eyed.

Philip nodded his head. "Of course, I meet you for the first time in the hospital that morning, so I went out and got you flowers to congratulate you on your pregnancy. I couldn't quite believe you were pregnant even though I had known for a few weeks."

I was so scared, I had no idea who this man was.

"Who are you?"

"If you sit down, I'll happily answer that question."

Every fibre of my being told me to get away from this strange man.

I stood firm. "I don't want to sit down. I do *not* know you and would appreciate it if you left this room immediately."

"I'm afraid I can't do that. Not when I finally have you alone."

Excuse me?

"What?" I asked, taking a step backwards.

Philip smiled at me as he stepped into my classroom. I observed his face a noticed the scarred side of his face didn't move, which made his smile that much more creepy. "I've been watching you for weeks now, but you're hardly ever alone, and when you are, it's only for short periods of time."

He'd been watching me? For weeks?

"Why have you been watchin' me?" I asked, a tremor of fear in my voice.

I was so scared I thought I would throw up.

Philip humourlessly laughed, "It's a funny story, actually."

I swallowed. "I doubt I'll see the humour."

"You wouldn't." He smirked.

I looked around for an exit. The windows were out because they were locked shut, but the classroom door was wide open. I glanced at the door, which was only a few feet away from me, then looked back to Philip, who was staring at me.

He evilly grinned. "Don't do it."

I ignored him and made a run for the open door, but within seconds Philip was on me. From behind me, he gripped my arms. He turned me to face him, and when I tried to dig my nails into his flesh, he stomped on my knee.

I screamed as pain erupted in my right lower leg.

"I ask you nicely to *sit down*, Aideen, just so we could talk," Philip sighed. "I didn't want to do that."

I couldn't think for myself or process what this horrible man was saying. All I could think about was the pain that I was currently feeling.

"Oh, God," I wailed.

Philip hoisted me up against his body and pulled me over to my chair where he dropped me. He forcibly slapped me across the face when his hands were free and snarled, "Stop. Screaming."

I instantly closed my mouth, but no matter what, I couldn't stop moaning in pain. I couldn't stop the tears that flowed from my eyes either.

"I don't know why women do this," Philip grunted to himself. "I tell them to do something, but they defy me like I won't punish them."

Punish?

"I don't know you!" I hollered. "Why would I stay and do what you ask?"

"Because," Philip chirped, "you don't want me to harm your unborn child or Kane, do you?"

I forced my eyes to focus on Philip. "What are you talkin'

about?"

How did he know about Kane?

"Your boyfriend and your baby, you want them kept safe, yes?"

I blinked my eyes and nodded my head.

"Then stop screaming and sit there like a good girl."

What was happening?

"You broke me leg!" I tried and used both of my hands to hold the area below my knee. I needed to hold it but couldn't directly touch it.

"I wouldn't have if you'd done what you were told."

"Fuck you!" I bellowed then whimpered in pain.

Philip chuckled to himself then walked over and shut my classroom door. He walked over to my desk and proceed to dig around inside my bag until he came up with the keys to the door.

He pocketed the keys then pulled up a chair from one of my student's desk and sat in front of me. He leaned forward, placed his elbows on his knees and just stared at my face.

I tried my best to glare at him, but I was in so much pain I couldn't do anything but cry.

"Are you okay?"

He was asking was I okay?

"Do I look like I'm okay? You bloody bastard!"

Philip laughed and sat back in the chair. "I can see why he is with you."

What was he babbling on about?

"You can see why *who* is with me?" I hissed.

Philip smiled. "Kane, of course."

Kane?

"Y-you know Kane?" I questioned, forcing myself to think of the conversation instead of the pain in my leg.

Philip laughed, "Yeah, Kane and I go way back."

I felt my eye twitch as I glared. "You want to clarify that?"

He cackled, "I bet he loves your attitude. People are terrified of him, but I'd bet my life that you backtalk him every chance you get."

I closed my eyes when the pain in my leg became too much.

"Don't you pass out on me."

I screeched when pressure suddenly gripped my leg and fresh pain shot through my body.

"Good girl, open your eyes."

I snapped my eyes opened and glared at the scumbag before me. He removed the hand that he placed on my leg and sat back in the chair.

"Tell me," Philip smiled, "what is the sex of Kane's brat?"

I placed my hands on my stomach in a protective manner.

"We don't know yet," I whispered.

Philip hummed to himself but said nothing.

"What do you want with me?" I asked, my body trembling.

Philip laughed, "It's a pity, but I need to hurt Kane and to do that, I need you. You just happen to be a good woman involved with the bad man."

That struck a nerve.

"Kane is a good man, and you won't be hurtin' him at all."

Philip snickered, "You're goin' to stop me, are you?"

You bet your arse I am.

"Does this make you feel like a man?" I asked. "Injurin' a *pregnant* woman."

Philip's face hardened. "I don't see gender, just a person who is my key to getting want I really want."

"Which is what exactly?" I snapped.

Philip didn't hesitate as he said, "Kane's misery."

I blinked. "Why do you want to hurt Kane?"

"Because *he* hurt *me*," Philip growled. "I tend to level the playing field."

My eyes automatically zeroed in on the scars that cover half of his face. Philip caught my staring and growled, "Yeah, he caused this."

I swallowed but said nothing.

"Why would Kane do that do you?"

Philip growled, "He did it indirectly."

I furrowed my eyebrows in confusion then groaned as a severe pain began to pulse in my leg.

"How—" I cut myself off to gather my bearings. "*How* could he do it indirectly?"

Philip set his jaw. "He set the fire to purposively burn someone else and got me as well as them. He locked me in a room to burn."

I blinked. "He wouldn't do that."

Philip sat forward, reached out and smacked me across the face so hard my head snapped to the right. I screamed and lifted my hands to my face, shielding it.

"You don't fucking know Kane Slater like I do. I created the prick, I know exactly what he is capable."

I uncovered my face and stared.

He created me.

My thoughts went back to a conversation I had with Kane over a week ago when he was telling me about his past. I stared at the man before me, annoyed with myself that it took me so long to figure it out."

"You're Big Phil," I murmured.

He laughed, "Big Phil is what my boys call me, you can stick to Philip."

"I prefer dickhead," I grunted then widened my eyes because I didn't mean to say that out loud.

Philip laughed so hard he had to wipe under his eyes. "Ah, I like you, darling."

I grunted in response.

"Can I ask you a question?"

I looked away. "I'm sure you will ask me anyway so go for it."

"Why Kane?"

That caused me to look at him.

"What?"

"Why Kane?" Philip repeated.

I blinked. "What do you mean 'why Kane'?"

"Well," Philip began, "most people judge him based on his appearance like they do me. They are frightened of him, and peg him as a bad guy. I mean, he must be bad to have so many scars, right?"

I growled, "He told me those scars are because of you and Marco."

"He forced my hand, he could have remained pretty as a flower had he done his job."

I seethed in anger.

"His life would have been a lot different. He looks big and scary now, but he wasn't always like that," Philip mused, a grin on his ugly face. "It's amusing to me that he got to look like a monster by trying to do the right thing."

I hugged my body. "What do you mean?"

"He told you how he got the scars, right?"

I slowly nodded my head. "He said they were from his old job, the shit *you* made him do."

"That's a no then," Philip chortled. "He didn't tell you the details because he thought you would see him as evil. Predicable Kane."

That piqued my interest.

"If you're goin' to tell me what you're talkin' about, spit it out," I growled. "I don't have all day."

Philip cackled to himself, "Little hellcat."

I glared at him.

"Okay, little miss pushy," Philip chuckled. "Your man is the best enforcer I've ever come across, it's like he was created to work for Marco just like his brothers. Alec has a knack for making people come, Dominic has a knack for knocking people out, Ryder has a knack for moving very fucking large shipments of product undetected, and Kane? That boy has a knack for making people scream in a very terrifying way."

My stomach contents rolled around my stomach.

"You see," Philip smirked, "Kane is very aggressive when he is mad. *He* has a tendency for blacking out during a fight. He turns into an animal without being aware of it, and I like to take credit for it."

"How can you take credit for somethin' like that?"

"Well," he began, "it was my idea to try shock treatment after the whippings became ineffective."

Lashings? Shock treatment?

"I-I don't understand."

Philip clicked his tongue at me. "Sure you do, you're a smart woman. Think about it for a second."

I did just that.

Kane received whippings and shock treatments from Philip... but why? The more I thought about it, the more the answer became clear to me.

"Y-you tortured him into becomin' a weapon for you?" I asked, my voice so low I didn't know if Big Phil heard me.

"Yes and no," he replied.

I looked at him. "What does *that* mean?"

"At first when Kane received a whipping, it was punishment, not torture."

I snarled at him. "Punishment for *what*?"

I didn't want to ask that question, but I had to know.

"Kane was the man to go in and hurt someone who fucked me or Marco over. Let's say a man owed some money for product, but he didn't have any money. Kane wouldn't hurt him, he would hurt his loved ones until payment was received. He only ever hurt the person in question, sometimes killed them, if nothing would come for simply hurting them."

I felt tears well up in my eyes.

"If he did all that, then why would he be punished?"

Philip smirked. "He didn't like hurting the kids and woman of the scumbags he had to extract payment from. For every refusal, he received a whipping."

"But he has hundreds of scars!" I bellowed.

Philip chuckled, "Why do you think I said we switched to shock treatment when lashings became ineffective?"

I wanted to vomit.

"He looks like a monster, but inside, he is actually a nice guy, which sucks for him because no one will stay with him longer than a few hours. He is pretty fucked up, you know?"

I spat in Philip's direction. "I'm with him. I *love* him."

"And he loves you," he replied rubbing his shoe against my side table to wipe my spit off, "and that is exactly why killing you will break him."

I stopped breathing.

"You... You're goin' to kill me?"

Philip smiled at me. "Yes, I am."

"Why?" I whispered.

"Kane let my son burn to death, so I'm returning the favour."

I widened my eyes to the point of pain.

Philip's son was the person Kane locked in a room that was on fire?

I shook my head clear and focused on the main point of what he said. "What do you mean *burn*?" I screamed.

Philip stood up and retrieved a plastic bottle from his coat pocket—I guessed it to be a seven hundred and fifty millilitre bottle. He uncapped the bottle and began to squirt the liquid around the room.

I gripped my knee as Philip moved over to my storage press. He opened the door and pulled out numerous books and boxes of blank paper. He kicked the lids off the boxes of paper, picked up handfuls and threw then around the room. He then squirted more of the strong smelling liquid.

My insides churned and panic set in when he reached into his pocket and took out a silver lighter. He swiped it against his thigh and stared at the flame he created.

"He killed my kid," Philip said as he stared at the dancing flame then flicked his eyes to me, "so I'm killing his and his girl. He'll know what it feels like times two. I'm not going to kill him, but I'm going to cause him so much hurt that he wishes he was dead."

He threw the lighter on the desk closest to mine and the desk instantly went up in flames thanks to whatever liquid he poured on it. The flames spread around the room. Wherever the liquid was squirted, a flame was there.

I looked around my room and screamed. I couldn't see a thing through the flames and the growing thick black smoke.

I heard a door slam so I looked back to where Big Phil was stood seconds ago, but he wasn't there. Through the flames I saw my classroom door was closed so I screamed as loud as I could for him to come back for me, but he didn't.

He left me to burn.

Tears streamed down my cheeks as I stood up off my chair and tried to walk towards my classroom door. When I put weight on my injured leg, I instantly fell to the ground, hitting the floor hard. I screamed so loud as the blinding pain took control of my leg. I began to cough then, and that snapped me back to reality.

I was going to burn to death.

The thought alone spurred me on. I used my good leg to push against the floor while I used my hands to pull myself. I felt around for my bag with every inch I gained, and I eventually grabbed the strap of it.

I coughed as I dug through it and fumbled with my phone as I gripped onto it with shaking hands. I couldn't see the screen because my eyes stung so bad and blurred with the mixture of my tears and smoke that filled them.

I focused and I used the swipe motion to unlock my phone. I saw the light grow bright, and I could make out the light-green phone app that brought me to my call list. I pressed it and then hit the last person who called me.

"Miss Collins?" I heard a shout from outside the door.

I screamed, "Help me, please!"

"Miss Collins!" a familiar young male's voice shouted. "Are you in there? I see smoke."

Caleb.

"Caleb!" I screamed. "Help me."

"Miss Collins!" his voice hollered. "I'm goin' to get you out of there!"

I heard banging on the door and I whimpered. He was trying his very best to kick it in.

"Aideen?" I heard a voice shout.

I didn't know who it was, my ears were starting to ring. I cried out as my mind refocused on the pain in my leg.

"Help me!" I cried and spluttered.

"Aideen!"

I blinked my eyes and looked down to my phone.

Someone answered my call.

"I'm at the school," I screamed. "He is goin' to kill me. He set everythin' on fire—" I cut myself off when a fit of coughing hit me.

"Aideen!" I heard his voice scream.

Kane?

I whimpered, "Kane. It's Big Phil. He's tryin' to—"

I coughed again and dropped my phone in the process. I couldn't see a thing so I tried to feel around for it, but I couldn't find it.

I screamed, "No!"

I searched for my phone. A table next to me collapsed and the burning timber fell against me and burned my arm. I bellowed in pain and kicked myself away from the fire.

"Miss Collins!" Caleb's voice screamed. "I'm goin' to pull the fire alarm- HEY! Let go of me!"

I looked up as my classroom door opened and a body was thrust into the room. The door slammed closed once more and this time laughter followed.

"There, you have a little brat to keep you company."

"You bastard!" I bellowed.

Philip laughed, "Give my regards to Marco, Miss Collins."

I was about to reply when I suddenly felt hands on my arms. I screamed with fright because I couldn't see anybody in front of me. The room was growing thick with smoke, and laying low on the floor seemed to be the only option.

"It's me," a voice said then coughed, "Caleb."

Caleb.

Oh, God.

"Caleb," I spluttered. "Get out of here right *now*."

"And leave you?" he asked, coughing. "No. Come on."

I cried, "Me leg, I think it's broken."

"Fuck," Caleb growled then hooked his arm around my waist and pulled. He grunted as he hoisted me up to my feet.

I instantly began to wheeze when I stood upright. The smoke was thicker, the flames were higher, and my throat felt like it was on fire.

"The window," I coughed.

I cried in pain as Caleb pulled me along with him. He rested me against a desk that wasn't on fire and tried to open the window closest to us, but it wouldn't budge.

"It's locked!" he bellowed and covered his mouth and nose with his hands.

I did the same thing.

"Try smashin' it," I said, coughing into my hands.

My throat started to feel like a razor blade was wedged in it, and the more I talked and breathed, the more lodged it became.

"Cover your face!" I heard Celeb shout.

I did as he asked and covered my face, seconds later I heard a loud crash as Caleb slammed one of the chairs into the window. I heard the glass shatter then Caleb's voice.

"Help us!" he roared out the window. "Please, we're trapped! Help us!"

I heard people's voices shout in reaction to Caleb's plea.

"There's a fire in the school!" a woman screamed. "People are trapped!"

A man shouted, "Call nine-nine-nine! Quickly!"

The school was situated in the middle of a housing estate so all around us were houses.

"Help us!" Caleb screamed again.

I leaned over the desk to rest a little. It was then I realised I couldn't feel the pain in my leg anymore. I couldn't feel anything, but the overwhelming tiredness that filled me.

"Miss Collins!" Caleb shouted.

I felt his hands on me then.

"Hey," he coughed, "wake up!"

I leaned into him and closed my eyes.

"Help me!" Caleb screamed. "I need help! Please!"

It felt like forever since Philip left the room, but for some reason it felt even longer since Caleb had smashed the window. It was like time slowed down and I was experiencing everything from a third person's viewpoint.

"We'll get you out of there, son," I heard a man shout as more glass shattered.

Caleb's hold tightened on me. "Me miss is with me, she's pregnant."

"Fuck!" a man's voice shouted. "We need to get them out of there."

I heard multiple voices then.

"The frame of the window won't break, I tried," Caleb said then coughed.

I gripped his arm. "You shouldn't... have come... back."

Caleb pressed his head on top of mine. "I was waitin' on me da to pick me up, he wasn't in the car park. I just said that so you would let me go early."

I laughed lightly, coughing whilst doing so.

"I heard a scream and was scared you went into labour or somethin'. I wasn't goin' to leave you all alone. Who was that man that did this? I didn't see him come up behind me."

I cried as I covered my stomach with my hands.

My baby.

"Aideen!"

I blinked my eyes open. "Kane?" I rasped.

"Mate, helped us break the frame."

"That's my girlfriend!" he shouted. "Move and we'll break it."

Kane.

"Hang on, Ado, we'll get you out in a second."

I heard loud bangs then.

"Stomp on it, Dominic! Force it."

Everything happened quickly then. A loud crunching noise sounded and people cheered.

"They can fit out! Quick, climb in and get them!" a woman's voice hollered.

"No, get her out first!" Caleb coughed.

I felt a few pairs of hands grab me then I was lifted into the air. One second I was inside a boiling hot, smoke-filled classroom, the next I was outside surrounded by cold, clean air.

I greedily sucked it down into my lungs.

"Aideen?"

Gavin? Why was he even here?

"Oh, God!" Gavin's voice cried. "Aideen!"

"She'll be okay, man. We have her."

"Look at her!" Gavin's voice cried. "She's not okay. I have to ring me da and brothers."

I wanted to reach out to my brother, but the best I could do was open my eyes and look up. I saw Kane's face first, and I instantly began crying.

"I'm so sorry," I spluttered, "for what I said—"

"Stop it," he cut me off. "You have nothing to apologise for."

But I did. What I said was wrong, and I hurt him.

"It was him," I coughed.

Kane tried to lift me, but I screamed when the pain returned to my leg.

"No!" I cried. "He broke it."

Kane looked down at my leg and a look of pure anger filled him.

"I'm going to make him sorry for doing this, babydoll. I promise."

I shook my head. "Don't leave me."

Kane took hold of my hand. "Never."

I began to cough hard then. Each cough felt like glass was cutting up my insides. I think I coughed up some blood—whatever it was it came up in little chunks.

"Oh, my God," my brother whimpered. "She's goin' to be okay, isn't she?"

I wanted to answer him, but my throat felt like it was burning.

"Yes!" Kane instantly replied to my brother and pulled me closer to him, wiping my mouth and chin with his hand. "She's going to be perfectly fucking fine. Where is the ambulance!?"

"On the way, bro," Nico's voice shouted.

I didn't know where he was, and I didn't care enough to ask.

"Caleb—" I began.

"Is fine," Kane cut me off. "Dominic is with him."

Oh God, that was good.

I wanted to ask if he was okay, but I couldn't get the words out. My body started to droop as tiredness grabbed hold of me. My chest was burning, my throat hurt terribly, my leg was pulsing with pain, and my eyes were starting to close.

I cried out when I felt my baby move.

I was relieved to feel her, but I was very aware that something was wrong with me. I felt wrong, I felt like... the end.

I was going to die.

"Save the baby!" I cried as the pain struck my chest. I squeezed Kane's hand as tight as I could. "Promise me th-that you'll choose her l-life over mine if it c-comes to it."

My voice didn't sound like my own, it sounded like two pieces of sandpaper rubbing together.

"Aideen," Kane spluttered and shook his head as he stared down at me. "You aren't going anywhere."

I didn't believe that. I felt like I wasn't going to wake up again once I feel asleep. My body didn't feel right. Everything was heavy, tired, and ready to give up.

"Promise me!" I repeated, tears streaming down my face as I began to cough again.

"Please, don't make me choose—"

"Promise!" I screamed through my coughs.

Kane wailed, "I promise!"

I tightened my hold on him. "I love you, okay? So m-much. You're perfect, inside and out—" I paused to cough once more, "you make me so h-happy."

"Stop it!" Kane bellowed at me. "Stop talking like that. Just stop. *Please*."

I slumped as the weight on my chest got heavier.

"Do *not* go to sleep!" Kane shouted and slapped my face with force, but I didn't feel it. "Keep your eyes open."

Sleep.

That sounded *so* good.

"Aideen!" I heard Gavin's voice whimper. "Please!"

I wanted to comfort him and Kane, but I couldn't move.

"Tired," I rasped.

"Just rest a little, but *don't* go to sleep," Kane said, his voice cracking.

I opened my eyes and gazed into his for a long moment and just in case I didn't wake up and see his face again, I said, "Bye."

The force of my words hit him like a train, I saw it.

Good-bye.

"No," he whispered, "it's never goodbye, it's I'll see you later, remember?"

I slid my eyelids closed when they became too heavy to keep open.

"Don't you think of leaving me, Aideen Collins. I need you. I love you, babydoll. Please, stay with me. You can do this, I'm right here with you. Me and you?"

Me and you.

I heard loud sirens then a lot of shouting and commotion. I

didn't need to open my eyes to confirm there were now loads of people around me—I could sense their presence.

"Sir, please, save her. I'm begging you. *Please.*"

Kane.

"She's thirty weeks pregnant, don't press on her stomach! Don't let me sister and nephew die. Please save them. *Please.*"

Gavin.

"Move back, we'll do everything we can, but you both have to stand back."

Everything became noise.

"Aideen!" I heard his voice through the cloud of haziness. "Stay awake, babydoll."

"Aideen!" This was Gavin.

I wanted to reply to them both, I really did, I just couldn't stay awake any longer. I let myself fall into darkness, but just before my mind when blank I saw Kane's smiling face and it put me at peace. I just hoped if I didn't wake up, he could somehow find peace, too.

CHAPTER TWENTY-SEVEN

Blinding white light.
That's what I was greeted with when I blinked my eyes open. It took a moment for my eyes to adjust to the light, but even when they did, I still had to blink a lot. They stung pretty bad.

I squeezed my eyes shut and lifted my hand to rub them. I lifted my arm and frowned, there was some sort of wire on my arm and I had no idea what it was. I tried to look down, but something on my face prevented me from seeing.

There was a mask over my nose and mouth.

What the hell?

I placed my hand on my bed and felt for Kane, but I just felt mattress then a rail?

"Kane?"

When I spoke, it sounded more like a rasp and it hurt like fucking hell. I erupted into a fit of coughing, and each cough tore through my throat.

Oh, God.

What was wrong with me?

"Aideen, it's okay."

Kane?

I opened my eyes and focused them until I could see his face. He was leaning over me and it looked like he just woke up.

"Where—"

"Don't speak, babe," he cut me off. "You're in the hospital."

The hospital?

"Wh—"

"There was a fire at the school, you were trapped for a little bit, but you're safe now. You're safe, babydoll."

A fire in the school?

I tried to think of a fire, but I couldn't.

My mind drew a blank.

I furrowed my eyebrows in confusion.

"You don't remember?" Kane questioned.

I tried to think hard, but nothing came to me so I shrugged my shoulders.

"It'll come back to you," Kane murmured.

I nodded my head and tried to sit up a little, but I yelped when pain shot up through my leg. I pulled the blankets off my lower half and stared down at the royal blue cast that covered my mid-thigh down to my ankle of my right leg.

What the hell?

Kane gripped my hand. "Your knee and shin bone were broken. You'll have to wear the cast for eight weeks until the damage repairs itself.

I blinked.

What the fuck happened to me?

I examined the rest of my body for any other signs of injury, and my eyes zeroed in on the white bandage that was wrapped around my left arm from my elbow to my wrist. I stared at it then looked up at Kane.

He frowned. "Second degree burns. You'll need a skin graph."

Fucking. Hell.

I checked out the rest of my body but saw nothing else, so I looked at Kane.

"You have a black eye, a swollen jaw, but that's it. Everything else is okay."

I slowly nodded my head.

"Are you in pain?"

Surprisingly no.

It hurt when I tried to talk, but other than that I was okay.

I shook my head.

"Good," Kane said. "Pain meds and some fluids are in the IV drip, they've had you on it since you came in last night. You've been here for sixteen hours now."

I've been here for sixteen hours?

"Are you okay?" Kane asked me.

I instantly shook my head.

I didn't know what happened to me, or why I was so busted up. It made me feel like a stranger in my own body. I didn't like it.

I looked down to my hands and stared hard at them. I tried so hard to think about what happened to me. I could remember going to school for detention. I had one kid to look after. One kid. My classroom. On our own.

One-second things were misty and dark, and the next images flooded my mind.

Philip.

Fire.

Smoke.

Caleb.

My baby.

I widened my eyes to the point of pain. "Baby," I rasped then fell into a fit of coughing.

"Easy, darling," Kane soothed and got me some water to drink. "Small sips, swallowing will hurt."

I whimpered in pain when I swallowed the little bit of water I had in my mouth. It felt like lava was sliding down my throat.

"There you go," he murmured and continued to rub his hand up and down my good arm.

I blinked my eyes and lifted my arms, though it was difficult because my body felt so tired. I pressed my hands on my stomach and was relieved to feel it was still huge and hard.

I looked at Kane, my eyes wild.

"He is okay, he is still in there."

The relief that flooded me almost caused me to throw up.

I began to cry and it upset Kane.

"Babydoll," he breathed. "You're both okay, I swear."

I shook my head.

"The baby is okay. The doctors don't know if there was any damage because of the smoke inhalation, but as far as they can tell, everything looks okay."

My tears were fast and furious then.

What if the baby had brain damage because of the smoke cutting off my oxygen?

All sorts of horrors flooded my mind, and terror filled me completely. I couldn't hear Kane speak. I realised why, it's because I was wailing.

"Baby!" Kane pleaded. "He is okay, I promise, he is okay."

"What if... brain... damage?"

"Don't think like that," Kane hissed. "You think positive alright. He is *okay*!"

I reached up and gripped my throat when the pain struck it.

I closed my mouth as hot tears spilled from my eyes onto my cheeks. The pain... God, the pain. I had never felt anything like it in my entire life. It was like someone was slowly running a saw over my throat.

"I'll get the nurse," Kane said and jumped up off the bed. He ran out into the hall and called for help. "She's awake and in pain. Please, hurry."

I blinked my eyes a couple of times, and when I focused, two nurses were next to me.

"Aideen, can you hear me clearly?" the first nurse asked. "Don't reply verbally, just nod for yes, and shake your head for no. Do you understand?"

I nodded my head.

"Good. Is your hearing okay? Does it sound like you're in a tunnel?"

I shook my head. My hearing was fine.

"What about your chest, does it hurt when you breathe?"

I tested it out and took a deep breath, which only result in coughing. I quickly pointed to my throat, which was the only pain I could feel.

"Your throat?"

I nodded my head.

"Okay, do you have any chest pain?"

I shook my head.

"Good, that's really good."

The nurse looked at Kane then and said, "Just to be safe, we're going to do a round of hyperbaric oxygen therapy. She will be placed inside a pressurised oxygen chamber here in the hospital, it will speed the replacement of carbon monoxide with oxygen in her blood."

"Is that safe?" Kane questioned. "She is pregnant."

The nurse nodded her head. "It's highly recommended for pregnant women who're exposed to carbon monoxide poisoning. Unborn babies are more susceptible to damage so this will be good for both mother and baby."

I wanted to do it. If it would eliminate any damage to the baby, I was completely on board.

I nodded my head.

Kane focused on me. "You want to do it?"

Again, I nodded my head.

"She wants to do it."

The nurse looked at me. "Okay, Aideen, we'll get the chamber prepared. We'll come get you in twenty to thirty minutes if you're able. Is that okay?"

I nodded my head.

The nurse pressed a button then and it caused the top half of the bed I was lying on to rise. She raised it enough until I was still lying, but in a more upright position. She leaned into me then and adjusted my oxygen mask on my face.

"Keep this on your face, sweetie," she said and fluffed the pillow under my head. "It'll make breathin' easier."

I nodded my head then looked at the door when it opened and in piled person after person. I gave a closed mouthed smile to my family when they gathered around the bed. My little brother was the first person who quickly leaned in and hugged me.

"Are you okay?" he whispered into my ear.

I leaned my head against his and nodded my head.

Gavin squeezed me tightly, kissed my cheek, and pulled back. He quickly wiped his eyes, and it only heightened the need for me to console him.

"I'm... fine," I rasped.

"No talking," the nurse chastised.

I ignored her and focused on Gavin, giving him a knowing look. He nodded his head to me and moved aside so my other brothers could hug and kiss me.

My father along with James stepped outside to ask the nurse some questions. I smiled when Keela shoved her way through Alec and Nico and almost climbed onto the bed to grab hold of me.

"I was so scared," Keela cried into my neck. "I thought you were gone when Kane called and told us what happened."

I tiredly lifted my good arm and put it around Keela. "I'm okay," I rasped.

"If you don't stop talking, I'll telling your dad," Kane warned me.

Keela laughed through her tears and I smiled.

She kissed me a bunch of times on the cheek, and then climbed off the bed. I hugged Kane's brothers and the girls. Alannah was shaken up pretty bad. She was worried about the baby, but Kane assured her that everything was okay.

"I'm *so* glad you're okay," she whispered to me when she gave me a cuddle.

I smiled at her when she pulled back; I looked at Nico when he murmured to Kane, "No sign of him."

Kane's body tensed. "Keep looking."

I focused on Kane. "Need... to... talk to... you."

"We'll have words, babydoll, just rest your voice a while." I needed to have a real talk with him about Philip. The man tried to kill me and my baby. I wanted to know what was happening.

Nico nodded his head once to Kane then looked at me and winked. "The kid that helped you is doing good. He is here in the hospital for another twenty-four hours as a precaution."

Thank God.

The news that Caleb was okay relieved me greatly. He was a little soldier, and without him, I think I would have died in that classroom. Images of Philip's flashing grin and flames entered my mind.

I squeezed my eyes shut.

"What's wrong?" my brother, Harley, asked me.

I swallowed and winced in pain. "I see his face," I rasped.

Harley leaned into me and said, "Kane told us what went down, and we're goin' to get this prick. Do you hear me?"

I nodded my head.

Harley smiled at me and wiped the tears from under my eyes with his thumbs. Everyone in the room sat down—the girls on the lads lap or on the windowsill. I leaned my head back and looked up at the ceiling.

I gasped when I felt movement inside me.

Once again, I burst into tears as I placed my hands on my stomach. I looked at Kane when he placed his hand on my belly and felt her move, too. I knew he was trying to keep my spirits up by telling me that she was okay, but I saw the relief that crossed his face when he felt her move under his palms.

"Thank God," he breathed and leaned down to me.

He kissed my mouth, then my cheeks and forehead.

"I love you so much."

I pressed my face against his. He stayed pressed against me for a few minutes, but when he pulled back, he sat back down and kept his hands on my stomach.

"He's wide awake," Kane murmured, looking at my stomach as she turned inside me.

You could see the shape of her elbow or knee poke out as she turned.

"That is freakin' me the fuck out," Dante's voice said from my right.

I looked at my brother and found his eyes, and everyone else's, on my stomach.

I smiled and shook my head.

He was such a man.

"I think it looks cool," Bronagh commented.

I smiled at her and found her staring at my stomach like it was the most interesting thing she ever came across in her life. I frowned then when her face paled, and she suddenly jumped up from Nico's lap. She ran for the sink in the room and vomited into it. Nico was right up after her, rubbing her back with his hand.

I looked at Kane who looked at me and smiled.

That exact thing happened to me about twenty odd weeks ago.

"I'm fine, just nauseous," Bronagh murmured and gargled some water, then wiped her face dry with some tissue Nico handed her.

They sat back down and Nico cuddled her to his body.

"Are you coming down with something?" he asked.

She swallowed and shook her head.

I smiled at her, and she glared at me.

She knew I knew.

"Don't look at me like that, Collins," she grunted at me.

I flashed my teeth at her and it pissed her off.

"You're lucky you're pregnant and injured."

I continued to smile.

"Stop!" she snapped.

Kane laughed then groaned, "I'm dreading your hormones. I can barely tolerate Aideen's."

Bronagh glared at Kane then looked at Nico when he tensed underneath her.

"Bronagh?"

Bronagh stood up and turned to face him. "I was goin' to tell you, but you've been goin' on about your stupid fight all week and I didn't want to distract you."

Branna was leaning against the door. "Tell him what?"

Bronagh looked at her sister and said, "I'm pregnant."

"Oh, for fuck's sake!" Alec shouted, throwing his hands in the air. "Is everyone going to have kids before me?"

My brother laughed at Alec while I watched Nico. He was looking up at Bronagh with a look of love and admiration mixed into one. He stood up and stepped towards her. She looked at him and began to play with her fingers. "Are you mad?"

Nico said nothing.

Bronagh groaned, "Please, Dominic, say somethin'."

He did.

He said, "I love you."

"Aww," Alannah cooed from the windowsill making Kane snicker.

"You... You aren't mad?"

Nico put his arms around Bronagh. "Mad?" he questioned. "We've been trying a while now. I'm happier than you could ever imagine. We're going to have a baby, pretty girl."

I started crying again.

Kane looked at me and smiled as he stroked his thumb over my hand.

"How long have you known?" Branna asked her sister.

Bronagh looked at her and said, "About a week."

Branna's face fell. "And you never told me?"

"I didn't tell anyone apart from Alannah because she was in the house when I took the test, Bran."

Branna nodded her head, but I could tell she was hurt.

"She's fine," Ryder said to Bronagh, who looked guilt-ridden as she looked at her sister. "She'll get over it."

Branna looked at Ryder, and I saw the moment her heart broke.

She looked at me then, her eyes filled with tears and said, "I'm sorry, Aideen. I'm glad you're okay, babe, but I have to leave."

I barely got a chance to nod my head to show her I understood before she opened the door and fled from the room. Ryder shook his head but made no attempt to go after her. Bronagh, on the other hand, didn't hesitate, she paused at Ryder and kicked him in the shin.

"Bronagh!" he snapped and grabbed his leg.

She pointed her finger at him and said, "That's for being an arsehole. Would it fuckin' kill you to be nice to her?"

Ryder set his jaw. "You don't know what you're talking about."

Bronagh shook her head. "When she plucks up the courage to leave you, and finds someone who truly loves and cares for her, you'll finally realise how incredible she really is and it'll be too late."

With that said, Bronagh left the room with an annoyed Nico in tow.

Ryder had waited about twenty seconds before he left, too. Alannah sighed from the windowsill and pushed herself to her feet. "I'm goin' to get some food, anyone comin' with?"

My brothers, Keela, and Alec all answered 'yes' in unison. They told Kane they would grab him something then they all left the room. It was just me and Kane, again.

"Our families are crazy."

I nodded my head and looked at him. I noticed his face looked so good compared to how pale and sullen it was weeks ago without his insulin.

I widened my eye then.

"Injections," I rasped.

Kane took my hand in his and smiled. "I did it myself."

I blinked in astonishment.

"I know," he chuckled. "When you were still asleep this morning I knew I'd needed it or I would be no good to you when you woke up. I didn't want my diabetes fighting against me when I needed to fight for you so I bit the bullet and injected the insulin myself. I wasn't scared... I'm not scared. Not anymore."

Tears welled in my eyes and I reached my hands out for him. He smiled and leaned into me, kissing my cheek and snaking his arm around my body.

"I love you," he whispered.

I hugged him tighter.

"Philip," I whispered gently, "told me things.

Kane pulled back and swallowed. "What he did tell you?"

"He was watchin' me for weeks," I whispered. "I met him in the hospital and in the p-pub without realisin'. He is the one who bought me the flowers that were sent to my classroom."

Kane's face hardened. "He must have seen you with me and wanted to know who you were."

I nodded my head. "He told me about your lashin's and the shock treatment."

Kane closed his eyes. "The bastard."

I waited for him to open his eyes and look at me.

"You didn't need to know those things, babydoll, no one needs to know any of what I was put through. No good comes from him."

I agreed so I nodded my head.

"He told me you killed his son," I painfully swallowed. "He said he was goin' to kill me and the baby the same way to make you wish you were dead."

Veins bulged in Kane's neck.

"He will die for this, I promise you."

I blinked. "Did you kill his son?"

Kane held my gaze. "Yes, I did."

Oh, God.

"How?"

Kane swallowed. "Big Phil's son, Colin, wasn't a nice kid. He was sixteen at the time... and I caught him doing something really,

really wrong."

I didn't want to know, but I didn't stop Kane from speaking.

"He had one of the guard's five-year-old daughters... and he was violating her."

Oh, Jesus.

My stomach churned.

Kane ran his hands through his hair. "I couldn't help it, I went crazy. He was passed out so I locked him in the room I found him in, then I brought the girl to her father and assured him I'd kill Colin. So that's what I did. I didn't lay a finger on him, but I made sure he would die painfully for being the vile creature he was. I just got a canister of gas and I poured it everywhere in the room I locked him in, and I set it on fire."

I grabbed hold of Kane's hand.

"I didn't realise Big Phil was in the bathroom of the room, but he was. I didn't know if he hurt the little girl either, but I didn't care. He tried to save Colin, but I poured gas over him so he was already dead within minutes. He died painfully. Big Phil got badly burned, but the fire was put how before he could die."

I squeezed Kane's hand.

"Marco asked what happened because cameras didn't work in that section of the compound—I'm sure it's the reason Colin took the girl there. No one would see what he was doing to her. I told him I had no idea, and that was it. Big Phil was in the hospital for a long time after that, but I forgot about him because it was around that time we came to Ireland. I hadn't given him a second thought just Damien's voicemail message."

I winced. "How do you think he knew it was you?"

"Maybe one of the guards told him?" Kane guessed. "I don't know; the girl's father wasn't the only one around when I brought her to him. Any of them could have overheard my plan."

I rubbed my thumb over his hand. "You did the right thing, Kane."

He looked at me. "I know, I couldn't let him live, not with her, and other kids, living on the compound."

I nodded my head in agreement.

"Don't think about this anymore, I will keep you updated on everything, but do *not* worry. I have help to get him."

"Help?"

Kane nodded. "Your brothers, your father... and Brandy."

I closed my eyes.

"I *need* Brandy to find him; I paid him for his help. I don't have to do anything bad, I promise.

That relieved me greatly.

I opened my eyes and looked at Kane. "I love you."

He leaned down and kissed my forehead.

"This is me ma's doin'," James's voice mumbled as the door to the room open. "She made her get with a Slater knowin' good and well I think they are a pack of pricks."

My father chuckled as he rounded the bed and reached over and took my free hand in his. I looked at him when Kane pulled away and sat on the seat to my left. My father's eyes welled up and when I reached for him, he leaned over and placed his cheek against mine.

"You frightened the life out of me, baby girl."

I squeezed him.

"I'm so happy you and the baby are okay."

My dad pulled back from me and didn't try to hide the fact that he was wiping his eyes.

"Where did everyone go?" James asked.

"For food," Kane replied.

James looked at our father. "Let's go join them, they're takin' her to that chamber thing in five minutes, and Kane will be the only one allowed to go with her."

My dad nodded and leaned in to kiss me once more before he stood up. He extended his hand to Kane, who clasped his hand and shook it firmly.

"Take care of our girl," he said.

I burst with love for my father.

He said, 'our girl' not 'my.'

"I will, sir." Kane nodded.

"I'll kick your arse if you don't, Slater."

I rolled my eyes at James while Kane snorted.

They left the room then and he sat down back down next to me.

"We have a few minutes before the nurses come for you."

I smirked.

"You have me all to yourself, germinator, what do you want to do?" I whispered, only wincing a little at the pain in my throat.

Kane locked his eyes on mine and with a smirk, he said, "When you come back here I want to turn on my laptop and watch season three of the *Sons of Anarchy* with you."

Fuck.

How'd I get so lucky?

"I love it when you talk dirty to me."

Kane laughed. "Then shut up and listen to me talk. Rest your voice; your throat won't heal otherwise."

"One more thing then I'll stop."

"What is it?"

"I love you," I whispered.

Kane's face softened. "I love you too, Aideen. You're my whole world, babydoll, but if you say one more word, I'll put tape over your mouth."

I smiled wide then leaned in to kiss him, but my face mask got in the way and so did the door to my hospital when it opened. I expected it to be a nurse or doctor, but the person who walked in was *not* a nurse *or* a doctor. He had a large bouquet of flowers, and I couldn't see his face because the flowers covered it, but I could see he had white-blond hair.

Oh, my God.

When the flowers were lowered and I realised who it was, I stared at him with my mouth agape. I shook my head, and for a moment, I thought I stopped breathing.

I couldn't believe who I was seeing.

"Kane," I whispered, not taking my eyes off *him* in case he disappeared.

"Aideen, what did the nurse tell you? You can't talk—"

"Look," I cut him off, my voice cracking and causing me pain.

I didn't care though—I was too astonished to focus on the pain.

Kane raised his eyebrows at me then stood up and turned around to see who was at the door and when he did, he almost fell on top of me. He stumbled but quickly steadied himself then took a hesitant step forward, opening and closing his mouth like a fish.

He was flabbergasted.

"I know, I'm ridiculously good looking and you can't help but fawn over the canvas that is my stunning face, but are you going to get your ass over here and hug me or stand there staring all day?"

Kane didn't move an inch. Instead, he repeatedly blinked his eyes as if to check if they were playing tricks on him. When he realised he was really here, and it wasn't some sort of joke his mind was playing, Kane took another step forward and whispered one word.

"Damien?"

NOW AVAILABLE

DOMINIC
SLATER BROTHERS #1

BRONAGH
SLATER BROTHERS #1.5

ALEC
SLATER BROTHERS #2

KEELA
SLATER BROTHERS #2.5

FROZEN
TRAPPED #1

COMING SOON

AIDEEN #3.5
RYDER #4
BRANNA #4.5
DAMIEN #5
ALANNAH #5.5
BROTHERS #6

ACKNOWLEDGEMENTS

Finally, I have reached the acknowledgments. That means *Kane* is complete. Thank you, God! I have my usual village of people to thank for helping make this book possible.

As always I'd like to thank God first and foremost, through Him all things are possible.

I wouldn't be where I am today without my daughter; you're the best thing ever to happen to me. I love you with all my heart, mini me.

My family. My crazy family. Thank you all for believing in me. Love you all!

My sister, my crazy partner in crime. I love you so much, and I'm so happy you get to share in this incredible journey with me. You're a star.

Yessi – I kind of like you. Kind of. That's the only nice thing I'm saying.

Jill – Thank you for being the amazing person you are, love you!

Mary – You always manage to make me smile, no matter what it is you do. Love you loads.

Jen, thank you so much for making editing a semi-enjoyable experience ;) Your witty comments and GIFs make the whole process better!

Jenny, the Goddess over at Editing4Indies, I love you for proofreading *Kane* so well! You're brilliant!

Nicola Rhead, thank you for also proofreading Kane, you're a gem!

Mayhem Cover Creations, you have done it again LJ. *Kane* is the sixth cover you have created for me, and I am absolutely in love with it. Thank you!

Jules from JT Formatting, your formatting is one of a kind. It's stunning. I adore it, and you. Thank you.

Last, but never least, my readers. I would not be typing the acknowledgments to *Kane* had it not been for each and every one of you. Thank you for giving me my dream job <3

ABOUT THE AUTHOR

L.A. Casey was born, raised and currently resides in Dublin, Ireland. She is a twenty-three year old stay at home mother to a two-year-old German Shepherd named Storm and of course, her five and half year old (the half is apparently vital) beautiful little hellion/angel depending on the hour of the day.

CONNECT WITH ME

Facebook: www.facebook.com/LACaseyAuthor
Twitter: www.twitter.com/AuthorLACasey
Goodreads: www.goodreads.com/LACaseyAuthor
Website: www.lacaseyauthor.com
Email: l.a.casey@outlook.com

Made in the USA
Charleston, SC
08 May 2016